DARK LIES

MAGIC SIDE: WOLF BOUND, BOOK 3

VERONICA DOUGLAS

Magic Side Press

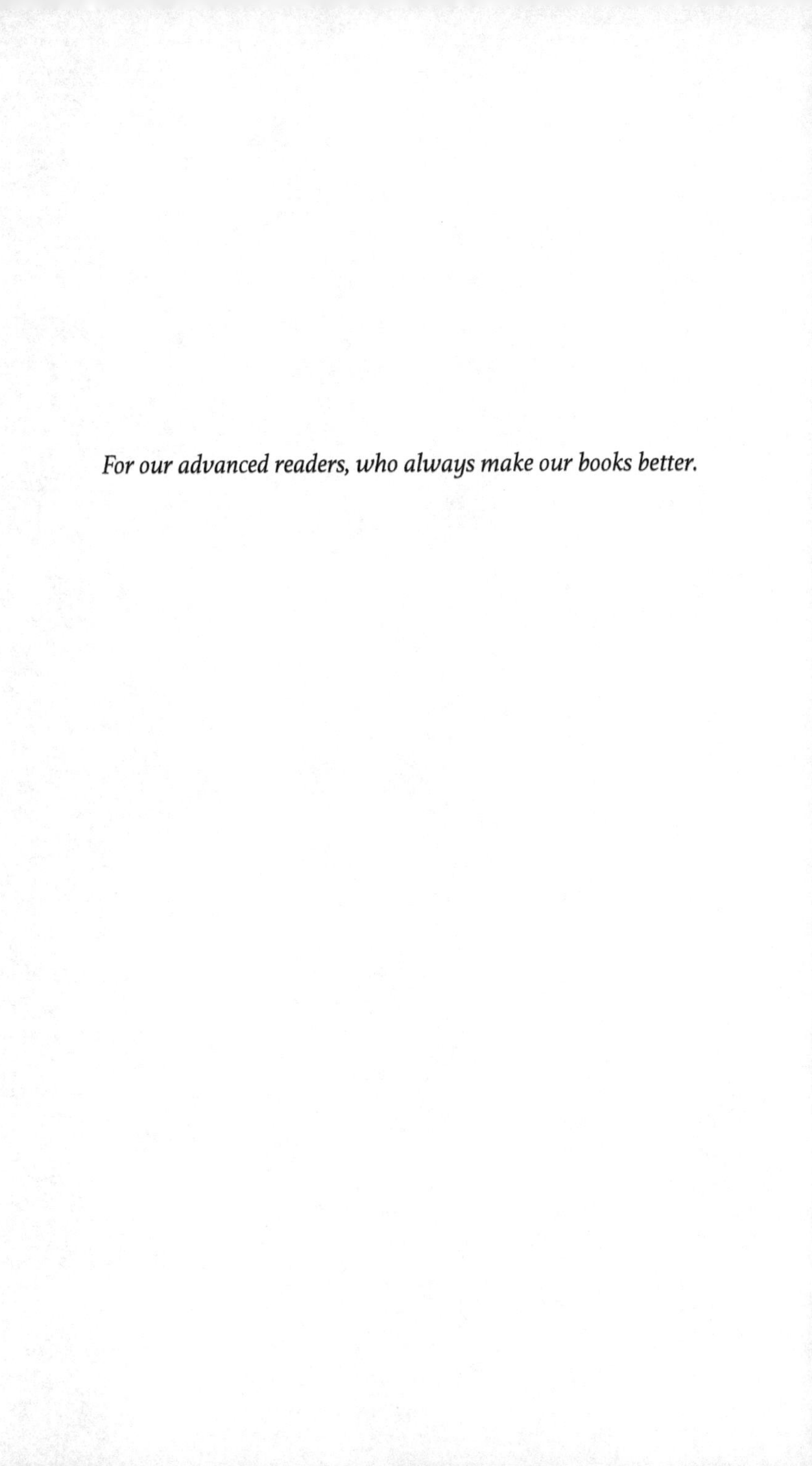

For our advanced readers, who always make our books better.

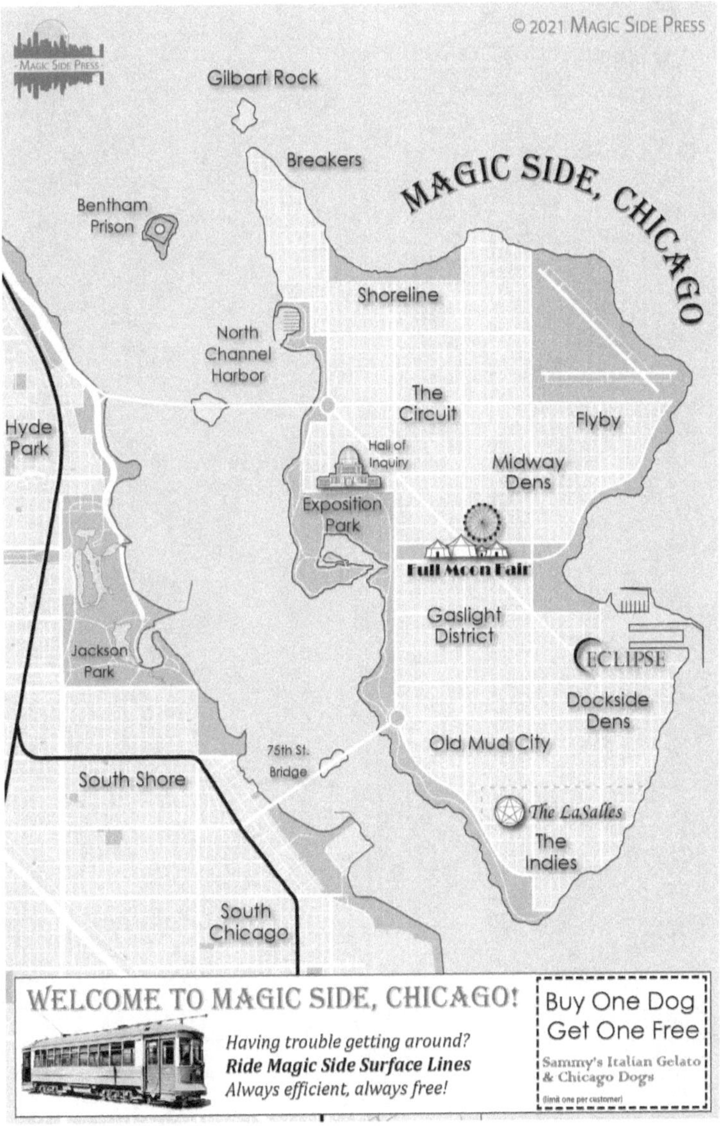

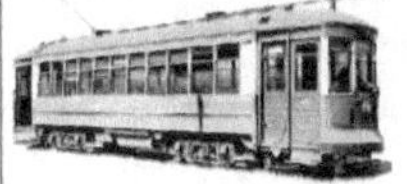

© 2021 Magic Side Press
Magic Side Press
Gilbart Rock
Breakers
Magic Side, Chicago
Bentham Prison
Shoreline
North Channel Harbor
The Circuit
Flyby
Hyde Park
Hall of Inquiry
Midway Dens
Exposition Park
Full Moon Fair
Gaslight District
Eclipse
Jackson Park
Dockside Dens
Old Mud City
75th St. Bridge
South Shore
The LaSalles
The Indies
South Chicago
WELCOME TO MAGIC SIDE, CHICAGO!
Having trouble getting around?
Ride Magic Side Surface Lines
Always efficient, always free!
Buy One Dog Get One Free
Sammy's Italian Gelato & Chicago Dogs
(limit one per customer)

PREVIOUSLY IN BOOK 2, UNTAMED FATE...

At the beginning of *Untamed Fate*, our heroine Savannah Caine was being hunted by the faceless man—the vile blood sorcerer who had her abducted in *Wolf Marked*. Jaxson discovered that the faceless man was actually Ulan Kahanov, a dangerous murderer who'd escaped from Bentham prison (see *Cursed Angel*). What Jaxson didn't tell Savannah was that Kahanov had given him an ultimatum: *hand over Savannah or the pack will pay.*

Kahanov also had a new trick up his sleeve—he'd stolen a magic book called the Grimoire of Nightmares and was using it to enter people's dreams. He put several members of Jaxson's pack into comas and made Savannah sleepwalk into the clutches of a monstrous Noctith Demon that was lurking outside her aunt's home. Unable to resist, Savy was almost captured, but at the last moment she looked into the sky and saw a mysterious image of a dark wolf in the clouds. An unfamiliar voice in her head said, *I will free you, if you free me.* Suddenly in control of her body again, she evaded the demon with her magic, but knew something about her had changed forever.

To make matters worse, the next day, Savannah began to

turn into a werewolf at a bonfire in the park, and fled. Jaxson found her clinging to life, half-shifted in the woods, and helped her finish the transformation. Savy was horrified at the new state of affairs, and they looked for answers to why it had happened.

Meanwhile, they discovered that Kahanov was after a dangerous weapon called the Soul Knife. With Amal's help (see *Dark Storm*), they tracked him to a mage's tower in Italy. Savy was wounded in the battle, but she drove him off and recovered the magic blade. He retaliated by putting twenty-one more members of the pack to sleep. Their desperate search for a way to stop him led them into a magical realm known as the Dreamlands, where they enlisted the help of a powerful maenad, Cavra. In return, they had to join her in a hedonistic revel.

Fighting the rising lust fueled by the revel, they slipped out to cool off in a starlit pool—but things only heated up. Drunk with the revel and Jaxson's warm embrace, Savy fell asleep—the one thing they had been warned not to do.

The magic of the Dreamlands transported her into a mysterious cave. Exploring the dark tunnels, she discovered the chamber where Kahanov had imprisoned the sleeping wolves. Before she could release them, he attacked and stole the Soul Knife. Wounded by the cursed blade, she escaped through a portal that exited from beneath the Tree of Life, in Forks, Washington. She hitchhiked into Forks, called Jaxson, and led him, Sam, and Neve (see *Wicked Wish*) back to the cave to free the sleeping wolves.

During the ensuing battle, Kahanov trapped her deep in the caverns and tried to steal her soul with the Soul Knife. But at the last second, she summoned the blade and cut out his soul. Rather than killing him, it released the ghost of Victor Dragan— an evil sorcerer who Savy's aunt had killed years ago—who'd been in control of Kahanov all along. Freed from possession,

Kahanov was bloodthirsty and looking for revenge, and tortured Savannah with his blood magic. She and her wolf joined their strength to kill him, but she was grievously wounded in the battle and couldn't escape the cavern.

Driven mad with anger, Jaxson fought his way to her and carried her unconscious body out of the caves. He healed her through the power of their mate bond. Intoxicated with euphoria from the magic, they kissed. Jaxson then revealed a truth that he'd hidden from Savannah since she'd first transformed: they were fated mates, destined to be together.

Savy was horrified and grew furious after she discovered that both Jax and Sam had known about the mate bond, but didn't tell her. She vowed to resist and make her fate her own.

Savannah returned to Magic Side a hero of the pack, but the words of Dragan's departing ghost still echoed in her mind—*I will have my vengeance!* Deep down, she knew that the battle wasn't over yet.

To make matters worse, she still had no idea why she'd turned into a werewolf, or how to reconcile with the new wolfish voice that had become a part of her soul. She couldn't risk telling her aunt and cousin the truth of what she'd become, though she suspected that aunt Laurel might have the answers she needed...

1

Savannah

Our paws pounded along the sandy lakeshore as the sunlight drained from the sky.

Our paws. It was a strange thought. Not *my* paws, because my wolf was in control. But they weren't just her feet, either.

Don't overthink it, my wolf chided. *Two legs think too much.*

I couldn't help it. It was still too weird.

Focus on enjoying the run. Like a massage or manicure—just relax and let me do the work.

I tried to let go of my incessant human worries and focus on the scents of the beach and the animals that came out in the twilight hours of the day. Whether I liked it or not, I had become part of something bigger than myself. An *us.* My wolf and me.

I'd driven down to the Indiana Sand Dunes to let my wolf run in the cover of darkness, a new ritual. Over the last week, the dunes had become our refuge from Magic Side, a patch of wilderness where we could avoid the city and all its complications.

The cost of gas was eating up my dwindling cash reserves, however.

My wolf sniffed the air. *Too many human worries. This is wolf time. There are many good smells here. Maybe we could catch a deer?*

I could smell the animal, not far off.

"No. Not a chance."

Just a bite? Or how about a rabbit? she pleaded.

Fine—but just chasing. No chomping. We can catch a plate of bacon on the way home.

It had been a week since my first shift, and I'd gotten a little more comfortable with being a werewolf. But there were some things I wasn't quite ready for yet, and murdering cute animals with my own mouth was definitely not on the agenda.

Okay. Just chasing, my wolf said, being an uncharacteristically good sport. *But I expect lots of bacon.*

She took another sniff of the air and raced off in the direction of the rabbit scent. We wove through the trees like it was an obstacle course, kicking up jets of sand with each step. She was so fast and far more agile than my human form.

You were pretty good at track for someone with only two legs, my wolf observed as we slid beneath a fallen tree trunk and leapt over a pile of brush.

She was clearly showing off for my benefit. But what was unsettling was that she had memories of my youth. I still wasn't sure how our relationship worked. Sam and Jaxson had told me that the wolf was just another aspect of my personality, but she didn't feel like a part of me. She felt like another soul sharing my body.

I pushed the unnerving thoughts from my mind and drifted into the rhythmic movements, running without an ounce of control, letting someone else steer.

It's good to run. It's good to let go, my wolf said.

I scoffed. All I did was run. I'd been running for weeks. First from Billy and the wolves, then from demons and nightmares, and finally from Kahanov, or Dragan, or whoever the hell the blood sorcerer was.

My wolf overtook the rabbit, and when it broke right, she shot left over the top of the dune toward the beach. I could feel her elation and smell the rabbit's relief.

We outran them all, my wolf said warmly.

That we did, Wolfie.

Yet I was still running. Perhaps only from myself, but running all the same.

Heart thundering, we dashed along the lakeshore until at last, my wolf slowed and stopped.

A million stars shimmered above us in the clear, moonless sky and reflected off the gently rolling water. I hadn't seen so many stars since I'd left Wisconsin, and then again, maybe not this many. A deep loneliness pooled in my gut. I missed my godmother, Alma, and all her kooky yard decorations.

I needed to get back there, but I'd just been...busy.

My wolf tilted our head back and let out a melancholic howl that echoed over the water. We waited.

No response.

When the echoes finally died away, my wolf asked, *Ready to shift?*

I hated this part.

Shifting is so much easier with Jaxson around. We should have him run with us. He'd come, my wolf said for the hundredth time.

My heart picked up a step, to my frustration.

I had no doubt that Jaxson would be here in an instant if he had any notion that we were running alone.

I shook our head as I braced myself for the shift. *We need to master this on our own. He won't always be there for us—like when we fought the sorcerer in the cave.*

I gasped as the transformation hit me like a blow to the chest. Agony raced down my spine and along my limbs as our body contorted. I tried to focus my mind on my human form, visualizing my long, pale legs and arms, thin fingers that were good at drawing, and red hair that always caught Jaxson's eyes.

My back arched and joints popped. We growled in defiance at the pain, but the growl became a whimper as bones cracked and strained. Through tear-glazed eyes, I watched paws become fingers clawing into the wet sand.

I touched my face with a shaky hand, feeling my familiar cheeks and jaw. My muzzle was gone, leaving only a human nose and mouth. Relief flooded me as the pain began to subside.

I flopped down naked and human in the wet sand and groaned for dramatic effect. "Damn, that sucks."

We did it, my wolf said. *That's eight times on our own.*

"One small step for werewolves. One giant leap for our independence," I muttered, still breathing hard as the residual pain echoed through my joints.

I closed my eyes and focused on the sensations of wet sand and the cold, dark waves as they raced up the shore and along the edges of my body. The feeling brought back memories of another beach on the far side of the country.

Lying in the Pacific surf nearly a week ago, I'd been at death's door after escaping the Dreamlands. But then *he* had brought me back. Jaxson. I'd been hanging in darkness until his healing magic had coursed through my body like wildfire. I'd never felt pain so close to pleasure. It was like having the sun rise in your soul, like being burned from the inside out.

I had woken with a gasp in arms that were strong like the rocky shore. Unyielding. Immoveable. Eternal.

His heart had beaten next to mine, each pulse in time with my own. And when his lips had found mine, all the sensations of the world had become like sunlight on my skin. As we'd flowed together like the sand and sea, that kiss had become everything we'd ever wanted.

There were moments after each shift when I could almost feel that magic again.

Too much. I pushed the memories from my mind and staggered to my feet in the gentle surf.

Everything ached. I waded unsteadily out into the cold lake and dove in. Cool darkness surrounded me, clearing my thoughts. The sensation was familiar, comforting. It was what my magic felt like.

For a second, I let myself drift, weightless. When I couldn't hold my breath any longer, I stood and pulled my drenched hair over my shoulders, and headed into shore.

We need to talk to him, my wolf whispered in my thoughts.

"I know," I said as I trudged up the beach to where I'd hidden my clothes. "I will. I promise, I'm working up to it."

Mm-hmm.

Fated mates. Totally fucked.

I grabbed my water bottle and took a long drink, then wiped my mouth with the back of my hand. I was pooped, but I needed to get out of there before it got too late.

Shivering, I tugged my underwear and shorts over my damp skin, trying desperately not to get sand in my pants. I pulled out my phone.

Two missed calls from Casey—typical. One from Sam, which had the potential to be interesting. And a text from Aunt Laurel: *Back in a couple days.*

She and Uncle Pete had split town not long after I'd returned from the Dreamlands.

I'd told them about killing Kahanov and about how—as far as I could figure—he'd been possessed by the ghost of Victor Dragan. Her eyes had gone dark at Dragan's name, and she wouldn't say much more than, "He was a very bad man. I'm glad he's dead. Again."

The next day, she was gone. The only explanation had been

a note on the table: *Now that we know you're safe, Uncle Pete and I must check on some things. Be back in a few days. Don't let Casey burn the house down.*

That was Aunt Laurel for you.

I sighed and snatched my shirt from the ground, then paused and touched the lingering scar on my shoulder. My fingers came away red.

Damn. It was seeping again.

After the battle in the Dreamlands, Jaxson's magic had healed all my wounds except one—the gash where Kahanov had rammed the Soul Knife through my shoulder. Even after drinking a couple of Uncle Pete's godawful healing potions, it still wouldn't fully close, and it bled every time I shifted or if I moved around too much.

Time to get that looked at.

I dumped some water from my bottle over my shoulder to wash it clean, and then I pulled on my shirt, contorting so I wouldn't have to move my right arm too much. The wound would be fine—it just needed a little more time to heal.

It and me both.

2

I fetched my car keys, which I'd hidden in the wheel well, and unlocked the door to my Fury. A cool breeze prickled my skin as I glanced around the empty parking lot. For the past week, I hadn't been able to shake the feeling of being watched.

It's just nerves, silly.

The leather of the front seat was warm under my thighs, sending another wave of shivers through me.

My phone binged. A text from Casey: *Grabbing drinks with Zar at the Hideout at 7pm. Bring your ass.*

"Sorry, Case, I've got a date with my bath and bed," I muttered, slipping the keys into the ignition.

A dark shape shifted in the passenger seat, and my heart seized.

"What the hell!" I jerked toward the door, hand ready to unleash a bolt of magic at the man who was sitting beside me, staring ahead.

He slowly turned his head toward me, and I froze as recognition dawned—the bastard who'd attacked me at the Tap House. Correction, the *dead* bastard.

Bile rose in my throat. *He can't be here.*

Crimson blood trickled from a wound on his forehead, and I swore I saw the tread mark from my tires on his neck.

Not freaking possible.

"Watch the road," he said. Then he disappeared.

I blinked twice at the empty seat beside me, then craned my neck around, but he was gone.

"Shit." I was either seeing ghosts or losing my mind, and I wasn't sure which scenario was worse.

I started the car and pulled out of the lot and onto the narrow road that led through town and to the highway back toward Chicago. I rolled down the front windows, hoping some fresh air would clear my head. Darkness settled over the tree-lined road, and I squinted at the three piercing lights that appeared in my rearview mirror.

My phone buzzed in my pocket. Slipping it out, I noticed Casey's name on the screen before I answered. "I'm not coming, Casey, so forget about it."

"Aw, come on. Do you have something better to do?" my cousin asked.

"Yeah. I'm driving back from the Indiana Sand Dunes, and when I get home, I'm taking a hot bath." With a pound of Epsom salts and a bottle of wine to ease the aches of my mind, body, and soul.

It's going to take a lot more than that, my wolf said.

I glanced in the rearview mirror again. Those lights were closing in. Three motorcycles, by the looks of it.

"What the hell is so interesting about the sand dunes?" Casey asked. "You've been out there several times this week. Have you joined a bird watching group or something? Meeting a secret boyfriend?" There was a pause on the line, and then he continued in a hushed voice. "Shit, Savannah. Don't tell me you're with Jaxson—"

"No! Are you crazy? I've just needed some space to process all the crap that's happened over the past month."

That, and I'm a werewolf now. Surprise.

"I get it. You do you, and if you need a shoulder to cry on, I'm here for you. Always."

Even if you knew what I'd become?

An awkward lump of emotions climbed up my throat, and I swallowed sharply. "Thanks, Casey, but I've got to go. I'll see you later."

I ended the call and tossed the phone onto the passenger seat. The bikers were still on my ass, and their lights were almost blinding.

"Pass me or back the hell off," I muttered, adjusting my mirror up to block the glare.

As if in answer, one of them pulled around to pass, the other two holding back. The man was riding a chrome Harley Davidson cruiser, and wicked ink covered his muscular arms. As he passed, he cast me a look that sent chills skittering down my spine. If his golden eyes weren't proof enough, his massive build told me everything I needed to know: he wasn't human.

What now?

He pulled in front of me and slowed down just as one of the other bikers came around and closed me in on the right. The bastards were trying to get me to pull over!

Memories of my car chase with Billy flooded my mind, and anger blossomed under my skin. I shifted the Gran Fury into fourth gear and pressed my foot into the accelerator. I wasn't the same girl I'd been three weeks ago.

The Fury rocketed forward and grazed the fender of the asshole in front of me. His motorcycle swerved, but he regained control and sped up, keeping a wider berth.

"Pull over, or you're going to end up in a ditch!" the biker on my right shouted. He was also covered in tats and solidly built, and if it weren't for the fact that he was trying to hijack my ride, or God knows what else, he'd be hot.

"Like hell I am." I swerved right, trying to ram him. Cursing, he careened away before my Fury clipped him.

Why was it that shifters kept trying to drive me off the road, steal my soul, and kill me?

Cause they're dicks, my wolf said.

Exactly.

The headlights of an oncoming car appeared around a bend. I hit the accelerator again, narrowly missing the guy on the Harley in front as he lurched right.

Beeeeeeeeeep, beeep.

The oncoming car laid on the horn but kept its course as the biker swerved off the road.

One down, two to go.

Heart pounding, I barreled down the empty road with two Harleys following in my wake.

I rounded the curve and squinted at the red flashing light a half mile ahead—a railroad crossing. My heart sank. The red and white arm was down, and the train's white beams were visible.

Suddenly, a gunshot sounded behind me, and I instinctually ducked

Bam! The Fury jerked right, and I fought the wheel for control.

Thump, thump, thump.

Bastards shot my back tire out. *Shit!*

My car bucked as pieces of tire flew across the road behind me, followed by the grating of metal on asphalt.

Cringing at the damage I was causing my baby, I eased up slightly. The two bikers were still on my tail, but the fact that they'd shot my tire and not my head meant they wanted me alive.

A horn blared from ahead. The oncoming train was rapidly eating up the tracks. My heart clenched. Could I make it across?

It was going to be a close call.

Steadying the steering wheel, I gently increased the pressure on the gas pedal, silently praying that I didn't wind up wrapped around a tree.

Another gunshot pierced the air but missed my car. Either that, or it was a warning.

The train's horns blared again as it barreled forward. *Come on, come on, come on.* I gritted my teeth and held my breath as I closed the distance to the tracks.

I wasn't going to make it. In a last, desperate attempt, I hit the accelerator. The metal of my bare wheel screamed on the asphalt, and deep pangs of regret tore into me.

The train's deafening horn blared as the Fury flew through an intersection and then launched over the train tracks.

The car's front tires hit the pavement first, and I barely managed to keep my head from smacking against the steering wheel before the vehicle swerved right and crashed into a stop sign.

The car stalled, and I leaned back in the seat, chest heaving, as I sucked in ragged breaths. The train rushed by, still blaring, but there was no sign of the bikers. *Thank fuck.*

I turned the ignition, and the Fury's engine rumbled to life. I put her in reverse, then eased her onto the road. After about a mile, I pulled onto the shoulder just before the exit to the toll road to Chicago and turned off the car.

Closing my eyes, I summoned my magic. Cool pulses of energy moved through me like breakers rolling into the shore. I focused on drawing the darkness around me, and within seconds, the Fury and I were enveloped in shadows.

And then I waited.

Five minutes later, three headlights appeared down the

empty highway. My nerves ratcheted up as the bikers neared. I'd been working on my mastery over shadows, but I'd never tried to conceal something as large as a car.

I held my breath and tried to still my heartbeat, focusing with all my strength on my magic.

I was certain it would fail or they would smell me, but the werewolf bikers didn't glance my way—just continued down the highway, oblivious to the fact that I was parked on the shoulder.

I didn't move. Not for three minutes. Not until I couldn't even imagine I could hear their engines anymore. With a cautious and slow breath, I climbed out of the car and popped the trunk, pulling out a tire iron and a jack.

I knelt and placed the socket over one of the lug nuts and had to bite my lip.

My heart surged as memories of my mom teaching me to change a tire bombarded me. "Who are you going to rely on if you get a flat and you're alone?" she'd said. "Yourself."

I missed her so damn much, and there were so many questions I had for her. Questions that I needed answers to. Like what kind of Magica she'd been, and why she and Dad had kept this all a secret. Questions that I planned on asking Aunt Laurel and Uncle Pete once they returned.

Changing a tire while maintaining my magic shroud of darkness was as easy as rubbing your stomach while patting your head. Luckily, multitasking meant that I couldn't dwell on thoughts of my parents. It had taken ten minutes, and the bikers hadn't returned, so I slipped into the car and headed up the tollway in case they decided to round back. I'd definitely need to get my car checked out to make sure I hadn't damaged the wheel.

Between the run and the toll of using my magic, I was exhausted to the bone and had to release my shadow shield. I wasn't going to try multitasking while driving.

We better tell our alpha, my wolf said.

"The hell we should," I murmured, squeezing the steering wheel until my knuckles stung. And he wasn't our alpha. We weren't pack.

Still, I knew she was right. A part of me ached to see Jaxson again, but I also knew that I couldn't trust myself to think straight around him. Whether it was our fated mate bond or the fact that he was six feet of pure man hunk, if I saw him again, I knew exactly what would happen. I'd had a taste of heaven, and like a kid in front of cake, I'd definitely want a bite.

A bite? You'd want to eat it all, Wolfie said.

I ran a hand through my slightly damp hair, sighing audibly. I was so screwed.

Grabbing my phone, I dialed Jaxson. It'd been a week since we'd last spoken, since I'd last seen him. A painfully long week.

The phone rang three times and went straight to voicemail. Seriously? I shot daggers at my phone and threw it back on the seat. *He* was ignoring me?

That's not ironic at all, my wolf said snidely.

She was a sarcastic bitch but not wrong.

Forty-five minutes later, I pulled into one of the only empty parking spots a block down from Eclipse. My nerves were shot, and my annoyance at actually having come here only made me more determined to find Jaxson. After all, I had to ask him if he knew anything about those biker werewolves. This had absolutely *nothing* to do with the fact that he'd ignored my call, nor that I was itching to see him again.

I spotted Jaxson's new truck in the back alley, and my pulse quickened. I was *so* screwed.

There was a line out the front of Eclipse. I recognized the beefy bouncer, and apparently, he remembered me, too, because he opened the door for me and stepped aside as I entered.

It was still early, but the bar was quickly filling up for a

Thursday. A rock band was playing tonight, and revelers crowded around the stage while thirsty patrons flocked to the bar. No sign of Sam.

I gave a quick glance around to make sure nobody was watching, and then I slipped through the *Employees Only* door. I'd been down this hall a few times before, and my nerves thrummed from panic or exhilaration, I couldn't discern which. Luckily, my annoyance at Jaxson ignoring my call trumped it all.

I twisted the doorknob of his office and stepped in. "After giving me crap about not picking up the phone, you have a lot of nerve—"

My stomach dropped as I took in the room of shocked faces staring back at me.

Jaxson stood before a monitor with a colorized map of the upper Midwest. He was wearing blue jeans and a tailored black shirt, the sleeves rolled up around his thick forearms.

"Damn," I whispered as he turned toward me.

Judging by the look on his face and those of the other ten people in the room, he was pissed.

3

Jaxson

Savannah burst into the room like a crazed demon. I'd sensed her presence the moment she'd entered the bar, but I hadn't expected her to barge into my office unannounced.

My mate.

I'd spent the past week scouring old pack books and lore, seeking a way to break our mate bond without breaking our minds. I'd come up short and was gradually coming to terms with my fate: Savannah Caine.

I clenched my jaw, willing myself to be calm, but her proximity was like a punch to the gut. Never mind her outburst, the pounding of her heart, that sheen of sweat on her rising and falling breasts. Hell, that fucking sweet scent of hers was enough to drive me over the edge. Yet somehow, I fought for control.

"And who are you?" Andre Vassilez, the beta of the South Dakota pack, eyed Savannah with an interest that made me murderous.

Savannah took a step back, scanning the room with a look of complete horror. Her hair was wild and unruly, and exhaustion tugged at her features. "I—I didn't know you were in a meeting."

Her embarrassment was palpable, and her flushed skin only heightened my sudden arousal.

"I'm so sorry for interrupting. I'll just step outside until you're finished." She backpedaled to the door and slipped out. I heard her slump against the wall and curse.

But even with the door shut, it was like she was still in the room. Her scent lingered, drowning my thoughts in desire. The images on the screen and everyone else's faces had become meaningless blurs.

I knotted my fist and cleared my throat. "I think I've outlined our stance on the trade negotiations. Take a few days to think it over, but understand that we won't budge. Ten percent, take it or leave it."

Andre's jaw ticked with irritation. This meeting hadn't gone as he'd hoped, but I didn't give a damn. If the South Dakota pack wanted in on our supply line, then they'd take what I offered them.

"This meeting is over." I eyed Sam, indicating for her to get them the fuck out.

Her chair scraped across the floor as she stood. "Let me show you gentleman to the bar. Drinks are on the house, of course."

Andre scoffed but knew better than to cross me. He stood and filed out of the room with the others. Sam raised her brow and gave me a look that said, *Better watch out.*

I could handle the redheaded she-devil. I was the gods-damned alpha.

"Send her in." I turned off the monitor and slipped the transport contract into my desk as Savannah stepped into my office, wringing her hands.

"Jax, I—" Her flushed red lips stopped moving under the weight of my silent gaze.

Heat pulsed through me, and my muscles strained as I fought the irresistible urge to press her up against the wall and breathe in the rich scent of her body. It had been difficult staying away from her this past week, but that was nothing compared to what I was feeling now. Judging by the agony on Savannah's face, she was struggling as well.

I leaned on my desk and dug my fingers into the sides as if somehow, I could use it to shield myself from her. "Ever heard of knocking?"

Anger flashed through her gorgeous blue eyes, and whatever reserve she'd entered with was redirected into fury. "Ever heard of picking up your phone?"

This was the woman I'd come to know, hotheaded and stubborn. So why did I want to taste those honeyed lips again so badly?

Because she is ours, my wolf pressed.

But it was more than that.

I owed her more than I could explain. When my packmates had been in danger, she'd found the way to free them from Dragan's clutches in the Dreamlands. She didn't shy from danger or a fight. She was a force of nature, and I was just a fool who had wandered out into the storm to see the tornado for himself.

Like the fortune teller had said, I had to find a way to tame her. Although all I wanted to do was get lost in her fire, I hardened my stance and expression. "How unbelievable is it that I might not be able to be at your every beck and call?"

She pinched her brows together with her fingers and closed her eyes for a second as a little of her fight faded. "Touché." With a sigh, she moved around the table and chairs to the far side of the room, putting some distance between us. "Listen, I'm sorry for barging in. I tried to call, but you didn't answer, and I needed your help."

Now that she'd reined in her ire for me, the undercurrent of anxiety rolling off her was unmistakable, scents of fear, anxiety, and adrenaline.

Everything in the room sharpened in an instant as the haze that had consumed me disintegrated. Protectiveness swelled through every muscle, and I took a step toward her. "What happened?"

She flinched and moved back. "I'm fine, but I was attacked by three men on motorcycles. Shifters, by the look of them."

Shock rocked through me as my senses went on alert. What was it about this woman that drew trouble like sharks to the scent of blood? I stalked around the table toward her. "Where? Explain."

Worry flickered in her eyes as she slid around the table away from me. "In Indiana. I was leaving the dunes after a run, and they came up on me. They tried to get me to pull over."

How dare they try to touch one of my pack?

Our mate.

Unbridled fury settled into my bones. "Can you identify them? I swear, I'll hunt those fuckers down and snap their spines."

Savannah put up her hands. "Take it easy, Jaxson, I'm *fine*. I just thought you should know, and I figured you might have an idea who these guys are."

Rage and frustration swirled in my mind. How in the hell was I supposed to protect her if I had no idea where she was?

"What the hell were you doing running at the dunes? *Alone*? Gods, Savannah." I turned, clenching my fists so I didn't put one of them through the wall.

"Listen, I didn't come here for a fight. Do you know who they might be or not?"

I scrubbed a hand through my hair and turned back to her. "Did you get a look at them? Were they wearing cuts or any distinguishing marks?"

By the way she knit her brows together, I knew the answer before she spoke. "I barely got a look at them. Just a glance of golden eyes and lots of tattoos."

Memories of the bikers Gretchen and I had tracked down before this shitstorm had started rose in my mind. "That's not a lot to go on, but I'll look into it."

It was nothing. There were several shifter MCs—motorcycle clubs—in Indiana and Michigan. Some were allies, others trouble, but the riders all had golden eyes and tattoos.

"Thanks." Savannah watched me expectantly, and color rose in her cheeks. "I'll get out of your hair. Sorry for interrupting your meeting."

She moved to leave, but I closed the distance and placed my hand on the door. "Where are you going?"

Savannah stopped abruptly, torn between wanting to retreat and wanting to draw near my body. Her damp hair hung around her shoulders, and the scent of lake water called up memories of swimming together in a starlit pool, of laughing together.

How long had it been since I'd laughed like that with anyone?

Not since my sister died. Perhaps not since before then.

Her pupils dilated, and her pulse quickened. "I'm going home. I need a shower and sleep."

Home. My irritation flared. She was a godsdamned werewolf now—her place was here with me and the pack. "You were just attacked. You should stay here until we can figure out what's going on."

Her eyes flicked to my hand on the door. "I'll be safe at the LaSalles', and I can't raise any suspicions with my family. Casey is already getting nosy, and he knows something's up. If they knew…" Briefly, her voice trailed off. "I just found them, and I don't want to lose them."

Letting my fingers slide from the door, I stepped up so that I was only inches from her. Her citrus sunshine signature surrounded me, bombarding my senses from every angle. She turned her head away, but I whispered, "But you're not the same woman you were three weeks ago, and not just a LaSalle. You're one of us now. Part of the pack. You belong with us."

With me.

Her eyes pricked with tears, but she raised her chin defiantly as she stepped back. "I don't know where I belong, Jaxson, or why I have a wolf inside me. Until I find those answers..."

Her voice caught, and she let the sentence die. But I could read the unspoken words. She wasn't ready to face the truth that she was a werewolf. That she was one of us. That she was my mate.

The distance she'd created between us with that single backward step burned. I closed my eyes and nodded. "Fine. It's your choice. Always has been." Her breath hitched as I reached around her and opened the door. "I'll look into the bikers," I added. "But if you notice anything out of the ordinary, call me. I promise I'll pick up."

For a moment, she lingered. Her hand hovered inches from my chest, and I could feel the prickle of electricity spanning the gap between us. Then she slipped by me and into the hall. "Thank you. I will."

I shut the door behind us and followed her down the hall with a hollowness in my chest.

For days, all I had wanted was a moment to speak with her about our mate bond. But it was clear that she hadn't even accepted what she was. Until she acknowledged that, nothing else would matter.

So that was the first step. I had to make Savannah understand what it meant to be part of the pack. That we were her family.

Then maybe we could face each other.

4

I hurried down the hall, heart pounding, and tried to put just a little distance between us. Going to Eclipse had been a mistake. I should have just gone home and called until Jaxson picked up.

Clearly, no part of my mind worked around him. One second, he infuriated me, and the next, I was weak in the knees. Delusional.

The moment Jaxson had placed his hand on the door and locked me in, a treacherous shiver snaked down my spine. Some deranged, traitorous part of my soul had wanted him to keep me there—hell, to pin me against the wall and never let me leave.

If that didn't go against every fiber of my being, and if things weren't so complicated between us, then maybe I would have let him. Even for a moment.

God knew I wanted it.

But things were complicated. And I wasn't about to face him and the apparent mate bond we shared—not when I could barely face my new four-legged reality.

I didn't even know how I'd become a werewolf, and until I got answers about that, there wasn't much more I could face.

Eclipse was bustling, but the crowd parted for us. Sam slid a cocktail across the bar to one of Jaxson's visitors and gave me a quick smile before turning her focus back on the men from the meeting.

I cringed at how all that had played out and felt my neck flush. Why did I always end up with one foot in my mouth?

Sam was so composed, whether she was in a gunfight or at the center of a whirlwind of drinks and gossip. I was jealous. I could barely keep my head screwed on straight.

As we pushed toward the door of the bar, Jaxson pressed his hand to my lower back. It was soft—just a light touch gently guiding me through the crowd—but even so, it sent a torrent of heat rushing along my skin.

Had he touched me like that in his office, I would have melted. And even though I was frustrated out of my mind and had bikers to worry about as well as the alpha, my thoughts were entirely focused on the way his lips tasted.

I wanted a bite of cake.

You want the whole *cake*, my wolf remarked.

Fair enough.

We stepped out onto the street, the cool night air cleared my head, and I moved away from him. I could tell from the dark clouds that had consumed his features that Jaxson was disappointed I wasn't staying. But just because I was a werewolf now and we had some kind of fated bond didn't mean I would automatically pack up my life and move in with him. I had too much to sort out and needed space and time.

As I walked up to the Fury, Jaxson stilled, his gaze taking in the loose bumper and the spare tire. "What happened to your car?"

The damage looked a lot worse now in the lights of the city

than it had in the shadows of the dark highway. My stomach twisted. *My poor baby.*

I gave him an uncertain smile. "Did I mention I rammed a couple bikers before one of them shot my tire out?"

Jaxson's appearance turned lethal. Darkness flooded his face as his muscles tensed. The man that had swum with me in the pond in the Dreamlands was gone, replaced by a killer. His signature was clamped down, but everyone around us could feel the change. Conversations stilled.

No one looked our way.

Jaxson stepped toward me, his posture rigid and radiating with fury. "No. You didn't think that part was important? That someone shot at you?"

Tearing my eyes from the hard contours of his chest, I looked up at him and shrugged. "I'm getting used to it."

But I wasn't, and I knew he could smell the lie.

Silence stretched between us as his anger hung in the air. I knew he would kill for me, and I hated how *hot* that felt, even as the terror of him trickled along my spine.

His wolf was so near the surface that I could see it struggling beneath the brilliant gold of his eyes. A part of me wanted it to come out, to see him off his tight leash.

Though the muscles in his jaw remained taut, the wave of rage began to subside. "Bring your car to Savage Body tomorrow. I'll have it fixed."

More dependency. More obligations.

I slipped around him and opened the car door. "I've already got a mechanic."

"You sure you have the money for that?" Jaxson gripped the top of my door, and I glared at him even as my stomach dropped.

I was dead broke, and he knew it.

It was beyond embarrassing, and I couldn't help but feel

inadequate standing next to him—a man who acted like he owned all or at least part of Dockside. Who wore designer suits and bought new trucks on a whim.

I had a few hundred bucks. Several bucks less after taking the toll road home.

"I don't take handouts," I said sharply.

He studied me for a moment, searching, and then his dark expression softened ever so slightly. "I wasn't offering a handout. I need help. I'll fix your car, and you can pay me back by working the bar with Sam this weekend. We've got a couple big gigs, and we're shorthanded."

I narrowed my eyes at Jaxson, searching for any hidden catch. He was offering me a way out. I wanted to shut him down and keep my pride, but I was broke, not stupid.

And hell, I *was* a waitress, for fuck's sake. I could tend bar. "Fine. And I'll pay for the rest once I have a job."

Jaxson nodded, and with that, I slipped into the Fury and pulled my door closed. I started the car, and Jaxson leaned down and rapped his knuckles on my window.

There was something about the way the massive man bent just a little to see me that sent the butterflies in my stomach fluttering like I was a teenage girl. *Damn, Savannah, get a freaking grip.*

I rolled down the window. "Yes?"

"Tony will escort you home and keep an eye on things," he said as headlights pulled up behind me. I could make out Tony and two others inside a black SUV. When the hell had he arranged that?

I started to object, but Jaxson cut me off, his voice commanding obedience. "If I can't have my eyes on you, then this is the alternative. It's *non*-negotiable."

He turned and left, and I slumped back in my seat, watching

him depart down the dark street. Was it too late to change my mind?

Sighing, I pulled out and headed back to the Indies with three werewolf bodyguards in tow. I prayed they wouldn't be spotted by any trigger-happy sorcerers and that they'd leave once they'd escorted me home, but I knew that was asking for too much.

My phone buzzed, and I eagerly glanced at the screen before answering. Not Jaxson. *Damn.* "Hi, Aunt Laurel."

"Hi, honey. Sorry I missed your call earlier. Pete and I are driving through Nebraska now and should be home the day after tomorrow. We have a *lot* to talk about." She emphasized that last line, worry evident in her voice.

"Right, I'm eager to hear more about my mom. You said we could talk more about her and Dad when you got home."

The silent pause on the other end of the line ratcheted up my nerves.

"Of course. We can talk about all of that, too, at some point. Is everything all right?" my aunt asked.

"Yup. Nothing to worry about. See you both Saturday." I hung up, feeling a sudden pang of deceit in my chest. Why was my aunt so evasive when it came to my mom?

But you know why, don't you?

She'd said we had a lot to talk about, which meant only one thing: she'd dredged up something on Dragan.

Dread mixed with an overwhelming sense of betrayal as I pulled into the driveway of my aunt and uncle's house. Casey's car was parked in the garage. "Great."

I climbed out of the Fury and glanced down the street to where Tony had parked. I waved my hand, dismissing him, but he didn't leave.

On the bright side, I wouldn't have to worry about bikers tonight.

The front door slammed closed behind me, and I slid the four locks into place. At first, I'd thought they were overkill, but now?

I headed into the kitchen and grabbed a pop from the fridge. As I was chugging the sugary goodness, Casey strolled in wearing a towel—and only a towel—wrapped around his waist.

"Your car sounded like a screeching bat when you pulled in. What the hell happened? Run over a werewolf or something?"

I choked, and pop shot out of my nose. "Why are you naked?"

Casey shot me a devilish grin. "I've got company, so keep it down. But first, spill the beans. What happened to the Fury?"

Ugh, now I was never going to sleep.

I took a long pull on my Coke. "Three werewolf bikers wanted to have a chat."

Casey's eyes bugged out. "Shit. Are you serious?"

"Deadly serious."

My cousin tipped his head back and laughed, causing his towel to slip loose. "You're like a shitstorm magnet!"

I snapped my head to the right to avert my eyes lest they burn out. "Thanks for your genius insight. Now if you don't mind, please put some clothes on, and let me have a little peace and quiet."

"I want to hear all of the juicy details, but I've got a lady friend waiting for me upstairs. Check you later." My cousin winked and sauntered out of the kitchen.

I slumped onto a stool and leaned on the kitchen island, rubbing my sore eyes. I was exhausted, but between Casey's lovemaking and the events of the day, I knew sleep was far off.

With a weary groan, I finally gathered the strength to stand and amble down the hall. Maybe a hot bath would help. But as I began climbing the stairs, my eye caught on the door to Aunt Laurel's study. It was slightly ajar.

I paused mid-step. Snooping was rude, but so was withholding information, and Aunt Laurel had been continuously dodging my questions about my mother. There was no way I could tell her what had happened to me, and I needed information.

Moving quietly, I sneaked toward the study. My heart leapt as several thumps sounded from the second floor, followed by an explosion and a crash. And then laughter.

What the hell were they even trying to do? My cousin was a lunatic, but at least I could be sure he was distracted.

I slunk into the study and gently shut the door behind me. I'd been in there a few times, and while it wasn't explicitly off limits, I'd always been invited in by my aunt.

Guilt and shame settled over me, and yet, I snooped the shit out of the place.

I started with my aunt's oak writing desk, which was filled with recipe books and spells scribbled on loose sheets. I shuffled through the papers but found nothing of interest. When I reached into the back of the top drawer, however, my fingers brushed over a cold metal object.

My heart fluttered as I stared down at the tiny brass skeleton key in my hand. It didn't fit in any of the keyholes in the desk, which were all unlocked. I scanned the room, and my gaze settled on the antique filing cabinet in the corner.

The key fit perfectly into the top drawer, and with a click, it slid open. Manila folders with printed labels filled the space. I flipped through them, not recognizing any of the names, until I spotted one that had grown far too familiar of late—*Laurent.*

5

Savannah

I snatched the thick folder out and spread its contents on the floor. Dossiers and photographs of each member of Jaxson's pack. What the hell?

My pulse throbbed in my temples as I seized two more folders. I didn't recognize them, but one appeared to be full of information about a pack from Grand Rapids and the other a pack in Duluth. I fumbled with the key and opened the lower two drawers, both of which were filled with manila folders about packs spread across the east and west coasts.

Bile rose in my throat, and I sunk to my knees. Laurel was keeping tabs on what looked like all the packs in North America.

I didn't know how long I sat there, shocked and numb, but a loud crash from upstairs jerked me back to reality.

Scrambling, I shuffled the papers back into their places and returned the folders to the drawers, careful to make sure each was in its proper spot before locking up and returning the key to Laurel's desk.

I tiptoed to the door and peeked out. All was silent except for the muffled moan from a woman upstairs. And that did it. There wasn't much more that I could handle for one day.

I gave the room one last look and—

Were those *photo albums* on the bookshelf?

Curiosity got the better of me, and I crept across the study and tugged out one of the oversized albums. Inside were old photos of Laurel and Pete and others I didn't recognize. I grabbed the other one and flipped through the plastic pages, then stopped when I saw my dad smiling back at me.

A choked sob escaped my throat as I dragged my fingers over the fading photo of my dad holding a frisbee at the beach. He couldn't have been more than eighteen.

There were more photos of him and Laurel and Pete on the next pages. And then of my mom.

Tears rolled down my face as I took in the happy faces of my parents. They were young and filled with so much love. One photo was of them canoeing, another of Dad with Mom slung over his shoulder.

I sat there for what felt like hours, memorizing every snapshot of their lives laid out before me. My grief mixed with the delight of seeing their faces again. When the fire had destroyed our home six years ago, we'd lost everything. Apart from the few photographs that my godmother had kept, these were the only surviving records of my parents.

I went through the photos again, settling on the one of them that included a man I didn't recognize. He was older and handsome, and very well built. I slid the photo out of its sleeve and flipped it over. On the back was my mom's handwriting:

Silas and me hiking with Dad at Crater Lake, 1992.

That man had to be my mother's father, Russ. I'd never met him. I flipped the photo over and stared at the man with his arm slung around Mom. He had the same eyes as her, but his build was like—

I dropped the photo and froze. His build was like Jaxson's, unnaturally large and ripped.

As if I could bury the truth, I shoved the picture back into its sleeve. But there was a folded-up piece of paper inside that I must have missed.

I tugged it out and opened it, immediately recognizing my dad's chicken scratch handwriting. I smoothed out the creases as I tried to make sense of the words.

Lauri-

I'm sorry we had to go without saying goodbye. This was never how I wanted to leave things, but you know why we had to. Tell Father I love him and that I hope he'll one day find it in his heart to forgive me. But Claire is my soulmate, and now that we're expecting a child, I will always choose them first. He can never know, and you must tell no one. Thank you for your kindness, dear sister. Love you always.

- Silas

My hands were shaking, and the room suddenly felt constricting. Panic washed over me as I jammed the note and photograph back in the sleeve. I couldn't breathe. I needed to get out.

The wound on my shoulder started to tingle, and I shoved the album back onto the shelf with my heart pounding.

"You dirty little half-breed snoop!"

I spun. An old man with a white goatee stood in the doorway. My lungs seized, and my mouth went dry.

I recognized his face. His picture was hanging on the office wall. Laurel's father. My grandfather. Simon LaSalle.

Who'd been dead now, according to Casey, for around fifteen years.

The ghost's face tightened with lines of hatred. "If my daughter found you in her office, if she knew what you really were, she'd skin you alive and spread you out at the foot of her bed like a rug."

Horror seized me, and I barreled toward the door.

My grandfather tried to block my way, but the ethereal figure dissipated into smoke as I charged through, leaving the doorway empty. It left the cut from the Soul Knife burning like the flames of hell.

My vision shifted, and nausea rolled over me. *Need to get out of here. Can't breathe.*

I staggered down the hallway in a daze and fumbled with the locks on the front door like my hands were encased in greasy mittens. I burst outside and stumbled down the front stairs before taking off across the lawn. Sobs tore from my throat, but I kept moving, knowing only that I needed to get away.

The ghost, my life, my past...

As if inhabiting another body, I heard a distant voice call my name, but it didn't register with my grandfather's words repeating over and over.

You dirty little half-breed snoop. She'd skin you alive.

I shuddered at the words I couldn't bring myself to believe—that my mother had been a werewolf.

But you've known the truth all along, a voice inside me said. Not my wolf, my own voice.

"No!" I cried, clutching my head. My foot caught on a garden hose, and I fell to my knees in a yard two houses down.

How did I get here?

I was too distracted by the litany of thoughts racing through my mind to dwell on the sting in my shins.

I didn't bother getting up. There was no way to run from the truth. My grandfather Russ had been a werewolf. My mother must have been one. And my parents fled Magic Side to hide me from Grandfather LaSalle.

I could still feel the hatred in the ghost's words.

"Savannah!" A distant but familiar voice broke through the din of my churning thoughts.

Strong hands gripped my shoulders, and when I blinked away the tears streaming from my eyes, I recognized the face staring back at me. "Tony?"

"What happened? Are you hurt?" he asked, lifting me to my feet and inspecting my body for injuries. The two other shifters who'd come with him prowled the street, looking around confusedly.

I shrugged out of Tony's grasp and wiped my face with my shaking hands. "I'm fine. Nothing happened. I just had a bad dream."

If only that were true.

"You're a bad liar," Tony said darkly. "You're in your same clothes."

"Hey!" My cousin's voice echoed down the street.

"Oh, no," I muttered, and turned in time to see Casey leap over the deck railing of Laurel and Pete's house.

"Get the fuck away from her, you ass turds!" he yelled. Summoning a ball of fire in his palm, he sprinted toward us.

"Casey, stop!" I stepped forward with arms raised. "It's just a misunderstanding."

Tony gave a brusque laugh and shook his head but motioned to the other two shifters and began walking back to his Jeep.

Casey watched them go with a scowl, then slung an arm around my shoulder. "What the hell was that? Did those dogs jump you?"

I rubbed my forehead, which was beginning to throb. "No. They're just here watching my back. Just in case the bikers show up. Everything is fine, I just—"

What could I tell Casey? That I'd raided his mother's office? That I'd seen the ghost of our grandfather? That I was one of those *dogs*.

I shuddered. "Panic attack. I had a rough day. Let's go inside."

Casey was watching me a little too closely with an expression I couldn't quite read, but he didn't say anything. He just squeezed my shoulder and led me home.

The second we stepped inside, my phone lit up and began buzzing. Jaxson.

Casey glanced at my phone as he strolled past me. "Deal with your business, but when that's done, you and I need to talk."

I shook my head as I stared down at my buzzing phone. I really didn't want to answer, but I knew that if I didn't, Jaxson would break the front door down in ten minutes.

Could this day get *any* worse?

I sucked in a shaky breath and tapped the screen.

"What's going on?" Jaxson all but shouted.

"Nothing, actually. I stepped out for some fresh air and... well, it was all a misunderstanding." Damn it, I was *such* a bad liar.

"Cut the bullshit. I'm five minutes away, and unless you want me showing up on your aunt's doorstep, you'd better tell me what happened."

"No! Don't do that!" My head was really throbbing now, and my cheeks burned with embarrassment. "It was really nothing, Jaxson. I just had a little panic attack. I'm okay now, though, I promise."

Understatement of the century. But I needed time to process, and the last thing I needed was Jaxson breathing down my neck.

"A panic attack? Why?" His voice hardened with concern. I was sure he'd gotten a play-by-play from his goons, and after humiliating myself in front of them on the neighbors' lawn, I didn't want to replay it over again to Jaxson.

I turned my back to Casey, who was grabbing a beer in the kitchen and without a doubt eavesdropping.

"I found some old photos of my parents, and then I lost it. I just need some time to process—it's been a rough day."

He was silent, and I wasn't sure if he was still on the line.

"Jaxson?"

He grumbled, "Okay, fine. But hand me off to Casey."

"You don't need—"

"I'll call him myself. My people are parked out front and not going away. I need shit to be crystal clear with your cousin," Jaxson growled with irritation.

I sighed and headed into the kitchen. "He wants to talk to you."

With an exasperated sigh, my cousin took the phone. "Yeah?" He frowned and nodded a few times, and then his eyes bugged out and locked on me. "*Of course* I'm not going to let her out of my sight. Yeah, yeah. Night, Laurent."

Casey hung up and handed my phone back. "You want to talk about it?"

"No."

The only people I wanted to talk to were long dead—my parents.

6

Savannah

The following morning, the house was thankfully free of ghosts, though I'd distinctly avoided my aunt's office on my way to the kitchen for breakfast.

With zero enthusiasm, I pressed my spoon into the brick of shredded wheat lying morosely in my bowl. It was...well, pretty damn unappetizing, to be honest. But I'd eaten more sugar in three weeks living with the LaSalles than I had in my entire life, and it was high time I started making changes.

I sorrowfully spooned a little milk over the dry haybale.

We should just switch to eating bacon every morning, my wolf whined.

"We're out," I said, rather mournfully.

Despite the prospect of eating what I was certain amounted to recycled cardboard, I felt pretty good, all things considered. I'd slept hard and late, and my nerves were chill. It might have had something to do with the whiskey and Xanax Casey had given me before bed.

A sweet aroma wafted through the room, and a moment

later, Casey clomped in. "You're not really going to eat that, are you?"

"Uncle Pete eats it."

"Yeah, but Dad also drinks his own potions. I think he might not actually have taste buds." Casey chuckled.

I looked down at the shreds. It was a fair point.

Casey dropped a pink box down on the kitchen table. The scent of sticky glazed donuts emanated from inside, and my mouth watered.

I looked up with pleading eyes. "Case, I can't keep eating this much sugar."

He opened the lid and made the box talk. "You know you want me. Just a bite."

I gestured to the fang marks on his neck. "Is that the line you used to pick up your lady friend last night?"

Casey grinned wide. "Vampire bites are an aphrodisiac. Don't knock it till you've tried it."

The doorbell chimed, and he glanced over his shoulder. "Are you expecting visitors?"

I shook my head and peered around him. *God, it'd better not be Jaxson.*

Casey's magic prickled the air around me, and he strode up the hall toward the door, muttering, "I don't like unexpected guests."

I shrugged and eyed the open box of donuts. Half were plain, while the other half were maple glazed with bits of caramelized bacon. He knew my type. The aromas were driving my wolf senses wild.

Bacon, please.

I seized two maple glazed donuts and started shoving one in my mouth as I heard Casey unlatch the four locks on the front door.

"What do you want?" he grumbled.

A woman's voice answered, "I'm looking for Savannah Caine. I believe she's living with you…"

I instantly stopped chewing and looked behind me, but I couldn't see all the way down the hall to the door. I could hear perfectly with my wolf ears, though.

Casey grunted. "Never heard of her. Is she somebody famous or a porn star or something?"

"Savannah Caine. Your cousin. Who put your address on her Magic Side ID. I know that's her car outside, Mr. LaSalle, so let's cut to the chase—she's not in trouble, and you're not in trouble. I just need to talk to her."

My pulse skipped a beat, then began pounding. A cop—it had to be. But why? About what had happened last night?

"'Mr. LaSalle,' is it now?" Casey asked in a tone I couldn't quite place.

My ears pricked at the sound of furious…chewing?

"That's the way it's always been," the woman snapped.

Great. Clearly, they knew each other—which, judging by my cousin's reputation around town, didn't bode well. I scooted off the stool. While I appreciated Casey's caution, there was no way I wanted him representing me to the cops.

"Coming," I said as I hurried up the hall and shoved myself between Casey and the open door.

The blonde standing on the porch wore a long brown coat and jeans and had an official-looking badge secured to her belt. She had gorgeous eyes and a curvy figure, and she was emphatically chewing on a wad of gum as she shot daggers at Casey. The way she had her arms crossed and hip cocked out said, *Don't screw with me, buster*. Her scent and posture told me she didn't like Casey, not one bit. I was pretty used to that reaction at this point.

I held out my palm. "I'm Savannah Caine."

The woman flashed one last deadly glare at my cousin, then

gave me a warm smile as she shook my outstretched hand. "Agent Harlow Blake. Special Investigations for the Order."

Casey put a hand on my shoulder. "Don't tell her anything. We don't have to talk to these people."

I used my hip to maneuver him back inside and gave him a brusque shove. "*You* don't have to talk to these people because they want to talk to me. Now buzz off. I've got this."

After making sure he'd truly withdrawn into the kitchen, I turned back to the woman. She was poised and confident in a way I wished I could be. Her scent told me she wasn't a shifter, but I couldn't place what she was. Her magic tasted like honeysuckle, felt like brushing your fingers over soft grass, and smelled like warm vanilla.

"How can I help?" I asked.

"We got a report that a gang of bikers tried to force your vehicle off the road last night."

My blood froze, and I inadvertently glanced at my Gran Fury. The bumper was still dragging on the ground, and I spied a bullet hole next to the spare tire. There was no plausible way to deny it, even if I wanted to.

"Where did you hear about this?"

"The bikers passed another car trying to get you. The driver had to slam on his breaks to avoid running over one of them. He called the highway patrol and reported that a gang of cyclists had shot out one of your wheels. Your license plate already had a statewide flag on it, so the alert made it back to our system."

A flag?

Jaxson had flagged my plate three weeks ago when I'd ditched him—as well as his truck keys—in Belmont. But I'd assumed he'd taken it off by now. Did that mean he was monitoring me every time I came and left Magic Side? I licked my suddenly dry lips as thoughts swirled in my head. "What's it to you?"

The special agent took off her sunglasses and pulled her blonde hair over her shoulders. "I'm running a taskforce that's investigating a crooked supernatural MC from Michigan. I was hoping you could tell me a little about your assailants."

I shrugged and leaned against the doorframe. "I didn't get a good look at the guys. I don't even know what they wanted—just that they wanted me off the road."

"Can you tell me anything about them?"

"Shifters, I think. They were big and burly with golden-yellow eyes. No helmets, but their faces were in shadow. Lots of tattoos."

"Did any of the tattoos look like this?"

She held up her cell phone, which showed a sketch of a two-headed wolf tattoo. *My* sketch.

Memories of the night I was attacked at the Taphouse by Dane and that woman bombarded me. She'd had that same tattoo, and so had one of the shifters who'd attacked Casey and me at the Magic Moon motel. Kahanov's goons, or rather, Dragan's.

I swallowed, but the lump in my throat wouldn't go down. "I don't know. How do you have that?"

She pulled a notepad out of her back pocket. "We should talk. May I come in?"

"No, she cannot!" Casey shouted from the other room.

Did he have werewolf hearing, too?

"Sorry," I said.

She opened her mouth, but Casey's voice interjected from the back. "You can ask her if she wants a donut. They like donuts."

I turned red and dragged my fingers through my hair. "I'm sorry. My cousin is—"

"Oh, I know." Her lips drew a thin line across her face, and she narrowed her eyes. "We *all* know who he is."

"I'm famous!" he shouted from the kitchen.

I stepped out onto the porch and pulled the door shut. "Let's talk over by my car."

Agent Blake glanced at my poor Gran Fury with its dangling bumper, bullet holes, and spare tire, and I instantly regretted my choice of location.

I strode in that direction as if the car's condition were perfectly normal and leaned against the trunk. "Okay, let's talk."

She smiled. "We've been tracking a gang of bikers. This tattoo started showing up around the same time they started moving a drug called Scarlet. Ever heard of it?"

"Nope."

"It's a magical blood-based drug with powerful effects on shifters. It makes them faster, stronger, and angrier. It's highly addictive and turns their eyes red for a time. Ring any bells?"

I remembered the first two werewolves I'd met—vicious, red-eyed, and capable of chasing down my car on the highway. Even Jaxson couldn't do that. I hesitated, not sure what to say. "It sounds like bad shit."

"The worst part is that the supply is drying up. Prices have quintupled. And shifters are going crazy trying to get their hands on it. People are getting hurt. Robberies have spiked." She started chewing on her gum. Hard.

"What does this have to do with me?"

She flipped open her writing pad but didn't look away. "Word on the street up in Wisconsin is that if they find the redhead, they can make more Scarlet."

My hand inadvertently went to my hair. *Fuuuuuuck.*

Her eyes locked on to mine in an unwavering stare. "I think they mean you."

There was no point in denying it. "I was abducted by a bunch of wolves who tried to drain my blood. I thought it was for blood sorcery, but..."

She nodded and responded, but I didn't hear her words. They were drowned out as memories of the sanitarium flooded into my mind. I felt the leather straps around my wrists and the needle pressing into my veins. Had they turned my blood into a drug? My heart started racing as my skin turned cold. They'd wanted to taste me...

Don't freak, my wolf interjected. *You're starting to freak. It's okay. We made it out.*

That was a miracle, I responded, trying to stop myself from shaking.

Not a miracle. We kicked their asses. And if those bastards come back, we'll kick their asses again.

I bit my lip. "Do you think they'll come for me again?"

"Perhaps. Any information you can provide might help us shut them down." Agent Blake looked up and met my eyes. "For instance, what's your relationship to Jaxson Laurent?"

I froze. That was one question I didn't know the answer to. I licked my dry lips. "Just friends."

She raised an eyebrow.

"When I was attacked by werewolves up in Belmont, he and his pack helped me find the people responsible and stop them. That's it. We filed a report with the Order."

"I've read it. I've read all the statements about your abduction, the sanatorium, the showdown at the cabin up in Wisconsin. There were a lot of bodies on both sides. Jaxson lost his brother-in-law, Billy. Your statement said he died trying to fight off one of the rogue wolves?" She flicked her eyes to mine.

My gut twisted. Billy, who'd pinned me down and tried to kill me. Who I'd killed instead by ripping his chest open with my claws and hurling him over a cliff.

I shuddered. "I was jumped by a bastard werewolf. Billy tried to save me."

She watched my eyes. *Intently.* Man, I hoped she couldn't smell lies.

"And what was your relationship with Billy?"

I cocked my head. "Didn't know him well."

"Yet he saved your life."

"I was lucky. He wasn't. It was the heat of battle."

She shook her head and gave me a warm smile that made the hair on my neck stand on end. "It's a funny thing. He had a well-known beef with your family, the LaSalles. There've been plenty of incidents before. And yet, he sacrifices himself to save a LaSalle. Pretty strange."

"I'm not really a LaSalle, so he didn't have a problem with me. I didn't know much about his past, just that he was Jaxson's brother-in-law. I've been through all this before."

"Of course. I'm sorry. I wasn't part of the original investigation. In fact, I had to go to an unused closet in the Archives to find the files, which was also pretty funny. And when I read through the statements, a lot just didn't add up."

I put my hands up in a helpless gesture. "I told them what I saw."

She looked down as she reached into her jacket and started fishing around. It was an overtly casual gesture, but I could tell she was still watching me out of the corner of her eye. Her voice was even in a practiced way. "I understand. I was just wondering if maybe everything wasn't so tidy. Maybe some pack members —like Billy, for instance—were involved with the rogue wolves who abducted you. Maybe Jaxson, well, convinced you to streamline the truth in your statement a bit."

My heart began beating faster. That was *exactly* what had happened. If the Order could pin the abductions on members from the Dockside Pack, they could hold Jaxson responsible and use it as an excuse to go sticking their nose where it didn't belong.

I shook my head and tried to swallow stealthily.

Fire burned in her eyes. "The pack are into some shady stuff. If they're responsible for pushing this drug, we're going to string them up by their balls."

The hair on my neck stood on end. "They're not. I'm certain."

"Do you have any idea what they do?"

I shook my head.

"Then maybe you shouldn't be so certain." She leaned close, subtly pressed a card into my hand, and spoke in a low voice. "I know that things between the LaSalles and Laurents are tense. If you're in some kind of trouble...if Jaxson is pressuring you or is holding something over your head..."

"He's not."

"Of course not. But if, for some reason, any reason, you need a safe place to stay, call me. If members of the Dockside pack are wrapped up with the MC, and the MC is out for your blood, things could turn out badly."

Yeah. Hindsight is 20/20. Fuck that traitor Billy and Kahanov and his rogue wolves.

I tried to manage a halfhearted smile. "I'm safe here."

Agent Blake turned and started walking to her car. "Just think on it. If you remember anything that might connect the pack with those bikers, call me. You have my number."

I looked down at my palm and then slipped the business card into my pocket.

Shit. My blood had been used to make drugs. Werewolves were still after me. The cops knew we were hiding what had happened up at the cabin and suspected that the pack had connections to the MC.

Our life is really messy, my wolf chirped. *But at least our love life is simple.*

I sank down on the Fury's trunk and put my face in my hands.

7

—————

Jaxson

I parked my truck in front of Savage Body a little before noon.

Savannah's Gran Fury was already pulled into the garage, and she stood with her back to me, hands on her hips. The way her gray jeans hugged her ass heated my blood.

A part of me was still shocked that she'd actually called, wanting to meet.

I tried to read her scent and body language as I approached. She looked nervous and agitated, though I wasn't sure if that was about whatever caused her panic attack the night before or about entrusting her precious car into our obviously unworthy hands.

She shook her head violently at my mechanic. "No, I just need you to fix the front bumper and check out my right back wheel."

She must have sensed my approach because she glanced over her shoulder. A faint blush spread across her face when she noticed me. "Hi."

I gestured for her to head inside. "You wanted to talk. How about my office?"

She nodded and started in, but she paused at the door and turned back toward the mechanic. "Don't touch anything under the hood, please."

My mechanic gave her a quizzical look, and I raised my brow at her. She shrugged and stepped into the shop office as I held the door. "The last time you had my Fury, your guys stripped her to pieces."

A soft laugh escaped my throat. "It needed new pieces."

Her expression only darkened. "It did not. That car is the last thing I have from my parents. Nobody tinkers with it, not without my permission."

I studied the hard creases at the corners of her mouth. She'd said her panic attack had been about finding old photos of her parents.

Some wounds cut deep. That, at least, was something I could understand.

I put my hand on the door frame, turned back to the mechanic, and growled, "Not a thing gets touched on that car without Savannah's permission. Treat that vehicle like it belongs to the Moon Mother herself, and make sure everybody in the shop knows it."

My mechanic glanced at the vehicle and swallowed. "Right, boss."

"Will that do?" I asked.

"Yes. Thanks," Savannah mumbled.

I took her into my office in the back and shut the door. Her tangerine citrus scent made me dizzy with need, and I had to take a deep breath to calm my desire. "Are you okay? What happened last night?

She swallowed hard, and her eyes lingered on my mouth

before she dragged her gaze to mine. "It...it was nothing. Just old photos. I'm not ready to talk about it. That's not why I'm here."

Confusion spiraled through my thoughts. "Then why *did* you want to talk?"

"I have some bad news." She paced back and forth, her unease unmistakable. "One of the Order's special agents showed up this morning. She had questions about the bikers who attacked me. And about you and the pack."

So much for a heart to heart.

If constantly dealing with the LaSalles and the out-of-state packs wasn't bad enough, the last thing I needed was the Order snooping deeper into our business. They'd been on our ass for a while, and when they couldn't pin the abductions and murders on us, I was sure it had upset a few agents.

My mood rapidly growing dark, I leaned back against my desk and crossed my arms. "What kind of questions?"

"She's investigating an MC in Michigan that's been pushing a blood-based drug called Scarlet, which I'm betting was made by Kahanov. Apparently, the supply has run out, and word on the street is that a certain redhead can be used to make more."

Fuck.

"Your blood." I recalled the shifter we'd tracked down after Savannah was kidnapped. Right before I'd torn his throat out, he'd said that Kahanov had wanted her for her blood. *It's like his.*

Savannah nodded. "She thinks that your pack is involved and that I helped you cover up the abductions and murders in Wisconsin."

"Of course the Order does." Trying to get a grip on my emotions, I reached down and sank my claws into the oak desk. It audibly cracked under the strain. "And what does this agent want from you?"

She stopped pacing and watched me closely. "To cooperate. To tell her the truth."

"What did you say?" My tone was harsh, and Savannah winced ever so slightly before frowning.

"Nothing. I'm not a rat," she snapped.

I relaxed. "I know. Sorry. I trust you."

Though she was a wildcard, I knew that Savannah would never put the pack in jeopardy. She'd proven herself loyal. More than loyal—she'd lied for us, covered up for us, and helped rescue members of our pack. We owed her a great deal. But she was still a LaSalle, and even though I trusted her, it was hard to forget.

Hard for you to forget? Or hard for your father to forget? my wolf asked.

I tightened my fist and pushed the thoughts from my mind. "I haven't really thanked you for what you did for our pack— rescuing so many from the Dreamlands. We haven't had a chance to talk about what happened..."

"It was my fault, Jaxson. The bastard was after me." She bit her lip and met my eyes. "The only reason your people were in danger was because of me. Because you wouldn't hand me over."

"*Our* people. You're part of us now, whether you accept that or not."

"I'm *not*, Jaxson. I'm fucking stuck in the middle. I'm part LaSalle, part wolf."

And you are my mate.

I wanted to say it, but as I reached up and opened my mouth, she moved to the other side of the room and wrapped her arms around herself, as if she knew what I was going to say.

"There's something you need to know." She looked up and out the window. "Right before I killed Kahanov, I discovered that it wasn't him who was pulling the strings. It was Victor Dragan."

"Dragan?" My mind reeled. He'd been a dangerous fucker, and the reason the LaSalles and the Laurents had made a pact to work together years ago. My father and Laurel had killed him. "He's dead."

"I know. It was his ghost possessing Kahanov or something. I think he wanted revenge on my family *and* the pack *and* the Order. He said we'd all have to beg the Dark God for mercy, right before I cut out his soul with the Soul Knife."

The hair on my neck rose as dread crept under my skin. Did he mean the Dark Wolf God? It was a thing out of buried legends and nightmares. If Dragan had been messing with such dark powers...

I dragged a hand over my face and tried to rein in my anger. I set my jaw. "Why did you wait until now to tell me this?"

Savannah's eyes flashed. "I was pretty messed up after nearly dying, and we haven't spoken. Plus, I told Laurel about Dragan shortly after we returned from Forks. She killed him the first time, and she and Pete are looking into things."

Fury twisted my muscles. "Moving forward, you will come to *me*. Do you understand? The Dark *Wolf* God involves werewolves, and so it's my business. I need to know everything you know."

Her temper flashed, but she pressed her lips together and nodded. "Fine. But it also involves me, so *I* need to know everything you know. What is this Dark Wolf God? Does it have anything to do with the twin-headed wolf tattoos we found on the rogue wolves working for Billy? You said once that it dealt with a myth, but that it was for wolves only. Well, I'm a wolf now."

I shook my head. "The Dark Wolf God is a thing of terrible myths and legends. It's not spoken of often, and it's not my story to tell. But we can ask the pack loremaster. She'll be able to tell us more."

Savannah took a hesitant step toward me. "Jaxson, this could be important. The Order agent said some of the bikers she was tracking had twin-wolf tattoos. I'm wondering if they're looking for revenge for what I did to Dragan."

"I thought you said they were after your blood."

She threw her hands up. "I don't know!"

I stepped closer and grabbed her forearms. She resisted for a second, but I let my power wash over her, calming her rising emotions. "Savannah. It's going to be okay. You killed Kahanov. You got rid of Dragan. These bikers, we're going to get rid of them, too."

She nodded, her chest heaving provocatively, and desire swelled within me.

I let go and stepped away, needing a clear head. Whatever was going on, all I knew was that I couldn't let her out of my sight. "You need to stay on pack lands."

She folded her arms and opened her mouth to protest, but I was ready for it.

"You don't have a choice." I crossed to the cardboard box in the corner, pulled out an Eclipse shirt, and tossed it to her. She caught it and held it up, frowning, and I explained, "You're working the bar tonight with Sam, as we agreed. Have you ever bartended before?"

Her jaw ticked in frustration. "I've waited tables."

"So no. Sam will show you the ropes, but it'll take some time to get up to speed. Tony will take you over now—he's waiting outside. He'll be your wheels and personal bodyguard while your car is being fixed."

I could smell Savannah's irritation. She hated being beholden to anyone. "Fine," she said, heading to the door. "But *only* until my ride is fixed."

"Until your ride is fixed and we take care of the bikers. And trust me—you have bullet holes in your car. You're not going to pay off the repairs in a single night."

With a low growl, she glared, spun, and stalked out the door.

A deep smile cut my face. I wasn't sure the customers in Eclipse were ready for her kind of fire, but it was going to be entertaining watching things sizzle.

I shut the door and braced my hands on the frame. Fuck. Things felt like they were spiraling out of control.

Pulling out my phone, I dialed Gretchen at the Order. She'd helped me investigate during the abductions several months ago and had been there when I'd found the broken vial of blood on the road. She answered after two rings.

"Gretchen, there's an Order agent asking questions about the pack and some MC in Michigan. Do you know anything about that?"

The lieutenant sighed audibly. "Harlow Blake. She's a force of nature and keeps her cards close. She's shut me out, no doubt because of my connection with the pack, but she's investigating a group of clubs that are dealing illegal substances."

"Did the lab reports on the blood in that vial ever come back?"

"Yes." Gretchen paused. "But there was a seal on the report. I can't share the results. Sorry, Jax, this is above me."

Special Agent Harlow Blake.

"I understand. Thanks for your help, and let me know if you learn anything more," I said, and hung up.

The last thing we needed was an Order agent poking into our affairs. We'd need to move quickly to figure out what these bikers were up to and just what they wanted with Savannah Caine.

A hint of pride sparked in my chest.

Whatever it was, I was certain that she'd give them far more hell than they'd bargained for.

Jaxson

I entered Eclipse from the back. It was just past nine p.m., and the line out front wrapped around the corner. It'd be a five-figure night, enough to cover the losses from returning the confiscated shipment to the LaSalles.

Casey LaSalle was getting on my nerves, and I would have sicced my wolves on him by now if I didn't have to tiptoe around the ridiculous situation with Savannah. It was more and more like having one of my wolves held hostage.

Actually, that was *exactly* what it was.

I cracked my neck as I strolled down the hall to my office, then dropped my keys on my desk. Savannah's signature tickled my senses, and I couldn't help but slip into the bar to see how she was handling her new job.

The bass of the metal band tonight pumped through the walls, and I greeted one of my servers as I stepped into the morass of bodies. Blue sparks sprayed off the drums with each beat, and orange flames cascaded across the stage as the bassist strummed his guitar. I scanned the room and settled on the bar, and then white-hot anger flashed through me.

Savannah was pouring drinks and wearing the white T-shirt I'd given her earlier. It skimmed over her busty chest and curves in ways that sent blood pumping through my body. Her hair was pulled up and half-braided, and as she slid three shots across the bar, she flashed a demure smile to the guys who were watching her like hungry animals.

Damn it to hell. This had been a mistake.

It had been the perfect way to keep Savannah within arm's reach. Here in the heart of our den, she was surrounded by my people. Not even a drug-crazed lunatic would try to take her.

Still, I hadn't planned on her becoming the center of attention.

I cursed under my breath, and the crowd parted around me as I strode to the bar, my fists ready to connect with the fuckers who were watching her a little too closely.

One of my bouncers stopped me on the way. "Things are getting a little rowdy, boss. Want me to call in backup?"

My attention was focused on Savannah, who'd spun around and was reaching up to grab a bottle of Patrón off the top shelf, with her ass cheeks and long legs on full display under those black high-waisted shorts. My jaw ticked, and murderous thoughts raged through me.

"Yeah, sure, whatever you think," I said, stepping around the bouncer.

Savannah poured a generous serving of tequila into a lowball glass and handed it to a *very* interested man in a black button-down. A vampire, judging by his pale skin and signature. As she slid the drink toward him, he brushed her hand, and though she smiled broadly, I smelled her displeasure.

Her eyes drifted up and caught mine, and she froze. "Jaxson."

I stepped up to the bar next to the vampire and gazed down at him, letting my signature loose so that he and every other asshole in this place was aware of me and what was mine.

The vampire gave Savannah one last, quick glance before getting up and leaving. I watched him snake off, then stared down the three shifters who'd been ogling her earlier. They shrank away, too.

Savannah slid a whiskey on the rocks over to me, scowl included. "Did you just deliberately chase off some of my customers?"

"I wanted a spot at *my* bar. And don't worry, I'm a better tipper than those pricks."

She reached down and grabbed a bottle from below the counter and waggled it at me. "You'd better be, or I'll start pouring you bottom-shelf stuff."

For the second time that day, I laughed—such a rare thing these days. "If you knew what kind of hooch was in that bottle, you wouldn't threaten me like that."

She slapped two shot glasses up on the bar. "I'm brave. I'll try it if you do. I'm used to moonshine."

I covered the shot glasses with my hand. "No doing shots with customers or at all while you're working. There are bikers hunting you. You're safe here, but you're also on display, and I need you sharp—not whiskey blind."

She dropped the bottle back into the well. "Are you really worried about the bikers in here, or just the other customers?"

With a wicked grin, Savannah headed down to the far end and leaned provocatively over the bar to tend to a couple of assholes. Darkness wound around my heart, choking my thoughts.

"This was definitely a mistake," I muttered as I watched her make their drinks.

There was a laugh to my left, and Sam reached over and topped up my glass. "You were the one who offered her the job."

"I was a fool." I polished off the drink, left a stack of cash, and headed to the front to check on the bouncers at the doors, but mainly to distract myself.

Spending the night staring at Savannah Caine was only going to get me into trouble.

~

Savannah

Jaxson stalked out the front doors, his power and energy trailing in his wake. The crowd surged around him like a wave.

"He's trouble," I whispered to my wolf as I did my best to ignore the women who'd inserted themselves into his path, hungrily watching him like they wanted a taste.

Could I really blame them?

Just watching him clear the bar so he could get my attention had set my mind in a muddle. I shouldn't have flirted. Not until I got my shit straightened out, which seemed every day less and less likely to happen.

I sighed in exasperation and took another drink order. What was it about him that short-circuited all my neurons?

Even if I couldn't keep my thoughts straight, at least I was making a killing on tips. It had only been a few hours, but I'd already earned four times what I'd make at the Tap House in a night.

If I could work here a few times a week...

"Hey, sweet thing." A guy in his thirties slinked up to the bar, followed by two other men. His signature smelled like sickly sweet chewing tobacco and licorice. "Give me a few vodka shots, would ya?"

I surreptitiously scanned his ink and froze. Among the slew of designs, was a wolf skull with two arrows through it, but no sign of a two-headed wolf.

My breath slipped out as my shoulders relaxed. I set three shot glasses down for him and his buddies, and filled them to the rim with well vodka, because I could tell that was the kind of guys they were—bottom-shelf.

"Ten bucks," I said, turning.

But the man grabbed my wrist and leaned forward, holding up a fifty-dollar bill in his other hand. "How about a fifty for a little taste of heaven?"

I yanked my hand out of his iron grip, my wrist stinging, and took his money and made change at the register. I slammed the bills down in front of him. "Not interested. And if you ever touch me again, I swear to God, you'll regret it."

He watched me closely, his jaw twitching, and then he chuckled and left ten bucks on the bar. "We'll see about that."

He slithered into the crowd with his sidekicks, and I couldn't help but feel sick to my stomach.

"You okay?" Sam asked, grabbing a couple of martini glasses from behind me.

I left the tip on the counter. "Fine. Just some assholes getting a little handsy."

"Seriously? Who?" Sam scanned the faces who filled in around the bar, looking like she wanted to fight.

I smiled and squeezed her arm. "Don't worry, I handled it."

The work was a whirlwind, and the hours zoomed by. I had to pass off most of the fancy cocktails to Sam and the others, but after I'd learned where everything was, I hustled fast enough to keep up with shots and server tickets.

Jaxson mostly roamed the edges of the unruly crowd like a pacing lion. Whenever I found him, his eyes were on me. It made my neck and thighs flush with heat every time, so I just tried to keep my own eyes on the bar.

As the night wore on, my tender feet began screaming in protest. I brushed a sweaty strand of hair behind my ear. It was getting hot with the mass of bodies crowded into the space tonight. I needed to sit down, even if it was for two minutes just to pee.

I caught Sam's attention. "Hey, can you handle the bar for a minute? I've got to use the ladies' room."

"Of course. Take five, I've got this." Sam shot me a smile and took another round of orders.

I slipped into the crowd and made my way to the bathroom. The music was no less pervasive in there, and the bass settled in my bones. I splashed some cool water on my face and neck and stared at myself in the mirror.

My skin was flushed with heat, and a dozen strands of hair had fallen out of my braid. I examined my clothes and admired the effect of the tight top pulled over my chest. I might look as disheveled as if I'd run a marathon, but at least my girls were still doing work.

There was a red speck on my shoulder. *Shit*. My cut. I dabbed it with a little water, and when that did absolutely nothing, I just pulled my braid over my shoulder and hoped no one would notice.

My phone read a quarter past one in the morning. No wonder my feet were killing me. Rinsing my hands again, I rushed back toward the bar.

People were jumping around, and someone bumped into me, knocking me into another. A pair of hands skimmed over me and gripped my waist, steadying me as I lost my balance. "Easy there, sweet thing."

His hot breath dampened my neck, and that tobacco licorice stench made me gag. I tried to shove him off, but he didn't let go. "You smell...*fuck*. You smell real good."

He pulled me closer, sniffing.

"Get off of me, asshole!" I elbowed him in the ribs and spun around to knee him in the balls, but he moved aside and grabbed my throat.

His eyes flashed amber, but before I could react, a shape moved between us, and I heard the man's wrist snap as his hand was yanked from my neck.

The air burst from my throat, and I stumbled backward into the crowd as two shapes dropped to the ground.

The revelers parted, revealing Jaxson crouched over my assailant. His fist rose and fell like a hammer, pummeling the man's face into a bloody mess. I'd never seen him like this. His eyes burned with golden light, and his body rippled with fury.

Oh, my God, he's going to kill the guy.

"Jaxson! Stop." I stepped forward and gasped as blood colored his fist.

Three bouncers pushed through the crowd, and it took two of them to pull Jaxson off the unconscious man. Shouting, the guy's friends picked him up, and the third bouncer escorted them to the door.

Jaxson jerked out of the bouncers' grips and turned toward me, his expression dark and furious. Shivers raked my skin, and a heady mixture of fear and arousal swept over me as his wolves pulled him away.

I couldn't discern my thundering heart from the drumming of the music, and I suddenly felt overheated and overwhelmed. A loud whistle cut through the commotion, and I turned toward the bar. Sam waved at me, a concerned look cutting her face.

Jostled left and right, I made it to the bar, and Sam slid me a shot of whiskey. I grimaced as it burned my throat. She poured a few more drinks and glanced at me. "You okay?"

I took another shot and nodded, my hand shaking.

"It's getting crazy in here," she said, opening a couple beers. "You should go to the back and check on Jaxson."

"Are you sure about that?" I'd never seen that look on his face before, and it scared the shit out of me.

Sam nodded. "You're the only one who can knock some sense into him. Trust me, he needs you."

I sighed. "All right. Text me if things get too wild and you need backup."

"Mm-hmm."

I slipped around her and accidentally kicked the bin of empty glass bottles, which was almost overflowing. "Want me to dump these in the recycling?"

She glanced down and frowned. "Would you mind? That'd be great. It's just out back."

Sam looked exhausted, and I could sense her agitation. She commanded the bar, but tonight was more hectic than I'd seen the place, and I could tell that Jaxson's outburst had unsettled her, too. "No problem, just take it easy and *text* me."

I could still hear the heavy metal ringing through the walls as I walked down the hall to Jaxson's office. The glass bottles clinked as I set the bin down outside of his door and knocked.

"Come." His voice carried through the door, and I was terrified what I would find on the other side. With a deep breath, I opened the door and stepped inside.

Jaxson was sitting in his chair, elbows on his knees as he cleaned off his bloodied knuckles with a white washcloth.

"Are you okay?" he asked, his gravelly voice sending prickles over my skin.

The room was dark except for a single desk lamp. It cut his face and features with hard light and deep shadows, emphasizing his muscles.

I couldn't decide if I wanted to run or to climb into his lap and let him consume me.

What the hell was I thinking? The man's hands had been covered with blood—and very little of it had been his.

My wolf snickered. *I don't blame you. He's a powerful beast.*

Oh, God.

Feeling flushed, I finally found my voice. "I'm fine. Are *you* okay?"

The way Jaxson looked at me made me want to melt into the walls. His presence was crushing, yet irresistible.

Before I could breathe, he was on his feet—just inches from me, sliding his hand behind my neck. He gazed down, his golden eyes smoldering as his molten heat drilled into me. *Fuck. Me.*

"I said I wasn't going to let anyone touch you," he growled.

I licked my lips. "You were looking murderously at every man I served."

His pupils dilated, and a sinful smile ghosted his lips as he traced his thumb over my cheekbone.

"Have I frightened you? You're shaking." His hand slipped around my waist, and I shivered with need.

"Am I?" I said breathlessly.

"I told you my wolf was possessive." He lowered his face and traced his nose along my neck, breathing me in. "And so am I."

The feminist part of me wanted to tell him to fuck off, but the other half? Right now, the other half wanted to bone the werewolf king.

"Jaxson..." I slid my hand up and grabbed the back of his head so that I could look at his face. I was trembling. Not from fear, but from the sheer weight of emotions that were washing over me. Fear. Lust. Desire. Uncertainty.

They were nothing compared to what I saw on his face. This man was awash with feelings, all conflicting and warring against each other. Did he hate me or love me?

There was a crash from outside, and he froze.

Just like that, the spell was shattered. I was in the arms of a man who, minutes before, had beaten someone unconscious with his bare hands.

A pounding fist shook the door. I quickly released Jaxson and stepped away. He regarded me closely, his eyes trying to bore into my soul. The pounding continued.

"Are you going to answer that?" I asked, my pulse hammering against my chest.

As if waking from a tortured dream, Jaxson tensed and glanced at the door. He looked down at me and growled. "Tony is going to take you home."

"But—"

He cupped my face with his hand. "Trust me, I know when the bar isn't safe, and that's now. Tonight, I'm your boss, and this discussion is final. You will go home, and Tony will give you a ride."

He stalked out of the office and shut the door, leaving me alone in the single light of the lamp. Low voices muttered outside. One of the bouncers mentioned a brawl that had broken out inside the bar.

I dragged my hands through my hair. This night was going off the rails. Jaxson's overbearing protectiveness was hot in the moment, but how was I supposed to deal with a guy like that?

Possessiveness and domineering were typically not my speed, but...

A knock sounded at the door, followed by Tony's voice: "Savannah?"

I popped through the door and nodded to the sandy-haired man, who was one of Jaxson's right-hand men.

He ushered me through the unruly crowd and out the front into the cool night air. One of the pack vehicles was already waiting.

I turned back. "Wait! My tips!"

"Sam will hold your share," he said gruffly. "Now get in."

I was pretty sure that whatever Tony's actual job was, he absolutely hated "Savannah duty."

Though not one to typically walk away from a fat stack of cash, I growled at Tony and reluctantly slipped into the passenger side and buckled up.

He was totally unfazed by my glare.

I leaned back against the seat as the Jeep pulled away, a little relieved, to my surprise. Jaxson was right. I had no desire to head back into Eclipse with the crowd all riled up. That, and my dogs were barking after four hours on my feet. I also smelled pretty sweaty, though I was too tired to care if Tony noticed.

It was time for a soak and bed.

Suddenly, the Jeep screeched to a halt, and the seatbelt dug into my chest. Gasping for air, I looked up as Tony cursed and hit reverse.

A white van had pulled out of the alley onto the one-way street ahead of us, blocking our path.

Tony hit the brakes again as a truck screeched to a halt behind us. The assholes had locked us in.

Neither vehicle moved, and my heart went haywire as I looked between them. "We're trapped!"

A bunch of burly figures barreled out of the vehicles. *Shit.*

Tony grabbed for his phone as an explosion hit the side of our ride.

His head ricocheted off the wheel as I slammed into the door, and the world spun.

9

Heart hammering in my chest, I pulled Tony off the wheel. He looked up, and a trail of blood dripped down his forehead. "Run!" he ordered. "They're here for you!"

Screw that.

As he went for his seatbelt, I unlatched mine and shoved open the door.

A bastard in a leather jacket lunged for me, but I kicked him back and rammed my boot into his face.

I leapt from the passenger seat and kneed him in the nuts as another one of the bastards took a swing. I wasn't quite fast enough to avoid the blow, which glanced off my cheek and sent me staggering back against the open door.

There was no mistaking the asshole who'd accosted me at the bar. The cocky bastards hadn't even bothered wearing masks.

The man grinned as he lashed out. "You're coming with us!"

I ducked and jammed my fist up into his jaw, wiping the smile off his face. His head kicked back with a sharp snap and ricocheted off the side of the vehicle.

I took one quick look into the Jeep. Tony was out on the other side, laying into two more guys.

They were everywhere.

As a third guy in a leather cut leapt in, I summoned my magic and released a cold burst of uncontrolled power into him. His body jerked, and he flew backward onto the street.

Then I was running.

Too many.

As I started to draw the shadows like a cloak around me, a red-eyed shifter soared over my head, rebounded off the building, and dropped into the alley. I tried to skid to a stop, but his arm clotheslined my neck.

I landed on my back hard, my throat aching. Another shape landed beside me from the roof, and the three thugs circled me. I kicked one of them in the shin, and he stumbled back, but the two others descended on me.

I screamed and clawed at their arms, but one of them pulled something out of his pocket, and then unimaginable pain coursed through my body, like bees crawling under my skin.

My muscles spasmed, and I lost all control.

Fear and dread settled over me as I lay there paralyzed, unable to speak or breathe. One of the men slipped a cloth bag over my head, then zip-tied my ankles and cuffed my wrists behind me. I was jerked over someone's shoulder, and seconds later, tossed into the back of what I assumed was the white van.

"Bastards," I tried to yell, though it came out more like an unintelligible moan.

Zap.

That horrifying pain returned, radiating from my thigh this time. My body convulsed, and I gritted my teeth as it went on for what seemed like forever. Then it stopped, and two doors slammed shut.

Though the pain was gone, my body was in shock. Literally,

because I'd just been tased. I couldn't move, but I heard their voices outside: "Bring her to the drop point, and don't mess around."

The van started, and I gasped as I finally managed to suck in air, though the bag over my face was causing me to hyperventilate. I rolled onto my knees and shook my head until the cloth slipped off. Just as I did, the van made a sharp turn and accelerated, and I flew across the cargo area, landing hard on my side.

I groaned as pain exploded in my shoulder.

Abducted?

No fucking way. I'd been here before, and I wasn't going to let it happen again.

Racking my brain, I struggled against my restraints. I probably only had minutes before they took me somewhere else. Luckily, the idiot who'd zip-tied my feet had secured the tie over my boots.

I shimmied my ankles until I could slip one of my feet out of my shoes, then the other. Once my ankles were free, I sat up and glanced around the van. The restraints on my wrists were going to be trickier.

The van swerved, and I rolled and crashed into the wall. Blood stung my eye.

Got to get out of here before these psychos crash, my wolf said anxiously.

"Yeah, I'm trying." I crouched on my knees and gritted my teeth as I began shimmying my wrists back and forth. The cuffs wouldn't budge, and the metal dug into my skin. Dammit.

I slipped my boots back on and scooted down to the double doors. There was no handle, so I kicked them. Pain surged through my ankles.

Shift, my wolf said.

"First, I need to get these open." I positioned my feet in the middle of the doors, where I imagined the handles to be, and then I kicked. The doors rattled, and I heard the muffled voices of the men in the front.

"A little help, sister?" I asked my wolf, bracing for another kick.

With a silent prayer, I kicked again and heard a metallic crack in the door. Adrenaline flooded me, and I started kicking the doors like a madwoman.

Finally, something snapped, and they flew open. *Shit, it worked!*

A pair of headlights blinded me, but I managed to brace the doors with my feet when they bounced back. They kept swinging, and I must have busted the mechanism that closed them because they would no longer stay shut, which was both a mercy and a pain in the ass.

I squinted my eyes at the vehicle that was following close behind. It sped up, and its lights switched to running lights. It was then that I recognized Jaxson's truck. *They'd followed me.* Sam was in the passenger seat, and Jaxson was driving, his expression homicidal.

The van accelerated, and I glanced at the blur of asphalt between the swinging doors. *Shit.*

We had to be going sixty. What would happen to me if I hit the road at that speed? Sure, I technically had healing powers, but only if I didn't snap my neck.

The van took a turn a little too sharply. My shoulder and head slammed into the wall again, and I groaned. The fact that I wasn't healing indicated that my restraints were magicuffs. So much for shifting.

Still, I had to get out of the cuffs so I could hold on to something. Potentially, I could summon the Soul Knife, but trying to use it in the swerving van seemed like a great way to slit my wrist or accidently slice out a chunk of my soul.

I rolled to my side and twisted my arms. With a cry of pain

and a pop of my shoulder, I brought my bound wrists under my ass. Then I rocked back in a ball so I could bring them around the ends of my feet.

My shoulder throbbed, and the cuffs dug into my wrists, but at least my hands were in front of me. It would have to do.

I stood and hurried to the open door, where I crouched and motioned for Jaxson to speed up. "I'm going to jump!"

I saw his lips move, and I assumed he was saying, "Are you insane?"

"Do it!" I screamed, though I doubted he could hear.

The truck accelerated, but the van swerved again, and I had to cling to the side rail with my bound hands for dear life.

As we straightened out, Jaxson punched the accelerator and roared ahead. The swinging doors of the van clanged off his hood, and I leapt.

I landed on the hood with a loud thump, fear clawing at my chest as my hands grasped for a hold in the gap below the windshield.

Jaxson began to deaccelerate, but the van slammed on its brakes, and we had to swerve around it.

I dug in my fingers, but my grip slipped, and I flew off the hood.

Everything went in slow motion.

Pain ripped through my body as I hit the pavement and tumbled to the curb.

Jaxson braked hard, and Tony's Jeep flew around the other side of him and ricocheted off the driver's door of the white van. The van screeched to the right, then accelerated to top speed as the Jeep pursued in a hail of gunfire.

I climbed to my knees. My shoulder was out of place, my arm ached, and my head was ringing, but at least we'd slowed to half speed by the time I'd been thrown off the hood.

Standing up, I winced as my shoulder wound began to burn.

Suddenly, a woman's voice gurgled behind me. "You think you're free? Dragan is coming for you. You won't escape."

I spun.

It was the backwoods woman who'd first attacked me in Belmont. Blood poured from the laceration in her neck where she'd torn her own throat out in Jaxson's jaws—several weeks ago.

I screamed.

Then Jaxson was there, hauling me to my feet. "It's okay. You're safe, Savannah. Are you hurt?"

The ghost was gone.

Either I was being haunted, or my brain had finally stepped off the deep end. I trembled in his arms. "I think I'm probably concussed, but I'm alive."

He regarded the magicuffs on my wrists, anger hardening his features. "We need to get those things off you."

Turning, he retrieved something from inside the truck—a pick. He jammed it into the side of the left magicuff, causing it to open.

I winced as my shoulder popped back into place, and the fracture in my forearm began to heal. "I'm going to cut out their fucking souls for this."

Jaxson shook with rage, and his claws ripped out of his hands. "Not if I get to them first."

"Hot tip: it was the jerks from the bar."

He growled, and I could hear the deep anger and self-reproach in his voice. "I should have sent more wolves with you."

Sam stepped up and slapped me on the back. "Damn, that was badass, Fury."

"What? The part where I got abducted again?" I muttered bitterly.

"The part where you nearly fought off an ambush of four

wolves, tore your way out of the back of a steel van, and then jumped onto a moving truck during a high-speed chase."

"Oh. *That*."

Jaxson gave me an approving nod, which sent butterflies spinning in my stomach. As much as Sam had come to mean to me, that small motion set me on fire.

"Is Tony okay?" I asked.

"They left him the moment they had you. He's after them now and looking to redeem himself," Jaxson said.

I put my hand on his arm. "Tony did what he could. This wasn't his fault."

He was a bit of a spook, but he'd fought for me.

"I know. This is my fault. I hold myself accountable," Jaxson growled. His expression turned savage as he glanced up the deserted road, and then back at Sam and me. "Let's get you home and cleaned up."

Having just skidded across the pavement at high speed, I was scraped, bruised, and coated with blood, dust, and grime. I couldn't imagine how bad I looked.

"Casey is going to lose his mind," I said.

Jaxson shook his head. "Not the LaSalles'. My place."

I tensed. "But—"

His eyes flashed gold. "You're a wolf. Until this blows over, I'm not letting you out of my sight. Period."

I sucked in a sharp breath as Jaxson's alpha presence hit me like a sledgehammer. It wasn't a gentle push, but rather an iron-hard directive, fueled by his rage.

Normally, I would have fought back, but I was so battered and bruised and drained that I just melted into it. For a moment, it was good to have someone else make decisions. And in all honesty, I didn't know what to say to Casey. Or my aunt and uncle, when they got home.

There'd be so many questions I wasn't ready to face. So many that I needed to ask—but that required a clear head, one thing I didn't have.

10

Jaxson

Violent thoughts plagued my mind during the drive back to the Dockside Dens. I gripped the wheel, considering all the ways I'd murder the bastards who'd laid their hands on Savannah.

Fucking echoes of my past.

I'd been the one who was supposed to protect my sister, and she was dead. I wasn't going to let the same thing happen to my mate—whether or not she was a LaSalle, whether or not she accepted me and the pack and our bond.

Fuck the world, I wouldn't let it take her, too.

The steering wheel cracked, and I looked down. Well, it *was* a new truck.

"Are you okay?" Sam asked.

"Fucking fine," I said as I looked over and reassessed the damage they'd done to Savannah. The skin on her wrists and ankles had been rubbed raw, and the gash on her head was still swollen and slightly blue.

My gut wrenched.

No. I wasn't fucking fine.

The fortune teller's words rose in my mind: *She cannot be tamed, but you must tame her to save her from herself. If you cannot help her, she will die and bring ruin to us all.*

How the hell was I supposed to tame Savannah Caine? The bar had seemed the perfect place to keep her safe. I hadn't expected her attackers to be so bold as to enter my den. I should have just locked her in the office. My arrogance had almost cost me everything.

Was her blood really so valuable that they would risk everything by entering the pack headquarters?

The metallic, sweet scent of her blood filled the truck, and damn me to hell, I wanted a taste of it myself. Was I just as crazed as they were?

Sam's phone rang. "Hello?"

I heard Tony's voice come on the line and monitored the short conversation as Sam nodded.

Finally, she hung up. "Not great news. The assholes ditched the van and escaped with a bunch of other creeps on unmarked bikes. Tony tried to follow but lost them. He'll apologize in person tomorrow."

Savannah tensed.

I was able to hear the sense of failure in his voice over the phone. His shame and regret would be repercussion enough if they were even a fraction of what I felt.

I ground my teeth. "Text him that I should have sent another team as well. Tell him to show up at my apartment with his people to keep watch tonight. No one that's not one of us comes in or out."

"There's more," Sam continued. "The van is currently on fire, and the fire department is on its way."

That meant no prints, no clues, and no way to cover it up. The Order would be looking into things and asking questions if they found out that all this had started at our bar. We worked with a lot of MCs to distribute our products, and I couldn't risk a clusterfuck Order investigation threatening pack business or our autonomy to pursue our own justice. Our own laws.

I sighed.

Nothing could ever be simple, could it?

~

Savannah

The moment we stepped into Jaxson's apartment, my phone made a strangled noise, and I pulled it out of my pocket. The screen was splintered, but somehow, the thing was still working. "Hello?"

Agent Blake's voice came across the other line. "I just heard from my little birdies that someone tried to abduct you tonight, and that there was a godsdamned car chase."

I tensed, with no idea what to say. I looked from Jaxson to Sam and put it on speaker. "Agent Blake, thanks for calling."

"The question is, why didn't you call me? Or the cops? I had to find out because someone left a burning van in the middle of the street. I told you to call me if anything happened or if you had any information."

The truth was that somehow, in this fucked-up place, I'd gotten used to the idea of vigilante justice. I didn't want to sit around and file reports and hope that in ten years, someone would put them behind bars. I wanted to hunt the assholes down and take them out.

I bit my lip. "I escaped. I'm fine. They're gone."

"And you don't think those assholes will be back?" she snapped. "You need to file a report. By law. There's no covering it up."

Her words were harsh, but I could tell from her tone that she was worried. And that she hated these bikers almost as much as I did.

But I didn't know her, and I knew she had an agenda.

Jaxson shrugged noncommittally, so I said, "Fine. I'll come in tomorrow."

Harlow cursed. "Tomorrow? Why not tonight?"

I was so in over my head. I had no idea where Jaxson stood with the Order, but I knew he was into something illegal, and I also knew he had people loyal to him at the Hall of Inquiry. I'd seen cops all around town treat him like a king.

But that was one minefield I wasn't going to wander too far into—not without coaching. "I'm pretty shaken at the moment and need to get fixed up. Tomorrow, I'll come in. Promise."

There was a long pause. "Do you need a place to stay? I can offer one, same as before."

Jaxson's expression went dark, and Sam raised her eyebrows.

I blushed and looked around at Jaxson's apartment. When I glanced back at him, his arms were crossed and muscles flexed, and he was boring into me with his eyes.

Danger. But not the kind she was thinking.

"I'm safe where I am. Goodnight," I said.

"Wait!" Harlow shouted across the line. "Can you tell me anything? Were they bikers? Did they have the twin-wolf tattoo?"

I paused. "They were bikers, yes, but without bikes. I didn't see anyone with a twin-wolf, but one guy had a big wolf skull pierced by crossed arrows. Does that mean anything to you?"

"Yes. That's the Arrowhead Disciples, an outlaw MC with people all over Indiana and Michigan. Do you think you could describe your assailants or identify them from photos?"

My heart leapt. That was something, at least. I was tempted to head down there immediately to find out more in person, but I knew Jaxson wouldn't have it.

"I'll draw them for you tomorrow," I said, and hung up as weariness overcame me. I just couldn't deal with it tonight.

Sam crossed her arms. "That's interesting. Arrowheads Disciples. It's not one of the clubs we work with. Do we know anything about them?"

Jaxson grunted. "No. They've never been in our territory, as far as I know, but our pack doesn't deal with outlaw MCs. That said, I can find someone who knows."

"So what's our plan?" I asked.

He worked his jaw and studied me intently. "I have my own thoughts, but you're the one with a bullseye on your back. What do you want to do? Rely on the cops?"

My fingers twitched. It was the logical choice: let someone handle it legally. But I just couldn't do it.

As a kid, my parents had warned me about the cops. Alma believed they were all in on some wacky conspiracy. My aunt and cousin were certainly on the wrong side of the law, as it seemed was Jaxson.

So far, the only things the cops had done for me was give me tickets and shrug their shoulders at my parents' deaths and my werewolf attacks.

I bit my lip. "Honestly? I want to hit those bastards back. An eye for an eye. I'm tired of running for my life."

Jaxson smiled. "Okay, then. Eye for an eye. They marched into my bar and tried to grab you on my turf. Tomorrow, we find out where the Arrowhead Disciples hang out, grab one of their guys, and make them talk."

God, I knew it was probably reckless and illegal, but a dark shiver of anticipation swept up my spine.

We knew who they were. And tomorrow, after long weeks of being constantly hounded and chased, I was going to be the one doing the hunting.

11

The first order of business, once Sam brought me new clothes, was to clean up and wash off the blood and gravel and the greasy touch of the chewing-tobacco-scented biker that covered my body. The shower burned my tattered skin but felt divine, all the same, soothing more of my poor, hammered bones and muscles. I had to be careful with my left arm. The fracture was already knitting together, but it still hurt like hell.

I've gotta stop getting my ass kicked by life.

Eh, Wolfie said, *we give as good as we get. And tomorrow, we're gonna make some bikers pay.*

With a huge breath, I shut off the shower and stepped out.

I dried off with one of Jaxson's plush, luxurious towels, then wiped the foggy mirror. So many scars, but at least they were already healing.

All except one.

It had torn open, though the skin at the surface was knitting back together a little. I rummaged in Jaxson's bathroom but couldn't find any Band-Aids. Not surprising for a werewolf with super-healing. I dabbed it with some toilet paper, then pulled on the clothes Sam had lent me for the umpteenth time. The bedrock of our relationship was literally built on hand-me-downs at this point, and I owed her majorly.

Jaxson was sitting by himself when I stepped out of the bathroom.

Shit.

Sam was also famous for leaving us alone in awkward situations, the evil genius.

I pulled my damp hair behind me, unsure of how I wanted to play things. "I'd better hit the hay."

Every nerve in my body instantly wanted his hands running over me, but I was stretched too thin. I could barely face what I was. How could I face the bond we were supposed to share?

Didn't I get a choice at all?

He put down his whiskey and stiffened. "Fuck. You're still bleeding."

I followed his eyes to my chest. A bit of blood from my shoulder was seeping into my T-shirt, blooming like a rose.

My hand went to my knife wound, which had bled through the wad of paper that I'd strapped under my bra. "Yeah, that's old. It's just taking a long time to heal."

"You're a werewolf. *Everything* should heal."

"I know," I snapped. "It's from the Soul Knife. The damn thing is cursed. I tried drinking a couple of Uncle Pete's potions, but it just keeps splitting back open."

"Let me see," he said as he stood and approached.

"It's fine." I turned to go back to the bathroom, but he put his arm out, blocking my escape.

My heartbeat went double-time as he bent his head low. "I want to see."

I froze, my back to the wall. A sharp *no* hung on my lips, but it wouldn't come out. Instead, I just breathed in slowly, letting his scent roll over my tongue. A quake passed through my body.

It was a command, firm but gentle. And although he wasn't using his alpha voodoo on me, just his proximity made we want to obey. That deep scent of forest and the taste of snow clouded every ability I had to think.

You're safe, my wolf said. *It's time to stop fighting.*

I took a deep breath and held it. Hesitantly, I reached down and grabbed the hem of my shirt, then slowly pulled it up over my head.

Jaxson's breath caught, and I could feel the tension vibrating off his body.

I dropped the T-shirt on the floor.

His eyes traced over my bare skin before settling on my wound. Everywhere they'd touched burned with warmth and desire.

He reached up, and I wanted him to run his hands across every inch of me. But instead, he simply traced a single finger along the edge of the wound, like he was caressing me with a feather. "This looks bad."

I tipped my chin up and gave him half a smile as I tried not to flinch. "It's from an evil magic knife. Who would have guessed?"

He breathed in sharply, and his eyes fogged. "Your blood. It smells...wild. Exotic. Powerful. No wonder everyone is after it."

I swallowed hard, not wanting to have to think about that aspect.

Jaxson stared at the red droplets pooling on my skin as if my blood were the only thing in the world. Hell, he looked like he was going to lick it up. The thought of his tongue dancing across my skin sent a flush of moisture to my center that I was certain he could smell, but I didn't care. He could know *exactly* what was on my mind.

Jaxson cleared his throat abruptly and looked away. "I have something that might help."

I bet he does, my cheeky wolf interjected.

Blushing, I scooped up my borrowed shirt and held it awkwardly against my chest. "You already tried to heal me once, in Forks. It fixed everything but this."

An almost uncontrollable desire welled up in me. Lying in bed alone at night, I'd relived that moment over and over—the heat of his magic surging through every inch of my body. I'd practically throw myself in front of a bus to feel that way again. Clearly, leaping out of a van hadn't done enough damage to warrant it.

"Not that," he whispered, his eyes twinkling as if he could read my mind. To my disappointment, Jaxson stepped back and dug a little jar out of a drawer. I stayed put, leaning against the wall, as he grabbed a cloth from the bathroom and dampened the corner.

My breath caught as he reached out and hooked his finger under my bra strap, where it crossed the bloody scar. "May I?"

Chest heaving with anticipation, I nodded.

Gently, he pulled the strap to the side and down around my shoulder. Goose bumps rippled over my skin. I didn't want him to be gentle like this. It was absolute torture.

I'd just survived throwing myself from a van at sixty miles an hour. I wanted him to rip my bra off then and there. To grab both breasts with his hands and ram his lips against mine.

But he didn't. He made me wait.

Without a word, he lightly dabbed the blood away from the open gash.

"Ow." I protested flatly, but the truth was, each touch sent shivers of ecstasy down my spine. With each press, my anticipation heightened.

Jaxson discarded the cloth, then opened the small jar, releasing a strong scent of ginger and spices that I couldn't place.

"I use this for stubborn wounds. We should probably visit a curse diviner, but maybe this will help."

He scooped a little out with his fingers and traced them over the laceration. Electricity and heat and pain followed his touch, and I gritted my teeth even as I savored the moment.

"There."

The sudden absence of his touch was more painful than the wound itself.

I realized my eyes were closed, and I opened them to meet his. They glistened in the dim room with a golden light of their own.

Pushing myself off the wall, I stepped up so that we were mere inches apart, letting sparks of magic dance in the space between us.

His hands brushed my skin, his touch agonizingly soft. Inviting. I relaxed into it, savoring every motion. He was a savage beast, and yet his touch could be so tender.

Suddenly, it wasn't.

With a swift motion, he grabbed my waist and jerked my body against his. My gasp was cut short as his other hand gripped the back of my head, and his mouth devoured mine.

His kisses were violent and hungry, and I met each one with the same savage intensity.

I moaned with delight, needing more.

He pressed me hard against the wall as desire wrapped around us like waves in the sea.

"Ow, fuck!" I gasped as pain shot through my shoulder.

Jaxson stepped back instantly, his eyes clear and alert. I looked down to find that blood was pouring from my wound.

He reached to touch it. "Shit, I'm sorry."

I winced. The damn thing—a goodbye present from Dragan. But had it really been goodbye?

I snatched the cloth from the floor and pressed it to my shoulder as a chill worked over my skin.

The ghost of the she-wolf had taunted me that Dragan was still out there. *You think you're free? Dragan is coming for you. You won't escape.*

A shiver ran through me as I recalled Dragan's twisted face after I'd severed his soul in the Dreamlands. His final words echoed through my mind: *I will have my vengeance!*

Was that what all this was really about?

I trembled.

"What's the matter?" Jaxson asked. "Are you okay?

I shook my head as I checked on my still-bleeding wound. "I think the bikers aren't acting on their own. I'm almost certain Dragan is behind this."

Jaxson tensed. "How? I thought you cut out his soul with the Soul Knife before you killed Kahanov."

Another shudder rocked my body as I recalled the gruesome moment and Dragan's howling, ethereal face. "He possessed Kahanov. Maybe I didn't kill him—maybe I just set him free. Could he possess someone else?"

"I don't know. How certain of this are you? Why do you think it's him and not just bikers working on their own to get your blood?"

I bit my lip. "Something someone said during the abduction. That he was coming for me."

He studied my face, and I prayed he wasn't going to press me about the source. I wasn't quite ready to confront the fact that I was either batshit crazy or seeing dead people. Or both.

Jaxson shook his head. "This is fucked, but it's nothing we can't deal with. Tomorrow, we're going to crack some skulls and find out who the hell is behind these attacks—whether it's Dragan or agents of the Dark Wolf God, or just freaks out for blood. We'll get our answers and shut this down. But until then, you need your sleep."

He turned to leave, and my stomach sank a little. Moments before, I was ready to have him throw me into bed, but the certainty of that moment had gone. The memories of everything that had happened in the past few weeks left me feeling tainted, and he seemed to sense that I didn't know what I wanted.

I was too tired, too weary to think. The adrenaline of the attack had faded, as had the euphoria of being in Jaxson's arms. All that was left was the sword hanging over my head.

My heart leapt a little as he paused at the door. "I'll be sleeping on the couch. You're safe, Savy."

I nodded. "Goodnight."

But doubt twisted in my gut. If ghosts were haunting me, bikers hunting me, and Dragan out there still, was there anywhere I would ever be safe again?

Harden up, Wolfie whispered in my mind. *Are you a predator or prey?*

A shiver of her strength worked through me, and I tightened my fist as a fragment of my earlier resolve came back.

I wasn't going to live in fear. I wasn't going to let other people fight my battles, whether it was Harlow or Tony or Jaxson. I was going to hunt. I was going to get answers. And if Dragan was truly behind this, I would bring him down and send him back to hell, where he belonged.

12

Savannah

The next morning, I woke in Jaxson's bed with a groan. My body felt like I'd thrown myself from the back of a van at sixty miles an hour.

Shocking.

On the upside, werewolf healing was amazing. A quick check revealed that my broken arm and almost all my lacerations had healed, and only faint scars remained. But that didn't mean every single part of me didn't scream bloody murder every time I moved.

I rolled over in the sheets, which smelled intoxicatingly like Jaxson, and searched the bed and pillows for my phone, but I couldn't find it. Rousting myself with a groan, I slipped into Sam's spare clothes and checked the bathroom. It wasn't there, so I stumbled to the kitchen.

There was a tall glass of carrot juice and a pile of painkillers on the black counter waiting for me. I popped them in my mouth and washed them down with the juice. It tingled and danced across my tastebuds, and I looked at the glass with surprise.

Sam stomped around the corner in tall black boots and a sexy leather jacket. "You're awake!"

"Apparently," I grumbled. "I assumed that this stuff was for me, but maybe I shouldn't have. What's in it?"

"Just a little drop of an elixir Alia whips up for us from time to time. After last night, I figured you'd need it. Also, you need lunch. It's not going to feel great on an empty belly."

"Lunch?"

She checked her phone. "Yeah. It's two p.m."

"Holy shit." I hadn't woken once. There was something soothing about sleeping in Jaxson's bed, surrounded by his scent, even if he wasn't in it.

If he'd been in it, you wouldn't have gotten much sleep, thus defeating the purpose, Wolfie observed.

Yeah. Probably. But as much as my libido was into Jaxson, I wasn't into domineering, over-possessive, thoughtless alpha types.

Sure, you're not.

I looked around. "Seen my phone?"

Busy in the middle of a text, Sam nodded absently to the table by the couch. "Jax got you a new one. It's all set up."

My eyes widened as I approached the end table. A brand-new iPhone sat atop its rectangular white box. The thing had to be worth over a grand, while my old one had been a bottom-shelf brick from Walmart that barely ran Google Maps.

With delight and trepidation vying for control of my nerves, I picked it up and turned it over. "Let me guess—no strings attached."

She laughed. "Plenty of strings. You're going to spend a lot of time on call for bar duty. The customers really like you."

I scoffed. "Yeah, I don't know about that plan. Some of those customers tried to take me home last night."

Sam tucked her phone in her back pocket. "That's why we're

going to pay them a visit. So grab something out of the fridge. Jaxson is on his way and will meet us downstairs in thirty."

"Where are we headed?"

"Jax got a lead on the Arrowhead Disciples, so the three of us are going to shake down a biker bar."

My fingers itched as images of the night before flashed into my mind: the greasy bastard who grabbed me at the bar, the asshole decking me in the face, the pricks who forced me down and bound my hands and feet.

I couldn't hold back my claws, which ripped out of my fingertips. "Let's go. I'm ready now."

Sam laughed. "Not looking like that, you aren't. We're taking bikes." She pointed to a stack of clothes on the couch. "I picked out an appropriate outfit for you this morning. Jaxson's expense, so I got *real* nice stuff."

Ten minutes and a Naked smoothie later, I was admiring myself in the mirror: killer jeans, T-shirt, and a hot-as-shit leather vest with straps and buckles, topped with a pair of designer shades.

Biker-chick chic.

But the best part of the outfit was something Jaxson had already bought for me: my Swiftley speed boots from The Cordswainer's Curiosities. Kicking ass and chasing down bad guys was the job they were made for.

The part that I wasn't certain about was my hair. Sam had quickly dyed it with a potion, turning it dark brown with a few faint red highlights. She figured that since the bikers were looking for a redhead, we shouldn't tip them off immediately.

It was going to take some getting used to, but at least it would wash right out. I pulled it to the side and wondered what Jaxson would think. Not that it mattered.

Turning, I checked out my *frankly amazing* backside. "You really know my size, Sam."

She laughed. "Duh. I'm like your personal wardrobe assistant at this point."

True. She was as tough as nails but patient and generous with me, despite my early attempts to push her away. I gave her a warm smile. "Owe you big time."

She shoved her hands in her back pockets and kicked out her hip. "Yeah, well, that's true. You can start paying me back by ripping those assholes a new one."

I flexed my claws as my wolf leapt against my chest. "Try to stop me."

Sam shot me a devilish grin and headed to the door. "The good news is you're going to look unbelievably hot doing it."

I retracted my claws and texted Casey as we took the elevator to the parking deck. He'd sent me a dozen alternately worried, angry, and mildly inappropriate texts.

Sorry. Worked late at the bar. Crashed with Sam. Jaxson and I did none of the things you're insinuating, so get your mind out of the gutter.

Not that some of his suggestions weren't mentally stimulating.

When I didn't pick up his subsequent call, he immediately hit me with a barrage of texts like a mother hen, so I had to put him on mute as we stepped out of the elevator.

Jaxson was waiting by a pair of Harleys in the parking deck. He tensed the moment he laid eyes on me, and his jaw dropped. "Your hair..."

I tossed it defiantly. "Sam dyed it—technically a temporary glamor—but it seemed prudent since they're on the hunt for a redhead. Her idea."

"Smart," he muttered absently as his eyes traced every curve and assessed every buckle. He was taking a long time, and it was obvious his mind wasn't on my words. I could feel his approval, a heady scent of desire and praise. Heat rushed into me, and part of me wanted him to be inspecting me with more than just his gaze.

"Up here, Laurent," I sniped, pointing to my eyes.

He jerked his head.

Jaxson was fucking hot himself, and to my embarrassment, I actually licked my lips. I couldn't help it. His muscles looked like they were going to rip his leather jacket apart at the seams.

Sam cleared her throat. "Savy's pretty as a biker chick, huh?"

Jaxson growled in irritation. "Are you two ready?"

I crossed my arms and cocked my head. "We're all dressed up. What's the plan?"

"I was able to track down some information on the Arrowhead MC. They're a werewolf motorcycle club known for running drugs and potions, but not magical weapons, so that's a plus. We found a bar where a few of their members hang out in Indiana, though it's not their main club. Just a place one or two guys frequent—which is exactly what we want."

"So we're going to tap one of them on the shoulder, and they're just going to answer our questions?" I asked.

He shook his head. "We go in and wait for a chance to get one of their members alone. They're werewolves, and though they're not our pack, I'm an alpha. I can make them talk."

"Something tells me they won't go quietly," Sam muttered.

"I can keep them in line," Jaxson muttered.

Sam cocked her head to the side. "And who's going to keep *you* in line? You think you're going to play nice and forget what their gang did? The last time you saw someone touch Savannah, you smashed their face in."

Darkness flushed his cheeks as his eyes turned a deep gold. I could see the first signs of a shift. "Then nobody better touch her."

His voice was ice, and the implication hung in the air, chilling the whole parking deck. He'd kill anyone who even thought about touching me. I could smell the undercurrent of rage, but there was something more. A scent, a look, that was utterly feral. Lupine.

He's alpha. They abducted his mate from his den, my wolf whispered in my mind.

My eyes flicked across the man, and suddenly, I saw him in a very different light. He was calm but operating with a razor-thin edge of control. He wasn't just ready to kill any biker who touched me. He was ready to gut the whole MC, if given an excuse.

Trembling beneath his steely gaze, I stepped up and laid my fingers gently on his arm. His skin immediately responded to my touch. The tension in his muscles drained, and just like that, he was back to normal, his iron control restored.

I shuddered. Possessiveness was one thing, but what Jaxson had was off the charts. I wasn't sure I was ready for the consequences of him thinking of me as his mate.

Or of *being* his mate.

He looked down at me, his voice low and gravelly, dragging over my nerve endings. "Are you ready to get answers?"

His words refocused my thoughts, and an angry rush of heat seared my neck. "Yes."

"Then let's ride."

I glanced at the pair of shining chrome and black Harleys behind him. "There's only two bikes. Does that mean—"

Jaxson swung his leg over the Harley and nodded. "You ride pillion with me."

Of course.

"Sucker." Sam laughed and winked as she mounted up on the second bike.

"Hey!" I exclaimed.

"Have you ridden two up before?" Jax asked as he pulled on a black helmet.

He knew I hated being a passenger. Sometimes, he could be absolutely infuriating. In this case, he was also correct. "No. I've never ridden a motorcycle."

He chucked me a heavy blue helmet, and I grabbed it instinctively when it hit my gut. He patted the seat. "It's simple. Just sit behind me and don't make any sudden movements. Lean with the bike, and don't try to compensate. It's just like a dance—follow my lead."

I flexed my fingers, put on my helmet, and popped the visor up. "Fine. Let's go dancing."

Jax took a moment to explain how to mount up, and I got on. Steadying myself with a hand on his shoulder, I put my right foot on one of the pegs, then swung my other leg up and over.

He looked back. "Sit up, but hold low around my waist, and don't grab my arms or shoulders."

I put my visor down and slowly slipped my arms around him in a soft embrace. I could feel his strength beneath my touch, grounding me. Even through the leather jackets, currents passed between us like prickling static on a cold winter's day.

I took a deep breath. "Okay. If we're going to do this, let's get out of here."

The motorcycles roared to life, and we rumbled out of the parking garage and down the road.

13

Savannah

An hour and a half later, my ass and abs were screaming. I was hot, sweaty, and battered by the wind.

Even though I wasn't steering and was clinging on for dear life, the racing air filled me with a sense of freedom I hadn't felt in a long time.

There was something hypnotic about the drone of the engine and the speed of the ground flying by. I pressed myself against Jaxson's back as we shot down the road—not because I was anxious, but because it made me feel like I was part of the machine. When he leaned, I leaned, and every move we made, we made together.

I hated to admit it, but riding with him was exhilarating— though that didn't stop my ass from hurting.

Just when I was starting to worry I wouldn't make it another mile, we began to slow. A roadside bar appeared up ahead, the Tattered Tire Roadhouse.

The building was covered in orange stucco. It was weathered, though not shabby or run down. About ten bikes were parked out front, and a big dude stood at the door, keeping his eyes on things. But there were also a number of cars parked off to the side.

Jaxson turned into the gravel lot and rolled to a stop. He held the bike steady as I started to dismount. "Watch the tailpipe. It's going to be hot."

Like I was an idiot. I flipped my leg over and dropped to the ground.

Jaxson pitched his voice low. "This isn't supposed to be a clubhouse, just a bar that a couple of the Arrowheads frequent. We want to get one of them alone and talking."

Sam removed her helmet and set it on the bike. "Keep in mind that this is Indiana, not Magic Side. No wolfing out, and no hocus pocus."

Jaxson nodded as he pulled off his helmet. "She's right. We don't want to make a big scene. If there are just one or two Arrowheads, I'll make them submit with my presence, and we'll escort them back to talk. Three or more, we leave, then jump them later on the road."

"And if there are none?" I asked.

He pulled off his gloves and surveyed the row of bikes. "Well, we wait and try to blend in as best we can. We're just weekend riders who need a cold drink."

I nodded, then followed Sam and him in, glad I was in the back so they wouldn't see my broken ass wobble. The big biker out front didn't even flinch as I staggered by.

The front entrance was covered with old fliers and a time-worn menu. The place was smoky and hot, and my throat imme-diately began to tickle. Despite the haze and the stink of beer and cigarettes, the bar was clean, and my feet didn't stick to the floor when I walked, which was frankly a miracle.

A mixed crowd filled the bar. Most were mainstream bikers, sitting at low tables in twos or threes and pounding back bottles of beer, though there were a number wearing cuts with outlaw insignia.

The classic rock was cranked up to cover the fact that there was very little life in the place. The bar, and the people in it, felt deeply road weary. Still, despite the general malaise, I could smell an undercurrent of tension in the room that made the hair on my neck stand on end. Three weeks ago, I might have missed it. But now, with wolf senses, it was like everyone was screaming at me.

While in some places, machismo was measured by blatant posturing, this place was the opposite. The inattentive expressions on the patrons' faces hid a practiced watchfulness. Everyone was broadcasting disinterest as hard as they could, trying to prove that they were big dogs by showing they had nothing to fear, that they were too busy to care.

Jaxson seemed to pick up on it, too, and toned his signature as low as it could go. He nodded to a group of stools over by an old, battered pool table. "I'll grab some beers."

I casually scoped out the room as Sam and I headed over to find seats. While there were a number of bikers with patches, it didn't seem like any of the Arrowhead Disciples were present.

Sam shoved some quarters into the pool table, and the balls tumbled into the trough. "Can you shoot?"

"Absolutely." I unzipped my jacket and grabbed a stick off the wall. I could shoot really well...just not pool.

Jaxson came back with three Budweisers. They were just slightly below cool, which wasn't a great temp for a Bud, but they were wet, which was all I needed after almost two hours on the back of a bike.

"This place feels like a powder keg," I muttered.

Jax just nodded.

I proceeded to demonstrate to them both how poorly my skill with firearms translated to shooting pool. To my horror, I was so bad that I soon found Jaxson pressed up against me, helping to line up my shot. His scent wrapped around me, far more intoxicating than a dozen beers. And while my mind rebelled against the display, I felt my hips press back into the warmth of his body like they had a mind of their own.

They definitely do, Wolfie teased.

Sam's eyeroll settled the situation, and I spun out of Jaxson's arms. "I think I've got it. Thanks."

He gave me a knowing grin. It wasn't like he couldn't smell what was on my mind.

I sank my next shot, which almost irritated me more than missing.

Circling to the other side of the table, my eyes flicked over Jaxson's shoulder as the door opened. Four big, bearded bikers strode in and bellied up at the bar in front of the NASCAR races on TV.

My hands froze mid-shot. The backs of their jackets had three-part patches with an emblem of a wolf skull and crossed arrow in the center. The top rocker read *Arrowhead Disciples*, while the bottom read *Indiana*.

One caught me looking, and out of instinct, I bent low to shoot, hoping my cleavage would distract the men from the fact that I'd been watching them. I shot, but the ball ricocheted off the corner.

My mind wasn't on pool. It was on *them*.

Four was more than we'd bargained for, but suddenly, the plan didn't matter. Those bastards were after me, and while none of them had played a role in my abduction, I recognized the prick who'd tried to get me to pull over at the dunes.

Fuckers. They'd have taken me right there.

My hands clenched on the cue as I stood up straight, and vitriol lanced through my veins. A deep, venomous voice in my soul urged me on. *Kill them all.*

I sucked in a sharp breath and stepped around the table, but Jaxson stopped me short by grabbing the cue still clutched in my hands.

With his back to the bar, he bent his head and whispered almost imperceptibly in my ear. "I feel them. Four—not one. And as much I want to gut them all, we need to stand down and leave so we don't make a scene."

But that dark voice didn't want me to wait. Those jerks had shot up my car and run me off the road, while their buddies had tased me and bound me and dragged me into a fucking van.

Looking at the sleazy bastards, I knew then and there that they wouldn't have stopped at draining my blood.

I had to clench my heart to stop it from running out of my chest.

I need to calm down. Help me, I begged my wolf as images of ramming my claws into that bastard's neck, over and over, flooded my mind. He'd be able to smell my hate across the room.

Close your eyes. Think of running. The beach.

Shaking, I shut my eyes, trying to recall how it felt to run as one with my wolf. Our paws pounding on the sand. The cool breeze and the stars reflecting on the water. The rhythm of our movement.

But still, all I could think of was my abductors shoving me down and binding my wrists.

The fury and rage built in my bones until they were vibrating. I tried to pull the cue from Jaxson's hand, but he held me firm and let his presence flow into me. Finally, my taut muscles began to relax.

But before I could breathe and turn away, the lead biker swiveled around and looked me up and down. It was a ponderous, oily, lust-tainted gaze that crept over every inch of my body. Everywhere his eyes touched felt grimy and rank, and I felt like he was inspecting a piece of meat. I could practically taste his arrogance and contempt, and it tainted my mouth like bile.

At last, his glare met mine. "What the fuck are you staring at?"

His friends turned around as well, and suddenly, in the hair-trigger atmosphere of the bar, everyone was looking at me.

Well, shit.

With his back still turned, Jaxson shook his head, even though his own eyes were blazing with golden fire.

But I knew it was too late to salvage our plan.

I met their look with a defiant stare. *Come get me now, assholes.*

The biker stood. "Don't you know to look down when a man talks to you? Or hasn't your pimp taught you—"

His buddy grabbed his shoulder and stood as well. "Fuck, man, that's *the* bitch. She changed her hair."

The remaining Disciples rose as their leader grinned. "What a fucking juicy piece. I'm gonna—"

With that, the Dockside alpha snapped.

14

Jaxson

I spun, ripped the cue out of Savannah's hands, and rammed it into the biker's open mouth.

His head cracked back, and I sprang forward and jammed my heel into his leg, dropping him to his knees. As soon as he was down, I grabbed him by the hair and slammed his mouth straight into the countertop, shattering his jaw and teeth.

It was over in a second. I let him drop to the floor in a bloody, moaning mess. I'd been in control until he'd opened his dirty mouth. Now it was shut.

A moment of stunned silence followed, and then the whole bar exploded.

The other three Arrowheads charged. Fists flew into us from all angles, and a set of claws ripped across my face.

Savannah was at my side, fighting tooth and claw, her eyes filled with a black rage.

One of the bastards grabbed her, while another knocked me against the counter, sending a burst of agony up my spine. I ignored the pain. The only thing that mattered was keeping them off *her*.

I shoved my attacker away and pulled Savy out of the other biker's grasp. His claws tore into her arms, and my vision went pure red as I saw her blood well up. I grabbed the half-shifted asshole by the arm, pinned it behind his back, and rammed his head down onto the countertop. Then, without letting go, I charged backward and hurled him across the room toward the entrance of the bar. The front door shattered as he flew halfway though.

One of the bastards immediately leapt on my back, but Sam and Savy pulled him off. I turned to see him backhand Sam across the jaw. Unfazed, she grabbed his vest and kneed him in the groin. As he bent double, I dropped my forearm like a sledgehammer on his exposed neck, driving him to the ground, and finished him with a kick to the face.

Three out cold.

But the Arrowheads weren't our only problem. The whole bar was against us now.

Razors of pain ripped through my skull as something shattered across the back of my head. Glass tinkled to the ground, and I spun. A random biker—human, with a broken bottle in hand. "Die, you freaks!" he bellowed.

I grabbed him by the shirt and punched him three times in the face. When I let go, he collapsed to the ground.

Humans were so much easier to deal with.

Unfortunately, we were overwhelmed. They were all around us, trying to bring us down. For one second, I saw the last standing, orange-bearded Arrowhead through the crowd. He glared at me, then bolted down the back hallway.

"Don't let him escape!" I shouted.

Savy leapt over the bar and charged after him.

I shoved a stool into the crowd to clear them off Sam, who was on the ground, but pain lanced through my side.

I twisted to face a human biker brandishing a broken pool cue, its end dripping with blood—*my* blood.

"Go to hell, you yellow-eyed monster!" he screamed as he rammed the shattered cue straight into my gut.

But he was human, and I was a wolf, and I had reflexes and strength ten times those of his. I grabbed the cue by the point before it dug into my flesh again.

The wound in my side and the sharpened stick brought forth memories of peasants with pitchforks hunting members of our pack—not my memories but those passed down through the magic of our lore master. Yet those echoes of our kind's hellish last days in France were almost as real as if they'd happened to me. For a second, he wasn't an asshole biker but a screaming villager, whipped into a bloodthirsty frenzy by the zealots of the Church.

I'd show him a yellow-eyed monster.

With a savage motion, I ripped the pool cue from his hand and grabbed him by his jacket. I lifted him, screaming, above my head with both hands, then slammed him down on the pool table.

The table shattered and collapsed around his limp body.

Fuck him.

All three Arrowheads inside were down. Sam was tangled with a couple of patrons, but I knew she could handle a dozen humans on her own. I had to get to Savannah.

But before I could move, the broken door burst open, and two people, a man and a woman, rushed in with badges held high. "State police! Everyone get down on the ground!"

Some idiot hurled a chair at the female cop. "Get the fuck out, fucking pigs!"

She staggered back into the doorway as two bikers jumped on her and her partner.

Fuck.

The female cop wrenched one of the assailants up by the arm, twisted it behind his back, and brought him to his knees. Not my problem. I didn't have time for this. I had to get to Savy and the last of the Arrowheads.

Pushing the cowering bartender out of my way, I leapt over the end of the bar top and charged toward the back.

Something slammed against the wall ahead of me in a cloud of smoke. A shockwave of magic raced through my body. My muscles seized in agony, and I crashed onto the floor.

Bikers and patrons collapsed around the bar.

Potion bomb. Stunner.

The male cop rose and hurled a second bomb to the other side of the room. Sam and the two bikers assailing her dropped to the ground.

These weren't state police. This was the Order. *Fuck them.*

I forced my neck to turn toward the back door. I strained with every muscle I had, but I couldn't move. But then a burst of pain shot through me. Not my pain—Savannah's.

No.

Fire poured through my veins as I fought against the power of the potion. I wouldn't let it hold me. My mate was in danger.

I pushed all my strength into my arm. Glacially, inch by inch, I pushed myself onto my knees. I turned my mind to my leg, and my muscles screamed as I forced them to my will. Slowly, I brought my leg forward and heaved myself up unsteadily against the wall.

With a roar, I shook off the chains of magic and hurled myself toward the back door.

Nothing would stop me. Not bikers. Not cops. Not sorcery itself.

∼

Savannah

I charged after the orange-bearded Disciple who'd ducked out the back door.

The moment I stepped outside, pain lanced through my jaw as his fist connected with my face. My head cracked against the wall, and bricks dug into my skull.

I slumped to the ground as the world spun. The biker brought his boot down on my knee, and something popped.

My head flew back, and I screamed.

The sky above me whirled, a beautiful kaleidoscope of white and blue. The sight was interrupted by the silhouette of the bastard biker as he stepped over me. I tried to scoot back across the asphalt, but he drove his foot into my ribs. I gasped as the breath burst from my lungs.

"I can smell it on you! I'm gonna make you bleed Scarlet!" he growled.

Unable to breathe or speak, I gurgled and rolled to my side to face a couple cars parked on the old, degrading asphalt. It was just another parking lot, and just another werewolf trying to kill me. The first time I'd met one, I'd been terrified out of my mind.

But not this time. This time, I knew what was coming. I was ready for it, I *needed* it. And when my breath finally came back, I actually laughed.

The werewolf biker grabbed me by my jacket. "What the fuck are you laughing at, you crazy little bitch?"

Wiping the blood from my lip, I gave him a crimson smile. "How screwed you are."

In a split second, I summoned the shadows around us and kicked out his feet. He shouted in surprise as he tumbled back against the wall. "What the hell did you do? I can't see!"

I rolled away and stood.

While I'd made the world go pitch black around us, my

power let me see. The bastard put his fists out in warning and looked left and right. "Who the hell are you?"

"I'm the wolf in the fucking darkness," I snarled as I hammered my clenched fist into the back of his head.

He staggered forward, then spun and swung wildly, fighting blind. "I can smell you! I can hear you, and I'm going to beat you to a pulp!"

Someone was shouting beyond the darkness, but I didn't care. I was focused on the asshole in front of me.

Fighting past the pain burning in my knee, I moved left. Unfortunately, my gimpy leg dragged on the asphalt. The biker turned his head and swung wildly in the direction of the noise.

Like Jaxson had taught me long ago, I stepped into the blow and deflected his arm to the right. My palm shot up and rammed into his chin with a deeply satisfying crack. I stood like a rock as he reeled back.

I attacked again before he could catch his balance, sweeping out his legs and dropping him onto his back. His head ricocheted off the asphalt just as hard as mine had hit the wall.

I was on him in seconds.

For a moment, he wasn't just a seedy biker who'd struck and dehumanized me. He was the pair of werewolves in the back lot of the roadside Taphouse. He was the bastards who'd grabbed me at the motel, as well as the ones who'd thrown me in the white van. He was every one of those monsters who'd hunted me, terrified me, and used their power to hurt me.

My fists rammed down into his face, again and again. He struggled, but I was faster, stronger, and propelled by an unrelenting rage. He cried out in the darkness, but there was no one here who cared.

Or maybe there was. A woman was shouting loudly now, but I didn't pay her any mind.

Savy, stop! We need him alive! my wolf commanded.

Fuck that. I called my claws, but they didn't come.

No. I refuse to do this, Wolfie growled.

Fine, I snarled back. *Have it your way.*

I summoned my Soul Knife and dismissed the darkness so that the bastard could see what I was about to do to him.

The tingle of magic raced along my arm as the cold copper blade formed in my hand. I swung my arm back, ready to ram the blade into his heart.

But it stopped short as strong fingers wrapped around my wrist. Electricity surged through my body.

Jaxson.

I struggled against his grip, but he was iron.

A woman shouted, "Nobody fucking move! Savannah Caine, drop your weapon!"

My head whipped to the side. There was a woman in a jacket, potion bomb in hand and badge raised. I recognized her.

"Harlow?" *What the hell?*

I looked down at the biker. His face was pummeled and covered with blood, which matted his hair and pooled behind his head. He was barely breathing.

Oh, my God, what had I done?

My body began to tremble, and I dropped the cursed knife. Jaxson's power poured through me. "Calm down, Savannah."

"Back away from the biker," Harlow snapped, kicking the blade away.

Jaxson helped me to my feet and pulled me close. I buried my face in his shoulder, but I could still see the biker's bloodied face in my mind. He'd assaulted me, but somehow, somewhere along the way, I was the one who'd become the monster.

Again.

15

Jaxson

Fuck everything.

I held Savannah close and ran my hands through her hair, letting my alpha presence pour into her to calm her trembling.

I sent my power blasting through the parking lot to subdue all the others. The Order agent with her badge raised. Her partner, a sandy-haired man who had his sidearm drawn but wisely held low. The stammering bartender, who'd been cowering behind the bar. And finally, the bloody bastard lying on the ground. He was a drug-crazed shifter twice Savannah's weight, and she'd absolutely annihilated him.

That, and she'd been one second from ripping out his soul.

Not good.

I didn't pity the prick. He was scum who sold drugs and treated women like disposable objects. But there would be fallout from this, either with the Arrowheads or the Order.

"Everyone stay the fuck where you are." The Order agent —*Harlow*—knelt by the body. "What the hell happened?"

"He attacked me...I fought back...I didn't know what I was

doing," Savannah mumbled, her voice distant and thin with shock.

My muscles tightened with rage as she lifted her head and I got a good look at her. Her face was bruised and battered. My claws ripped out of my hands. "What did he do to you?"

Savannah's hands dug into my jacket, and she whispered, "Please, no more violence."

Harlow backed up quickly and held out a warning hand. "This is not the time or place to shift, Laurent."

An asshole had battered my mate, and he was sitting five feet away. It sure the hell *was* the time to shift and rip his throat out. But we needed him alive. I tried to calm my breathing and glared at Harlow. "His buddies jumped us inside as well."

"Is this true?" Harlow asked the bartender, who was human.

"One of the guys at the bar stood up, and then—" The bartender pointed at me with a trembling hand, then froze. "Shit, why are his eyes yellow? Like those freaks inside?"

The hair on my neck rose in frustration, and I gestured to the doorway. "You're in shock. Go back inside and start cleaning up."

I let my alpha presence slam into him like a baseball bat. He gulped and scuttled back into the bar.

Harlow cursed and knelt to check the unconscious biker over. "Well, this doesn't surprise me in the least. I've got a file on Big Red here. He's got a history of starting fights and beating women. He may rethink that after today."

"He'd better," Savannah hissed.

Harlow looked up at Savy. "Let me be clear. Whatever he's done in the past, you're not within your rights to *stab* the man, so it's better for all of us that your knife is over there on the ground and not sticking out of his chest."

Savannah nodded, and with the flick of her wrist, she discreetly returned the blade to the ether.

Harlow turned to her partner as she rose. "Okay, Max, go cuff the other Arrowheads before they wake up. Then call this in. We'll need a cleanup crew and some mind mages on the scene, ASAP. I'll take care of the mess out here."

Harlow's henchman headed inside, and I grabbed Savannah to follow.

The cop crossed her arms. "Nuh-uh, Laurent, I'm not through with you two."

"We need to check on our friend, the blonde woman in the biker jacket," I growled.

"She's fine, just out cold from the potion bomb. First, you two need to answer some questions, like what the hell were you thinking"—she checked around the corner to make sure that the bartender wasn't eavesdropping at the door—"starting a brawl in a human bar? Are you insane?"

We were forbidden to use our powers in the presence of non-Magica. The punishment could be dire.

Crossing my arms, I turned back to Harlow. "These assholes tried to abduct Savannah a few days ago. We came here to figure out why. We weren't looking to cause a fight, just ask questions. We thought we might be able to talk to one alone. But four showed up, and they thought they could grab her."

Harlow cursed as she rubbed her forehead with her fingers. "What a mess."

"What are you doing here, anyway?" I snarled in irritation. "You got here suspiciously quickly."

Harlow pulled out her phone and began texting someone. "We've had eyes on you two since Savannah was attacked, and we got an alert that you were headed out of town, dressed as bikers, so we followed. Seemed like a good bet that you were going to get yourselves in trouble."

What the fuck?

I balled my fists. "So what, you were just sitting outside in your car, waiting to see what would happen?"

She shrugged. "Until someone threw a half-shifted werewolf through the front door. Speaking of which, we need to get the other shifters from inside. Help me restrain this asshole."

We grabbed the huge shifter and set him up against a telephone pole. Harlow pulled his hands around his back and slapped a pair of magicuffs over his wrists, binding him in place. "That should hold him. Come on, let's see the damage you did."

We followed Harlow back into the bar. Chairs and tables were overturned. The front door was smashed in, and the countertop was decorated with blood and loose teeth. The pool table was snapped in half, with an unconscious man in the center.

The place looked like ground zero for a hurricane or an MMA match.

The patrons were all passed out, slumped over chairs and tables, and lying on the floor. Potions affected humans a lot harder than they did Magica.

Harlow's partner bent over Sam. "Is this one yours?"

"Yes." My heartbeat accelerated, though Sam only had a few scratches. I couldn't afford to lose her for my sake, or Savy's.

The agent—Max—lifted her up and gave her a sip of a potion he'd pulled from his coat.

Sam sputtered to consciousness and gagged. "Holy shit. What happened?"

Savy dropped to the ground beside her. "Are you okay?"

"A little woozy. Not sure my legs are going to cooperate for a bit." Sam turned to Harlow's partner. "Who the hell are you? What did you give me?"

He stood. "Max. I'm with the Order. I gave you a revival potion. The sleep bomb should wear off shortly."

Sam gave him an appraising, almost lusty look. "Thanks. Then again, you're the asshole who KO'ed me with a potion bomb in the first place."

She staggered to her feet with our help and gave me a

wicked grin as she looked around the joint. "We're in trouble, aren't we, boss?"

Harlow put her hands on her hips as she surveyed the wreckage. "I should chuck the lot of you in Bentham for having a rumble outside of Magic Side."

"That's not going to happen," I growled.

"Oh, I'm not naïve. I know I've got no chance of that, not with your friends and connections," she snapped, eyes burning with resentment.

She was right.

"We want the same thing," I said as I crossed my arms and pushed my alpha presence at Harlow. "You want to stop these bastards from selling Scarlet. We want to stop them from going after Savannah. Give me a couple of minutes alone with the prick out back, and I'll tell you what I learn. I can make him talk."

She opened her mouth to object, but I pressed with my power until she nodded. "You can ask your questions, but I'm going to be there."

"Fine." I didn't care what she did as long as she didn't get in my way.

Max nodded to the bartender cowering in the corner. "Heads up—this guy called the cops before I could stop him."

"Damn it! Not what we need." Harlow cursed and pointed to her partner. "Max, you and Laurent drag the other Arrowheads out back."

I hefted one of the unconscious assholes off the floor. It was the guy whose teeth I'd knocked out on the counter. A better man would have cringed at his broken face, but I wasn't a good man. Just the monster my father and sister had trained me to be.

And shutting him up mid-slur? That made me happy.

Savy helped Sam hobble to the bar where she could sit.

I paused. Savannah made me better, or she at least made me want to be better.

As if she could feel the heat of my eyes on her back, she turned and met my gaze. Fortunately, the bastard hanging over my shoulder was facing away from her. She'd seen enough gruesome work today already.

Her eyes drifted to the zip ties that bound his ankles and wrists behind his back. Practically the same thing they'd done to her.

"Seems like a fitting end," I said.

Savy just nodded, and I hauled the guy to the back lot and dumped him against the wall.

"You motherfucker!" the biker cuffed to the telephone pole snarled. Apparently, he'd woken up from his nap. He strained, and the thick wood pole cracked a little. "Let me go!"

I slammed him with my alpha presence. "Sit still and be quiet, and don't speak until you're spoken to."

He slumped against the pole and set his jaw.

As I stepped back into the bar, Harlow was speaking to Savannah in hushed tones. "Are you sure you're safe? With him? You don't have to be a part of this."

"I am a part of this. Part of the pack," Savannah said with defiance.

"Part of the pack? Like, Jaxson's pack?" Harlow asked. "I thought you were a LaSalle."

"I'm a werewolf, now, too," she said.

My muscles tightened at the despair in her voice, and a deep wave of failure cut through me.

So far, all that being a werewolf had brought her was trouble. She didn't understand what it was to be part of a pack. She only knew the bad side, and that had to change.

I had to change it.

16

Jaxson

I stepped around Max as he struggled to drag the last of the unconscious Arrowhead Disciples out the door. "Big Red is awake and pissy, but I think he's willing to talk."

With an unreadable look, Savannah and Harlow broke off their conversation and followed me outside.

Big Red began struggling violently as soon as he saw Savannah. "Don't let that psycho bitch near me! Look what she did!"

I grabbed him by the jacket and shoved him back against the telephone pole. "Were you part of the crew that grabbed the redhead outside of Eclipse?"

He spat in my face. "I'm not answering your questions."

I pressed him back so his shoulders popped, then rammed him with my alpha presence as hard as I could.

"Ah, fuck, don't..." he whined as I bared down. "Yes! It took me a second, but I recognized that little slut even with her brown hair. I could smell her blood. Wanted the Scarlet." He gave Savy a licentious look as I released a little pressure. "I would have taken more than that."

She hauled back and slapped him, then snarled, "Who sent you after me?"

He turned his head in resistance.

"Answer our questions." I let the weight of my alpha presence drop on him like a sledgehammer, commanding his submission with every fiber of my body.

"Fucking alpha," he spat, but he scowled and submitted. "According to our president, if we got you, we could make more Scarlet."

"How?" I asked.

He twisted to face me and bared his teeth. "I don't know! I just push the stuff! We were supposed to hand her over to the alpha of the Central Michigan pack. I don't know why."

"Lucius Grayling?"

Big Red snorted. "Yeah, he used to be called that. But he's changed. Now he just calls himself the Dragon, or something. That fucker is out of his mind, but if he could deliver the Scarlet..."

Savannah clenched my arm, and I could feel the urgency tingling in her fingertips. Not Dragon. *Dragan.*

Her claws dug into my skin. "Why do you say he's out of his mind?" she pressed.

"I haven't met him. But the guys he hasn't brainwashed say he's batshit crazy. Argues with his wolf aloud. Fucking acts like some kind of prophet."

Damn. It had to be Dragan.

Harlow didn't miss a beat. "You two know this guy?"

Savannah's eyes burned with emotion. "Victor Dragan. My aunt killed him decades ago, but he won't stay dead. His ghost possessed Ulan Kahanov, and he's been hunting me. Seems he's found a new host."

"Possessed?" Harlow asked. "And Kahanov? The prisoner who escaped Bentham several months ago?"

Savy nodded. "He's dead."

Sam tensed. "Time's up, boss! The fuzz are on their way. I can hear them."

"What?" Harlow asked.

I perked up my ears, catching the faint noise though the cars were still miles away. "Sirens in the distance. You'll hear them soon enough."

"Shit! We've got to wrap this up before more humans arrive." Harlow turned back to Big Red. "Where can we find this Dragan, the Dragon, whatever he calls himself?"

"I don't know."

I gripped the biker by his vest and pulled him forward so his cuffs caught on the pole, his shoulders straining in his sockets. "*Where?*"

He growled and clenched his teeth, but at last, he spoke. "There's supposed to be a rally up in Michigan three nights from now. I'm certain that he'll be there. I wasn't going to go. Those two-headed freaks are involved and pushing it hard."

I let him slump back.

Harlow glanced at Savannah. "Two-headed freaks?"

Big Red glared at us. "Yeah, they've all got these freaky two-headed wolf tattoos. I think it's like some sort of doomsday cult. There's a few in every pack and MC around."

Harlow's eyes burned. "Have they ever approached you? Told you what they wanted?"

For some reason, he looked at Savannah. "They say the Dark Wolf God is coming back. That we won't have to live in fear of humans anymore. We won't have to hide. I told them I'm not afraid of any human. I just want to sling dope, get paid, and get laid."

Harlow looked over her shoulder in the direction of the approaching sirens. "I hear them. I've got to get this prick back to the Hall of Inquiry. Laurent, you three better get your bikes and ride. The cleanup crew is going to have a hard enough time setting all this straight without you getting caught."

Savannah knelt and looked Big Red in the eye. "Where and when is the rally?"

He trembled in front of her and looked away. "Monday night, an hour before midnight at Pere Cheney Graveyard. Too fucking freaky, if you ask me. That's all I know, I swear."

I could feel the truth of his words.

Harlow pulled Savannah back. "You've got to go, *now*. I'll let you know if I learn anything else. For now, this guy needs to take his nap for transport." With that, she pulled a potion bomb out of her pocket, uncorked it, and splashed a little in Big Red's face. He flinched, but as the liquid began to steam, his head lolled forward. "He won't be begging to call his lawyer anytime soon," the agent muttered.

Savannah turned to go but paused at the door. "Thanks for the bailout and for not busting us."

Harlow nodded. "You three aren't out of the woods. Don't go vigilante again. If you do, I don't care what friends you have up top—I'll throw you in lockup myself. We'll help you get Dragan, but you're working with us, under our rules."

Savannah nodded. *Fucking hell.*

"Let's go, boss!" Sam shouted from inside the building.

The three of us raced through the bar.

"Don't come back, now!" the bartender said meekly from the back corner.

I turned and took a step toward him. "If I hear you open your mouth about our role in this or say anything to the cops, I'll come back and gut you myself."

They'd wipe his memory, but it was deeply satisfying to see him start trembling.

I followed Savy and Sam through the broken front door. Our bikes were still outside and in one piece.

Savannah wiped her eyes and started fiddling with her helmet. I could feel her strangled sense of despair pulsing through me, a deep melancholy that was not my own. "Are you okay?"

"Not really. I messed that guy up pretty good. If you hadn't stopped me..." She looked away, in the direction of the approaching cop cars.

I reached out and brushed away a tear, then gently traced the bruise on her cheek. "Don't cry for that prick. He and his friends were planning to abduct you and drain you dry. Do you think you're the first girl he's hurt to get what he wants? Harlow knew him by name, and she's got a dossier on him. The beating you gave him—he probably deserved worse."

She pulled away and tugged her helmet on, concealing her face. "And I've done worse, Jaxson—I've killed people, for heaven's sake. But today—that wasn't me, and it wasn't my wolf. I was so angry. For a moment, I was just...somebody else. I'm becoming something I'm not. A monster."

I grabbed her by her shoulder and spun her toward me. "No. You're a wolf, and you're fighting to survive. You're not alone, Savannah. You're part of a pack. We all wrestle with our beasts, but I swear, you are *not* a monster." I let my presence wrap around her, soothing her emotions.

There was so much more I wanted to say, but the sirens were almost on us. I glanced down the road as my fists clenched in frustration. "Fuck. We've got to go."

Sam gunned her Harley and rumbled out of the lot. I swung my leg over my bike, and Savy hopped up behind, just like I'd taught her. She wrapped her arms around me and squeezed tightly. Her magic and signature flowed through me, and although I could sense her despair, for one second, in a bloody fucked-up day, everything was all right.

I fired up my bike, and with Savannah pressed close against my back, we rumbled out onto the open road.

17

Savannah

By the time we got back to Magic Side, my despair had turned to numbness.

Although I'd been pretending nothing was happening, the truth was that I was no longer that naïve girl from Wisconsin. I'd become a werewolf and a killer and had made my bed with criminals. I could command shadows and darkness, and I could summon a knife from thin air that would tear out your soul.

Despite what Jaxson had said, there was no doubt I was a monster. Something dark inside of me was growing every day. Something that wasn't my wolf, and that wasn't my magic.

Maybe it was just me. The real me—the part that hated my parents for dying and wanted to strangle every one of the bastards who'd ever laid their hands on me.

I wrapped my arms tighter around Jaxson's waist just to have something solid to cling to as the daze took hold and the city streets passed by.

Finally, Jaxson's bike rolled to a stop in front of Savage Body, and I looked up in surprise.

"Your car's done," Jax said.

My heart leapt as I caught sight of my Gran Fury sitting in the front lot, freshly washed. I eagerly slipped off the bike and hurried over.

The rear wheel had been replaced, and the bullet holes had been patched and painted. I let my fingers drag along the restored side of the vehicle and trunk, savoring the moment. I could almost feel the magic tingling beneath my fingertips.

My father's magic.

A sense of limitless freedom rushed through me like wind on a warm summer's day. And the darkness that had consumed me on the ride back from the bar evaporated.

Footsteps approached from behind, and I turned to face Jaxson.

"Everything in order?" he asked.

More than ever.

I nodded. "Yes. Thanks."

I hoped he could sense my gratitude because words couldn't explain what my Fury meant to me.

"Good," Jax said laconically, and crossed his arms. He looked like an absolute hunk in his biker jacket. Tall. Strong. Confident.

His signature mixed with the intoxicating scent of his sweat, and I drank it in as a comfortable silence stretched between us. Comfortable, that is, until I became aware of it.

Aw, shit, was I staring?

Heat crept across my neck, and I suddenly felt hot, sweaty, and grimy. I hadn't seen myself in a mirror, but I was betting my face was covered with blood and bruises and my hair was wild and wind tangled from the road. Add to that the stink of exhaust, blood, and perspiration, and I probably seemed like one hell of a catch.

I awkwardly gestured to the car. "I'm going pay you back. I owe you a lot of hours at the bar for this."

An indecipherable smile tugged at the corner of his mouth,

and he shrugged. "As you wish. But not tonight—I certainly have had enough of bars for today."

I let out a deep breath. "Tell me about it."

Sam strode over. "I, unfortunately, have bar duty tonight. But before you two get lost staring at each other's eyeballs, I want to know what the plan is."

My cheeks burned, and I glanced away.

Jaxson, always the confident one, was totally unperturbed. "Well, it appears that Dragan is back, and he's possessed Lucius Grayling. That, or Grayling is trying to use Dragan's old network for power—but given what we know, I'm going to bet he's possessed."

"So how do we stop a ghost?" I asked.

"Instead of killing him, we'll have to capture him," Jaxson said.

Sam checked her phone. "Sounds like he'll be at the rally on Monday night with all his minions. If we can catch him there, along with a bunch of his drug-crazed cultists, we could potentially knock out the threat to Savy in one fell swoop."

"What do you think they're up to?" I asked.

Jaxson's face darkened. "I don't know, but we need to find out before we go in, guns blazing."

A slow, sinking feeling of trepidation weighed down on me. "I think it's time I talked to my aunt."

Jaxson's eyebrows rose.

"She killed him the first time," I explained, "and she and Uncle Pete went off looking for more information. If anyone knows, it'll be her."

"Or my father," Jaxson said flatly. His voice was level but dripping with an emotion I couldn't quite place. Resentment? Frustration? Wariness?

Whatever was there, at least he wasn't going to have to tell his father he was a wolf.

Of the two questions I needed to ask Laurel, I knew which terrified me more, and it wasn't, *What's Dragan up to?*

It was, *Was I born a werewolf—and why didn't you tell me?*

Half an hour later, I pushed through the front door of the LaSalles' house and dropped my car keys in the brass bowl by the door. I'd quickly changed out of my biker clothes and washed most of the magic dye out, so my hair was almost back to its normal color.

My sweaty hands were practically shaking, and I wiped them on my jeans as I reevaluated my plan. Maybe I'd wait to ask Aunt Laurel about being a werewolf until after we'd sorted things out with Dragan. And although I wanted to know what she knew about my mom, the potential fallout could be catastrophic.

Things were too up in the air. It was best to wait.

Better to rip the band-aid off, Wolfie murmured in my mind.

Easy for you to say. You don't have to look her in the eyes.

"Savannah, is that you?" My aunt whipped her head out of the kitchen and smiled. The smell of cinnamon and butter wafted down the hall. Cinnamon cookies.

At times, she could be positively warm and domestic. But I'd seen her other side—one as hard as iron. A woman who could command demons and disintegrate monsters with a single flick of her wrist.

"Welcome home," I said, trying to keep my voice steady.

"It's good to be home." My aunt pulled me into a warm embrace, and I awkwardly wrapped my arms around her.

A part of me wanted to just get it done with, to scream, *I'm a werewolf! Did you know?*

I knew she was hiding something from me, but I couldn't believe she knew the truth. She'd welcomed me into her home

—why would she have done that if she knew what I was? Any time someone mentioned werewolves or the Laurents, I could feel the heat of her hatred, like standing next to an open fire.

The odds were fifty-fifty that she'd lose her shit and kick me to the curb or chain me in silver.

We'll claw her eyes out first, my wolf said defiantly.

Laurel handed me a heaping plate of warm cookies. "Take these into the drawing room. I'll be right there. We should talk."

Oh, yes, we should.

I set the cookies on the coffee table and took a seat on the antique couch. Laurel swept in with two steaming mugs of milky tea. She handed one to me and sat. "Casey tells me that you didn't come home last night."

I nearly choked out my half-eaten cookie. *That snitch!*

Not that it mattered. I was going to have to tell her. I wiped my mouth. "I was attacked, and I stayed the night with a friend."

The mug froze halfway to her lips, and I could see the fire in her eyes. "Attacked? By whom? Are you okay? Should I call in Uncle Pete? And why, for the sake of the gods, didn't you come back here where it was safe?"

I reeled from the impact of the rapid-fire questions, though I recovered quickly. I had answers to all of them except the last.

"I'm okay. It was a bunch of werewolf bikers."

She leapt to her feet, and magic crackled around her. "Werewolves? The Dockside pack? I told you not to get involved with them or Jaxson Laurent."

"No!" I snapped—more harshly than I should have, seeing as all she wanted was to protect me. "Jaxson and his people chased them off. The jerks who jumped me were part of a biker gang, and I think they work for Dragan."

My aunt went ashen as she slowly sat. "Dragan..."

"The bikers were supposed to hand me over to the leader of one of the Michigan packs, who's suddenly calling himself the

Dragon or Dragan. I think he's possessed, just like Kahanov was. And he's up to something."

Her eyes were wide. "What?"

"We don't know," I said matter-of-factly between overflowing mouthfuls of cookie. "Whatever it is, it involves me and a bunch of cultists with tattoos of a two-headed wolf. So *my* question is, what did you and Uncle Pete find out on your trip, and what was Dragan up to before you disintegrated him?"

My aunt let out a sigh and ran her hands through her hair. "This is very bad. Dragan...Dragan was a monster. Part sorcerer and part wolf. He had access to forbidden magic—and it seems he has unfinished business."

"Why did you hunt him down?"

"I was called in to help solve a string of murders. He left his victims in the middle of pentagrams inscribed with sorcerous runes. It was all part of a ritual we didn't understand, but the werewolves seemed to know about it. Something about releasing an ancient evil, though they wouldn't tell us what."

The Dark Wolf God.

My skin prickled as a cold draft moved through the room.

Laurel looked me in the eyes and continued, "Your uncle and I are afraid he's trying to do so again—except this time, he intends to use you as a sacrifice."

"What about the cultists? Or the two-headed wolf tattoo? What do you know about those?"

"Little. Dragan had cultists to help with his rituals back then, which scaled up and became more elaborate with time. Your uncle and I returned to the place we killed him, an ancient graveyard in what was Czechoslovakia. He'd collected a dozen people to sacrifice and murdered six by the time we killed him."

"Why go there?"

"I wanted to know why he was able to come back and possess Kahanov. Ghosts are rare, and with the spell I used to disintegrate him, returning shouldn't have been possible." She looked down at her hands. "I still don't know why or how he came back."

"You and the Laurents worked together to bring him down?"

Laurel tensed and snapped her head up. "Yes, but it was a mistake. If that's what you have in mind, hanging out with Jaxson Laurent, you can forget it. He'll betray you the same way they betrayed us in the end."

I sat on my hands to pin them in place. "What happened?"

My aunt's eyes burned, and iron replaced the bitterness in her voice. "Nothing that can ever be changed."

Her words were final, and silence filled the space. A silence that begged for a question and was leading me there, step by step.

I took in a shaky breath. "So why is Dragan after me?"

Laurel shuddered, and the fire in her eyes disappeared, dowsed with sorrow. "To inflict revenge on our family for killing him, I suspect."

My voice approached a whisper. "But Casey hasn't been attacked. Your own son. Wouldn't Dragan attack him first?"

She looked away, toward the hall and stairs that led to Casey's room. "Perhaps he thought you were an easier target— though thankfully, you've proven him wrong on that."

I dug my fingers into my jeans and fought down my trepidation.

"Do you think that maybe it's not because of who I am, but *what* I am? What my mother was?"

Her pupils shrank to laser points, though a fake smile hung on her face. "What do you mean, dear?"

Before I knew her, I would have been fooled. But not now. I'd lived with Laurel for weeks, and I'd learned a few of her tells and tics. I could smell the fear that her lie would be uncovered.

I *knew* that she *knew*.

Narrowing my eyes, I slowly set my mug down. "Let's cut the bullshit, Laurel. Tell me the truth, starting with my mother. I know what she was."

Way to rip the band-aid off.

Laurel flinched. "Excuse me?"

"A *werewolf.*" I paused, watching the shock roll off her like heat waves above hot asphalt. "She and Dad left because she was pregnant with me, but you already knew that."

"How—who told you this?" Anger flashed through her eyes, and I sensed her alarm. Defensiveness. Fear. Shock.

"I had my suspicions, but then I found a letter that my dad had written to you. Did you know about me?"

"I don't understand." Laurel had stopped breathing, and her eyes turned glassy. "Did something happen to you?"

Her confusion mixed with anxiety, making a heady aroma that burned my nostrils. But it was the underlying hint of affirmation that made me sick to my stomach. She'd known all along.

"*Happen* to me? No, I was born this way. But my family was too disgusted by what I was, so my parents fled and lied to me my whole life. You're just as guilty as they were for keeping this from me."

Laurel's face had turned pale. "Born this way?"

Her voice rang with the horror of a truth she knew but couldn't accept.

I slowly extended my claws as I held back tears. "Born. A. Werewolf. Except I didn't turn into one until I came here to Magic Side."

For an infinite moment, Laurel stared at my hands in shock. Then she bolted to her feet and pushed back the chair as she staggered away. "How? This isn't possible."

"I'm not sure I understand your question. My mom was a

werewolf, and I'm a werewolf. I grow fangs and fur and run on four legs."

And eat rabbits and bacon, my wolf added, snickering.

With her eyes wide and unfocused, my aunt began to quake and clutched the wall for support. "It's not possible...we bound your wolf. It shouldn't be possible..."

My head spun as I took in her words. "*Bound* my wolf?"

Laurel looked at my claws in terror and then wrung her hands. "It's okay. It will be okay. We can do it again. Your mother and father aren't here, but I can teach Pete and Casey."

Oh, my God.

The world around me twisted and warped like it had been demented by a carnival mirror.

She did this to me? And my parents helped?

Laurel approached tentatively. "Don't worry, Savannah. I can fix this—"

I bolted out of my seat and maneuvered to the far side of the room. "What do you mean, *fix this*?"

She pressed her hands to her mouth. "You must be so scared. But don't worry, I can make it go away."

My wolf surged in my chest, and my fangs sprang out. *Traitorous bitch! She'd bind me again?*

Confusion and desperation spun in my mind as I tried to maintain control of my wolf.

She could make it go away.

At first, all I had wanted was to make it go away. When I'd thought I was a werewolf because Billy or Kahanov had infected me. But this was different.

I was born a wolf. Wolfborn. And Wolfie was a part of me now.

A part that I hadn't wanted. But in that moment, staring down my aunt, I knew I couldn't give her up. That I'd *never* give her up.

You'd better not! Wolfie growled, still raging and fighting for release.

I backed away from my aunt, who'd betrayed me, who'd lied to me, who'd help tear out a part of my soul.

"Savannah," she said, reaching out. "Don't be afraid. I can help."

My wolf tore at me from within, and hair burst along my arms.

"I don't want your help!" I snarled in a feral voice that made my aunt's eyes go wide. "I want to know why you lied to me! Why you did this—why my parents did this!"

Laurel paused and looked at me with terror and confusion. "To protect you. Your parents and I bound your wolf with a spell to keep that half of you a secret. We wanted you to lead a normal life."

"A normal life?" I scoffed. "Never knowing who I was or what I was capable of? A life without magic? A life with only half a soul? Did you hate what I was that much?"

Betrayal sank its bloody fangs into me, and a sob lodged in my throat.

"None of us ever hated you." Laurel's eyes brimmed with sorrow and determination.

"Not my grandfather?"

She froze, and I could sense her panic. "He wasn't the reason."

"Then what was?" I growled. "What was so important that you took that half from me without ever telling me the truth?"

My skin itched and tingled, and I could sense a shift coming on.

"You were born just after Dragan died—"

Horror took me as the room spun. I cried in pain as the shift began—as who I was began to melt away into something else.

Dragan. Had they worried I was going to be like him? A monster? Was that the truth?

Were they right?

I howled and charged for the door of the drawing room, but Laurel flicked her hand, and it slammed closed.

"You can't leave, Savannah. It's not safe. I can help turn you back."

"I don't want to turn back!" I screamed. "I want to be who I am!"

I hadn't fully shifted yet, and I struggled for control. I needed hands to get out of this damned house.

Someone pounded on the door and started shouting. Casey? Panic seized my mind. If he came in and found me as a wolf, would he shoot me on sight?

I summoned every ounce of willpower to keep the shift from taking over, but I could barely think with my wolf raging in my chest. I jiggled the doorknob, but the door was stuck. "Let me out!"

"I can't let you leave," Laurel said calmly. "It's not safe. Not with Dragan out there. This may be the reason he's after you. Please calm down. You need to stay here with your family."

White-hot rage flashed through me like a thunderclap, and my body trembled. "You're going to lock me up? Like you did my wolf?"

Laurel began to cast a spell, and terror clutched my mind.

Was she going to bind me right now?

I tried to channel my magic into the door, but it became a vortex, swirling inside me. Dark shadows moved across the wooden floor, coalescing at my feet. My body jerked, and a cry of pain tore itself from my throat as the shadows poured into me and then exploded out in the form of a black wolf. I threw my arms wide, and the shadow creature lunged forward, tackling Laurel and surrounding her with darkness.

My aunt screamed and crashed to the ground, desperately fighting at the shadows.

Abject horror filled my mind as I stood paralyzed.

An explosion knocked me to the floor as a burst of flames blew the door off its hinges. Casey stormed in, fireballs in both hands. He looked between Laurel and me. "What the fuck is going on?"

"Casey, don't let her leave!" my aunt shouted as she struggled with the shadows.

She did this to you, a voice said in my mind. Not my voice or my wolf's, but one that I vaguely recognized. An avalanche of rage drowned out any reason I might have mustered. "No!"

I would burn this fucking house to the ground.

Suddenly, Casey was shaking me. "Savannah, stop!"

I twisted free as his shouts reeled me back to reality.

Laurel was crawling to her feet, and streaks of blood—claw marks—marred her skin. What had I done? Horror hit me like a sledgehammer, and I stumbled back with a gasp. The shadows engulfing Laurel evaporated as Casey ran forward and cradled her. He glared at me. "What have you done?"

Shock and terror cut across his face as his eyes fixated on my hands. On my claws.

On what I had done with my magic, to my aunt.

Stabbing agony settled in my chest, and I tried to speak, but no words came out. Instead, I turned and fled.

18

Savannah

I leapt into my car and drove.

My phone rang a dozen times, but I just drove and drove, looking for a place in Magic Side that wasn't full of LaSalles or Laurents. Without sorcerers or werewolves. But I didn't know where that place was.

Normally, when I was distraught, the thrum of the Fury's engine soothed me, but not tonight.

I could feel my father's magic—magic that he'd once woven with his sister and my mother to bind my wolf.

Magic wrapped in lies.

The car began to feel like a constrictor, and it became hard to breathe. I'd almost torn my loving, treacherous, protective, deceitful aunt to pieces. I'd seen Casey's face. There was no going back.

Eventually, I found my way to the Midway Dens and pulled over. I scrolled my phone.

I couldn't call Jaxson or Sam. They were werewolves, and they'd probably go nuclear when they found out what my aunt had done. And Casey had quickly become my best friend. I kept scrolling and scrolling. Most everyone in it was either a LaSalle or a Laurent—that, or a human with no idea that magic was real.

Like I had been once.

My finger hovered over my godmother's number. Had she known? What would she even say if she hadn't? Now *I* was the crazy one?

Finally, at the very end of the list, I found Zara's name—the only friend I had who wasn't wrapped up in this mess.

I dialed, and her voice came across the line. "Hey, Fury, what's up? Ready for roller derby this weekend?"

"Hey, Zar. Um—" My voice choked up. "Look, something really bad has happened, and I don't know who else to talk to. I don't know where I can go, and I need a drink, preferably without any LaSalles or Laurents around."

"Hey, hold on there, waterworks. Are you okay?"

I nodded, though she couldn't see me, of course. "Yeah. Just need to talk. And drink."

"Meet me at the Rift on Razorback?"

I sniffed. "Yeah, I'm close. Thanks."

"See you in five. I'm already on my way."

It only took me a few minutes to get to the Rift, but finding parking was hell. In the end, I had to walk four blocks through the cool night air.

Casey kept calling, but I muted him. I just couldn't face what had happened. Not yet, not sober.

If I could take what had happened back, I would. But I couldn't.

The Rift was in a building constructed from dark glass cubes. It had an animated neon sign of a sexy she-devil dancing above the door that reminded me a lot of the jammer of our derby team, Rayne.

The hulking blue-skinned demon outside the door just waved me through. Sometimes, it was good to be a girl.

The pulse of the music worked into my bones as I pushed through the grinding bodies. My hands were shaking, and though I felt disconcertingly numb, deep down, I knew I was a bomb ready to detonate.

I wedged myself into a spot at the bar to wait for Zara and motioned to the bartender, who strolled on over. He was handsome and ripped and had two gray horns protruding from his forehead like Zara's, though hers weren't always visible. "Two tequila shots, please."

He nodded and poured the tequila as I looked around. The bar was covered with car racing paraphernalia and filled with every kind of Magica I could imagine. A mouthwatering scent of barbeque filled the air, and between the flow of people and alcohol, it seemed like a good place to get lost, which was just what I needed for a while.

Most importantly, I didn't see anyone I knew.

Screw werewolves. Screw sorcerers. And screw Dragan and my aunt and my parents and all the shit they were wrapped up in.

The bartender slid the shots across the bar, and I noticed the wicked tattoo under his sleeve—a bird of prey. The colorful feathers on its wings were striking against his blue skin, and they shimmered like they were reflecting the sun.

I handed him my credit card. "Nice ink!"

He glanced down at his arm and grinned. "Alana at Devilish Inks is the best in town. Looks like you could use some more." He gestured toward the tattoo on my arm. "She works just down the street."

I'd always wanted another tattoo.

"Maybe. Thanks for the tip." I downed the first shot, wincing at the burn.

At the far end of the room, a curvy woman with a tail was

hanging upside down from a stripper's pole. She was really flexible.

Hell, I kinda liked this place.

As soon as I saw Zara pushing through the crowd toward me, I downed the second shot and ordered another round for us both, as well as a double whiskey on the rocks.

The bartender slid it and the four shots across the granite top as Zara shoved the guy next to me aside to make room for herself. She eyed the two empties and the four full tequilas. "Rough day?"

"You could say that. Help me celebrate."

Zara downed a shot and nudged one over to me. "What happened?"

I tossed it back. "Well, this afternoon, I nearly beat an asshole to death in a biker bar, and then I ended the evening by finding out that I've been a werewolf my whole life, except that my parents *bound my wolf* to hide what I was, and my aunt was in on it. I nearly killed her on accident and then fled, but not before revealing what I was to Casey—an absolute fucking monster."

"Shit. That's a pretty fucked-up day," she said, and shot another tequila.

"Pretty much. How was yours?"

"Same." She motioned for another round. "I visited my dad in prison today. Parents are shit."

"Damn, I'm sorry." The fourth shot went down easier than the first three had. "What'd he do?"

"Oh, you know, summoned a demon army and tried to take down the world. And he was the well-adjusted parent." She grabbed my wrist and towed me into the crowd. "Come on, fuck today. Let's dance."

Well, at least I wasn't the only one with a totally fucked life.

Clutching my whiskey, I followed her to what I presumed

was the dancefloor. The crush of bodies and thrum of the bass dulled my senses, and before I knew it, I'd lost myself in the music.

I'm sure it has nothing to do with the tequila, my wolf quipped.

Touché. Though ever since my wolf had been released, it had been much harder to get drunk.

This was what I needed: a moment to forget all the shit that had unfolded. And I had to, because tomorrow, there'd be bigger problems to face. Like figuring out what Dragan was up to.

My aunt and parents were assholes for what they did, but Dragan was the fucking root of it all. I could feel it in my bones. Once I killed him—or whatever that equated to when you were already dead—I could try to put the pieces of my life back together. *If* Casey or my aunt would ever speak to me again. If I could bring myself speak to her.

Just dance.

After another round of shots, I was blissfully unaware of my troubles.

I let my body move me and soon found myself grinding up against a guy who I was pretty sure was a demon—but not the ugly, bloodsucking kind. He had hot horns, silver and black hair, and an open shirt that displayed his muscles. All in all, he was pretty attractive, though not my type. I apparently only liked dangerous, possessive alpha holes.

Plus, the demon was getting a little handsy.

I shoved him off and wound through the crowd. My thoughts began returning to Laurel's words—*we bound your wolf*—which only meant one thing: I needed more tequila.

I ordered another shot and checked my phone. In addition to the barrage from Casey, I had three missed calls from Jaxson, two from Sam, and a slew of messages. I opened the first of Jaxson's:

Your cousin called, blaming me for turning you into a wolf. Where are you?

The image of Casey's shocked face bombarded my mind, and I fought back a sob. He'd never forgive me for what I was or for what I'd done to his mother.

I'd just lost my best friend.

I downed the tequila and disappeared back into the crowd, unable to face any more reality than that.

Head spinning, I stumbled a little. Hands gripped my waist and pulled me in. The demon I'd been dancing with slipped his hands around my ass and began grinding against me. Tears pooled in the corners of my eyes, but I went with it until he nuzzled his face in my neck, and his hot tongue traced my skin. "What do you say we get out of here?"

Rage tore through me, and I stomped my boot down hard on his foot. "Not interested. Now get your hands off me!"

If I'd wanted a booty call, I knew just the wolf to hit up. But for one moment, I didn't want to be a wolf or a sorcerer or a nice piece of ass. I just wanted to exist in a space where none of what had happened was real—to dance and forget everything.

Unfortunately, the creeper didn't appreciate my reaction, and he shoved me back. "Bitch!"

Before I could react, a blonde woman stepped up and slammed him to the ground.

"Sam?" I yelped as I lost my balance and landed on my ass.

She gripped the demon's neck and leaned close to his shocked face. "If you ever touch her again, you'll be a dead man."

What the hell was Sam doing here?

The room spun, and I had to blink to focus on her. She was frowning, but she looked hot, and—*oh, my God, I'm going to puke.*

My head buzzed.

Did I say that out loud?

Sam and Zara scooped me up and pushed through the crowd. The next thing I knew, I was doubled over and retching on the sidewalk. Once I'd emptied my stomach, Sam handed me a travel-sized bottle of mouthwash.

"Thanks." I swished my mouth out and spat it on the street. The minty flavor stung my cheeks.

Sam opened the passenger door of Tony's Jeep. "Get in."

Drunk though I was, I knew better than to argue.

"How'd you find me?" I asked after a few silent blocks.

"Zara called. Said you were on a bender and that she couldn't reach your cousin." She glanced over at me, the oncoming lights of a car highlighting the irritation on her face. "You're lucky that *I* was the one she called and not Jaxson. Fuck, Savy, what the hell happened?"

God, this wasn't how I'd wanted this night to end. I tried to dry my eyes with the back of my wrist. "The truth caught up with me, and I made a mess of everything."

Before she could speak, Sam's phone rang, and she picked up. "I've got her. I'll bring her right over."

Even drunk out of my mind, I recognized the voice on the other end of the line. Jaxson.

I put my face in my hands. It seemed my evening parade of humiliation wasn't over.

19

Jaxson

My body rippled with pent-up fury as I downed a finger of bourbon. Savannah Caine was going to send me to an early grave.

The empty glass rang on the countertop as I slammed it down.

After her lunatic cousin had thrown a half-dozen baseless accusations at me, I'd called Savannah to figure out what the hell was going on. But she'd screened all my calls, leaving me with a burgeoning sorcerer–werewolf war on my hands.

I'd nearly lost it.

Clearly, she had. All I could get out of Casey was that they'd discovered she was a werewolf and that she'd attacked Laurel, and they were holding us responsible.

None of the rest of anything he said made one lick of sense. What could have possibly happened?

All Savannah had to do was go to the LaSalles and ask about Dragan. Simple. Instead, she'd outed herself at the worst time possible.

It made me furious. The screened calls. The crazy LaSalles.

The fallout. But the thing that had crippled me with anger was having to sit on my hands.

I could feel her sorrow like a noose around my neck. As soon as we'd figured out where she was, I'd wanted to run to her—I could feel her pain pulling me—yet Sam had stopped me.

Made me wait.

Apparently, according to her, I didn't have the requisite temperament to extract Savannah from her current predicament, whatever the hell that meant.

But I listened to Sam. When it came to Savannah Caine, I knew I was blind and beyond reason.

Savannah's signature hit me as she and Sam stepped out of the elevator. Citrus trees on a hot summer day. Every sense I had was on alert, and I could hear the swish of her pants and feel the erratic stomp of her boots as she came down the hall.

She was definitely tipsy, a miracle for a werewolf. What had happened?

I poured another finger and tossed it back, setting the glass down firmly as the pair entered.

"Should I give you two a moment?" Sam asked when I rounded the corner.

"Stay." My voice was rough as I took in the mess that was Savannah. The scent of her shame and grief mixed with the sweet and spicy aromas of tequila and something else. "She'll fall over if you put her down."

Savannah stepped forward on her own—somewhat unsteadily—her eyes flashing with defiance. "I'm not sure what crawled up your ass, Jax, but I just had one of the worst nights of my life, so lay off."

"Is that so?" My jaw tensed, but I remained calm as I prowled around her. She wasn't just tipsy—she was drunk on bottom-shelf tequila and Jack Daniels.

I gripped the countertop and dug my claws into the underside as another aroma cut the air: demon. Male.

"It smells like you had quite a good time," I said, having to grind out each word.

Someone has touched our mate, my wolf growled.

My claws and fangs erupted as jealousy tore into me like a wild animal, and Savannah flinched as I leaned in and brushed her hair away from her neck, where the scent of demon was strongest. "A *very* good time."

Sam awkwardly disappeared into the kitchen.

Images of the man who'd had his hands—and mouth—all over her made me homicidal, and I had to fight the urge to put my fists through something.

Ours, snarled my wolf.

Fury spiked in her eyes, and she seized the lapel of my jacket. "Screw you! You've got no idea, so back off!"

Even as she pushed me, I gripped her wrist and pulled her close. The warm contours of her body pressed into me, causing heat to coil inside. "I have some idea," I snarled. "But why don't you fill me in on the details?"

Savannah jerked out of my grip and took several steps back, putting distance between us.

The scent of rage and alcohol boiled from her, but somehow, I knew it was a façade, masking a deeper truth.

I took a deep breath and drew on every sense I had. Pain and regret vibrated from every inch of her body, and I could practically taste the salty hint of tears. Her sorrow churned in my gut like it was my own, and I could feel the ache of blood pounding in her temples. I exhaled slowly and took a step forward.

Savannah took another step back, and I paused.

It was like a knife.

We studied each other in the silence of the room. My mate

was broken and in pain, and nothing I felt mattered. Whatever jealousy I had, I slew it then and there.

"I'm sorry." Speaking the words made my jaw tic, but it was right. "Please tell me what's going on."

She glared at me with a burning hatred that seared my skin like a wall of flame. But then it broke, and she looked to the side with a single tear hovering at the corner of her eye. "I fucked everything up. I attacked my aunt, and now my cousin knows I'm a wolf."

I nodded. "So I gathered. Casey called me, blaming the pack. What happened?"

She sighed and rubbed her face, the fight in her completely faded. "After you dropped me off, I talked to Laurel. The conversation twisted, and I found out that I'd been born a werewolf, and that she knew."

My heart stopped for a second, then began to slowly accelerate.

She'd been born a wolf. The implications for our mate bond were staggering. But that wasn't the most surprising aspect. I reached for my glass, but it was empty. "Laurel...*knew*?"

That was practically unfathomable. She'd never have accepted Savannah into their house if she'd known...

But Savannah nodded and bit her lip.

"Then why did Casey accuse me of turning you?" I asked, mentally flipping through scenarios. All of them landed on Laurel.

"He didn't know." A choked sob escaped her throat before she continued. "It was a secret. Laurel and my parents used sorcery or spellcraft or something to bind my wolf when I was born. I guess she hasn't told him."

"*What*? How's that even possible? Your whole life—your wolf was bound with magic?" The horror of it tore into me as images of animals in cages bombarded my mind. Stunted, insane from a lack of freedom. A tremor of disgust and hatred shook me. My muscles coiled beneath my skin, and I flexed my fists, feeling my knuckles crack. I'd be paying Laurel a visit tonight.

"I don't know how they did it. All I know is that my parents fled Magic Side because of what I was: half werewolf, half sorcerer, just like Dragan. I'm a fucking monster, Jaxson."

She put her face in her hands and started to drop to her knees, but I closed the distance between us in a flash. Shaking, she buried her face into my shoulder.

Her agony was a dagger in my heart, and each silent sob twisted the blade deeper.

I breathed out, long and slowly, trying to get a handle on my heartache and fury. "I need you to listen. You're not a monster, Savannah. You're a wolf. There are those who can also work magic, like you. Dragan is different. He's broken and tainted with evil."

She shook her head and looked up at me, eyes red and swollen. "*No*. There's a darkness inside of me—I can feel it."

I grunted. "We all—"

But she broke away and began pacing the room. "Laurel tried to keep me at her house, Jax, and said it wasn't safe for me to leave and that she didn't want me around you and the pack. When she locked the door, I just lost it." Savannah wiped her eyes and looked at me with a distant expression. "I hurt her with my magic really badly, and if it wasn't for Casey..."

I strode over and cupped her face with my hands. "You were in shock. Your powers are new. Being a wolf is new. The same could have happened to anyone in your position."

She tried to shake her head, but I tipped her face up to mine. "Hey. While you're a pain in my ass, Savannah Caine, you're no monster. You're a good person who's had monstrous things done to her. Do you understand me?"

Every fiber of my body screamed for me to kiss her, but I

knew that wasn't what she needed, so I fought down the urge with every ounce of strength I had.

Finally, she nodded, but her solemn eyes betrayed her lack of conviction. She was burned out. Spiritually, emotionally, mentally.

She needed someone to take control. And while tequila had been her first choice, I could do a much better job of it.

I grabbed her by the shoulders and held her at arm's length, pushing my power into her. "You've had your night to grieve a bunch of fucked-up shit. But we have a real monster to fight: Dragan. So tomorrow, you're going to tell us what you learned about him. Tonight, you're going to get a shower, get to bed, and sleep this off. I need you fresh. Got it?"

"Okay," she whispered, relief palpable in her voice.

I spun her and pushed her toward Sam. "Make sure she goes to bed. Give her my room, as usual. I'll be on the couch."

"Right, boss," said Sam.

I grabbed my keys and headed toward the door.

Sam gave me a questioning look. "Where are you going, Jax?"

I paused partway through. "Taking care of some business."

It was just past one a.m. when I parked out front of Laurel's house. The neighborhood was quiet, the houses dark. All except hers.

The front door opened, and the devil herself strode out, arms crossed. "Where is she, Laurent?"

I stopped at the edge of the front lawn, my wolf and my fury reined in on a tight leash. "With her pack. Where she belongs. Meanwhile, you and I need to talk."

Anger flashed across Laurel's face, and she stormed down

the front stairs. The air in front of me cracked, and a patch of sod near my feet was torn loose and hurled fifty feet away.

My lips curled, muscles flexing. "Was that a threat?"

"You'd better believe it. If you think you can turn her against her family, then you'd better prepare yourself for fucking Armageddon."

My gaze lingered on the pulsing artery in her neck. It would only take half a second to close the distance and tear it out. She'd be dead before she even realized it.

I bent my head and growled low. "It seems that you're doing a fine job of turning her against her family on your own."

My wolf surged in my chest. *She stole our mate.*

Laurel shot a blast of green lightning toward my feet, leaving a pattern of jagged seared lines across the grass and sidewalk. "Don't test me, Jaxson. I want my niece back here, ASAP. And I don't want her to have any more contact with you or your kind."

"My kind?" My claws slipped out as rage rippled over me. "Savannah *is* my kind. And she's my mate, so there will be no negotiating. She stays with me."

Laurel sucked in a razor-sharp breath and froze mid-step. "You're lying."

"I'm not." My words were iron.

In the beginning, I'd fought against it. I'd seen how the bond destroyed Billy and my sister. I'd tried to convince myself that Savannah wasn't a true wolf. That the bond was somehow false.

But I knew it to be true, now, without a doubt.

Savannah Caine was mine.

Laurel's face contorted in a tortured expression, and her voice was hushed. "Are you certain?"

"As certain as the sun rises in the east," I growled.

She froze for a moment, then dragged her hands through her silver hair. "Those damned fates!"

I bared my teeth as my temper threatened to boil over, but

my words were slow and hard. "I'm going to ask you a question, Laurel, and I'll know if you're lying, even in the slightest. Did you use sorcery to take my mate's wolf away from her?"

Hatred and murder burned in her eyes, but finally, she forced out a confession. "Yes. Her parents and I did it to protect her."

My fury turned cold and brutal, like the wind in the arctic. "For whatever reason, Savannah still cares for you. But if I ever hear you've cast such a spell on her again, my pack and I will burn the Indies to the ground. There won't be a sorcerer left in Magic Side."

She didn't flinch, instead locking me with an unyielding stare.

I turned to go, but she grabbed my arm. I spun, claws out, but the pleading in her eyes stopped my hand.

"We did it to protect her from your father."

My heart froze as the words sank in. I didn't lower my hand. "What?"

"Jaxson, if she's anything more to you than something to possess, if you care about her in the least bit, you need to listen to me. Savannah is in danger, and so are you. We bound her wolf because of what your father might have done if he found out about her."

I paused, my confusion and anger rising. "Savannah said that it was *your* father who was the danger."

Laurel waved her hand dismissively. "Simon was a bastard who hated wolves and a good many more people, but he's dead, and he's not coming back. But mark my words, Jaxson, Alistair must *never* know who or what Savannah is."

I grunted, unsure of how to react. I could smell the truth of her words, which only meant she believed her own delusions. While my father hated the LaSalles as much as Simon LaSalle had hated us, would he really harm Savannah if he knew she was a wolf? That she was my mate? Impossible.

I turned to go, but her voice caught me.

"I can see you don't believe me, but trust me in this, if nothing else in life. Ask him about Dragan. Ask him about the prophecy," she said. "And whatever you do, *don't* mention anything about Savannah. Ever."

Silently, I walked away.

"I want my niece back, Jaxson," Laurel called after me. "She's safer with us than with you. And if you ignore me, you'll learn the truth far too late."

"Never chain a wolf again," I snarled as I got into my truck.

But as I turned the key, my mind was on her warning. I only knew of one prophecy.

The prophecy of the Dark Wolf God.

20

Savannah

I woke to a blaring alarm. Head throbbing from seven different angles, I rolled over to shut off my alarm—but it wasn't my phone.

"Make it stop," I groaned.

"Rise and shine. It's ten a.m., and you've got to get ready for work," Sam chirped as she came into the room and switched off a bedside clock.

I pulled the sheets around me and sat up. "What?"

The blonde vixen smiled cruelly at me, or at least smiling seemed cruel that early in the morning. "Jaxson assigned you to the lunch rush, waiting tables. So you'd better get up and get going."

I flopped back into bed and rolled over. "No way. I have a headache that extends to my knees, there's a possessed lunatic trying to kill me, and I've fucked up most of my life."

She grunted. "Jax said you'd probably protest, so he took your keys and picked up your car from the Rift. If you want them back, you'd better get over to Eclipse."

I bolted upright, not caring if Sam saw me naked. I was ready for blood. "That bastard!"

"Yup!" She tossed me a waitress outfit, which I caught out of instinct. "Better get going."

Sam, my cruel taskmaster, marched me into the shower, fed me a frozen burrito, and then physically hauled me to Eclipse.

Unfortunately, my hangover came along for the ride. Why wasn't my werewolf healing kicking in?

Well, you did have whiskey on top of a full bottle of tequila, Wolfie remarked.

I groaned as my stomach did somersaults. Somewhat more unfortunately, Sam's proposed cure was a beer with clamato and a raw egg.

She handed the vile concoction over. "This is a redeye. Drink up. Your shift begins in five minutes."

The fizzy, tomatoey, eggy concoction was just as bad as I'd imagined, though frankly, a lot better than anything Uncle Pete had ever brewed.

As soon as I drained the red drink from the highball glass, I groaned again, regretted every tequila shot I'd ever drunk in my life, and raced to study the menu.

The lunch rush was more of a feral stampede.

Once, before my existence had turned into a perverse nightmare, I'd eaten the most fabulous meal of my life at Eclipse. I could still practically taste it: bacon-topped figs, charred brussels sprouts, and endive cups filled with some kind of cheese and herbs.

Suddenly, all those exotic dishes I'd enjoyed were flying at me like a hail of bullets.

"Don't these people have jobs they have to be at?" I screamed at Sam as I grabbed a couple of martinis from the bar. "How do this many people have time for lunch?"

"We have a two-week waitlist!" she shouted back as I dodged another server.

And I thought bartending had been wild.

My beleaguered brain had to race at top speed to master a new menu and handle my section. Thankfully, other servers whirled around me, helping me fix orders and make salads. I had no idea how they kept on top of me as well as their own work.

Everything moved three times faster than it did at the old Lakeside Taphouse up in Wisconsin. I'd been a pro there, but at Eclipse, I suddenly found that I was once again at the bottom of the food chain. And everyone belonged to the pack, so they all knew *exactly* who I was.

I was red in the face from wheezing and embarrassment the whole shift. At least I had my Swiftley speed boots to get me back and forth fast enough to fix orders when I screwed them up.

By the time my shift ended at three, my mind and body were mostly broken. I staggered out the back door and leaned against the wall, breathing hard. Once, Jaxson had slipped me through that same door to hide me from the pack, worried how they'd react to a LaSalle.

Now, they were the only reason I'd survived the shift.

Funny how things change.

After a couple of minutes of staring at the sky, waiting for the world to slow down, the door opened. I didn't even have to look over; I knew him by his scent.

"Jaxson, you're a merciless bastard," I growled.

He chuckled. "I hear you did extremely well."

I scoffed and glared at him. "I was a disaster."

"A beautiful disaster," he purred, which set my nerve endings alight. He was so handsome in his suit. I was, by contrast, sweating through my shirt with my hair all knotted up and tangled. I probably had five pens hidden in there.

It was absolutely infuriating.

"I did your dirty work," I groaned. "Now give me my keys back."

He pulled them out and spun them on his finger. "I think not. I like having you where I can keep my eyes on you."

"What? Are you worried I'm going to go crawling back to my aunt? Not after what happened. Not after what she did to me." I spun on him, tears of frustration verging in my eyes. "I don't have anything, Jaxson, and nowhere to go, so you don't have to worry. I just want the freedom to leave."

He crossed his arms and leaned back next to me. "Have you been worrying about what happened last night?"

I gave an incredulous laugh and glared at him. "I haven't had time to think of anything but side orders and drink orders and making change all day! Not Dragan, not Casey, not my aunt. I swear to God, if a couple of those Arrowhead Disciples had come in this afternoon, I would have gotten them two waters and a menu, and run for a basket of bread."

A slow, self-satisfied smile crept across his face. "Good. Then you're the barback for happy hour, so you'd better wrap up your break."

Shock hit me like a two-by-four to the face. Was that the point? "You conniving bastard! Is this all just to keep me distracted?"

He smiled and held out a wad of cash. "Is it working?"

Refusing to acknowledge him with an answer, I slowly reached out and took the money. "What's this?"

"Tips from the other night."

I licked my lips. "I thought you were keeping my tips to pay for the car..."

"I'm garnishing your wages to pay for repairs. Hopefully, the tips are enough to keep you afloat."

It was more money than I'd made in a month at the Taphouse. If I could pick up more shifts, I could afford my own place. My own car repairs.

"But...but Dragan is out there," I stammered. "I don't have time—"

"The rally is tomorrow night. I have people getting everything ready. You'll be there."

"But—"

He put his hand on my shoulder, and tingles raced over my skin. "Savy, breathe."

I met his eyes and could feel the deep concern churning within him. "Look, my sister was supposed to be alpha," he murmured. "Not me. My father didn't train me for it, didn't do anything but drop it in my lap. The hardest lesson I learned is that you don't have to do it all yourself. It took me years, but that's why I have Regina and Sam and Tony and once, Billy."

I shook my head. "Dragan is after me. I need—"

"To let me and Sam handle getting ready. Meanwhile, you need to learn that you're part of a pack. That means no matter what, you're never on your own. You don't have to do everything yourself."

A part of me wanted to believe it, but I couldn't.

He headed for the door. "Also, that reminds me. Tonight, we have the Lakeshore run. Hundreds of werewolves will be there. You're coming."

Yes! Wolfie shouted in my mind.

"Are you trying to kill me? No way. Tonight, if I'm not hunting Dragan, I'm going to rent myself a hotel room and take a long bath with Epsom salts. I owe it to my paws and back."

Jaxson paused in the doorway and tossed me my keys. "It's

part of being a wolf. Plus, I already told the pack you were coming, so you can't back out now."

We're going, my wolf said as I caught the keys.

I frowned. "I thought you were holding my keys hostage."

"I'm an asshole but not heartless," he said. "I know how much that car means to you."

My anger at the cocky man subsided a fraction, but I still didn't want to join the pack tonight. "Maybe I'll go on the next run."

He grinned. "Sorry. Alpha's orders. Anyway, you once told me you were the state champ for the four-hundred-meter in high school. I'd hate to think such a fierce competitor would shy away from testing her mettle against a pack of wolves."

With that, he slipped out the door.

"Jackass," I grumbled.

You like it when he bosses you around, Wolfie noted.

Shut up, Wolf.

21

Savannah

I was exhausted after my shift, but Jaxson showed me no mercy. He'd made it clear that I was going to run with the pack.

Sam drove us through Dockside, and I watched the lights of Magic Side drift by. There was no moon tonight, but I couldn't see the stars because of all the city lights.

I remembered driving this road on my first night in Magic Side with Jaxson. The place had been so foreign. Now, it was home...or had been home. I didn't know any more.

I was feeling a very light buzz, which helped me forget my sore feet. Sam and I had grabbed a couple beers after the happy hour rush.

You'd think after my bender and spending the afternoon at the biker bar the day before, we would've taken an evening off, but I had a lot to come to terms with.

The situation with my family was still messed up, and I had no idea what to do about it. Sam listened but pushed me to focus on the problems at hand, which miraculously seemed so much more manageable than the prospect of dealing with my aunt: Dragan was back, and he'd rounded up a bunch of psycho cultist bikers to do his bidding.

That, as well as a rumor that we'd really pissed off the Order...which seemed fair.

But none of that was my immediate problem—the pack run was.

Jaxson had insisted I participate. *It's part of being a wolf.*

Wolfie and I had been fine with our solo runs along the lakeshore. And despite her early enthusiasm, neither of us was quite sure how we felt about running with a hundred werewolves.

Sam pulled her truck up into a packed parking lot, and I let out a low whistle. "Man, that's a lot of vehicles."

A hundred werewolves might be an underestimate.

What are you complaining about? my wolf asked. *All you have to do is strip in front of a hundred people. I'm the one who has to avoid getting trampled by a bunch of furry lunatics.*

I took a deep breath as we slid out of Sam's ride.

There were shifters everywhere, all talking, laughing, and drinking in the glow of the headlights. So many people. Most I didn't recognize, but they probably all knew about me by now. The new wolf. The redheaded LaSalle in their midst.

Ex-LaSalle.

"Ready to run?" Sam asked.

"For sure—but I'm thinking of maybe running in the other direction."

"You'll be fine, Fury." She laughed and grabbed a beer from someone as she pulled me headlong into the milling crowd. Sam was aglow and totally in her element. I, on the other hand, was as far as I could be from mine.

People I'd never met jostled me left and right as we waded through the bodies. None of them looked directly at me, but I could feel their eyes on my back.

It was all too much. The lights. The voices. The music blaring from someone's car. The scents of anticipation and excitement and comradery. My breathing quickened as the crowd began closing in around me.

We've gotta get out of here.

A few people that I didn't recognize came up to Sam and gave her a hug. She started laughing and joking with them, and I took that moment to slowly back away.

I wasn't running, just taking a breather.

I slipped past the periphery of the crowd and slunk off into the shadows of the trees. Pressing my back against a trunk, I closed my eyes and focused on breathing in and out and let the cool darkness wrap around me like the waters of the lake.

"You okay?" a woman asked as she approached across the grass. Not Sam. Regina?

I glanced her way, and my face flushed. "I'm fine."

Regina crossed her arms and studied me. "You don't look fine. You look like you're having a panic attack. What are you doing over here alone?"

My heartbeat raced as my embarrassment blossomed into anger and shame. "What's it to you?"

She held up her hands apologetically. "Hey, I'm just checking in."

"Well, I'm fine. This—this meetup is just a lot." I turned back to the darkness. But I wasn't fine, and I was certain she could smell my panic and hear my racing heart.

So many people I didn't know. My pack.

I'd stared into the gaping maw of a living nightmare, yet tonight, the prospect of all these folks was more than I could bear.

Regina slowly circled the tree. Her eyes flashed gold, and her power vibrated the air around us, pressing in on me. "Savannah, you need to stop worrying. You're going to be all right. I know this is more werewolves than you've ever been around before, but you're one of us. It's okay."

I caught the scent of hickory, and the taste of cinnamon burned my tongue.

"Don't use your alpha voodoo on me," I growled, but in spite of my resentment, my panic had drained away. I hadn't known she had powers like Jaxson, but then again, she was his second in command, and probably for good reason.

Her presence didn't let up. "You don't need to be afraid. You're one of us now."

Her voice soothed my nerves, and my heartbeat slowly returned to normal. That irritated the hell out of me. This woman had no right using her power on me or playing with my emotions.

"One of us?" I laughed. "That's rich coming from someone who wanted me tried for murder and strung up under the Old Laws. I was abducted and drained and almost killed, and you wanted me dragged before a pack of wolves to plead for my life."

Anger clouded her expression for a split second, but then her eyes flickered, and the gold was replaced by a shimmer of shame. Regina shifted uncomfortably and looked down. "Look, I'm sorry for that. It was out of line. You were a LaSalle, and I didn't think we could trust you. Billy's involvement could've landed the pack in deep shit, and I was afraid you'd turn on us because of everything that had happened to you." She looked up at last and met my eyes. "I shouldn't have threatened you like that. It was wrong. *I* was wrong."

I'd been so traumatized at the cabin that I could barely think, horrified that Billy had been planning to execute my family, and then she'd dropped that bombshell on me.

"It was fucked up," I snapped, surprised by the sob in my throat.

Silence stretched between us. Finally, she shuffled her feet and said, "I know. But I was scared and fucked up, too. You'd just..." Regina's voice caught for a second, and when she spoke again, her voice was low and soft and sorrowful. "You'd just killed my best friend's husband. And sure, he was a monster and a bastard, but I'd known him as a good man almost my whole life. He was all I had left of her."

She looked away. A hairline fracture in that hard, hard exterior.

My stomach churned. Seeing Regina's unbreakable façade crack a little was like cracking myself. I could smell her sorrow and practically feel the ache in her heart. I'd killed a monster, but that monster had been her family.

Billy had fucked up both our worlds.

I started to take a step toward her, but Regina tensed and snapped her head up, all signs of the fracture gone. "I was looking for someone to blame for everything falling apart—someone other than myself. For that, I'm sorry."

I absently touched the unhealed wound on my shoulder and steeled my nerves. "And I'm sorry that I took someone that mattered to you. I didn't want to kill anyone. I was running for my life, and things got out of control."

She crossed her arms again, closing herself off like the gates of a castle, and raised her chin. "I don't expect you to forgive me for the way I've treated you, and I can't entirely forgive you for what happened."

I started to open my mouth, but she held up a hand. "I know that's unfair, but I have my own demons, and that's the way it'll be for a while. Still, you need to understand this: you're not alone, not with us, not even when you're off standing in the shadows. Regardless of how I feel, I'll always fight to protect you, and so will the others."

I swallowed, unsure of how to respond. "Okay."

"And not because you matter to Jaxson or Sam. You're part of this pack now because *you* earned it. You fought for us the way we'll fight for you. We're family now."

I hung my head, not feeling strong enough to make eye contact without breaking down.

Jaxson and Sam had told me I was part of the pack before, but coming from Regina, someone who couldn't quite let go of her anger and hatred, that was different.

And for the first time, I really understood the stakes. Yesterday, I'd lost so much. Casey. Aunt Laurel. Uncle Pete. The last of my family.

Could the pack really replace the thing I'd come to value more than anything I'd ever owned? Was this why Jaxson insisted I come? I wasn't sure, but at least Regina was offering an olive branch.

"Thanks," was all I could muster.

Regina gave an undecipherable huff. "For what it's worth, none of us would have followed through with the threat. They're called the Old Laws for a reason."

"Well, they're fucked-up laws," I muttered bitterly.

"They are. Because they come from a fucked-up time. Our pack was almost hunted out of existence." Her voice was hard and angry—though not with me.

Hunted out of existence?

A knot slowly formed in my stomach. Had that been my family's doing? My grandfather Simon, and those who came before him? Dread coiled around my heart, and the darkness pressed in.

Biting my lip, I looked up out of the corner of my eye. "Was that here? In Magic Side?"

An inadvertent snarl twitched at the corner of her mouth. "No. It was before we came to the New World. Before Magic Side and all the trouble with your kin."

"Oh." Relief flooded me. The LaSalles had done a lot of messed-up shit, but at least not that.

Regina looked at her nails. "Our ancestors were from southern France. After generations of living side by side with humans, things started changing. Witch hunters and zealous priests whipped the local people into a terrified frenzy, and they turned on us. The Church paid for each wolf pelt they could bring in."

She met my gaze. Suddenly, instead of the reflections of headlights glinting in her eyes, I saw flickering flames. Howling wolves hunted down and skinned alive.

Not just my imagination. Magic. Actual memories of horror. My stomach twisted. "You fled."

"Not at first. We fought back. To survive, we had to become the monsters they'd been taught to fear. We abandoned the restrictions that had kept the peace and adopted new laws of reprisal—what we call the Old Laws now. If an outsider hurt a wolf, we killed them. If they killed a wolf, we made their family bleed three times over."

Regina's words were bitter, as if she'd witnessed each atrocity herself.

I dug my nails into my palm. "I'm gathering that the Old Laws didn't work in the end."

Her body trembled with anger, and she hid her hand behind her back as her claws erupted. I could smell her disgust. "Oh, the laws worked. The villagers who'd been our friends learned to live in fear, and the land became polluted with blood and hatred. In the end, the Church stopped sending priests. My family, the Laurent family, and the other families here all left the pack and sought a new life in the New World, but we've kept the Old Laws ever since. That way, we never forget that our first duty is always to protect the pack."

The hatred in her eyes was fresh and raw and unforgiving. I

studied the lines of her face. Had she witnessed all of that? She couldn't be that old, could she? How long did werewolves live?

"You speak like it was yesterday...you weren't there when it happened, were you?"

She snorted. "What are you implying? Do I look like an old hag?"

My face heated. "God, no. I just realized I don't know how long werewolves live..."

Regina gave me a wry but reassuring smile. "Time comes for us all, just like most people. But we keep a living history. Our loremasters have powerful magic that helps us remember the past. When they tell a story, it's almost like being there. We die, but the pack remembers. You'll experience it tonight."

"What do you mean?"

"At the end of the run, the pack loremaster always tells a story. It's...a magical experience. Remembering is part of who we are. Part of being wolves."

An eerie howl suddenly cut through the air. The hair on my neck stood on end, and my body jerked forward involuntarily, like someone had just yanked on my shirt. *Jaxson.*

Regina moved slightly, too, called by the howl. "The run is going to start. Stay with the pack and follow Sam and Jaxson, and you'll be all right. We're all watching out for you."

"Thanks."

Regina turned to go.

"Hey, Regina?"

She paused and looked back over her shoulder.

I shrugged. "Perhaps it's time for new laws."

She looked me up and down. "I know, but it's hard for us to let go. Sometimes, it still seems like the world is against us. I'm sure you know how that feels."

Boy, did I ever.

22

Regina turned and walked back to the pack.

Huh. I think I like her better now, but maybe not a whole lot better, Wolfie said.

You and me both. I studied the dense crowd of milling were-wolves. So many bodies.

We're going to get trampled to death, my wolf chirped with mad glee.

I straightened my shoulders and headed toward the crowd. *It's like a track meet or a marathon*, I told her. *Only this time, we're all going to be snarling, panting, wolves.*

My wolf's irritation prickled. *Honestly, when you used to run track, you did plenty of snarling and panting and wheezing, so maybe you shouldn't throw stones.*

I laughed aloud, drawing glances from several people as I passed. I had absolutely no idea where Sam was, and there were too many scents to single her out. I could sense Jaxson, though, with every fiber of my being. His magnetism pulled on me and guided me through the crowd.

Someone jostled me. I stumbled, but they grabbed my arm

and set me upright. "Hey, you're the new girl. Are you okay? I didn't mean to knock you."

It was a guy I'd never seen before. White-blond hair, blue jeans, bulging wolfy muscles. Not bad, if I'd been anyone else.

I shrugged. "First time. Just a bit lost, looking for Jaxson and Sam."

The guy grinned. "Have you ever seen one of those stampedes of African wildebeest? It's like that. Don't get trampled."

Great. I was just hoping I could keep up. "Honestly, I don't even know where we're running to."

"Ah, we kind of all memorize the route. Just follow the pack. We run out to the point." He winked. "First one to jump in the lake wins."

"Thanks." I wasn't sure how I felt about diving into the water as a finish line.

I pushed through the crowd of muscles and asses until another voice called out, "There you are! I turned my back, and you disappeared!" Sam grabbed my arm and started pulling me forward. "Where were you?"

"I just went for air. Ended up having a chat with Regina."

She stopped and planted her hands on her hips defensively. "Was she giving you a hard time?"

"No. Actually, she wasn't a bitch—to my surprise. And I guess I got a better perspective on things. Pack history."

"Cool. Reggie has a little loremaster in her, so she doesn't tend to forgive and forget. Glad you guys are working things out. She's good people. Fierce. Loyal."

Sam pulled me out of the crush of bodies and over to the side under a tree.

"What are we doing?" I asked.

She tossed me a cheap pink nylon bag that had my name on it: *Savannah "Fury" Caine.*

Not LaSalle. *Caine.* I'd forgotten that for a time.

Sam yanked her T-shirt over her head and then popped off her bra.

"Whoa, lady!" I gasped.

She laughed. "It's go time. Throw your shit in the bag, and Regina and her people will make sure it gets to the bonfire."

"Isn't she running?"

"Nah, she's supervising the bag team tonight. Glad you guys have made up so she doesn't order them to *accidentally* misplace it," Sam added, laughing.

I really hoped she was joking about that.

I looked around as Sam unclasped her jeans. Half the werewolves were stripping. Wolfborn, like me. The others were shifters and could transform, clothes and all.

If I was going to be a werewolf, why couldn't it have been the other type?

Because being wolfborn is more fun. Who needs clothes, anyway? They're kinda silly and pretentious, Wolfie observed. *Now get naked. I want to run.*

I glanced at the mass of bare asses. Men, women. Nobody seemed to care. This was going to take a *long* time to get used to.

"Come on, slowpoke," naked Sam said. "It's cold, and I want my fur coat."

I sighed and stripped as quickly and discreetly as possible, then stuffed all my shit in the pink bag. Clothes, wallet, cell phone. I assumed it would be safe, or they wouldn't do it this way, right?

Where was Jaxson?

I looked around wildly, then saw him among the trees. A massive wolf, staring back at me with deep golden eyes. A shiver ran over my skin.

It felt like he was looking through me, into me, seeing whatever was truly inside.

Then he put his head back and howled.

It was unlike any howl I'd ever heard. Low and unearthly, it vibrated the world around me. But the howl wasn't for me—it was for my wolf. I gasped as she leapt in my chest, and then the transformation came, swift and fierce, like ripping off your lover's shirt.

One second, I was a woman, then every part of me broke at once. The breath was ripped from my lungs, and I didn't even have time to scream. I collapsed onto my hands, and when I landed, I was a wolf.

Holy. Shit.

All around, the werewolves shifted in a great wave of fur and fangs. Jaxson had called us all, commanded us all. And we had obeyed instantly as one.

My wolf staggered forward, dazed. *I think...I think it's better shifting quickly, but "holy shit" is right.*

Suddenly, I understood.

Jaxson had been treating me with a gentle hand. His presence and touch had always made shifting easier, but he'd only used his power to give me the barest support I needed. He could have called my wolf out in a second, but he'd let me fight through the shift each time, pushing me to master it on my own.

The truth was, he could control me with a single howl—God, with a single look.

In that moment, I knew his power for what it truly was: complete. I was his to command, body and soul, whether I liked it or not.

And I didn't like that one bit.

Yes, you do.

It wasn't just me. The entire pack had shifted. A wolf nearby snarled and yanked a pair of torn jeans off her leg with her teeth. Apparently, she hadn't finished undressing when the call came.

Sam followed my look, and I could almost read her

thoughts: *Yikes. Those were expensive. That's what happens when you spend your time chatting.*

A single howl, and we'd all obeyed instantly. I shivered.

Sam shook her silky fur with joy, then gave me a look. *You okay?*

I nodded, understanding her intent in my mind. It wasn't quite telepathy that we shared—there were no words, really—but something deeper, more primal. Meaning conveyed by a myriad of small motions and scents and expressions I never knew existed, but that I could somehow read.

She flicked her head around, and I followed her gaze.

Jaxson was waiting at the far side of the clearing, staring back with impossibly gold eyes that said one thing: *Come to me.*

Instantly, we were padding across the grass. I felt my wolf's excitement mix with my own.

He could call me anytime.

The wolves watched me pass. I must have stood out with my red and brown fur.

I ignored them all. Jaxson was a whirlpool, drawing me in and consuming my attention.

While the pack had wolves of every shape and size, Jaxson stood head and shoulders above the rest. Some were lithe and lanky, but he was all tightly bound power and muscle—a beast from a prehistoric age. A monster out of legend.

Our mate.

The fates had bound me to a savage that could break my neck with a single bite.

Jaxson took a step forward, and I found myself trembling and down on my belly, looking up at his powerful jaws.

He met my eyes. *You are beautiful, red wolf.*

His praise sent a shiver of pleasure though my body, and the fur on my back trembled.

Our mate approves.

I hadn't realized we'd stopped breathing.

Are you ready to run? Jaxson asked in my mind, speaking with his eyes and his posture and the primal voice that wasn't words, but images and sounds.

The feel of the grass, the thunder of paws, the scent of a hundred wolves all around me.

Do not be afraid. Once you run, you will know what it is to be one of us. You run with your family now.

The voice of Jaxson's wolf was strange. So much more formal than that of the man. He spoke as a king to his queen, not as a man to his lover.

Jaxson cocked his ear as if hearing my thoughts. *We do not know each other yet. I am eager to know you in this form just as well. Are you ready?*

I just hope you can keep up, my wolf replied.

Had I been in human form, I would have clapped my hands over my damn sarcastic mouth.

Jaxson's eyes just sparkled with laughter. *Can you?*

Then, without warning, he turned and ran.

23

Savannah

We sprinted forward, and the whole pack was suddenly in motion, a rolling wave of fur and teeth and claws.

Our feet pounded against the grass as my wolf wove back and forth, struggling to keep us from being trampled.

This wasn't a track meet. It was a stampede. Wolves were everywhere, jostling and colliding into each other.

Sam was at my side, snarling when other wolves got too close. *Follow me!*

Heart racing, I clung to her heels and let her run interference. *This is insane!*

A wolf I didn't recognize whipped around my side and careened in front of us. Wolfie growled and nipped at him.

Sam gave me a wink that said, *Now you're getting the hang of it.*

The hell I was.

Rather than fight the flow, I let my wolf take full control as the hairy maniacs of the Dockside pack bounded and sprang around us. *This is not what I had in mind!*

Sam ran confidently by my side, and the primal sense of her

thoughts flooded my mind. *Don't worry. The hierarchy will sort itself out.*

Clearly, everyone just wanted to be in the lead, by Jaxson. He was already far ahead.

Wolfie gave a growl of frustration. *There's no way we're going to bring up the rear.*

We began to pick up speed, which brought us back into the chaos that boiled in Jaxson's wake. We dodged and wove, trying to gain ground, until my wolf finally gave up and eased off the gas. *We're going to break an ankle dodging these idiots.*

Frustration tore at us both. This was a terrible way to run a race.

This is a 5K. We need to pace ourselves, I said to my wolf, and concentrated on my memories of running cross country. Sprinting at the beginning was a great way to lose. We needed to find a pace we could sustain. We didn't know the course, so it was best to meter others.

This pace feels pretty good, but it's all teeth and tails ahead, my wolf responded.

The pack had started to split into clusters, and she decided to hang with half a dozen wolves that were drafting just behind the lead group.

After a few minutes, the chaos settled down, and we left the wooded park and pack land behind. Wolves all around me howled as we crossed Razorback Avenue.

We joined in the howls as our claws skittered across the road and we leapt back onto the soft grass of the Midway Green, where the Full Moon Fair had been held a few weeks ago. It was just open grass now.

The pack had settled into a steady pace, though we were breathing hard.

Sam glanced over at me with her tongue hanging out and a very human expression that seemed to say, *Are you okay?*

My wolf gave a determined snarl back. *Fine.*

She nipped at me in warning. *Don't overdo it.*

My wolf just gritted her teeth and put her head down. I could feel her determination matching my own.

Running with the pack was like nothing I'd ever experienced. As we settled into a rhythm, we became one with the wolves around us. Our stride, our breathing, was like the low thrum of a hypnotic dance.

Soon, we left the Midway behind and turned to run south through Exposition Park, which was lit by antique-looking streetlamps. We tore around strolling pedestrians and late-evening bikers with reckless abandon. A few people shouted and cursed, and some even threw beverages or ignited warning spells over our heads. But overall, the Magic Siders were remarkably unfazed. Apparently, a pack of rabid-looking wolves running through the city wasn't all that uncommon. Anywhere else, the hapless citizens would be screaming at the top of their lungs, running for their lives. But this was Magic Side. People here had seen *a lot.*

We raced down the shoreline, with the lights of South Side Chicago twinkling back at us across the waters of Lake Michigan. Unfortunately, a deep throb of exhaustion began creeping into our muscles, and we began to lose ground.

My wolf gave a frustrated growl as Jaxson slipped further ahead. Sam stayed with us, though I knew she wasn't equally winded, which sent irritation bubbling beneath my skin.

Wolfie stumbled a little but pushed on. *I could use a little help, here.*

How? I asked.

I'm not exactly sure how it works. But I helped you free your ankle in the forest of shadows and gave you strength to break out of the van.

Could I do the same for her now? I focused my mind and will on running.

We tripped and slammed snout-down in the grass.

Sam skidded to a halt and turned back as wolves zipped by. She gave a soft whine that said, *You need to take it easy.*

No! We scrambled to our feet and tried to catch up. We were hopelessly behind the second cluster by now.

My wolf got back into rhythm and focused on her stride. *That didn't work. Maybe I should just drive.*

A melancholic sense of failure seeped into my heart. *Fine.* Helping her run didn't work. I gave a defeated sigh and just focused on remembering my races in high school—what it had felt like to run, to have strength in my limbs. The runner's high. The soothing rhythm of the road.

I'd been a star once. I would've won a scholarship if I hadn't gotten hurt in my senior year, and I would've gotten the hell out of Belmont and Wisconsin a long time before this.

As memories of those meets whirled in my mind, we began to pick up speed.

Keep doing whatever you're doing, Wolfie said.

Holy shit, we were running *fast.*

A surge of elation coursed through my veins. We could do this. I thought of the thunder of my sneakers on the trail and track, the thrill of passing rivals, the wind in my face.

The sweet taste of victory at hand.

We broke out of the second cluster and began to gain on the lead pack. We started passing more and more stragglers, and then suddenly, Sam and I were on the heels of the leaders. She was breathing hard and gave me a surprised look: *Where the hell did this come from?*

I grinned at her. *Second wind.*

Then I felt it. The drug. Not just a runner's high, but the

intoxicating knowledge that we could win. That our rivals were all tired, and that somehow, we'd found a new store of strength.

My wolf and I had never been so in tune, so connected.

We surged forward around the edge of the pack, leaving Sam behind. Leaving them all behind. I'd come to run with Jaxson, and that was what I was going to do.

We focused on him, the massive wolf at the head of the pack. He was a comet, and the rest of the us were a silver tail strung out behind him.

That asshole. He'd invited us to run, then left us behind.

I focused my frustration on him and felt it entwine with that of my wolf. He'd let us run with the stragglers, eating his dust like we were just another wolf. But we weren't. We were his mate, weren't we? He sure didn't act like it.

It should have been him guiding me through the crowd. It should have been him running at my side, not Sam.

My wolf dug her claws in with every step. Ran like she hated the earth and all it stood for. I focused my mind on all the memories I had of ever taking the lead. Watching runners fall away until there was only one left.

We slammed into a burly wolf and ricocheted off another until we finally broke free of the cluster. And suddenly, there were just two of us. Jaxson and me.

He looked over, and I let the resentment burn in my eyes. *You left me!*

A wry grin spread across his face, and his own yellow eyes glowed with...pride? *I knew you would catch up. My mate is strong. Agile. Fast.*

We almost stumbled as a burst of delight threatened to spoil our hard-earned frustration. His approval was like smoky whiskey that tasted divine and spread warmth through your chest.

I wasn't going to let the beast sucker me with a smile. But his intoxicating scent wrapped around me, and it was all I could do to think. The musk of exertion and the rich notes of forests and moss—it was desire and freedom and limitlessness, all wrapped into one.

I could run forever.

He was so much larger than me—I had to take two strides for every one of his—but somehow, our pace became one as the lights across the lake flashed by.

This is what he'd wanted. To run side by side. Just the two of us. Free.

Jaxson nodded to the far promontory ahead. *Almost there.*

The point. The finish line.

Desire sparked in my mind. I realized I could win, no matter how big he was, no matter how fast. I was *strong.*

I gloried in the knowledge.

Memories of old races and past victories flooded into my mind. The final sprint. The burning in my muscles. The intoxicating call of the finish line. The tape breaking on my chest.

Once, a decade ago, those moments of victory had been everything to me in a bleak and lonely world.

My wolf and I surged with a strength and speed neither of us knew we had. We left Jaxson behind, Sam behind, the entire pack behind and shot forward. A cocktail of elation and triumph poured into our veins as the dark trees flew by and the grass tore beneath our paws.

The shoreline, with its limestone seawall, loomed ahead. Beyond it was only the dark water of Lake Michigan and the distant lights of Chicago. This was it.

We run out to the point. First one to jump in the lake wins.

I would win.

I would show Jaxson I was stronger, faster, and more worthy than any wolf in his pack. Now that we knew where we were going, we couldn't be stopped.

With a final burst of speed, we bounded over the terraced limestone seawall and leapt out high over the water.

We did it! I thought with joy as the waves sparkled below.

And then...I began to shift.

What are you doing? I screamed at my wolf.

I hate the water. Good luck!

Aw, hell.

24

My body contorted in the air as I plummeted toward the water—no longer a graceful dive, but rather an ungainly tumble of thrashing limbs.

Oh, Go—

A painful splash drove the breath from my lungs as I plunged into the cold darkness. I lashed out frantically with my paws as they turned into hands. My joints popped and bones cracked as the pain of the transformation tore through me. At last, I felt my face change, and the hair across my body retracted, exposing my bare skin to the chill of the water swirling around.

I kicked upward and broke the surface with a desperate gasp, and immediately directed my ire at my wolf. *You should have warned me!*

You were fine, she replied. *Shifting is so much easier with Jaxson nearby, even when he doesn't help us.*

Treading water to stay afloat, I slicked back my hair and looked around. Where *was* Jax? He'd been right on my heels.

Jaxson stood atop the tiered limestone seawall, still in wolf form. His head was cocked curiously to the side.

Behind him, the rest of the pack was staring down at me with befuddled expressions. I whipped my head around in all directions. I was alone in the water.

Oh, goddamn it.

Nobody else had jumped in. Of course, they hadn't. Wolves *hated* water. Some jerk had just made an ass out of me.

Jaxson descended the tiers and shifted effortlessly into human form. Why was it so awkward for me when he could do it so gracefully, like pouring whiskey into a glass?

He crouched down, completely unconcerned that he was stark naked in front of me. And his casual unconcern made it unbearably hot.

The faint light glinted over his muscles and left dark shadows that set fire to my imagination. He was a study in contrast, every curve of his body, traced in light and darkness. I wasn't sure I could breathe, and it took all my strength to train my eyes on his.

"What are you doing in there?" Jaxson asked, his voice low and amused.

Well, that broke the spell.

I bared my teeth, barely able to repress my frustration long enough to talk. "Someone told me that everyone jumped in the water at the end. That the first one in was the winner."

"But...werewolves hate water."

"I know that!" I hissed.

Jaxson narrowed his eyes, rose, and turned back to the pack. "Whose idea was this?"

His roar reverberated across the stones, and all the wolves hung their heads with shame. I felt his alpha power wash over me like a thunderclap, and even I suddenly felt guilty for what had happened. Power and anger radiated off him in waves, and the air grew heavy and hard to breathe.

He loomed naked above me like a colossal statue of a Greek

god, draped in robes of soft shadows. The view was frankly amazing, if abjectly intimidating.

Whoever sculpted those buns was a true master of their art.

Jaxson's head whipped back at me, and his eyebrows rose.

Oh, God.

Had I directed that thought at my wolf or Jaxson? Or had he just caught the scent of my desire? Dread filled my veins, and I let myself sink down as low as possible in the water.

He turned back as the pack parted, and a silver-white wolf groveled his way forward over the grass onto the stones. Jaxson ascended a level and glared down at him. "Is this your idea of a joke? To isolate and trick a new pack member?"

The silver wolf whimpered, and the tenor of Jaxson's voice set my stomach churning. I reached out. "Jaxson, it's okay. I like swimming! It was just a joke, and I probably misunderstood. I'm going to get out. Don't wor—"

He held out his hand to quiet me, then addressed the pack. "This is a good lesson to us all. The run is not about winning or being first. It's about running with your alpha, running *together* as a pack. We are one, tonight and every night. We don't turn on each other. We don't take advantage of each other. Savannah is as much a part of this pack as any of you, and it is your duty to guide her on this journey."

A few yips of solidarity erupted from around the pack, and Jaxson glared down at the silver wolf, deciding what to do.

I could feel the tension in the air. The whole pack was braced. Most had surmised by now that Jaxson had chosen me, which meant Blondie had just fucked with the alpha's mate.

There was a sudden blur as a brown wolf raced forward, bounded down the steps, and leapt out over my head. It hit the water with a yelp and a sudden splash.

I wiped the water from my eyes, and seconds later, Sam's grinning face popped up out of the water. "Man, that's cold!"

"What are you doing?" I demanded.

But rather than respond to me, she turned to Jax. "I'm surprised you're willing to settle for third place."

His mouth opened, and surprise flooded his face. One of the wolves on the shoreline looked up at him and down at us, then plunged into the water. Sam cocked her head. "Fourth, then?"

Jaxson frowned. "But it's not a race…"

A few splashes echoed from further down the seawall, and Sam gave me a wink. "Not even top ten?"

My heart leapt with every splash around me. I'd been alone. A fool. And suddenly, Sam was here at my side.

Jax looked down at the woebegone wolf before him and picked it up by the scruff. "Fine. It seems like we're all going for a swim, per your suggestion. Therefore, you get to be the last one out."

Then, with an enormous heave, Jaxson hurled the hapless creature skyward and out into the lake.

He smiled warmly down at me as more wolves plunged into the lake all around us. "It seems you've started a new tradition."

He crouched, and then, with a powerful leap, he cannonballed himself into the air, spinning head over heels. Before I could react, he slammed into the water with a splash that washed me shoreward. Sam was cackling and trying to wipe the water out of her eyes.

Following Jaxson, the whole pack flooded into the dark, cool waters of Lake Michigan. Howls and hoots erupted around me.

Laughing as Sam splashed me, I whipped my head around, searching for Jax. He was nowhere.

Powerful hands grabbed me from below and thrust me into the dark sky. My subsequent unacrobatic bellyflop cut my surprised scream short.

I kicked my way back to the surface and found Jaxson watching with a wicked grin.

"You bastard," I snarled playfully as I leapt at him. He evaded me with ease, and Sam laughed.

She wasn't as fast as Jax or prepared for me to turn on her, and she let out a surprised squeak as I shoved her under the water. When she popped back up, she was laughing even harder than before. All around us, werewolves were playing in the water, wrestling, swimming, and doing flips off the seawall.

It was like a raucous adults-only pool party. Everyone was wet and naked, and having a good time.

It was perhaps the craziest thing I'd ever done—skinny-dipping with werewolves. But somehow, for the first time in almost a month, I felt inexplicably normal.

25

Savannah

Twenty minutes later, everyone was cold, sodden, and in desperate need of towels and a warm bath. Lake Michigan, even in the late summer, was pretty chilly.

I wrapped my arms around myself and looked at Sam, teeth chattering. "I think maybe we should have thought this through —no towels."

"You're the towel. Just get out, shift, and shake off. They've got the bonfire going, so we can dry by that."

Bonfire? Oh, right.

I sniffed the air, which was redolent with the scent of burning wood. Several types. Elm and maple?

Man, my senses were getting better, or at least more finely tuned.

Sam heaved her naked ass out of the water and quickly shifted. I glanced up apprehensively at the wolf. The water was cold, but there was a bit of a breeze, and Sam looked pretty bedraggled.

She gave me a devilish look and shook herself off, spraying me with a shower of icy droplets. I screamed and dropped back down in the water—which, granted, made no sense, but somehow, drops on exposed skin felt a lot worse than the lake itself.

Jaxson swam over. "You okay?"

I dipped down to my chin in the water out of instinct. "Cold. Just trying to decide if I'd rather face the night air and shifting again or die of hypothermia."

He chuckled. "I'll help you shift."

"I hate how easy you make it. Why can't it be natural?"

"It will be. With practice."

I sighed and looked at the shore.

Jax coughed. "I'm sorry about Eric—the silver wolf. That was a nasty trick to play on you on your first run."

"Don't worry about it. This was actually a lot of fun. And I don't think he meant for this to happen."

"It won't happen again. My wolves will respect you."

I shook my head, remembering the way Regina had spoken to me. "I'd rather earn it than you command it, Jax."

"I have no doubt that you will." He heaved himself halfway out of the water and looked back with a wry smile. "Especially now that you've beaten the alpha in a race."

I put my hand over my face. "I'm not going to live this down, am I?"

"Not a chance. Now get out. It's past time to gather at the bonfire." Jaxson leapt up onto the stone, and in a single fluid motion, he shifted into a wolf again.

I was sad not to have a longer view.

I'm perfectly happy, Wolfie chirped.

Fair enough. I admired the massive silver and brown wolf out of the corner of my eyes. His fur practically shone in the starlight. To be fair, he was a damn fine-looking wolf.

Was I really thinking of a wolf as attractive? Shaking my head at how far down the rabbit hole I'd fallen, I clambered out of the lake, and then, with Jaxson's help, I shifted.

A quick shake sprayed water in a fine mist around us. Unfortunately, I was still pretty damp and chilled to the bone.

Jaxson gave me a look. *Let's go.*

Instead, my wolf glanced out at the lake as more werewolves climbed out and shifted. *Give me a minute.*

Jax followed my gaze to the pale blond man treading water at the back of the pack. The douche who had tricked me—Eric, apparently.

Jaxson grunted. *Find me when you're done.*

I waited until Eric was the only one left and padded down to the shore.

He looked up guiltily from the edge of the seawall. "I'm really sorry, Savannah, I was just joking around. I didn't think you would take me seriously or be able to keep up—"

My wolf put our paw on his forehead and gently but firmly pushed him down into the water.

"I won't do it again, it was poor judg—"

There was a brief gurgle as his head plunged beneath the gentle waves. When she let him back up, she—we—gave him *the look.*

Blondie froze.

I'd never really understood the look and its effect on people. It was just something I'd had growing up. But I knew it for what it was now: weird-ass wolf voodoo.

I guess it always had been. At least I knew exactly what to do to put him in his place.

He slunk down in the water to the level of his chin. "I think I'm going to wait here in the water a little longer."

We nodded, removed our paw from his head, and sauntered off.

There were a few large fires burning further along the point, and we padded toward them across the dark grass.

Jaxson was waiting, as was Sam. Werewolves were everywhere. The pack had formed a ring around a pair of roaring bonfires. Most were lounging around in wolf form, though a few were still human.

Beyond the fire, three burly werewolves stood in the shadows of the trees—Jaxson's guards. I got the sense they were watching for interlopers. Apparently, this was a werewolf-only event. Not that anyone—well, other than Casey—would be crazy enough to barge in on a pack of wolves.

A pang of loss cut through me, and suddenly, everything I'd gained seemed a little hollow.

The look of horror on Casey's face had wounded me just as deeply as the Soul Knife had. Would that cut heal with time or remain oozing and dripping?

Your crazy cousin will probably come around, Wolfie said, somewhat reluctantly.

In my heart, I knew she was right. Casey wasn't entirely lost to me. But I knew our relationship would never be the same. Not after what I'd done to his mother. Not with what I was. He might hold his tongue, but I would always know what his beliefs were.

Maybe, with time, my aunt and uncle would even accept me. But there would always be prejudice, a desire to *cure* me and bind my wolf and turn back time so that things were like they once were.

That was one thing I knew I could never let happen.

Damn straight, sister, Wolfie said.

Jaxson led me toward the fire. Sitting werewolves rose and moved out of our way as we approached, clearing a spot for us close to the flames. I felt self-conscious walking beside Jaxson. He loomed over me, and every step betrayed his power. No wonder they all treated him like a king.

My earlier confidence left me, and I felt like an imposter, a hanger-on. At least it would get me a spot by the fire, and I wasn't too proud to take it.

We flopped down and basked in the warm glow of the hypnotic flames, and I breathed deeply as the heat began to work its way in beneath my skin. My front was too warm, and my back was too cold, but my wolf and I gave a collective sigh of relief.

After a moment of basking, the hair on my back rose. I glanced behind me. Jaxson was staring back, devouring me with his golden eyes. I couldn't quite discern his expression, but I got the sense that he hadn't been able to look away since we'd arrived.

My wolf rolled lazily to the side and stretched out for his benefit. *Do you do this every time the pack runs?* I asked, using that strange not-quite-telepathy that we shared.

Jaxson gave me a wry look. *Not the swimming part.*

With a huff of feigned annoyance, I turned my attention to the wolves around us. Those in human form were chatting in low, almost expectant voices. Most were in wolf form—six or seven dozen, in every size and fur color imaginable.

These were my people now, but they weren't family. Not yet.

The murmur of voices stilled as an expectant hush filled the air. The wolves on the far side of the circle rose and parted as an old woman with a walking stick shuffled out of the shadows and into the firelight. She walked to a spot between the flames and bowed her head to Jaxson. "Alpha."

Jaxson bowed his head in turn. *Grandmother.*

She brandished her stick at him. "My grandchildren can call me that. You can't. Makes me feel old and decrepit. It's 'Loremaster.' My stories are old, not me."

Something about the exchange told me that it had all been said before. That this, as much as anything, was part of a well-worn ritual.

The loremaster sniffed and gave a filthy look at two shifters whispering on the far side of the circle. She pointed her walking stick. "The gods, bless their teeth, gave us all two forms. One is for talking, while the other is for listening. Which should you be in?"

The couple looked sheepishly at each other, and in a swirl of magic, they transformed into a pair of wolves. The remaining shifters did so as well until after a few moments, the pack was only wolves and one old woman.

She jabbed her walking stick into the ground. "Now is the time for me to talk and for you all to listen. You're here for a story. But what should I tell?"

A few wolves yipped, though I couldn't understand what it meant.

The loremaster shook her head, waving her hand. "No, no, those won't do. I've told the story of the Wolf Queen too many times already, and the others aren't right for a night like tonight."

She turned to me. The firelight—or perhaps something else—glinted in her eyes. "We have a new wolf among us. We'll let her decide."

The ancient woman leaned on her cane as she made her way over to me.

I lowered my head onto my paws and looked around, unsure of what to do. I didn't know how to speak in wolf, and I didn't know any wolf stories.

"Bah." She scoffed. "Of course you do. You might not have grown up in this pack, but you know the stories, if not by their name. The stories are part of us. They make us who we are."

I blinked in surprise. Apparently, the loremaster could read my thoughts.

The old woman scrunched up her face as she studied mine, then straightened as her expression fell into shadow. "Oh. I see. *That* story."

I looked at Jaxson, my head spinning. *But I didn't ask for anything! Or even think it!*

The loremaster laughed and waved her hand as she walked back over to the fire. "You don't need to say anything to ask for a story, silly pup. Your eyes are saying it, your body is saying it, you're begging for it with every movement you make. I know the story you crave."

She turned to the assembled werewolves and raised her hands. "I have been asked for a story."

Silence. Instant, utter silence. Jaxson commanded attention like a general, a king. But this woman demanded absolute stillness with her words—like an actor standing before the opening curtain, the audience hanging in the moment. No one spoke. No one even breathed.

What story had I chosen? The hair on my back rose, and my chest constricted as a slow dread filled me.

The loremaster's words cut through the air as she haltingly circled the fire. "Our new wolf has asked for a very old story, a story that I have not told for a long time. We *are* the stories that we tell ourselves. Some we do not like to speak aloud, but we must tell them all the same."

She spun and looked directly at me with eyes that burned with bright red flames.

"Tonight, I tell the story of the Dark Wolf God."

26

Savannah

"It is fitting that there is no moon to watch over us, for she would be jealous of us speaking of her old lover," the loremaster said as she spread her hands wide and began to walk around the circle of gathered wolves.

As her words thrummed in the air, the bonfire grew larger, and the wolves around me shrank, until all that was left in the darkness was the loremaster, the fire, and her voice.

"Once," she continued, "Moon and the Dark God were lovers."

The fire rose, and the image of two people appeared in the curling flames: a woman in a long silver dress and a man shrouded in black.

"Their nights and days knew no boundaries, and they lost themselves to each other beneath the sky."

My pulse quickened as the loremaster's story unfolded before my eyes—Moon and the Dark God weren't just lovers, but passionate and wild. They came together with feral heat, their skin soaked with sweat and their bodies tense and quivering with need. They growled and fought and rutted like animals until their lust was spent and they could no longer move.

I could feel their hunger and taste their passion—a heady mix of earth, salt, and raw musk—and I suddenly found myself completely drunk. The vision was so real and visceral in my mind that my own need awoke, summoning the moisture of my body and leaving me hungry with desire.

The loremaster bent low and came close, as if telling us a secret. "But love can be fickle, and being strong and beautiful, Moon and the Dark God had many suitors. In the end, their jealousy tore them apart—but not before Moon gave birth to the wolf people."

She stood upright. "In those days, people had both animal and human forms. But as the world grew older, they forgot a part of themselves. The wolves forgot they were human and began walking on four legs, while the humans forgot they were wolves and chose to walk on two. But all were beloved by her."

For a moment, I saw humans and wolves and shifters peopling the earth, but then the loremaster swiped her hand, and the image dissolved into shadow.

"And yet, despite the Moon Mother's love, the two-legged people did not love the land she had given them. They burned the forests to make fields and cities, and they poisoned the rivers and land with their waste. At first, in his bitterness, the Dark God ignored the children of Moon—but soon, the two-legged people spread, pushing the wolves and other animals off their land. Their greed was insatiable, and when there were no more forests to claim or land to despoil, the people began to fight each other for the scraps that remained."

My heart clenched as I saw it all in the flames of the fire. The destitute human cities, sick with crime and greed and cruelty. Parched lands that had once been lush, despoiled with salt and ash and blowing away in the wind.

Wherever humankind went, death followed in its wake.

The loremaster flung her hands wide, and a dark shadow rose above the flames.

"A black rage seized the Dark God, and he took the form of a wolf to speak to the packs. He told them, *We must make war on the two-legs. They will kill us all if we do nothing. We must make the world pristine, as it once was.* With venomous words, he spread fear and hatred among the wolves until they agreed to slay all of mankind."

Haunting visions consumed me. I saw the Dark God take a hypnotic form that was both a wolf and not a wolf. He slipped from shadow to shadow, whispering vindictive words in the ears of our pack. His rage and warnings wound around my heart until my own pulse was pounding with fear and hatred and I, too, was ready to see all two-legs slain and their cities torn to the ground.

But just as quickly as she had summoned the black vision, the loremaster swept it away, leaving us with an image of Moon weeping on her bed.

"While the Dark God only saw evil in men, Moon loved her offspring. She saw that they were only children who had not yet grown wise—that they had the capacity for great good as well as evil and would create both magic and beauty in the world."

For a moment, I saw a child playing on the ground—her red hair short and oddly cut. She looked up at me and smiled with such joy that my heart strained with sorrow, weeping for the person I had become.

"Moon was a ferocious mother and would fight to protect her offspring, but she knew she could not hope to stand against the Dark God and all the wolves of the earth. Thus, clever Moon went to her friend Night Sky and asked her to weave a cloak of darkness to conceal her movements. She wrapped the cloak around herself and slipped quietly into the Dreamlands, and with her bright glow hidden, the Dark God did not know where she was."

With a flourish, I saw the beautiful moon wrap herself in darkness like an eclipse until only a sliver of her light remained.

"When she returned from the world of dreams, she called the Dark God to join her at a feast. She told him, *You are right*—because that is what all foolish men wish to hear. She told him, *I've seen the truth—the people are cruel and corrupt. Tonight, let us make the world anew together.* Then she loosened her silver dress so he could see the graceful curves he had never forgotten."

In my mind, I saw her rise and let the slit of her dress part. My chest ached at her beauty, and I knew no man could resist her alluring skin or smile. She summoned the Dark God to her with the crook of a finger, even as the loremaster's words began again.

"They danced and drank, and all the while, Moon topped his wine with water that she'd stolen from the river of dreams that carries us all through the land of the night. At last, she took him to her bed. They rutted into the dawn like wild animals, and when they were spent, the Dark God fell into deep dreams, from which he did not wake."

The vision faded, but for some reason, the fire didn't return to its former brightness, and strange shadows flickered in the flames. The loremaster raised her hands, and the light grew. "That is how Moon saved us from the Dark God—and yet, the legends say his slumber grows restless, and if we do not care for creation or nature, he will wake to bring destruction upon us all."

I blinked at the simple moral. It was no more than a child's story to teach young wolves. Yet the loremaster's hands were still raised, and I shivered as a chill wind rose. It began as a breeze, but it soon whipped savagely around us. My fur was buffeted in the wind, which howled like wolves in my mind. I pressed myself to the ground as a dark shape rose above us, blotting out the lights and stars.

The wind was madness, screeching in my mind and choking my throat with violence and hate. It whipped the bonfire into a frenzy, and soon, all the trees were alight. Black and grey smoke billowed from the distant skyline and skyscrapers that lined the shore.

I tried to move, but my bones were frozen stiff with horror.

The eyes of my packmates had turned white as snow. They howled and raged and became abominations—half man, half wolf, their minds torn between.

I knew that it was a vision, but it felt more real than my own flesh and fur.

All around me, people were running as wolves hunted and slew anything that walked on two legs. An image rose in the flickering firelight—Casey's corpse burned and tattered, lying in a pool of blood.

My stomach churned, and I wanted to retch or howl or even just cover my ears with my paws. Laurel's distraught cries from the darkness were so real, they left me quaking by the fire.

The vision shifted, and the crumbled stones of ruins entwined with trees rose around me, roots wrapping around rusting cars and the bones of the dead.

Then the image disappeared, and I came back to reality with a gasp.

The loremaster put down her hands. "The Dark God may slumber, but now you have seen his dreams."

All around me, wolves were down on their paws, whimpering and scared.

Yet Jaxson rose and stood, solemnly staring into the fire. His presence flowed over me, hotter than any flame. I didn't understand his power to speak to us without words, but I felt the message burn into my soul: *We will be vigilant, and we will defy.*

His strength building within me, I rose to stand at his side. All around us, the pack clambered to their feet until a hundred wolves stood waiting in silence for what one day might come.

The return of the Dark Wolf God.

That night, I slept restlessly, and when I dreamed, it was not of Jaxson or Kahanov or the bikers, but of him.

27

Jaxson

Dawn softened the sky above the tall trees that lined the dirt road. I drove along until I saw my father's old blue pickup. It was weathered, worn out, and perfectly suited to this place—just like the man.

I'd known where to find him first thing in the morning: his favorite fishing spot. After he'd stepped down as alpha, my parents had turned their backs on the city and all its problems. They lived in the lake lands in central Wisconsin, as far as they could get from anyone else.

I tightened my grip on the wheel. I had to be very careful what I asked. Laurel said Savannah's parents had fled Magic Side because of him. I wasn't certain why, but for some reason, I believed the old witch.

I shut off the truck, opened the door, and dropped down from the cab. He'd know I was here by my scent, if not the telltale sound of the engine.

Pushing overgrown branches aside, I followed his smell through the woods.

I hadn't seen my parents much since my father, Alastair, had stepped down, even though they were only four hours out of Magic Side. I'd come up a few weeks before to tell them about Billy's death. That hadn't gone well, and I hadn't planned on coming back for a long time, but none of us had that luxury anymore.

I stepped to the shore. My father, sporting rubber waders, stood up to his thighs in the glistening water. His back was to me, and he didn't turn around. "Alpha."

My neck grew warm, and my muscles tightened. "Father."

He flicked his pole, making the fly dance across the surface of the dark water. "Don't scare the fish."

So I stood there, silent as a ghost. Frustration churned inside my gut, but I kept my composure and scent even. I wouldn't take the bait, even if the fish did.

Finally, he looked back. "Your mother misses you."

I crossed my arms. "I know. It must be hard for her to be away from the pack."

After he'd stepped down, they'd moved north to the lakes. He said that it was to give me space to lead, but I knew it was to get away from the wicked city that took my sister.

They were bitter at the world and everything in it.

My father returned to casting. "It's not too hard. We've washed our hands of pack life. She misses her friends, of course, but we gave the pack our daughter, our son, and our lives. We don't have more to give. You'll understand that feeling one day."

The man had never been the same after my sister's death. He'd groomed her from birth for the job and simply taught me how to do her dirty work. When she died, he was done. He'd held on for a few years, but he'd become a ghost of the man he'd once been. In the end, he dumped it all in my hands and faded away.

His fishing line flicked in the air. "I'd tell you to come up more, but you and I know that's not going to happen."

I leaned back against the tree. "Things are busy right now."

"They always are. And you wouldn't be here if you didn't need something. What is it?"

I watched his motions alertly. I knew he was measuring me, even with his back turned, just as I was measuring him.

"We had a run last night," I said.

He laughed at that. It was just a short exhalation of air, but from him, it was a surprise. "I admit, I do miss the lake run. But there are other lone wolves out here. We run with them when the moon is right."

"After the run, the loremaster told the story of the Dark Wolf God."

If I hadn't been watching like a hawk, I would have missed the subtle tensing of the muscles in his neck. His casting didn't lose even a scrap of fluidity, but I could tell that had surprised him. "Not a story I wish to remember."

Even though he was no longer alpha, my father tended to keep his cards close to his vest. Even with me. I focused on every movement, every scent, every twitch. "What can you tell me about Victor Dragan?"

I hadn't needed to be so attuned.

He stopped short, and the fly dropped to the water. I held my breath as he considered his words. "Dragan was a monster. A twin-soul."

"That I know. Half sorcerer, half wolf."

He turned suddenly, his eyes blazing gold. "No. *All* sorcerer, *all* wolf—just trapped in one body. Two souls vying for control, ripping his mind apart. It drove him mad...drove him to do unspeakable things."

The hatred and anger in his voice could have boiled the river dry. I'd rarely seen my father react to anything with such ferocity. He was typically measured. Tactical.

My mouth turned to sand as memories of Savannah arguing

with her wolf flooded into my mind. I'd told her not to worry, that her wolf was just a different aspect of her personality…but what if it wasn't? What it she was like Dragan, a twin-soul, two spirits trapped in the same body?

Would she go mad? She talked about a darkness in her…

I shivered and realized my father was studying me intently, so I cleared my throat. "What did Dragan do?"

"Dark magic. Rituals. Sacrifices. He pursued forbidden knowledge and turned his own abilities to perverse spells. He seduced good wolves with power and the promise of vengeance on a world that despised and feared us."

All things Dragan had done while possessing Kahanov. All things we suspected he was trying to do again with the bikers.

I shifted my stance as curiosity pulled me in. "Why?"

"A lust for power. To take revenge on us. To summon the Dark Wolf God. But that's in the past."

Alastair began fishing again, but instead of deftly teasing the top of the water with his fly, he lashed out as if whipping a man in a pillory.

"The loremaster mentioned the prophecy, but people only ever allude to it," I said. "What is it, exactly?"

He gave me a suspicious look. "That a twin-soul would bring the Dark God back. That they would take the souls of our pack."

My heartbeat accelerated. There would be no hiding it from my father. "I need to know the exact words."

He studied my face a long time in silence. His scent had gone from mild irritation to a low, simmering dread tinged with echoes of old hatred.

He closed his eyes, and after a moment, he spoke. "I will tell you what the old moon-gazer told me: the rabbit is in the house of the wolf, and we have entered an age of darkness. A twin-soul will come to power. They will be the harbinger of destruction. In the night, when the moon has turned her back, they will make a sacrifice before the Dark God, and in seven days, he will walk the earth once more, spreading madness among the living. The twin-soul will steal the wolves from every werewolf who resists them and will leave your people weak before the Dark God."

Darkness swelled in my chest. *This* was what was coming, what Dragan was trying to achieve. "That's why you hunted him down? Because he was prophesied to do a ritual to bring back the Dark Wolf God?"

My father bared his fangs, though not at me. "Dragan murdered and stole and corrupted. If we hadn't done something, he would have brought back the Dark God. He would have stolen our souls somehow. That's why I even stooped to working with those filthy LaSalles."

Fuck. Hadn't Dragan wanted to take Savy's wolf?

Suspicion filled my father's eyes, which focused on me like lasers. "Why are you asking so many questions about a dead man?"

I didn't flinch. "I believe he's returned."

"Impossible. I saw Laurel LaSalle disintegrate him with my own eyes. His body turned to dust." My father's words were confident and filled with anger, but his scent—although masterfully controlled—betrayed his shock.

I focused all my senses on reading him. My father knew something more. "Dragan's soul survived. He was possessing a blood-sorcerer, Ulan Kahanov."

My father's rod dipped until it touched the surface of the slowly flowing water, creating a thin wake like a knife slicing into skin. "The sorcerer that Billy helped?"

I nodded.

His face contorted with rage, and his muscles tensed. Fur erupted along the backs of his hands, and his claws dug into the cork grip of the rod. When he spoke, his voice cut the air like a scream, but it was no louder than a whisper. "The fucking fool."

My father and mother hadn't taken Billy's death well, and I knew they blamed me. He'd been their son-in-law and their last link to my sister, just as he had been to me.

I hadn't told them everything he'd done. I owed them that. "I don't think Billy knew who Kahanov truly was, only that he promised revenge on the LaSalles."

My father's fingers twitched, and pain and bitterness filled his words. "We *all* want that, but Billy was a fool just the same."

"We hunted down the sorcerer and killed him. But we think Dragan is still out there, that he's possessed another."

My father locked me with an iron glare. "Then you and the pack must do anything you can to stop him. Make deals with warlocks or devils or vampires, but you *must* destroy him. If the Dark God returns, he'll revert the earth to its natural state. Cities will crumble before him. Technology will fail, and humankind will be hunted until there's nothing left but animals to walk among the ruins."

His words stirred the memories of the loremaster's story. I saw the darkness rising and the ruins of Magic Side hidden in the mist. There were no machines or noises or people—just overgrown stone and pavement, and birds flitting warily from tree to tree.

"Can you tell me anything more about how to defeat him?" I asked.

"If I knew that, I'd have done it myself." He turned back to his fishing. I knew it was a dismissal, and I could tell his heart was no longer in it. "But Jaxson..."

"Yes?"

"Don't stop until you've destroyed Dragan's soul."

I nodded, though he couldn't see it. I turned to go but paused and warily placed my hand on the trunk of a pine. I kept my voice even, using every ounce of power and control I possessed. "And if I ever discover another twin-soul, what should I do?"

"Kill them. No matter who it is, no matter the cost, do it without hesitation. It's what I would do. It's what your sister would have done. If the Dark God returns, we're all as good as dead."

I left before he could smell the dread rising in my chest.

Was this what Laurel feared? Why she'd bound Savannah's wolf?

My guts knotted as I climbed the hill. I had no idea whether Savannah was a twin-soul, but that didn't matter. If anyone even suspected...

I had to protect her.

That meant no one could ever know the truth. Not Sam, not Regina...

Not even Savy herself.

28

Jaxson

When I got back to my penthouse, Savannah was gone.

That wasn't entirely surprising. The woman was possessed by the gods of chaos themselves and went wherever she wanted.

I should have never given her back her keys.

Calling and texting her proved useless. The damn woman never answered her phone—which I'd bought for her *specifically* so that I could contact her.

Fantastic. Dragan was going to try to release the Dark Wolf God *that night,* and she was nowhere to be found.

At least I'd had the foresight to install an emergency tracking app on the phone.

I turned it on and braced myself for the results, desperately hoping she hadn't gone off to Michigan on her own to hunt down the bastard.

Luckily, she wasn't far, only a few blocks over in the Midway Dens—demon territory.

While the Midway boss and I maintained a fragile truce, he wouldn't like to have me in his domain uninvited. Again.

Screw it.

I drove past the Rift, the demon bar that Sam had rescued Savy from two nights before, and headed along Razorback Avenue until I got to 53rd. I turned right and pulled up in front of a shop with a dark wood façade and its name etched on the glass windows: *Devilish Inks*.

Savannah was inside. I could feel her pull on me, a whirling vortex drawing me in. It was getting stronger every day, which was both a blessing and a curse.

I gripped the steering wheel of the truck and took a deep breath. My father's words had shaken me to the bone, almost as much as what Laurel had done to Savannah had shaken her—a crime I would never forgive, no matter her justification.

We did it to protect her from your father.

I slid out of the cab and slammed the door. What a gods-damned mess.

Two steps took me to the front door of the tattoo parlor, and I pushed inside.

The place was clean and tidy with white plaster and brick walls, faded black furniture, and pale wooden floors. The sound of buzzing tattoo needles filled the air. Framed artwork, oil paintings, and photos of completed tattoos hung on the walls. The work was impressive.

That was a good sign, at least.

As I stepped in, Sam looked up from the long wooden bench she was sitting on—an old church pew, by the look of it. "Shit. So much for the surprise."

"This is surprise enough," I grumbled.

Savannah was in the back in a parlor chair, under the needle. A she-devil with horns, short black hair, and a pierced lip bent over Savy's right arm. I could sense my mate's discomfort as if it were my own.

"Why don't you ever answer your phone?" I snarled.

She looked up, and her eyes dilated.

"What are you doing here?" Savy grunted through her clenched teeth.

I pushed through a low decorative gate and strode over to her chair. "I'm tracking down a rogue wolf. Want to tell me what you're doing here?"

"Getting a tattoo, obviously. You were gone this morning, so where were you?"

Speaking to a man you can never meet.

"Gathering information." Irritation writhed beneath my skin. I wasn't going to let her put me on the defensive. "What on earth possessed you—"

"Sam said that we had time before—" She cut off her words with a glance at the tattooist. "Well, before we head to Michigan this afternoon, and since I didn't know what you were up to, I decided to take advantage of your absence."

"Seems rash, considering—"

She bared her teeth. "This isn't something out of the blue. I've wanted new ink for a while—I've just been broke."

I swallowed uncomfortably as a modicum of guilt tugged at me.

Sam put down her magazine and grinned at me from the waiting area. "I think you're going to fucking love it when it's done, Jax."

I ground my teeth. Her body, her choice, yes...but part of me still wished I'd had a say in the matter. It wasn't like tattoos were *permanent.*

I stepped forward. "Fine, let's see it."

The she-devil paused her work and met Savy's eyes. Savannah nodded, and the tattooist leaned back. Although the woman was only two-thirds of the way through the outlines, I could see the whole design from the residual imprint of the thermal stencil.

The face of a wolf. And not any wolf—Savannah's wolf.

My breath caught.

Fuck.

Savy raised her eyebrows expectantly. All her initial fire had been a ruse, and I could smell her sense of expectation, even trepidation. The work was excellent, deeply lifelike. I'd seen enough of her artwork to know it was her design.

And it would mark her as a werewolf forever.

I nodded slowly, taking in the implications. "It's...beautiful. Perfect."

When Savannah Caine burned bridges, she used napalm.

The she-devil returned to her work, and the buzz of the tattoo machine filled the air.

"I love it, but why now?" I asked softly.

Savy bit her lip, then hardened her eyes. "I didn't want there to be any mistake any more about who I am."

My pulse accelerated.

The way she'd fought at first, I'd been afraid it would take her months or years to truly accept what she was. But now that the truth had come out, she was all in—just like that.

Part of me was elated. If Savannah could accept her wolf, she could accept the pack, and maybe she could finally face our bond.

But the rest of me boiled with fury.

All it took was her losing everything.

I fought down my anger at the fucking LaSalles and looked around the shop.

There was a big horned demon working on a vampire in the corner. I chose my words carefully. "Why this shop, rather than...down in Dockside?"

Implication: why the hell are you getting a tattoo of a wolf done by a devil rather than one of your own kind?

The she-devil paused her work and narrowed her eyes at me. "This area is for customers only."

I didn't budge.

Savy flinched and gave the tattooist an apologetic look. "I met a demon bartender at the Rift with unbelievable ink—colored tattoos on blue skin. I asked him who did the work. I figured that if you can work on blue skin, you can do anything. So I wound up here with Alana, who's an *unbelievably* awesome artist, by the way. That's her stuff on the wall over there."

Alana, the she-devil, dipped her needle in an ink pot and returned to inking. "I'm just tracing the lines. You drew the design. I bet you could do this kind of work, if you wanted. You have a lot of talent. I can see it in your other tattoo as well. I can tell it's your design."

Savy winced at the pain but forced out a smile. "Thanks. But I just cope with this bat-shit crazy world by sketching."

The original drawing was lying on the table, next to the transfer paper. It was more than just pencil and lines—it had vitality. I could feel her in every stroke. "It looks exactly like your wolf. It's perfect."

She met my eyes. "I've drawn her from every possible angle a hundred times, trying to come to terms with...all of this."

I nodded slowly. "I understand."

But did I? What would it be like to not know your wolf your whole life?

Savannah cocked her head to the side as if listening to someone. "Also, my wolf wants you to know that she hates having to pose for me in front of mirrors, which I think is BS, because I reward her with bacon."

My skin turned cold.

Often, I referred separately to my wolf, but it was just a feral, more noble part of my personality—one that was in conflict sometimes with my more human drives.

But the way Savannah spoke about hers, it was like a completely different being living inside of her.

Was she a twin-soul like Dragan? Fully sorcerer and fully wolf, doomed to tear each other apart?

Or maybe she was simply wounded. Her wolf had been torn from her as a child. I couldn't even imagine the trauma left by that vile spell. Savy never had a chance to understand that part of her personality growing up, so maybe the two parts of her soul were still suturing together like the edges of the wound on her shoulder.

I had to hope that was the truth. But it begged another question: would she ever be whole?

Yes, said the part of me that was a wolf. *Give her time.*

My knuckles cracked as anger threatened to consume my calm. Laurel LaSalle had stolen Savannah's identity and chained her very soul. She'd ripped Savannah's mind in two. I couldn't think of a crime more perverse to commit against a werewolf. Against a member of *my* pack.

Her words cracked through my mind: *We did it to protect her from your father.*

My gut twisted, and my claws slipped out. Savy tilted her head to the side. "What's wrong?"

This wasn't the time or place to discuss these things, if there ever would be one, and so I set my jaw and reined in my wolf. "When will you be finished? We need to talk things over before we head to Michigan. The situation there is more dire than I anticipated."

Savy looked at me with curiosity, then turned to the tattooist. "How much longer?"

The she-devil didn't pause. "Two hours, give or take. We're mainly doing outlines and some shading today. Finishing touches and color will take another session or two."

I fished a wad of cash out of my pocket and counted off a grand or so. "Your best work. Please."

Savannah's eyes widened at the stack of bills. "I can cover it, Jax. This is for me, not you."

"Fine. Then that's the tip." I turned and strode away but paused at the door. "Meet me at Eclipse at two. We've got a biker rally to break up."

29

Savannah

Sam and I pulled into the parking lot of Eclipse just after two.

My arm was still throbbing, and I was eager to get to a mirror. The tat had looked amazing at the shop, but I wanted to see it in the light of day.

Alana had wrapped it to keep it clean, but I could tell it had already almost fully healed. Being a werewolf was freaky but definitely had its perks.

Jaxson was out back with Tony and half a dozen other wolves. He broke off their conversation and approached as I parked my Gran Fury and got out. "How's your shoulder?"

"Fine, but under wraps for the moment." I hoped that he couldn't tell how much his approval meant to me.

Jaxson nodded and led us to the back of the lot. "Good. We're almost ready."

"You dodged my question in the tattoo parlor. Where were you this morning? Not that I need to know, but..."

My words trailed off as his body grew tense and shadows crossed his face. He'd had the same reaction in the tattoo shop.

Whatever errand he'd been on hadn't been a pleasant experience.

I was ready to drop the subject, but Jaxson stopped and turned, the lines of his face grim and set. "I was visiting my father and checking into the legend of the Dark Wolf God and Dragan's connection to it. Things are worse than I feared. Our pack has an old prophecy: Dragan will attempt a ritual of sacrifice on a moonless night, and if he succeeds, the Dark God will return in seven days and bring destruction to the world of the living."

A cold wind blew across my skin, though the air was still.

"It's new moon now," Sam whispered.

Jaxson nodded. "We need to stop him. *Tonight*. My source said to do anything and everything in our power to destroy him."

I swallowed hard. "Is everything ready? You had me waiting tables and running marathons instead of helping."

He leaned close. "Yes. To clear your head after what happened. To show you who you are and what you're a part of now. We're going to need to rely on each other tonight. Guns and ammo are easy to get a hold of. Trust isn't."

I glanced at the wolves loading equipment into the trucks. Jaxson's best people. Some I recognized, others I didn't. All were ripped and lean and looked like professional killers.

My pack.

Jaxson cleared his throat and stepped close to Sam and me. "There's more," he whispered. "The prophecy said that Dragan would steal our wolves."

Shit.

"When I spoke to Kahanov—I mean Dragan—in the Dreamlands, he asked for my wolf," I hissed.

And you almost gave me to him, Wolfie snapped.

Guilt tore at me.

Jaxson tensed, but his voice was calm. "Don't speak of this to anyone. Only the three of us know, and we need to keep it that way."

Sam and I nodded, and Jaxson turned toward the trucks. "We'd better go."

I followed after. "Well, I'm not sure it'll help, but for what it's worth, I did some investigating into Pere Cheney Cemetery while waiting for my appointment."

Jaxson glanced back at me over his shoulder. "Learn anything useful?"

"Maybe?" I shrugged, unsure what could possibly count as useful, given that our plan was to disrupt a biker rally—but with magic places, you never knew.

"Pere Cheney was a ghost town that was wiped out in the eighteen-nineties by diphtheria or plague, or perhaps"—I allowed myself a little dramatic pause—"a witch's curse. Legends say that her restless spirit still haunts the graveyard."

He grunted. "Humans are barbaric. Most people hanged as witches were just young girls who spoke their minds or got pregnant."

Slightly deflated, I said, "Yeah. The stories also say that, but it's kind of less exciting and more depressing. Either way, the town's gone, and the graveyard's just an overgrown clearing in the middle of nowhere."

Reaching the trucks, I lifted up the tarp to see stacks of guns and ammunition. It was a lot, though I guessed most of the team would be in wolf form. That was how we'd attacked Billy's cabin.

At that moment, three black SUVs with tinted windows pulled into the lot. The werewolves pulled the tarp back over the weapons, and Tony slowly slipped a shotgun out of the back seat.

Jaxson stopped and waited as the lead SUV rolled to a halt.

Agent Harlow dropped out of the driver's side with frustration boiling off her in waves. "Looks like you're planning a party. Why wasn't I invited?"

Jaxson's face betrayed no emotion. "Because you're not."

She nodded to the all-too-suspicious tarp on the back of Jaxson's truck. "I thought I told you three not go vigilante again. That we'd help you take down Grayling, or whatever he's calling himself now."

"Dragan," I said.

Her sandy-haired partner, Max, and four other Order agents climbed out of the vehicles. I could practically taste the tension in the air.

With his hands stuffed in his pockets, Jaxson stepped up to the woman and glared down from his towering height. "The bikers are werewolves, making this werewolf business, or did you forget that? Moreover, you're on pack land. Not Magic Side land, *our* land. So, I suggest you step back and settle down."

She stood her ground, though I could smell her fear and mistrust.

Waves of tension rippled through the assembled wolves and agents. Hands were at hips, and claws were ready to spring out.

I think I've seen this movie, my wolf said. *Spoiler: everyone dies.*

Time to jump on the grenade, then.

"Harlow!" I shouted, and ran over, waving like I wasn't walking into the middle of a showdown. "I'm so glad you decided to join *us*."

I gave her *the look* and tried to will my thoughts into her brain. *You want to play? You do it our way.*

I could almost feel her resisting me, but I had a better understanding of my wolf mojo now, so I pushed—smiling broadly, with all the confidence I could muster.

"You called her?" Jaxson's voice was low and smooth, but I could feel the fury beneath the surface.

I nodded, hoping the rest of the wolves wouldn't be able to

smell the lie if I didn't speak it aloud. "The pack and Magic Side are in danger. You told me that we needed to do everything in our power to bring Dragan down. Well, luckily, Harlow has agreed to provide Order support for *our* operation. We'll coordinate. That way, we won't get in each other's way."

Harlow studied my expression. This was clearly not how she'd planned this encounter to go. I pled with my eyes. *I'm offering an olive branch, here. Take it. He's not going to give you a better offer.*

At last, she backed down just slightly, and her shoulders relaxed. "Yes, the Order is *willing* to coordinate *our* operation with the pack. But the stipulation is no casualties. Our goal is to bring Grayling in without a bloodbath like there was at the upper Michigan cabin."

Jaxson tightened his fists. I knew the Order was pissed over the gunfight at Billy's place, but this wasn't the time to poke the bear.

I gave Harlow an *Are you kidding me?* glare, then turned to Jaxson, eyes pleading. We couldn't communicate as we did in wolf form, but I hoped he could read my expression. *We need all the help we can get. I'm offering everyone a chance to save face.*

His jaw ticked, and his eyes dilated in a way that said, *We're going to discuss this chain of events.*

But finally, he crossed his arms and turned back to the waiting agent. "We'll be calling the shots. This isn't just a manhunt. We think Dragan is attempting to summon a god from werewolf legends who's a direct threat to the pack."

Harlow pulled off her sunglasses. "Wait a minute. What do you mean?"

"The bikers are going to do a ritual to summon one of the gods of werewolf lore. We think there'll be sacrifices," he said, his voice low but strained with anger.

She tucked the shades in the top of her shirt and gave Jaxson a hard look. "All the more reason not to go in claws out and guns blazing."

Jaxson grunted. "You have a better idea? We can't risk failure, no matter the cost."

She unhooked a small cannister clipped to her hip and held it out for us to see. "We have access to riot guns and sleeping potions. If they won't come quietly, we gas them and knock down the stragglers."

Jaxson jammed his hands in his pockets and gave a low laugh. "It won't be so simple. Unless your potions are super-concentrated, werewolves will shake off the effects in seconds. And as soon as they scent you, they'll either attack or flee."

Harlow flipped the canister around. It had a yellow label with silhouettes of what I assumed were some kind of goblin, orc, ogre, giant, and a dragon. The ogre was marked with a red X. Above it, the label read *High Potency* and had tons of warnings.

Damn, this was industrial stuff.

She smiled and clipped it to her belt. "We have sleeping gas canisters capable of knocking out ogres. Shifters should be no problem. Moreover, it's my understanding that this entity you call Dragan is possessing Lucius Grayling, potentially against his will. We don't know whether Grayling is culpable for this mess, so we need to make sure to take him alive."

If things were as bad as Jaxson said, then we could really use their help. I held my breath and looked from one to the other. *Please put down your egos and work this shit out!*

Jaxson glanced at me, and as if reading my mind, he ground his teeth and turned back to Harlow. "Here's the deal: I'm calling the shots. We'll go with sleeping gas like you suggest, but if that doesn't work, we're taking those pricks down by any means necessary. The safety of our pack is at stake here, and I will *not* risk letting the ritual succeed."

After a moment, Harlow nodded. "I want to know more about what's at stake and what we can expect, but we agree."

In Michigan, the rogue wolves had gassed us with wolfsbane. We were turning the tables.

Unfortunately, I couldn't banish the images of that battle from my mind. I shuddered, recalling how horrifically it had played out.

We had to learn from our mistakes.

I licked my lips and placed my hand on Jaxson's arm. "When we attacked the rogue wolves at the cabin, their leader tried to escape down the back roads. The MC will have bikes and might try to pull a similar trick. We can't let them get away."

Harlow nodded. "Good point. We'll need to set up road-blocks at all access points."

Jaxson shook his head. "It's not enough. They're wolves— they'll just ditch their bikes and run through the trees. They'll overrun and outrun you, particularly if they have any Scarlet left. We'll need to surround them."

Annoyance still vibrated beneath his words, but his scent had changed. He was no longer resisting the idea, just solving the problem.

I let a faint sigh of relief escape my lungs.

"Can your pack secure a perimeter and subdue them without killing anyone?" Harlow asked.

He shrugged. "Sure, but if the bikers resort to lethal force, then I'm not going to have my pack members fight with their claws tied behind their backs."

After a long pause, she nodded. "Stop the ritual. Rescue the prisoners. Arrest the person calling himself Dragan."

Jaxson gave me a subtle nod and held out his hand to Harlow. "Welcome aboard."

30

Savannah

Eight hours later, we were at the head of a convoy of Order agents and werewolves racing north through central Michigan.

I rested my head against the window and watched the high beams of Jaxson's truck sweep the road ahead of us. Dark trees rose on all sides, and a heavy layer of clouds blotted out the night sky.

It was as if those high beams were the only light in the outside world.

Another road north. Another showdown. I sighed.

Jaxson looked over from the driver's seat. "That's the first noise out of you for hours. What's up?"

Had it been that long?

I took a deep breath. Apparently, I'd lost myself to road hypnosis, yet somehow, the silence between us hadn't felt weird or strained. We'd both been comfortable in that quiet space, deliberating about the task that lay ahead.

I turned toward him and stretched my legs. "This reminds me too much of the road north to Billy's cabin. I just hope..."

"That it's not another nightmare?" Jaxson asked, finishing my thought.

"Yeah."

"It won't be," he said with certainty, and turned his head back to the road. "They don't know we're coming. Billy did. They aren't sitting on an arsenal of wolfsbane. Billy was. And this time, we've got sleeping gas."

Considering our last run-in with rogue wolves, I wasn't sure how I felt about going in with sleeping potions instead of bullets, but Harlow insisted on *no casualties.*

With werewolves involved, good luck.

I bit my lip and turned back to watching the winding lane lines. "I don't want to make the same mistakes."

Jaxson tightened his hands on the wheel. "We won't. First, I won't leave your side. We'll do this together. No solo vendettas, no matter how much you want to take this guy out."

I let out a mock huff. "What, you don't want me to steal your truck and chase Dragan through all the backroads of central Michigan?"

"Not my baby," he purred as he patted the dash. "I'm keeping the keys on me."

I let my head drop back against the seat. "Yeah. This hulking monstrosity is too slow. We should have brought my Fury."

He shrugged. "Maybe. But we didn't have time to stop for gas every thirty miles."

An involuntary smile forced itself along the corners of my mouth. "Did you just make a joke?"

"Nope. Just stating the facts."

I laughed and relaxed a little, but it wasn't easy to calm my mind. Still smiling, I returned to watching the road. "Frankly, I'm surprised that you agreed to work with the Order."

He grunted, not taking his eyes off the road. "Not like you gave me any choice. But it was the right call. You did well."

I shrugged. "Well, hopefully, that won't wreck your bad boy reputation. We wouldn't want anyone to think the Dockside alpha has gone soft."

Jaxson's smile faded, and for a second, his eyes flashed gold. "Dragan is a monster. What he's doing will destroy our pack. My father's exact words were, 'Don't stop until you've destroyed Dragan's soul.' He worked with your aunt to take the bastard down once. I'll do whatever it takes. The Order is nothing."

There was a hardness in his words that made the hair on my neck and arms stand on end. For a second, I saw beneath Jaxson's civilized façade and glimpsed the savage beneath—a beast who'd forged his reputation in blood and would rip the world to pieces to protect his pack. To protect me.

I shivered and opened my mouth to speak, but the shape of a person flashed in our headlights.

I sat bolt upright. "Holy shit, Jax!"

"What?"

Pivoting in my seat, I craned my neck to check the road behind us. "We almost ran that guy over!"

"What guy?"

"Beside the road! A hitchhiker." I flopped back in my seat, heart pounding.

Jaxson shook his head. "Maybe a deer, but I would have seen something."

I rubbed my eyes with my palms and tried to recall the man I'd seen. He'd been pale. All of him—almost translucent. And he hadn't been flagging us down. He'd pulled a finger across his neck while staring straight at me.

Not a hitchhiker. A ghost.

I turned my head to watch the shadows of the road go by. "I must have been drifting off. Sorry."

Another ghost. But why? Was it a warning or a threat?

Google Maps jarred me from my thoughts: "Turn right onto West 4 Mile Road."

We pulled off the Interstate and onto a dark, two-lane road. I took another deep breath, letting my chest swell to bursting and then fall.

Dragan was out there. He had a new body but all his old tricks. When he'd possessed Kahanov, he'd had the powers of a blood sorcerer as well as his own magic...whatever that was.

What powers would he have now? Could he cast spells? Lucius Grayling, according to Jaxson, was just a werewolf.

Just a werewolf? Someone is all high and mighty now, my wolf chided.

You know that's not what I meant. But you know we're different.

I wasn't just a sorcerer. Wasn't just a werewolf. And although Sam and Jax assured me there were other people with mixed heritage, it was troubling that of all the people in Magic Side I'd met, Dragan was the one most like me.

We're the same, he'd said.

We weren't. I knew that. But he was a dark mirror. And now I had to bring him down once again.

Maybe it's not really him, Wolfie said. *Maybe it's someone using his reputation to control the werewolves.*

I smiled. *Wouldn't that be nice?*

In that case, perhaps everything that had happened with Kahanov wouldn't have been for nothing.

We saved two dozen werewolves from the Dreamlands. Amal. Cara. So many others, she said.

True.

But the bastard was still out there, and until he was dead for good, we would never be safe.

Our pack would never be safe.

～

A few minutes later, our convoy turned south to approach the cemetery from its northern access point. Some of the agents and wolves had turned off earlier to secure the southern exit near Staley Lake Road and the south half of Center Plains Trail.

We slowed to a creep and rolled over a set of train tracks, then pulled to a stop just off Cemetery Crossing Trail.

A pair of Order SUVs drove a little ahead with lights off to set up a roadblock just in case the bikers decided to hop on their bikes and blow past us.

"Here we go," Jaxson said as he slipped out of the cab.

I jumped out and pulled my bulletproof vest from the back. We weren't sure if they'd be packing heat, but the vests also worked well against claws.

I'd found that out the hard way.

Behind us, the rest of the pack trucks pulled up, and werewolves hopped out.

Those that were wolfborn started stripping to transform. Others, like Tony, were shifters and could transform clothes and all. I'd never stop being jealous of that trick.

Sam, already a wolf, brushed against me as she walked by, and I let my fingers drag through her fur in a friendly way. She'd be backing up the agents, ready to do what was necessary if they weren't. Tony, third in the chain of command, was organizing the wolves that would be in the deep woods to the east and west. They'd be ready to take down the bikers by any means.

All around him, Jaxson put people in place he trusted with the fate of his pack. Sam. Tony. Regina. Even Billy, once.

Did he trust me to do my job, to understand what was at stake beyond my own fucked-up battle to the death with Dragan? Did he wonder if I was here for myself or for the pack?

Turning to meet him, I placed a hand on his chest, rose up on my toes, and let my lips lightly brush across his cheek. Waves of energy raced along my skin, but I gently lowered back on my heels. "I'm with you."

His eyes dilated.

I glanced at the guns and the wolves around us, then walked over to Harlow to check the agents' status. Perhaps I could have said something more to Jaxson, but I hoped it was enough.

A few minutes later, Jaxson pounded on the hood of his truck. "Okay, everyone, gather up."

Agents and wolves formed a tight circle around him.

Jaxson leaned casually on his truck, but his presence pressed heavily over all of us. "Lucius Grayling is possessed by a monster known as Victor Dragan. He and his biker gang are performing a ritual. If they succeed, it means the end of our pack and catastrophe for Magic Side. Stopping the ritual is our number-one priority. Catching Dragan and bringing him in is number two. If we fail at both of those things, we're fucked. There is *no* room for failure, does everyone understand?"

Our team voiced their assent as one. A good sign.

Jaxson looked to Harlow. "You brought maps?"

Everyone gathered around, and Harlow spread some maps out on the hood of Jaxson's truck. "The southern roadblock is here," she said, tracing her finger over the paper. "We'll come from the north. We assume that they'll be holding the ritual in the cemetery, so we'll spread out in the woods north of there. If Grayling doesn't surrender, we'll nuke him with gas."

She looked at the werewolves that had already shifted. "Stay clear of it, or you'll be out cold in seconds."

Jaxson nodded to Tony and his team. "If the bikers try to escape, bring them down. But keep in mind that taking out Dragan is our priority. If we cut off the head, the rest will follow."

Jaxson finished reviewing assignments, and the six Order agents grabbed their riot guns and sleeping potions.

With a low growl, Jaxson gave us all a bloodthirsty grin. "Let's go fuck this ritual up."

31

Jaxson and I stayed in human form while we scouted ahead so that we could communicate with Harlow and the agents—one of the many things that annoyed him about the operation.

We left the roadblock behind and started down the dusty two-track road on foot. The wolves padded silently along the side, while the agents crept behind us. For all their effort to stay quiet, to my ears, it sounded like the agents were stomping.

No wonder Jaxson had wanted to run an all-wolf operation.

It wasn't the agents' fault, of course—I'd never realized how heavy-footed I was until I'd turned into a werewolf. You had to be able to hear how noisy you were to correct it.

Hopefully, those psychos are all focused on their ritual, Wolfie said.

I crossed my fingers.

As we walked, Jaxson scanned the trees along the sides of the trail, as did the wolves. We had no intention of getting ambushed ourselves.

While the old road was dark, it wasn't unnavigable. The diffuse glow of towns in the distance reflected off the low clouds, giving them a dull pinky-gray glow. That was, all except to the south, where the clouds were pitch black and pooling in a circular eddy right above the spot where the graveyard should be.

Not a good sign.

A quarter of a mile down the road, something pricked at the edge of my senses, and I froze.

Harlow raised her hand to stop the agents behind us. "What is it?"

I concentrated for a second. "Chanting. In the distance."

Jaxson nodded. He could hear it, too. It was nearly inaudible, almost drowned out by the sound of our breathing, but my wolf senses were highly tuned. I could feel it almost more than I could hear it, a deep, rhythmic pulse of wrongness.

We moved along the road until the sound grew clear—gruff voices chanting words not meant to be shaped by human tongues.

Harlow tapped her ear. She could hear it now, too.

We proceeded cautiously along the washboard road, clinging to the side beneath the shadowy trunks of the trees.

Moments later, Jaxson stopped us and sniffed the air. "One of the bastards is close. Has to be a sentry."

Thankfully, we were approaching from downwind, or he'd have smelled us, too.

I turned from him to Harlow. "Let me investigate. I'm quiet, and I can move under the cover of darkness."

Without hesitation, Harlow passed me one of the sleeping potions they'd brought. Then she raised her arm and held her shirt sleeve taut. "Rip my sleeve with your claws. If there's a sentry and you can get a jump on him, poor a little potion on the cloth and hold it over his mouth."

I wavered for a second, then extended the claw on my index

finger. I pierced her sleeve and tore it a ways down. She finished tearing it off and passed it over.

"I'll come with," Jaxson whispered.

I shoved the cloth in my pocket. "You can't see in my darkness."

"I'll hang back, then, in case things break down. But I'm going to come. Two pairs of eyes and ears are better than one, and we are *not* separating."

I remembered Billy's cabin and nodded.

Jaxson and I clung to the edge of the road, treading softly on the grass and avoiding the fallen leaves and loose gravel as best we could. Maybe without him at my side, I would have felt trepidation, but his presence surrounded me like armor.

I was ready to do this.

We're ready to do this, my wolf reminded me. *But I wish we could shift. Paws are so much better for stealth.*

I could tell she wasn't bitter but just wanted to be a part of things. I sent her warm thoughts of praise. *Yeah, boots aren't ideal, and your senses are better. But we need to use my magic. Who knows, maybe we'll get to run one of these bastards down.*

Hopefully. I'm in a mood to give someone a good chomp.

The road ahead began to glow with a faint light as we approached. Jaxson stopped me and pointed.

Straining my sensitive eyes, I stared as hard as I could, trying to pierce the darkness. Finally, I saw it—a faint silhouette of a werewolf standing beneath the trees a few hundred yards ahead. I nodded.

Jaxson's eyes locked on me. *Ready?*

I pulled out the potion, and using every ounce of control I had, I uncorked it silently. With a quick shake, I doused a little on Harlow's shirt sleeve, then handed Jax the stopper and potion.

He corked the bottle, then briefly grabbed my shoulder, giving me a look that said, *I can be there in two seconds flat.*

I pulled the shadows around me and moved along the edge of the trees, inching closer to the sentry. With every footfall, the chanting grew louder, but I still moved as quietly as I could—there was no accounting for werewolf hearing.

Partway there, I reached down to grab a stone, but I wobbled and had to brace myself on the ground with my outstretched fingers.

Shit. The sleeping potion. I could smell it faintly on the cloth —a marshmallow scent—and it had to be affecting me. I held the cloth as far from my body as I could and pushed through the dizziness.

As soon as I found a good throwing stone, I proceeded on.

Within a matter of footsteps, I was so close, I didn't dare breathe. The biker was silhouetted by light streaming through the trees ahead, but I didn't take my eyes off him to check the source. Our element of surprise counted completely on this, and I couldn't let my guard down.

The biker froze, looked up, and sniffed. *Shit.* The scent of the potion was too potent.

Without hesitation, I tossed the rock behind him. He spun, and I sprang.

With my werewolf speed and my Swiftleys, I was on him in half a breath. I clamped the cloth firmly over his mouth and nose and wrapped my left arm around him.

Help me hold him! I called to my wolf.

Vitality flowed through my veins as her power merged with mine, and we clenched down with a strength I'd never had in human form.

He fought, but I was stronger by far. He bit into my hand, but I held back the scream that tried to escape and pressed harder, trying to muffle his sound.

Finally, he weakened and began to slump.

Normally, I would never have been able to support the weight of a two-hundred-fifty-pound man, but with my wolf's strength, I pushed power into my legs and was able to lower him gently to the grass.

As his head rolled to the side, I finally let myself have a full breath.

The chanting pounded against my eardrums. It was eerie and insidious and sent a shiver down my spine.

While I quietly positioned the sentry on the side of the road, my fingers brushed the grass, and I paused in surprise. Something was wrong with it.

In the pale light streaming through the trees, the grass seemed peculiar. Since I was concealed in a cloud of shadow, I slipped my phone out and flicked the screen on to illuminate it. The grass was a faint green and infested with some kind of strange moss or lichen.

Something about it made me feel deeply uneasy. A thought came to my mind unbidden: *Corpse grass. Welcome to the land of the dead.*

It wasn't the voice of Jaxson or my wolf, but rather a young woman's voice. With all the apparitions that had haunted me, I didn't have time to contemplate the source.

Putting the grass out of my mind, I left the damp cloth over the biker's nose. *Hopefully, that keeps him down for the count*, I told my wolf.

I rose and peered through the trees, but I couldn't make out the source of the dull light ahead. I'd need to push on, so I stepped out of my cloud of darkness and waved Jaxson forward. The wound on my hand where the sentry had bitten me burned, but I could feel that it was healing.

After a moment, Jaxson crept out of the shadows and joined me. "Nice work."

A tingle of pride ran down my spine. I hated it, but I yearned for his praise and delighted in his approval.

Turning quickly to hide my blush, I pushed the cloud of shadows ahead of us and led Jaxson along the edge of the road. Finally, we neared a clearing, and I lowered the veil partway so we could both see the source of the light.

A dozen chanting bikers ringed a blazing bonfire in the center of an open field. Tumbled and broken gravestones cast long shadows over the infested corpse grass like dark arrows pointing back to the fire.

And at the center of it all was Dragan. He had a new body and a new face, but I could sense his familiar, twisted presence all the same.

A deep melancholy pressed in on me. I'd known it would be him, but some part of me had hoped that I'd truly killed him in the Dreamlands, that the man here was an impostor.

I craned my head and stepped slightly to the side, immediately gripping Jax's hand. "There are two people bound at his feet. This is a blood ritual."

He bared his teeth and squeezed my palm. "Then we've got no time to lose."

32

Jaxson

Savannah and I headed back to where Harlow and the rest of the agents were waiting and brought them with us as quickly as we could.

With the sentry out and the werewolves chanting loudly, we could afford to abandon a little stealth.

Why did we have to bring noisy humans? my wolf snarled, though he was well aware of the situation.

By the time we neared the perimeter of the light, the chanting had ascended to a fever pitch. The words cascaded off the werewolves' tongues in obscene ways that made my ears ache and thoughts twist. Whatever they were speaking, it was a foul language. I didn't know its meaning, but I understood its intent: to bring a being of pure evil into our world.

Savannah shivered, and I didn't blame her.

Those words were the only thing standing between us and calamity. When the chant ended, Dragan would kill his sacrifices, and a doorway would open—one we might never be able to close again.

Harlow turned to her agents and whispered, "Okay, this is it.

We'll fan out into the woods as planned. The trees should conceal our positions and provide some cover from firearms. Masks on, everybody."

I turned to the cluster of werewolves on our flank. "Fan out on the other side of the road. Be prepared to pursue and incapacitate stragglers."

They faded noiselessly into the darkness. I secured my gasmask, which made it impossible to breath or see correctly, then helped Savannah put hers on. "This had better fucking work."

"I hate this thing," she whispered as she shimmied it in place on her face.

I followed her, Harlow, and the masked Order agents cautiously into the woods. As planned, Sam and two wolves stuck with us to provide pursuit and fangs if we needed it. Unfortunately, with the potion bombs, they wouldn't be able to directly enter the fight.

I flexed my claws, regretting working with the Order for so many reasons. Gods, every step the agents took was like a tree falling in the forest. Could they be less discreet? At least Savannah had learned to walk quietly, like a reasonable creature.

Savy and I took up the first position with Harlow and another agent I didn't know. Sam continued on with Max and the others, while Harlow crouched down and waited, her megaphone on her knee.

I didn't like this plan one bit. It would have been better to have killed all the bikers and let the hells sort them out. But gods alive, if my father could work with that fiend Laurel LaSalle, then I could work with the Order.

My wolf's voice rose in my mind: *If it all goes to hell, we do it the werewolf way—with tooth and claw.*

I took a deep, satisfied breath. *Here's hoping.*

Sensing Savannah's anticipation, I turned to my mate. "Ready?"

She nodded solemnly and whispered, "I'm going to fuck Dragan up."

I grinned. She was so beautiful. The faint light of the fire traced the perfect lines of her cheekbones and glinted off her red hair.

So much fight. A strong mate, still needing to be tamed.

Two brief pulses of static came over Harlow's radio. Sam and Max were in place. A triplet of blips followed a moment later, indicating that the third team was set.

Looking through the brush, I could just make out Dragan in Grayling's body among his circle of cultists. I'd had dealings with Grayling many times over the years, but tonight, he looked deranged. His hands were raised, and he was swaying in front of the bonfire, which had taken on an eerie purple-black light. The glow had crept out of the flames and begun forming symbols and radial patterns on the ground.

Not good.

Savy shifted her bulletproof vest, and I caught a brief flash of pain cross her face. Was her wound bothering her again?

She half rose and looked into the darkness behind us, then turned to me with wide eyes and hissed, "Jaxson, it's time! The spell is almost done!"

I hadn't heard the chant change, and teams four and five hadn't checked in. "How do you know?"

Cold and pale, she looked like she'd seen a ghost.

Savy grabbed Harlow's arm. "We need to do this now. One hundred percent now. Go, go, go."

Hell, she didn't even bother whispering.

For one second, Harlow froze, and then she pulsed her radio six times, took a deep breath, and raised the megaphone to her lips. "Victor Dragan, Lucius Grayling, this is the Order. You are surrounded. Everyone raise your hands, kneel on the ground, and cease your sorcery, or you will be incapacitated. This is your one and only warning."

Grayling paused and turned toward the sound of her voice. His eyes flickered with the purple light of the fire. With a malicious grin, he opened his palms wide. "My brethren, the Dark God has delivered new sacrifices into our midst, just as promised. Make sure their cries of agony are loud enough that he can hear!"

The bikers turned slowly toward us, almost like zombies, and a chill passed through my bones. For the first time, I could see their eyes. They weren't yellow like wolves' eyes, or red like those of drug-crazed madmen, but pure white, with no irises.

"Something's not right. Fuck your protocols, and take these bastards down before shit gets wild," I snarled.

The bikers' mouths opened in silent howls, and their hands erupted into claws.

Harlow raised her radio. "These guys want to play. Disperse the potions."

The agent beside us hurled a cannister in a high arc. It dropped at the edge of the circle and began spewing out a jet of pinkish gas. Four more potions flew from the darkness, and plumes of gas billowed up where they landed.

Harlow raised her radio. "Do not engage unless necessary. We incapacitate the bikers and apprehend Dragan-Grayling."

With streams of smoke filling the air, two bikers stumbled to their knees. But it wasn't enough. The rest shot forward, roaring like rabid dogs.

"Knock 'em down," she shouted into the radio.

Riot suppression guns cracked next to us. Beanbags flew from the darkness and slammed into the chests of the advancing werewolves, each puffing on impact with little bursts of magic.

Three wolves flew back and landed hard, and the agent beside us tossed a sleeping gas potion beside them.

But the werewolves moved like the wind. Six made it through the barrage and crashed into the brush around us, roaring and shifting into wolves.

One leapt above us, shifting in midair. I lunged up, tore him from the sky, and rammed him into a tree. Behind me, another burst from the bushes and trampled an agent, before charging Harlow, fangs bared.

I hurled the wolf in my claws back into the woods and spun, but Savannah was already there. Her claws extended, she caught the wolf by its neck, and then, with a thunderclap of dark magic, sent it spiraling head over heels.

I shivered as the freezing shockwave rolled over me. That was new.

She caught my eye. "We need to get to Dragan."

I nodded. Sam and the others could protect the agents. We had to bring him down.

We raced out of the brush into the graveyard, the haze of sleeping gas now thick in the air.

"Dragan!" I roared through my mask. "This is the end!"

With a snarl, a shadow stumbled out of the plumes of smoke and into a patch of clear air. A deep sense of fury and horror filled me.

His claws and head were that of a wolf, but his body was that of a man. His form twisted and shifted as he lurched forward.

He had become an aberration. A true monster.

Riot guns cracked from the trees, and a beanbag slammed into his side. Dragan stumbled but held his ground, and with a howl, his head turned back to that of a man.

"We will tear you to pieces!" Dragan roared as he charged— and even as he did so, he lurched and craned his neck as his head became lupine once more. With each step he took, his body continued to twist and change.

He couldn't seem to hold his form. What the fuck was wrong with him?

I braced for impact, but Savannah snapped her hands up, and Dragan was suddenly swallowed in a ball of darkness. "Shift position, Jax!"

I darted right as she darted left.

Dragan stumbled out of the black cloud of Savy's magic, his back to me. *Just like bullfighting.*

I pounced and drove him to the ground with an elbow blow to his back.

He snapped at me with his wolf jaws. Pain shot through my arm as his fangs tore through my flesh and into my bone, but then his jaws released as his head became human again.

"Fuck you, Laurent!" he snarled as my blood poured from his mouth. Dragan thrust his claws toward me, but before they hit, a blast of green flame raced over my skin. It was an inferno of pain and heat, but I held on to him even as the shockwave pushed me back. Agony lanced through my chest as he ripped his claws along my ribs. But I fought through the pain and squeezed his neck like a vise. He kicked and gurgled as his eyes bulged. He tore at my hand, but I didn't stop.

All I had to do was let my claws out, and they would rip through his jugular. Instead, I froze.

This wasn't only Dragan. This was Lucius Grayling, alpha of the Central Michigan pack. He was a bastard, but a bastard I knew well. Plus, if I killed him, chances were that Dragan would just possess another.

With a roar of rage, I heaved him skyward into the ring of smoking potions.

Grayling's body landed with a bone-rending crunch. The impact cleared the fog for just a second, revealing his form lying atop an ancient gravestone, and then it swirled in, obscuring him from view.

The crunch hadn't sounded good, but he was a werewolf—as long as the landing hadn't snapped his spine or neck, he'd live.

Savannah was at my side in a second. "Shit, Jax. You're burned and bleeding everywhere!"

"We need to make sure Grayling is down." I moved toward the cloud of gas.

As soon as we entered the pink-gray smoke, our vision dropped to feet, then inches. The haze was building instead of dissipating, and we had to step cautiously over unconscious bodies on the ground. Some were bikers, while others were bound prisoners. All were just shadows in the dark grass, almost impossible to discern until you were standing on top of them.

Savannah grabbed my arm. "What was that?"

I took a fighting stance and scanned our surroundings, but I couldn't make out anything—not through the smoke and the thick, charred lenses of the clunky gasmask. "Keep your eyes peeled."

We started moving forward again into the depths of the cloud. Nothing. No movement, no motion.

My foot hit something hard. I grabbed Savannah's wrist and bent down to examine it.

The gravestone.

I stood. "Grayling's gone."

Savannah scanned the pink-gray cloud. "Well, fu—"

Her voice cut out as her wrist slipped from my grip, and she vanished into the smoke.

I didn't hesitate or let the horror of the moment take my mind. I didn't need to see—I could *feel* her being pulled away. I barreled forward in the direction my heart was tugging.

I was on them in seconds. She struggled as Grayling—Dragan—pulled her through the clouds of potion. She elbowed him in the face, causing his grip to loosen, and she spun out of his grasp.

With a roar of rage, I lashed out and hurled him to the ground. Pinning him in place, I rammed my fist into his face over and over. He was holding his breath to keep from succumbing to the potion, but he'd have to breathe sooner or later.

He clawed at my gas mask, but Savannah ripped away his hands. Together, we restrained his arms.

Dragan thrashed and cursed. His hands and face shifted back and forth from human to wolf to human again, but we maintained our iron grip. Eventually, he roared and took a breath.

I slammed my fist down on his chest, and he gasped again.

His head flopped back into the grass as he finally submitted. His eyes grew glassy, and he looked at something we couldn't see.

Then he spoke, his speech slurred with drowsiness. "You think you've defeated me, Alistair? This is just the begin..."

His head rolled to the right as his body relaxed into slumber.

My heart was racing, and Savy's beat matched my own. Tentatively, she released her grip.

"Jax, I think—"

A swirl of spectral light surged up from Grayling's unconscious body. It emitted an unearthly howl that echoed through my mind.

For a second, the apparition of Dragan hung before us, and then, like a wolf seizing its prey, the ghost leapt straight into Savannah.

33

I reeled backward as the alien presence rammed into me, sending a bone-cold chill through my body. My lungs ached, and I shivered as the shockwave dissipated, leaving my skin cold and tingly.

What the hell happened?

I looked down at Grayling's body, then up at Jaxson.

With a burst of pain, my claws ripped out of my fingers, and I slammed my hand into Jaxson's face, tearing at his mask.

Oh, fuck! my wolf shouted in my mind. *He's in us!*

Jaxson blocked my wild blows and shoved me back.

However, Dragan, laughing in my mind, seized control of my legs. I leapt to my feet and darted into the smoke.

A gravestone caught my foot, and I tumbled to the ground. Jaxson was on me instantly.

As horror filled my mind, my leg shot out and rammed into his knee. He grunted and stumbled, and I rolled to the side.

This can't be happening!

Oh, but it is, honey, Dragan whispered in my mind.

That fucker.

Dragan forced me to my feet even as I fought against his control. Jaxson grabbed my arm, but I spun and slammed my forearm into his skull.

His grip loosened for a second, and I ran.

Wolfie! I screamed in my mind. *Help time!*

We can fight this! Take control of one leg together! Left!

My wolf and I focused our will on my left leg, willing it to seize up. But I kept running.

We strained, and suddenly, my knees locked. My body twisted out of control, and I tumbled headfirst into the grass.

Eat that, Dragan!

"You think you can stop me?" he said in my voice as he fought for control of my legs.

Fear iced my skin. Oh, *hell*, no. I would *not* let the bastard take my voice.

My will rose like a burning torrent of power, and fighting for every syllable, I seized control of my vocal cords. "Fuck you, asshole. I'll never submit."

I felt him try to speak again, but I wouldn't allow it.

Dragan forced me to my feet as Jaxson barreled out of the clouds of gas.

With a swift motion, Dragan thrust the claws of my left hand against my jugular, and his voice croaked from my mouth. "Don't move, Laurent. You need her alive more than I do, and her claws are razor sharp. One more step, and I'll tear her throat out."

Jaxson froze midstride. "Fight him, Savannah!"

Fight him, Savannah, Dragan mocked in my mind as he took a cautious step backward.

You're a fucking monster! I shouted at him, the words echoing though the caverns of my mind.

Yes. A monster. But you see, we're the same, Savannah. Two murderous monsters. That is what this corrupt world has taught us to be. Forced us to be.

Even as Dragan made me walk into the mist, I bared my teeth and took control of my voice once again. "I'm nothing like you."

You're exactly like me. Two souls sharing one body. An aberration. A monster. If they knew what you truly were, they'd kill you where you stand, Savannah Caine. They'd kill you without a second's hesitation.

My wolf's voice cut into my thoughts. *Sorry, asshole. This is already a duplex, and you're the odd freak out!*

Her strength poured into me, and we stumbled as the whole left side of my body came back under my control.

Dragan gave a bestial roar as he pushed back, leaving us as three souls vying for control of one body.

Fool! Dragan bellowed as his strength began to return. *Together, our power would be unimaginable. The Dark Wolf God will grant us each our own form, but we could have the strength of all of us combined!*

Our grip started slipping.

Suddenly, Jaxson was there, pinning my arms to my sides. His strength poured into me and cleared my thoughts, like plunging into the icy waters of the lake, like a sunrise on a cold winter morning.

I gasped and spoke. "I'm the one Dragan wants, Jax. Pull off my mask. Now!"

"What?"

"Trust me! Do it before he takes control!"

Growling with desperate fury, Jaxson reached for my mask. The second he let go, I kneed him straight in the nuts, and my traitorous right arm shot out to tear his mask off instead.

Jaxson seized my right wrist with both hands and pulled it

free of his face, leaving my left arm—the one I still had control over—uninhibited. It was all I needed.

My wolf and I galvanized our will and grabbed the buckles of my gas mask with my left arm. I began to pull. *Mindfuck someone else, asshole.*

No! Dragan roared in my mind as he struggled against us all. He tore my arm out of Jaxson's grip, but it was too late.

I ripped my mask free and took a deep breath of the sleeping gas. "You're not going to control me!"

Dragan released his power over my arms and tried to take my legs. In resistance, I pivoted my waist and used my body weight to tip myself over and drop into the strange, lichen-infested grass. Then I crawled forward, hand over hand, like a zombie toward one of the smoking gas bombs, my legs jerking and dragging behind me.

Stretching with all my length, I snagged the spewing potion and brought it close to my face. *Nighty-night, asshole.*

I breathed in deeply as Jaxson dropped down to my side.

The gas tasted like bubblegum and smelled like marshmallows. A soothing sense of freedom washed over me like warm rain on a summer's day. Every muscle in my body began to relax.

I didn't have control anymore. But neither did Dragan, and that was all that mattered.

His rage and fury strained against the limits of my soul, and then, with a sudden release of tension, he was gone, and I was at peace.

I rolled onto my back as darkness closed in around my vision.

All I could see was Jaxson's mask bending over me and tree branches swimming in a sea of clouds. I clumsily reached up and brushed my fingers along the edge of his mask, and laughed.

"Savannah, are you okay?"

I frowned as my vision spun. "I was just thinking that you kind of look like Darth Vader in that thing...but in a sexy way... Darth Jaxson. Hot Vader. I'll workshop it..."

"What?" he asked, confusion dancing in his voice like the waves of darkness that danced in my eyes.

I felt my arm drop to the ground. The strange grass was soft, like an old linen comforter. I realized my eyes were closed. An absolutely crucial thought ran through my mind, and even though my lips felt leaden, I forced the words out. "You know, I've only ever watched the original..."

Darkness took me.

34

Jaxson

I roared with fury and spun, searching for the spirit among the haze.

But the apparition of Dragan had fled, slithering from Savannah's body like a ghostly eel the moment she'd gone unconscious.

Fuck!

I checked her over for a third time. No wounds other than the one that had never fully healed. She was just sleeping peacefully—probably for the first time since she'd learned about Magic Side.

Turning slowly, I scanned the clouds of gas. I couldn't see anything, so I booted the still fuming potion as far as I could.

Where the hell had Dragan gone? Could the asshole jump bodies whenever he wanted, or did his host have to die or lose consciousness, like Grayling and Savannah? Was he going for another host or just lurking in the woods?

I had to warn the pack.

I lifted Savannah gently, heaved her over my shoulder, and stormed out of the billowing cloud of gas.

As the haze thinned, someone shouted, "Halt! Don't move."

"It's me, asshole," I growled as I strode forward.

I shifted instinctually—even before I heard the gun fire—and snatched the hurtling beanbag out of the air. My arm jerked back in its socket, and a burst of magic numbed my arm, but I didn't stop.

Moving like the wind, I darted out of the haze and smacked the riot gun out of the agent's hands. I handed him the beanbag. "I said, *it's me*. Where the fuck is Harlow?"

He stammered, so I didn't wait.

The battle was over, and most of the agents were busy cleaning up—recovering potions, untying the sacrificial victims, and cuffing the unconscious bikers.

I laid Savannah down on the grass and tore off my mask. Then I kicked my head back and howled—a deep, rage-filled bellow from the depths of my lungs. It told my pack that our quarry had escaped and to not let anyone leave the woods alive.

If that bastard tries to possess one of my wolves...

"Jaxson!" Harlow shouted as she rushed over. "Is she okay?"

I dug my claws into the earth, and it took every ounce of patience I had to keep my voice steady. "Savannah gassed herself so Dragan couldn't possess her."

Harlow looked over her shoulder. "But we found him unconscious—"

"Nope, that's just Grayling now. Dragan jumped ship. He could be anywhere."

"What?" she exclaimed.

I fixed her with a glare. "Tell me you have something to neutralize this shit and wake her up."

Harlow fished a vial out of her pocket and bent down, holding it under Savy's nose. Seconds later, Savannah sat up with a gasp.

"Jaxson..." She rubbed her head. "Is Dragan..."

It was all I could do to stop myself from shifting in rage. "We're fucked. I saw his ghost leave your body, and then he disappeared into the mist. He could be back in hell, for all I know, or in someone here."

Savannah ran her hands through her hair and dropped back down into the strange grass. "Goddamn it. He could be in anyone."

I took her hand and hefted her to her feet. "I don't know about that. He barely seemed to be able to control his form in Grayling—parts of him kept shifting. And when he was trying to control you…"

She looked down at her ripped jeans and shirt. "Please tell me I wasn't wolfing out like that. It was horrific."

She could smell the truth, so I wasn't sure what to say. "You're fine now."

"Crap." She covered her face. "Dragan was so close to taking over."

I grabbed her shoulders and pushed my power into her. "He wasn't. I saw you fighting him. You were the stronger one, I could feel it. He just caught you by surprise."

Savy shook her head and nervously pulled her hair over her shoulder. "I don't know, it felt like he was so close to winning. That's why I gassed myself."

"He was desperate. You're strong—more willful than anyone I've ever met." That was the truth.

A howl echoed from the far side of the woods, and we spun.

Three bikers stepped out from the trees onto the road. One had his hands in the air, while the second was dragging the third along. "We fuckin' surrender!"

A pack of Dockside wolves emerged from the darkness behind them.

Three agents converged, riot guns raised. "Get on the

ground, assholes," one of them barked. "You're under arrest for participating in black magic and profane rituals!"

We headed over.

As soon as the bikers were on their bellies, the agents cuffed them. "We've got one wounded," the lead agent reported.

His leg had been torn to shreds, and all three had bites and scratches.

I checked in with my wolves. "Nice hunting. Is anyone hurt?"

Sam padded over in human form. Blood matted her shoulder. "They weren't hard to bring down."

I growled low in approval. "Clearly, they've spent too much time riding and not enough time hunting."

Headlights swept over us as a pair of Order SUVs slowly trundled down the road. A man crossed through their low beams as they approached—Max, Harlow's sandy-haired partner. He pulled off his mask. "The wolves brought in one more on the other side of the graveyard. We've got Grayling and thirteen others unconscious, making eighteen. There's eighteen bikes up the road, so I think that's everyone, unless they were riding two up, which"—he looked down at the beefy, well-built bikers—"I think is unlikely."

"Congratulations," Harlow said as she turned to us. "We got them all."

Savy crossed her arms. "Nope. *Grayling* had a passenger—Dragan, who got away."

Silence hung heavy.

I looked from Harlow to Max. "We need to make sure all your people are accounted for. Round them up and check if anything is strange. Dragan might have possessed one of them."

Harlow nodded at Max. "Do it."

I turned to Sam. "Us, too. Dragan was having trouble controlling Grayling's forms. He might have trouble with a shift."

Sam rounded up the wolves as Max and Harlow inspected their agents.

Savy hugged herself tight. "How do we fight a ghost if he can just jump hosts?"

"No idea. But we're going to find out," I growled.

Moments later, Sam dashed around the corner of the SUV. "Jax, Tony's gone."

Fuck. It couldn't be.

I turned to my wolves. "Who saw Tony last?"

Two of them nodded to the road, back where the Order's SUVs had come from. I turned to the cluster of agents. "Did anyone see a wolf or man heading that direction?"

One of them nodded. "There was a guy grabbing one of the trucks when we were going for the SUVs. I thought he'd be here by now."

I stilled my breathing and tuned my ears.

Nothing. No sound of wheels on dirt.

I spun on my pack. "Spread out. Find him, *now*. Sam, take two and head for the trucks. The rest of you go parallel to the woods. Howl if you encounter him—track, but do *not* engage."

My wolves tore off into the darkness.

"I might be able to get there faster in my Swiftleys!" Savannah shouted.

"Do it."

"Okay, Wolfie, sprint time," she said, and with a burst of speed, she shot into the dark, propelled by werewolf strength and her magical boots.

Harlow ran up. "What the hell is happening?"

"I think Dragan may have found his ride out of here in one of my people," I snarled. "Get these asshole bikers in custody. We'll track Dragan down."

I pulled out my phone and called Tony. With every ring, my hope faded. Finally, it went to voicemail.

Tony was gone.

I reared my head back and roared.

35

Savannah

We were born to run, I told my wolf. *Help me do this.*

Her strength poured into me, and I accelerated to a break-neck pace. Thankfully, my eyes were sensitive enough that I could partially see the dirt road and the hundreds of protruding rocks, roots, and potholes.

I flashed by the pull-off where the bikers had parked their rides, and soon, I was ahead of the wolves and on my own, dashing through the darkness.

The pack's trucks appeared up ahead, but one was missing.

I skidded to a halt, almost wiping out on the loose gravel. A quick inspection told me everything I needed to know: we were screwed.

Tony—technically, Dragan puppeteering Tony's body—had ripped up the tires of all the remaining vehicles. A quick inspection revealed he'd taken the keys, too. We were dead in the water.

Jaxson and the wolves arrived seconds later.

I pointed. "He's fucked our rides and taken one of the trucks! Can any of you smell which way he went? I'm not certain."

In wolf form, their senses were much stronger. Sam and the others checked the road for the smell of tires and exhaust, and then she nodded. *North.*

Jaxson pulled out his phone and dialed. A soft glow and buzz emanated from the bushes. "Well, fuck. He ditched his phone, so we can't track him that way. We're going to need Harlow's SUVs."

I grabbed Jaxson's arm. "How many of your wolves can ride a bike? Because there are eighteen Harleys parked back there."

With a grim expression, he turned to the waiting wolves. "Who can ride?"

Harlow retrieved keys from the captured bikers, and five minutes later, Sam and three other werewolves roared up the road. The reality was that there were half a dozen turnoffs between Pere Cheney and I-75, and Tony had one hell of a head start.

He wasn't going to be found unless he put the truck in the ditch.

Harlow contacted the state police and flagged the vehicle as stolen. There wasn't much more we could do without a Seeker on hand—a type of Magica skilled in finding things.

Jaxson rammed his fist into the side of his truck. The force of the blow made it lurch and pivot a couple feet to the side. He shook his wrist and walked away, leaving a huge dent in the bed.

I stepped over and put my hand on his back, letting that familiar electricity between us warm the tense muscles beneath his jacket. "I know you and Tony are close. We're going to find him."

We stood silently like that for a moment, and Jaxson's breathing calmed.

He turned slightly so he could look me in the eyes. "I know. I don't like being out-maneuvered. And I hate not being on the road, hunting him."

I let my fingers trace down his back, rising and falling. "Trust me, I get that. But Sam's taking a shot in the dark. Tony could be anywhere. Our job is to figure out how we're going to stop Dragan and get him out of Tony once we find him. We need to figure out how to fight a ghost."

He let out a gruff laugh that sounded thin on hope.

An insidious melancholy hung over the assembled team, and I felt it creeping into my bones. And why shouldn't it? I'd come so close, only to fall short. Dragan had gotten away. *Again.*

If I could knock a truck around like Jaxson, I would have.

We stopped the ritual. That's something. My wolf had a lot more perspective than I did. *The pack is what's important.*

I took a deep breath. Dragan had been seconds away from summoning a nightmare from the darkest depths of werewolf lore. If he'd succeeded, our pack would have been doomed. He would have stolen our souls and destroyed Magic Side.

That was huge.

So why did I feel so defeated? We'd won the battle, but not the war. The bastard was still out there, and until we caught him, no one would be safe.

Tonight, they're safe, Wolfie said.

I nodded. True. Maybe that was enough. Another night, another week. He was on the run, and we'd get him soon.

I opened my eyes as boots approached across the dirt road. Harlow. She brushed her hair from the side of her face. "We found four captives, all Magica. They're terrified out of their minds, but none of them were physically harmed. We sent them back to Magic Side via transport charm."

"What about the bikers? Do any of them know where Dragan might be headed?" Jaxson asked.

She shook her head. "Most of them don't remember a thing, or at least they claim not to."

"I can get the information out of them," Jaxson growled.

She held up her hand. "That was a onetime thing—when no one was watching. I want to make sure these bastards get locked away, so we're doing this by the book. I'm sending them to Bentham, where they can be processed and questioned properly."

I could sense his irritation, but he didn't push the issue.

Harlow crossed her arms and gave me a suspicious look. "How did you know that Dragan was about to finish his ritual? You had me spring the trap early."

My face heated, and I looked between her and Jaxson. "Honestly?"

She nodded, and Jaxson narrowed his eyes at me.

I gave a pained smile. "Well, I see dead people."

Jaxson's eyebrows shot up. "You're joking, right?"

Suddenly ashamed, I looked down at my Swiftleys and shook my head. "I don't know why I didn't mention it earlier. I thought I was hallucinating at first, then that I was being haunted. Now, I think they've just been helping me. A woman appeared in the woods and warned me that the ritual was almost done."

Jaxson cocked his head to the side. "That's right...I saw you turn and look off into the trees, but I couldn't see what you were looking at."

I nodded. "That was her."

Harlow tucked her hair behind her ear and gave me a warm smile. "There's supposed to be a ghost at Pere Cheney—a witch. Lucky for us, it seems."

The Witch of Pere Cheney—it had to have been her.

Suddenly, it hit me. I grabbed Jaxson's hand as he started to turn back to the others. "Holy shit, Jax!"

"What?"

I looked from him to Harlow. "You wanted to know how to stop a ghost? How about we go ask one?"

Savannah

We raced back down the two-track trail on the back of a commandeered Harley. I clung tightly to Jaxson. It was dark, and the road was poor, and we didn't have helmets. I closed my eyes against the dust and pressed my cheek into his strong back.

After just a few minutes, Jaxson slowed the bike, and I looked up. We'd reached the clearing surrounding Pere Cheney cemetery.

The graveyard was dark and mostly abandoned. The cursed bonfire had burned to embers, and most of the agents and their detainees had taken transport charms back to Magic Side. The clouds that had been spiraling like a cyclone above the ritual were mostly gone, and the stars were bright. Without the diffuse reflection from the overcast sky, everything was far darker than before.

Jaxson parked the bike, and we dismounted. He surveyed the shadowy edge of the woods. "Where to?"

I rested my fingers gently on his jacket. "I should go alone. I don't think you'll be able to see the ghost, and she might not show up if others are around."

He took my hand softly but possessively. "You don't know that's the case."

His touch made me want to never let go, to take him with me. But he was over-protective, and this was my task.

I checked the woods ahead, then turned back to him. "Normally, the ghosts only appear when no one else is there, so I'm afraid you're out. Trust me. I have a gut feeling about this one."

Jaxson ground his teeth, but after a moment, he inclined his head—just slightly. "Okay. But ghosts can be dangerous. Speaking with the dead is generally forbidden in our pack."

"I'll be fine. Our pack is superstitious."

He gave a low, appraising growl. "You called it *our* pack."

He'd caught that. And I could tell from the tension in his body that this was a question. An important one.

They were my pack now. All I had.

I took a deep breath and nodded. "Our pack. Still too superstitious, especially now that you have a sorceress in your midst. I *will* be fine, Jaxson. The only ghost that's given me any trouble is Dragan."

He let me go. "All right. Just don't get possessed by some ugly old witch."

I pulled my hand free and smirked. "Yeah, I'm definitely leaving you here. It's a diplomatic decision now."

He grunted, which I took as a laugh. Striding with far more confidence than I felt, I turned and headed into the woods in search of a ghost.

With the firelight gone, the forest was darker than before. At least the clouds had parted. Patches of the strange grass, old leaves, and twigs crunched beneath my boots as I wove my way through the trees. Soon, their overhanging branches were dense enough that the leaves blocked out almost all the starlight.

I could have turned on my flashlight, but my sensitive werewolf eyes quickly adjusted to my surroundings, and it seemed more appropriate to hunt for the ghost in the dark.

Passing agents and werewolves had trampled the brush down, and the scent of our pack was everywhere. Their passing had revealed old, hidden gravestones—once part of the perimeter of the cemetery, now overgrown by forest.

I'd hoped to find the exact spot where I'd seen the witch before, but it was impossible in the dark, so after a while, I simply shouted, "Hey! I'm looking for the witch of Pere Cheney! I think you helped me tonight?"

I held my breath. A minute passed. Nothing.

Cupping my hands to my mouth—and with no real conviction that I had any idea what I was doing—I called out again, "Hello! Ghost! Thank you for your warning. It saved our pack! But I need your help again!"

Still nothing.

I gritted my teeth. For all the sneaking up on me that ghosts had been doing, shouldn't they have the decency to come when I called?

Since I didn't have a Ouija board and didn't know the first thing about summoning ghosts, I just kept shouting.

Pretty soon, my vocal cords began to itch. The stars turned overhead, but no ghost appeared. The whole thing was futile.

"Savy, it's time to get out of here!" Jaxson shouted from a surprising way away. "This isn't working. It was a good plan, but we'll find another way."

I sucked my teeth. Crap. He was probably right, and I'd wandered far.

With nothing left to do, I gave the gloating trees *the look* and shouted one last time, "Hey, ghost lady! Show the fuck up!"

Nothing. Just dark, smug trees rustling their leaves gently in sarcastic applause.

"Yeah, screw you, too," I muttered, and turned back—straight into the pale, intangible face of the witch.

Too shocked to scream, I stumbled back, tripped over a broken headstone, and landed in some brambles.

The ethereal figure floated over and looked down. It was the woman who'd warned me earlier. She was young—maybe eighteen—with ratty hair and a soiled dress. Although she was translucent, I couldn't see through her.

My wound began to ache, and a frost crept from it across my body.

Her head twisted, and she gave a hungry grin as she held out her hand. "Have you come to bargain for your soul?"

My breath hitched, and I dug my fingers into the dirt. "What? *No!* Absolutely not!"

"Pity." The young woman drifted between the trees.

With a sharp intake of breath, I scrambled to my feet and began to draw shadows to me out of instinct.

The ghost laughed. "Ah, yes, such deliciously dark magic, so deliciously cold!"

I couldn't tell if it was just the shadows or the trees themselves, but they seemed to bend and bow with her passing as she circled around me.

"Please, I *need* your help," I begged, slowly turning to follow her spin.

She stopped short. "I already helped you. I will not do so again—not without a bargain." Then she slipped half behind a tree.

The word *bargain* sent a shiver down my spine, but I licked my lips and took a step forward. "Why did you help me? Why not again?"

In a flash, she was inches from my face. "I helped you because you are one of us."

My skin turned to ice—because of the deep cold that radiated around her, and because of the words she'd spoken. "I don't understand. Because of your magic?"

She pointed at my shoulder. At my wound. "Because you are dead and with us in the underworld."

The frost on my skin penetrated deep within my gut. "I'm not dead."

"A part of you is. A little sliver. It's here with us." She laughed and zipped away.

I touched my wound. A little sliver of my soul was dead?

Fuck.

But there had to be more. "Dragan is dead, too, but you helped *me*. Why?"

The ghost slowly turned and laughed in a far too sweet trill. "He won't be dead for long, my love. Not if he can bring back your god. The Dark God will give him a new form, and no one wants that—not the living or the dead."

I swallowed, though it made no difference to my dry throat. "Then please, help me!"

She twisted her hair and came so close that my teeth began to chatter, and my wound screamed. "Help *me*. Then I'll help you."

Jaxson's voice echoed through the woods. "Savannah!"

He was closer. I turned and shouted, "I'm all right! Give me a minute."

When I turned back, the ghost was gone.

Damn it!

I spun, searching the trees. "I'll help you—how?"

Silence. Then a voice whispered in my ear, "Bring me a gravestone. A beautiful one that will never fade."

I yelped and spun around, finding myself once again inches from her.

My breath caught as she pulled down the high collar of her dress and held back her head so I could see the dark bruises ringing her pale, translucent neck. "They left me hanging in these woods—never gave me a proper burial. Left my bones to be taken by wolves!"

I raised my hand to my mouth. "I'm so sorry. Why—"

She unleashed a wail that pierced the depths of my mind, and I squeezed my eyes shut, as if that could block out the unearthly sound. "They accused me of witchcraft and threw me out of my town. Hanged me from a tree!"

The ghost slumped down at the base of an oak and began to sob gently with her hands over her face.

I wanted to reach out to her, but every instinct told me not to touch. "I'm so sorry."

Quelling her tears, she folded her hands in her lap, straightened her spine, and spoke in a soft and controlled voice that burned with underlying intensity. "I showed them. I brought plague and disease and misery until they and all their children were buried. Until not one person remained. Now they are forgotten."

My stomach tightened at her gentle smile. She rose and sashayed from tree to tree. "Now their headstones are rubble. Their graves are looted and forlorn. Bring me a gravestone that will never crack, that will never weather, and I will be able to rest knowing that of everyone who lived in that cursed town, I will be the only one remembered!"

I needed her help, so I nodded. "If you tell me what I need to know, I'll bring you the gravestone."

She shook her head. "A poor bargain. Bring me the stone first, and then I will tell you anything you want to know."

"I can't. I need the information now. It's now or never."

The ghost witch slowly started to stalk toward me. "Very

well. I will give you three answers, but you must swear an oath to fulfill your part of the bargain."

"I will."

She suddenly vanished, and cold crept over my back. I didn't move a muscle as she whispered in my ear, "If you betray me, I will hunt down that missing sliver of your soul and make sure you never sleep again. That every waking moment of your life is filled with cold and pain."

Okay. Ghosts were bad.

But Dragan was slipping away. No ghost had ever talked to me before like this, so the witch might be my only shot. And she only wanted a headstone.

Muscles tense and aching, I turned to face the phantom. "I swear I'll bring you a gravestone if you answer my questions. The ghost of Dragan possessed our friend. How do we stop him from taking control?"

The ghost cackled and drew back. "You didn't need me for that. Kick him out with an exorcism, of course!"

I ground my jaw. "But how do I stop him from possessing someone else?"

She smiled. "This is a better question. You'll need to get his bones. A ghost always wants their bones. I wish I had mine, but they're long gone. They left me to hang like curing meat. The wolves took my flesh and bones."

The way she looked at me every time she said *wolves* made my skin crawl. She'd given me an answer, but not enough of an answer. "You haven't explained what to do!"

"Find someone who can cast a curse, fool girl. Draw him in! Trap him!"

"You're a witch. You could do it."

She pulled on her long, stringy hair. "I wish, but you'll have to find yourself a living witch! Now get out of my woods and bring me my headstone, or I will make you suffer like you have never imagined!"

The ghost whipped through the air like a silver streamer and vanished through the trees.

I looked around frantically. "You haven't answered all my questions!"

But there was no response.

I'd needed to ask where his bones were, or more about the wound caused by the Soul Knife, and what she'd meant when she'd said I was like them—the ghosts. But that opportunity was gone. Traitorous creature.

Somehow, I imagined she would still have no compunctions about enforcing her end of the bargain.

The pull of our bond led me easily back to Jaxson, though I still had to pick my way carefully through the downed trees.

He was waiting there in the shadows, a deep, warm presence that smelled of amber and moss and pine. Somehow, the darkness made every sensation stronger, bolder, and more enticing than ever.

His fingers ran over my skin.

"You're frozen," he said in low tones that sent a shiver down my spine.

I felt the cold so much more now that I was close to him. I nodded and pressed close, relishing the heat of his body. I realized I could see my breath, a faint plume in the warm summer night air.

Jaxson didn't shy away or do anything except stand, letting me take his heat. Finally, he spoke. "Did you find what you were looking for in the woods?"

"Yes," I said at last. "But to get the information I had to promise to bring the ghost an unbreakable headstone."

"That's going to be tricky. I hope the information was worth it. What did she say?"

"To catch Dragan, we need to collect his bones."

Jaxson gave a low growl of approval. "Well done, Savy. Did the ghost know where he was buried?"

I gave a deep, forlorn sigh. "I didn't have a chance to ask. But I think I know who might."

Aunt Laurel.

37

Savannah

Since Jaxson's truck was out of commission and all the Order's transport charms had been used to move captives and prisoners, we rode back to Magic Side with Harlow.

Exhaustion and defeat weighed on us all, which made it an awkward ride. When we pulled over for gas at a Mobil station after only an hour, I practically barreled out of the vehicle.

Only three and a half miserable hours to go.

"You okay?" Jaxson asked as we exited the vehicle. "You've been quiet."

Because I didn't want to talk about the next step. I knew what I needed to do: call Laurel. She'd killed Dragan and was the only one who might know where we could find his bones.

But it was a call I was loath to make.

I'd spent the drive reflecting on each interaction that I'd had with my aunt and uncle over the past month.

All that time, they'd said nothing. Swept the truth under the rug.

I couldn't shake the sense of having been violated, like a piece of me had been taken against my will. The fact that it had been my parents and aunt who'd done it...that cut the deepest, like rubbing salt in a festering wound.

But there was no way around making the call.

I coughed to loosen my parched throat. "I'm all right, but I need to call Laurel, and I don't want to do it in the car. Can you have the cops wait?"

Jaxson looked at his watch. "It's nearly two in the morning."

"I have a feeling she'll answer, and we don't have time to wait."

He nodded, and I headed around the side of the J&H convenience store and leaned back against the red brick wall.

I pulled up Laurel's number on my cell phone, my finger hovering over the call icon on the screen. *Suck it up, Savy. Stopping Dragan is more important than your personal beefs.*

The phone rang four times, and just as I was about to hang up, Laurel answered drowsily, her voice a mix of relief and concern. "Savannah? I'm so glad you called."

Uncle Pete's voice came over the line. "Who the hell is that?"

I could envision him lying in bed in his silly nightgown and eye mask, trying to figure out who would call at this time of night. I'd gotten to know them so well in just a few weeks.

A staticky sound came across the line as she muffled the phone, and I heard her whisper, "Shh. It's Savy. I'm going in the other room."

Her voice returned a second later, and I could hear her walking on the creaky floorboards. "It's two a.m. Are you okay?"

My gut twisted, and tears burned the back of my eyes, but I kept my voice steady. "Let me be clear: I haven't forgiven you for what you did to me, and I don't want to talk about it. I'm in a bind, and I'm afraid that you're the only one who may be able to help. *That's* why I'm calling."

There was a pregnant pause.

"I understand. I'll help any way I can." Her voice was hard

and measured, and I could practically feel the push of emotions she was holding back.

I swallowed the budding ache in my throat. "Dragan is back. His ghost took over the leader of a werewolf biker gang. We stopped a blood ritual tonight, but he escaped by jumping into a new host. A friend."

She sucked in a sharp breath. "That's worse than I feared. How can I help?"

"To stop him, we need his bones. Do you know where they are?" My heart pounded in my chest, and I dug my nails into my palm while I waited for her answer.

"My." Laurel's voice was distraught, and I could easily picture the familiar furrow that cut her forehead. "That might be tricky."

"Tricky or impossible?"

The long silence on the other end didn't give me hope.

Finally, she spoke. "When I killed him, I disintegrated him. His body was nothing more than ashes that are surely long gone by now."

The last thread of hope I'd had unraveled, and I rubbed my tired eyes. "We'll have to think of something else, then. Thanks."

"Wait!" she said as I was about to hang up. "Don't go. Let me think for just a second."

I held my breath.

After a moment, she spoke again. "Victor Dragan had a nickname: Ninefingers. Years ago, a vampire cut off one of his fingers as punishment for stealing from him. If you could find it..."

My mind raced. A finger? That was all that was left?

The vampire could have fed it to his dog or thrown it in the trash, or anything. It would be impossible to track down.

The hope that had welled up in my chest collapsed into a black hole. "Shit. What's the chance that the vampire kept the finger?"

My aunt sucked her teeth. "Well, better than zero, so that's something. He was known as a collector of odd things and art, so maybe he kept it. Hell, a sorcerer's finger probably could be used to make a powerful potion, for all I know. I could ask Uncle—"

"Do you know his name?" I interrupted, not wanting to even know that Uncle Pete could potentially answer that question.

There was a long pause. "No."

Shit.

"He was a dealer of magical artwork and artifacts. I think he resided in Mexico. I'm trying to remember what Dragan tried to steal..."

A car door slammed, and I looked up. Harlow and the others were waiting. "Thanks. I really appreciate it. Text me if you can remember his name."

I pulled my phone down to hang up, but her voice stopped me. "I know about you and Jaxson. He told me about the mate bond."

My breath hitched as a cold sweat dampened the back of my neck. Her words hit me in the chest harder than a bullet.

Damn you, Jaxson.

"It's not that simple," I whispered as I shut my eyes tight with frustration.

As if I needed one more complication in my life. If either of us did. Hell, the moment he told me about the mate bond, I'd gone into a rage, and he'd said, "Do you think I'm any happier about this than you are? Do you think I want this? Because I don't."

Complicated would be an understatement.

"I've seen how he looks at you. I won't tell you what to do, but you have to realize that it's extremely dangerous to be with him. His father—"

"His father has nothing to do with anything. Nor do you. Or the fates. You and my parents took the choice of being a wolf from me." I clenched my phone, almost to the point of breaking the screen. "If Jaxson and I end up together, it won't be because three crazy old crones decided it was so. It will be *my* choice. Just like being a wolf is my choice now, despite what the three of you did."

My throat seized up, and I disconnected the call.

The phone rang, but I muted it. I was certain an apology was hanging on the other line, but I didn't want to hear it.

I'd had to funnel my anger just to hang up, because although we'd only known each other a short time, I missed her voice. Like my car, she was all that I had left of my parents, and I didn't know how to face their betrayal, or hers.

I didn't know how to face Casey. He was the closest thing I had to a brother or a best friend, but I knew he'd never get over what I was or that I'd kept the secret from him. We might make peace, but would he ever look at me the same now that I was a wolf? Now that I was the goddamned Dockside alpha's mate?

I swiped away the tear that slipped down my cheek.

"Everything all right?"

I jumped. Jaxson.

His broad frame was silhouetted against the lights of the station. Powerful. Composed. Whole.

Everything I wasn't.

Just being close to him made my body buzz with anticipation, and all I wanted to do was fall into his strong arms and sob.

Instead, I growled and narrowed my eyes. "You told Laurel about our mate bond."

"I did," he said calmly, but his jaw tightened. "She needed to know."

A lie. Telling Laurel had just been a way for Jaxson to hurt her. A way to stake his claim on me. Fuck that.

I jabbed my finger into his chest. "Let me set one thing straight, Jaxson. You don't own me. Got it?"

An infuriatingly confident smile ticked up at the corner of his mouth. "I wouldn't dare. The insurance premiums would be too high, even for me."

My jaw dropped as shock washed over me. "You ass. You think you can make a bad joke, and this all goes away?"

"It's my second of the night. That has to count for something."

I shook my head. "It doesn't."

He held out his hand. "Gas station burrito? You have to be starving."

The aroma of it was...all right. But it was food, and my treacherous stomach grumbled, just as it had on the bridge to Magic Side when we first met.

I took it defiantly. "Yes, I'm starving. But what is it with you and burritos? You own a world-class restaurant, and it's the only thing you have in your freezer that even resembles breakfast."

"I thought you liked them, so I stocked up."

I bit into the warm burrito but managed to snarl at him between bites. "I ate them because it was the only thing you had."

He shrugged. "They remind me of working the docks as a kid. It's what I took for lunch. Things were simpler then. Grab a burrito, go to work."

I chewed less aggressively at him. After all we'd been through, were we really arguing about burritos? Was he just trying to distract me from the shitstorm headed our way, like he had by making me work the lunch rush at Eclipse?

No way I was going to let him manipulate me that way, either.

A horn honked, and he looked over his shoulder. "Harlow wants to roll. Are you ready?"

I swallowed the last bite of warm, bean-and-cheese-filled goodness. "My aunt disintegrated Dragan, so there aren't any bones, except—and this is gross—his finger, which a vampire art collector cut off ages ago. So we're probably fucked."

Jaxson's eyebrows went up. "An art collector?"

"That, and magic artifacts, according to my aunt. He lives in Mexico. He also would've had to have kept the finger, which seems like a long shot. We probably need to find another solution." I grunted as I wadded up the used wrapper, almost wishing I had another.

Jaxson rubbed his beard. "Maybe, but it's something. Sounds like we need someone who knows the artifact trade to figure out who he is, as well as a Seeker to find the finger. Good thing I know the perfect pair—and they owe me a pretty big favor."

With that, he turned and headed back to Harlow's SUV, leaving me bewildered, with my emotions a mix of fear and anger and heartbreak.

And for a moment, the slightest sliver of hope.

38

Savannah

Despite my churning thoughts, I passed out on the ride back to Magic Side.

The day had taken every ounce of strength and energy I had. That, and my mom also gave me sleep-anywhere genes, and the car was about as good a place as any to catch a little shut-eye.

I vaguely remembered Jaxson carrying me up to his penthouse when I woke the next morning at twenty past eleven in *his* bed once again.

I *had* to get my own apartment, or at least my own sheets. Waking up to his scent each morning was not conducive to clear thinking, and I needed to keep my head on straight. As much as it irritated me, my aunt was right. *It is extremely dangerous to be with him.*

That was, if I wanted to make my own fate and not get enraptured by our goddamned mate bond.

Jaxson was waiting for me when I emerged. "Sleep well?"

Nuh-uh. This wasn't going to be a precedent. I put my hands on my hips. "We're not together. I need to get my own place and stop waking up in your bed."

"And yet, here you are again. I wonder how that keeps happening?" With an infuriating smirk hovering at the corner of his mouth, Jaxson handed me a cup of coffee. "Ready to hunt down a vampire?"

I gratefully took a sip as hope blossomed in my chest. "We've got a lead?"

The get-my-own-place conversation could wait.

Jaxson grunted. "Well, I contacted Neve Cross and Damian Malek. They say they can help, and we can head to their place as soon as you're ready."

Excitement thrummed in my chest. I'd met Neve and Amal the day we went to Bentham to question the Ripper. She'd then saved our asses in Forks. Though we didn't know each other well, part of me had hoped we'd see each other again. I cocked my head. "I didn't know Neve had a partner. Why does Malek sound familiar?"

"He's the one who gave us the tip on where to find the Viper. That, and you might have seen Malek Tower in the Circuit."

Oh, right. *That.* It was a black spire that dominated the land-scape of downtown Magic Side like a dark lightning bolt shooting toward the sky.

I set my coffee down as the hair on my neck stood on end. I'd heard rumors about him. "Isn't he..."

"A fallen angel? Yes. That, and a crime lord."

Fantastic. A fallen angel crime lord. What would he demand for helping us? Our own fingers?

"Why him?" I asked nervously. And why would Neve, who was a detective at the Order, be working with a dangerous crime lord?

Jaxson shrugged and set down his own coffee. "He made his fortune running bounty hunters and recovering property—at least, *recovering* is what he calls it—among other things. He's also a Seeker. Between him and Neve, we should be able to track the damn thing down."

I scoffed. "She works for the Order. Do you think you can convince her to work with him?"

Jaxson gave me a sly smile. "Oh, they're together."

My eyes widened. Talk about a conflict of interest.

I quickly pulled together a patchwork outfit from the pile of old clothes Sam had left me. At least my hair was back to normal. It had taken a couple of showers to wash Sam's potion out completely.

Jaxson drove us north in his *spare* truck, a well-loved beater, arguing that there was no time to grab my car from Eclipse and that I didn't know the way to Malek's place.

I was certain he did it just to rub my nerves the wrong way.

After about thirty minutes, we were cruising through an upscale neighborhood on the northern tip of Magic Side. "Welcome to the Breakers," Jaxson said.

Giant houses lined the glistening lakeshore. While Laurel's house was larger and more ornate than anywhere else I'd lived, the Breakers made the Indies look like a slum.

We turned down a long drive and pulled up in front of a two-story house with massive windows looking out over the water. Apparently, crime did pay.

The tail end of the morning breeze caught my hair as I slid out of Jaxson's ride. We were parked next to a glistening black Porsche, which contrasted with Jaxson's old blue pickup in every way imaginable.

The truck was like Jaxson. Rugged and powerful. Reliable. Ready to take on whatever you threw at it and give it hell.

I wondered what my Gran Fury said about me.

Watch out, other drivers, Wolfie quipped.

Shut up, you.

How about "Hell on wheels"? Or "Doesn't brake for werewolves"?

I ignored the continued suggestions from my wolf as we headed up the driveway. Beyond the tree-lined yard, the skyrises of Chicago and the outline of Bentham flickered in the hazy distance across the waters of Lake Michigan.

A butler opened the front door and let us in the bright and modern house—not the dark and tortured abode of a fallen angel, as I'd expected. Paintings and unusual artwork hung on the walls, suggesting a life of exotic adventures in long-forgotten places.

Yet there was an unmistakable precision to everything.

The butler led us into a palatial kitchen that was so perfect, it made me miss the warm confines of the LaSalles' and the endless boxes of Froot Loops shoved in the cupboards.

Neve was sitting at the counter, sipping a coffee from a tiny glass. Her dark red hair seemed to float in the breeze, though the air was still. I inadvertently touched my own hair.

She stood immediately and gave me a hug. "I hear your adversary just refuses to die."

I hugged her back. "Well, it's more that dying doesn't seem to be a problem for him. Thanks again for helping me kill him *last* time."

A man entered the room, immediately drawing my eyes. His signature bombarded my senses with the scent of windswept forests and the sound of crashing waves.

I hadn't known what to expect from a fallen angel, but Damian Malek was so handsome, it was almost painful—a tall man with piercing green eyes and perfect dark hair.

He extended his hand to Jaxson. "Jaxson, it's good to see you again."

The fallen angel turned to me and smiled broadly, making my pulse quicken. "And you must be Savannah. My name is Damian. Neve has told me a lot about you. It's great to finally make your acquaintance."

Holy damn. This man was gorgeous, and judging by his signature, extremely powerful and dangerous. Still, he paled in comparison to Jaxson in my eyes. Where Damian held a sophisticated grace about him, Jaxson was rugged and all beast—a study in contrasts like the two vehicles parked out front.

I know which one you want to ride.

SHUT it, Wolfie!

Neve lightly touched my arm. "Can we get you anything? Coffee? Tea?"

My eyes darted to her glass, which was still sitting on the counter. "Your coffee smells divine, and I didn't get much sleep last night. Do you have extra?"

"One jet fuel, coming right up," Damian said, and set a strange copper cup with a long handle on the stovetop.

Apparently, a gazillionaire fallen angel was about to make me fancy coffee. My life had really gone to strange places since the Taphouse.

Neve returned to her spot at the counter. "I've got some good news. I think I've identified the guy you two are looking for."

My jaw slackened. "Seriously?"

Jaxson had only called her this morning. I figured we had a snowball's chance in hell.

"Alejandro Rivera, a notorious dealer of magical artwork. He lives in San Miguel de Allende, a mountain town a couple hours north of Mexico City. He's known for his exclusive parties and extravagant acquisitions, which he auctions at exorbitant prices."

"And do you think there's any chance he might still have this *fingerbone* of Dragan's?" It sounded absolutely ridiculous. Why would a wealthy art dealer keep someone's finger?

Neve took a sip of her coffee and smiled. "Oh, for sure. This guy is creepy. Not only is he known for his black-market dealings in antiquities but also for his—how do I say it—impulsive temperament? He holds longstanding grudges, and if Victor Dragan was caught trying to lift one of Alejandro's objects, then I'd bet he has a special showcase devoted specially to Dragan's withered finger."

This guy sounds like a maniac, my wolf said.

I crossed my arms. "Delightful. How soon can we arrange a meeting with him?"

"She's fiery," Damian whispered to Jaxson, perhaps assuming I couldn't hear, as he stirred the coffee.

Jaxson locked me with a heated look that sent a whisper of tingles up my thighs. "You have no idea."

Damian poured the coffee into a set of little gold-rimmed glasses like Neve's. "You can meet him tonight. He's holding an art auction, and I've negotiated admittance for myself and company."

"Really?" My breath caught as I tried to temper my excitement. "You would do that for us?"

"Of course," Damian said. "I owe Jaxson and the pack a favor. Plus, you're Nevaeh's friend."

Neve smiled at me warmly and winked, and something in my chest clenched. I'd been in Magic Side just a short time, but already, I'd met more people that I cared about than I'd known growing up.

I eyed Jaxson, wondering what he'd done to deserve this favor. Damian was a crime lord, and I knew the wolves had underworld dealings.

Probably best not to ask too many questions.

"Thank you. That's amazing," I said as I sipped the coffee. It was dark and sweet, with aromas that brought far away lands and exotic places to mind. "The coffee is, too."

"It's Turkish," Damian explained. "From near my homeland."

"Once you've had it, you never want anything else," Neve

said, smiling at Damian. The way she looked at him made me wonder if she was talking about the coffee or the man.

How in the hell did an Order detective wind up with one of the biggest criminals in Magic Side? And here I'd thought Jaxson and I were opposites, I mused as I sipped the dark brew.

A cop and a criminal, my wolf remarked. *The sex must be explosive. I wonder if they use handcuffs?*

I choked on my coffee, and the others all looked at me. "Sorry. It's hot."

I bet it is.

Shut UP, Wolfie. You're going to make me choke to death.

"We can't thank you two enough," I blurted as my face heated.

"Well, you can return the favor," Neve said, putting her empty glass in the sink. "I can't go to the auction—there's no way Alejandro is going to let an Order operative in—but from what Jaxson has told me, you're an incredible artist and have a picture-perfect memory. Once you get back, could you make sketches of the people you see buying objects?"

I blushed harder. Jaxson had told them that I was an incredible artist?

"I don't have a photographic memory, and I'm not an artist. I'm proficient and sketch a lot. But I'm happy to try."

"I saw the sketches you did of the werewolves that attacked you in Belmont. You're very good."

Brushing my hair aside, I looked at the floor, unsure whether I should be embarrassed or proud. "I'll help any way I can."

"Thanks," she said. "These black-market art and artifact dealers think they're untouchable, but sooner or later, they all mess up. If we can build a database of who—"

She squeaked as Damian pulled her close, adoration and fire flickering in his green eyes. "Detective Cross is a champion of world heritage. No thief stands a chance."

Color flooded her cheeks, and she swiveled out of his arms. "That's right. No thief *or* fallen angel."

I knew it, my wolf chirped.

Oh, my God. I needed to put a muzzle on her.

"Now that that's settled, we need to find you an outfit for the auction," Neve said. "The word on the street is that these are extravagant affairs."

Nerves flittered in my stomach, and I suddenly felt out of my element. I'd never been to anything fancier than a fish boil before.

I looked down at my old shorts and boots self-consciously. Yeah. Not going to work.

"You two talk business," Neve said as she grabbed my arm and towed me out of the room. "We're going to do some shopping."

Oh, no. I hated shopping, and my bank account had five hundred dollars in it, last I'd checked.

As Neve all but dragged me down the hall, I heard Damian say quietly to Jaxson, "Alejandro is a shady fucker. His business is acquiring ill-gotten artifacts, but his hobby is collecting *people* he finds appetizing."

Great.

Hopefully, we weren't going to be on the menu.

39

Apparently, *shopping* meant something completely different if you were shacking up with a bazillionaire and not the owner of a three-figure bank account.

Neve took me to lunch at a fancy lakeside café, and then we headed back to Jaxson's penthouse. There, we were met by a pretty blonde woman with at least five designer shopping bags full of clothes and a couple of bottles of fancy champagne.

"I'm Jeanette." The blonde smiled, her hands full. "Ready to try on some amazing outfits? Where should I put all of this?"

I let them in with the key Jaxson had lent me. *Temporarily.*

"Uhm. In the bedroom?" I glanced at the shoeboxes and makeup bag that Jeanette had shoved into an oversized tote. "That's a lot of stuff."

Neve grabbed three champagne flutes from the kitchen. "Are you kidding? You're going to be mingling with millionaires tonight. You've gotta fit in."

A light dizziness overcame me. *Mingling with millionaires.*

What's this obsession with clothes? Wolfie asked. *You've already got a perfectly fine fur coat.*

I helped Neve and Jeanette haul their stuff upstairs and dropped several bags of clothes onto Jaxson's bed. I felt like a vagrant, with no home or belongings, squatting in Jaxson's luxury apartment and taking handouts from Neve. "Are you sure we need all of this?"

Neve watched me closely, seemingly reading my unease with the situation. "Absolutely. I love clothes, and Jeannette is a stylist at Madison & Main, so technically, this is part of her job. She gets the latest fashions each month and decides which styles are selected for the store's main display. We're helping her."

"Really?" I raised my brow at Jeannette.

"Really." The woman nodded, and I couldn't detect a hint of dishonesty. "Since Neve has started helping me, I've gotten two promotions. Girl's got an eye for fashion."

"That's right." Neve popped the cork off a bottle of champagne and poured three glasses, handing me one. "Now strip. We've only got three hours to find the perfect dress and do your hair and makeup."

Why had so much of my life started to revolve around getting naked in front of other people?

The first problem we had to address was the wound on my shoulder, which was seeping a little again.

"It really won't heal?" Neve asked me for the third time as I self-consciously covered my chest with my hands.

"Trust me, it won't. It's from a cursed knife. Every time I think it's getting better, it just starts bleeding—and I've even got werewolf healing now. I've tried potions and ointments, and Jaxson can, uh...heal me, too."

Neve raised her eyebrows. "Mm-hmm. Healing magic is so *hot*, isn't it?"

Heat flushed my cheeks, and I'm sure I turned as scarlet as the lipstick Jeanette had picked out.

We settled on using a bunch of tiny bandages to suture it

closed. "Hopefully, that works. I don't think it will show or bleed on the clothes," Neve said.

Then it was on to the dresses.

Two hours, ten outfits, and two bottles of champagne later, Neve was on the floor cracking up at something Jeannette had said, and Jaxson's bedroom was strewn with tissue paper, bags, and makeup.

Maybe this would make him think twice about getting me my own apartment.

Slightly tipsy, I giggled as I sucked in and zipped up a red silk dress that fit me like a glove. So far, I'd selected a silver tulle number and a slightly more modest black gown as potential options for tonight.

I definitely shouldn't have eaten linguine alfredo for lunch, I thought as I adjusted the satiny fabric over my hips and turned to face the bathroom mirror.

Holy tits. Literally. The plunging neckline and embroidered lace panels that hugged my hips accentuated my curves. I turned to examine my derriere and smiled at the open back.

Hussy, my wolf said.

Maybe. But when else would I have a chance to wear a—I glanced at the tag, *Vera Wang*—dress and feel like a million bucks?

I stepped out of the bathroom, and Neve and Jeannette's laughter cut off.

"Holy fates, Savannah." Neve stood up and strode around me. "I think we found the winner."

"You don't think it's too much?" I'd never worn anything like this before, and though trying it on in the bedroom with the girls was one thing, wearing it in public was another. Butterflies —or the bubbles from the champagne—churned in my stomach. What was Jaxson going to think?

I'm pretty sure I have an idea, my wolf chirped.

"This dress was *made* for you. But...it's missing the most important part." Neve scooped up a black shoebox from beside the bed and shot me a wicked grin. "Jaxson had Jeanette pick these up."

Huh? Why the hell would Jaxson have ordered shoes for me?

Because you're a hobo, Wolfie answered.

Heat rushed up my neck as I flipped the box open and pushed the turquoise tissue paper aside. Oh. My. God.

My heart skipped two beats, and I froze as I gazed down at the gorgeous pink platform heels I'd fallen in love with the day Jaxson had taken me to buy my magic boots.

Jeannette grabbed my arm and peered into the box, her eyes bulging. "The newest line from Andrea Todorova? You *lucky girl.*"

Jaxson had remembered that day and bought these for me.

Something stirred in my chest, and I suddenly felt flushed and breathless. I set the box down and rushed into the bathroom. Leaning on the white marble sink, I splashed water over my face and breathed in and out slowly. Why was I freaking out? It was just a nice pair of shoes, that's all.

Because there are definitely strings attached, Wolfie said.

"You okay?" Neve asked, stepping into the bathroom.

"Yup. Just a little nervous about tonight. I haven't been to a fancy party before. I wish you were going."

Neve handed me a bottle of water. "You'll be fine. Jaxson and Damian will be there. They know how to navigate."

Damian, I had no doubt. But I hadn't really thought of Jaxson that way. He was so rugged and down to earth. I knew he had political connections—hell, he owned half of Dockside— but he seemed more fitted to a truck than a tux.

Surprised the Wolf King might have a different side? The waitress sure does.

I looked at myself again in the mirror as my stomach twisted. *I hope I do.*

Neve stepped up holding my new pink pumps. I glanced down at my red dress and frowned. "Unfortunately, I'm going to need to pick a different dress to wear with those shoes."

"They'll be perfect. Trust me, I know shoes." She laughed and slipped my feet into them. Maybe she knew shoes, but was Neve colorblind?

As soon as they were on my feet, I glanced down and gasped. They felt like walking on clouds, but more importantly, the leather on them began shifting its color, like a chameleon changing its skin, until the pumps matched the red of my dress.

My jaw dropped, and I looked to Neve and Jeannette. "They change?"

Jeanette looked personally offended and frowned. "They're Todorova heels. What did you expect?"

Neve laughed. "They feel good, right? They're magic. Not only can you run in them like sneakers, but they change color to match whatever outfit you're wearing."

Holy hell. "I might never take them off."

"You'd better not," Jeannette said enviously.

They spent the next half hour doing my hair and makeup.

Jaxson had returned in the meantime, and I heard the shower down the hall running. A fluttery feeling filled my chest, and my mouth went dry. I was beginning to see the softer, kinder Jaxson beneath that hard exterior, and I liked it.

Jeannette finished with my mascara and stepped back, admiring her work with apparent satisfaction. I glanced at myself in the mirror, and a smile spread over my lips. She'd put beach waves in my hair, and my smoky eye makeup made my eyes pop. Subtle yet sophisticated. I looked like a freaking movie star.

The doorbell rang.

Neve glanced at me in the mirror. "Ready for the ball?"

In this dress and these pumps? I was ready to slay.

Neve was right, I thought as I sauntered down the stairs. These heels were like walking on freaking clouds.

Damian and Jaxson stepped into the room, their gazes falling on us. I inhaled sharply as Jaxson tracked my movement like a predator, pupils dilated, assessing me carefully. He wore a dark charcoal three-piece suit that accentuated his broad shoulders and slim waist, his five o'clock shadow adding to the alluring effect.

Now that's a Werewolf King.

"You clean up nicely," I said awkwardly as I stepped up to him, sure that he could hear my heart thudding against my ribs.

His eyes fell to my lips "So do you. I'm going to have to keep a tight leash on you tonight."

A deep, aching need flashed through me.

"Mm," I said, like tasting a delicious dish. My eyes went wide as soon as the sound was out of my mouth.

His chest rose rapidly as he sucked in air, and I could smell the heady mixture of desire, possessiveness, and something else.

"Thanks for the shoes," I blurted. "I love them."

"It's nothing. You needed shoes."

Neve's voice startled me back to my senses. "Are we all set?"

Damian nodded. "A car will pick us up from the portal to take us to Alejandro's. Unfortunately, according to my source, he always watches the attendees from his balcony but never mingles."

"So how do we talk to him?" I asked.

"Sometimes, he grants audiences to people who acquire a favorite object of his. The showpiece tonight is an enchanted sapphire and diamond brooch that once belonged to the Romanovs. I'm guessing Alejandro will be keeping a close eye on that sale. That's how we'll reel him in."

The Romanovs, like Anastasia? Man, the price of that would be staggering. Was it Damian's intention to buy the brooch just to help us out?

Apparently, he owed Jaxson a *mighty* big favor.

"What if we don't catch his eye?" I asked.

"Then we do things the hard way." Damian cast Jaxson a knowing look and drew a folded set of blueprints from his pocket, which he then unfolded. "We steal it."

40

Jaxson

We emerged from the Magic Side portal onto a stone platform overlooking an open, shrubby landscape.

"What is this place?" Savannah asked, her voice lost in wonder as she slowly turned and took in the sprawling ancient complex.

"Cañada de la Virgen," Damian said.

But the ruins meant nothing to me. I couldn't take my eyes off her in that fucking red dress as she turned. It hugged her curves too closely and made me want to devour every inch of her.

At last, I forced my gaze away from the woman to assess the scene. We stood on the highest platform of a step pyramid, illuminated by the warm glow of the fading light. Our vantage point revealed that the whole complex was oriented east to west, to the rising and setting sun.

"It must be ancient," Savannah said, her voice tinged with awe.

Damian smiled. "It's an astronomical complex that was built

by the Otomi peoples fifteen hundred years ago. We're standing on the House of the Thirteen Heavens."

"I've never seen anything like it. I mean, I've only left the States twice."

"You should visit when you're not trying to shake down a vampire." Damian laughed. "The place is actually a tourist attraction, though the park is closed to visitors after three p.m. That allows Magica to use the portal undetected as long as we arrange it ahead of time with the landowners. This way, now. The car should be waiting."

Damian headed down the long stone staircase. It descended to a sunken patio covered in sparse grass and surrounded by raised walls and another staircase at the opposite end.

Savannah glanced at me quickly and followed.

With her red hair flowing over her pale shoulders and her crimson dress clinging to her hips, she was like the setting sun, yet more captivating by far.

I gave a low growl and followed, not liking how easily she ensnared my mind.

Shrubby trees and newly sprouted grass covered the sprawling landscape. A black limousine with tinted windows pulled down a dirt road. We couldn't have been more out of place if we'd tried.

The limo wound through old roads until fifteen minutes later, we entered the small town of San Miguel de Allende. Historic buildings in various hues of red and orange lined the cobblestone streets. It was a wonder how the driver navigated through the narrow thoroughfares.

At last, we came to a stop in front of a deep russet mansion. Not just a mansion, I reminded myself, but a *vampire's lair*.

A man in a tuxedo stepped up and helped Savannah out of the limo. I drank her in as her dress slid over her skin.

The man in a tuxedo noticed the alluring effect as well.

Jealously flared within me—that, and doubt.

Parading her in front of a vampire *dressed like that* was probably a bad idea. Werewolves were already after her for her blood. And while most vampires were civilized, they were all blood addicts. It would be like offering a crack addict coke on a silver platter.

She shouldn't have come along.

I glared at the man in the tux and, taking her arm, I leaned into her ear. "I want you to stay close to me tonight."

What I meant was, *If someone touches you, I'll gut them.*

Her fiery beauty and unconscious flirtations had a way of bringing out my murderous side, and once unleashed, there was no telling what would happen.

More men in tuxedos escorted us through a pair of carved wooden doors that opened into an ornate reception area with a double staircase and central dome. The place was bustling with pretentiously dressed men and women, who pretended not to watch us as we came in. Most of them were Magica, but a few didn't have signatures, which meant they were humans. An interesting and potentially problematic mix.

Damian checked us in with the auction organizer while I scanned the space, memorizing the exits and the guards who patrolled the balconies of the second floor.

"For your convenience." A young man in a double-breasted tuxedo handed Savannah and me a silver phone-sized tablet. "Please enter your financial information. If you see an item that strikes your interest tonight, simply select it and enter your bid."

I grunted and scrolled through the items for sale. A surprising collection of art objects *and* people.

Savannah tensed as she examined the auction listings, and I could sense the bitter tang of her sudden shock and outrage. "There are people on the menu."

Despite all that she'd experienced over the last month, she was naïve and far too innocent.

I gestured to the artists working around the reception hall. "Contracts, I'm guessing."

Though I suspected some might be more than that.

We passed through a hall lined with Greco-Roman statues that led to an open-air garden surrounded by a candlelit portico covered in vines. The place was flamboyant and ostentatious.

I could only imagine how conceited Rivera had to be to live in a place like this.

"It's gorgeous," Savannah muttered, eyes lingering on the fountain in the center of the garden.

"I think you mean garish," I said, scanning the guests.

She shrugged. "I like what I like."

I gave a noncommittal grunt. We couldn't be more different, and yet, something kept pulling me to her—more than just the power of our mate bond. A taste of all the things I couldn't be. Impetuous. Free. Completely herself and uncorrupted.

"Ladies and gentlemen!" a voice boomed from above, drawing my gaze to a second level balcony where a man in a black suit scanned the garden like a lion. *Alejandro Rivera.*

The asshole was just as I'd imagined.

The bloodsucker wore a flashy smile and tailored linen suit, the top three buttons of his shirt left open to reveal his muscled chest. Rings adorned the hand he rested on the stone railing, and his manicured nails and gelled curls screamed pomp.

A pretty brunette hung off his arm like the year's newest fashion accessory, and more groupies hovered behind.

Everything about him and the entire place revolted me.

"Welcome to my home, my friends. *Please* make yourselves comfortable and enjoy the refreshments while you peruse the pieces and people on sale tonight. The auction will begin at the top of the hour, and as always, I promise this night will be one to remember."

For one moment, before he turned away, his eyes rested on us. But I knew it wasn't me he was looking at. His gaze was lecherous and made me want to throttle him.

I grabbed a glass of tequila from a passing waiter and downed it while Damian broke off to find the brooch.

"Nervous?" Savannah raised her brows as she took a sip of champagne. Several men around us were watching her closely, and the scent of their lust burned in my throat. My muscles tensed.

"I'm eager to get what we came for and to get you out of here," I said as I felt the heat of the room's eyes on her.

What Alejandro noticed, *everyone* noticed.

My wolf struggled in my chest.

Savannah's eyes dilated, and I knew she'd sensed the change in my signature. She gave me a sly grin. "What are you worried about, Jaxson? Alejandro? Or the other men?"

And why shouldn't I be?

My mate was a feast for the eyes. Fiery and beautiful, and more than any man could tame. But she hadn't accepted our bond and did whatever she wanted, unpredictable as an autumn leaf on the wind.

I couldn't stand being so close to her and not having her.

"You are my mate, and my wolf is the jealous type." I stepped closer, pressing my hand to her lower back, causing a shiver to work down her spine. Blood flushed her cheeks, while for me, it travelled somewhere else.

Almost instantly, she clamped down the overwhelming scents of her delight and arousal and fixed me with an iron stare. "I'm not yours, Jaxson. I am my own."

She tilted her glass back to down the last of her drink, and the pale skin on her exposed throat drew me helplessly in. "You have no more claim on me than anyone here. Now, I'm going to go look at the things that *are* available for sale."

With that, she snatched another glass from the waiter and pushed into the crowd.

41

Savannah

My head buzzing with champagne, I moved through the dizzying crowd. I could still feel Jaxson's gaze burning into my spine as I wound through the huddles of ritzy guests.

I was desperate to put some distance between us so that I could peruse the *goods* for sale in peace and quiet without having to bask in the jealous glow of an overly possessive wolf.

Greek statues, mosaic panels with erotic scenes, what I assumed was Renaissance artwork, and clusters of ancient objects...perhaps plundered artifacts?

I tried to memorize the more suspicious objects, as well as the faces of the people bidding on them, to take back to Neve.

My third glass of champagne didn't help, and I decided I'd better slow down.

The most bizarre part of the auction was the *people*. Alejandro had somehow acquired various artists and performers who were dispersed throughout the garden on display. A violinist with a current bid of thirty-seven grand was playing in the corner of the room.

As I stepped onto the portico, I glanced over my shoulder.

Jaxson was surrounded by women, as if he were on auction. A beautiful brunette in a cream corset dress had sidled up to his side—the same one I'd seen earlier hanging on Alejandro up on the balcony.

She dragged her manicured finger over Jaxson's chest, a sly grin tugging at her painted lips. Jaxson was smiling and talking to her like she was an old acquaintance.

Is he trying to get a meeting with Alejandro or sampling the wares?

A flicker of jealousy burned through my chest, stopping me in my tracks as my claws slipped out. I dug my fingers into my palms to hide my transformation.

I knew it was irrational.

Hell, I'd left him standing there because he'd made it obnoxiously clear that I was *his*, whether either of us liked it or not.

Even so, anger and irritation blazed through me like a wildfire. My eyes locked on a woman beside me who was all but drooling over him.

"See anything you like?" I hissed.

She gave me a wicked smile. "As a matter of fact, yes."

I showed her my fangs, and she immediately scurried to the other side of the room.

Rather than watch the feeding frenzy, I hurried back to the main hall.

Alejandro was still on his balcony, watching the proceedings intently. Business was brisk, and I suspected that at least a dozen pieces of art had already been sold, as they'd been taken down.

Hoping to clear my head, I strolled over to a painter who was seated in front of an easel near the central fountain.

The silver tablet I'd been given glowed when I stepped near, and the artist's starting bid pulsed across the screen: *fifty thousand dollars.* I wasn't sure I was ready to contemplate the implications of that.

The artist was middle-aged, dressed in a green linen tunic and pants, and seated on an ornately carved stool with a canvas bag full of art supplies propped next to it.

He dragged a sweeping stroke of shimmering blue paint across the white canvas. The paint soaked into the material, and then, like water seeping through a cracked landscape, the color snaked across the painting, moving in animated rivers. Picking up another brush, he dipped the tip in a deep red paint and touched the edge of the canvas. The color wrapped around the blue, spreading across the page like blood seeping from an open wound...

"How do you do that?" I blurted, in awe of the beauty.

The artist turned and looked me up and down slowly. "I don't think you'd appreciate the finer points."

"Try me," I growled, and he sat back in surprise.

"Steady on, Savannah," Damian chuckled from behind.

I turned and brushed aside my hair. "Hey. Any luck?"

He passed me a note. "Unfortunately, no. It seems Alejandro is not coming down tonight, nor is he interested in speaking with us."

I unfolded the note to reveal a message scrawled in red ink. *Dear Damian, please, visit us again next month. Perhaps we can talk then. Bring Nevaeh. I'm sure she'd be interested in many of the items on offer.*

My stomach sank. It was a put-on. Alejandro was having a laugh.

"Jaxson is speaking with some of the shifters here to see if they have any connections, but I'm not hopeful. Vampires and shifters tend to be a combustible combination."

We didn't have time to wait a month to speak to Alejandro, if it was even a real invitation. Dragan was out there, and only the fates knew what he was up to.

The low pulse of panic began to throb in my veins. "So what do we do?"

Damian pitched his voice low, sending vibrations along my skin. "I'm afraid we might have to go with plan B. You stay and mingle, and I'm going to have a look around the grounds to see if I can find the access point to his vaults."

With that, Damian moved off quickly into the crowd.

Shit.

Well, I sure as hell wasn't going to just stand around looking at art while the men tried to flirt and sneak their way to a solution.

Moreover, with all the guards around, I was liking plan B less and less. Damian might have a reputation as a brilliant thief, but Alejandro had cut off Dragan's finger for trying to steal from him.

I didn't want us to end up in the same predicament.

The irony would kill me.

Minutes later, my heels clicked on the floor as I moved across the central room at the reception where we'd entered.

The two guards at the bottom of the double staircase stared at me gruffly, the closest one adjusting his grip on the gun slung over his chest. I painted on my most charming smile but could immediately smell their suspicion and the restrained violence masked by their casual stances.

Nope. Hard pass. *Maybe* I'd try a back entrance. There had to be another way upstairs.

Feigning drunkenness, I swayed a little before turning around and stumbling back down the hall. It seemed to work because the scent of their suspicion quickly turned to distaste.

As soon as I was out of sight, I hurried the other way. I passed a few locked doors, silently cursing, and was about to give up when I noticed a lonely guard standing watch at the end of the hall.

He didn't look more than eighteen, and his eyes dragged over my body as I sashayed toward him.

If Jack-ass-son was going to give me a hard time for looking good and smiling, I might as well use it to my best advantage.

I pressed my hand to my chest and hurried over. "Oh, my goodness, I'm glad I found someone in this maze of a place. I was wondering if you could help me with something."

His brown eyes twinkled with interest and desire, and he swallowed hard. "Of course. How can I, uh, assist you?"

"Wonderful. I've been running all over, but haven't found anyone competent at all." I glanced up at him through lowered lids and flashed him a coquettish smile. "I travelled all the way here from Chicago, and well, I was hoping to make Alejandro's acquaintance, but it seems he won't be coming down tonight. Is there any way that you could arrange a meeting for me?"

He shifted with unease, glancing down the hall behind me before smiling awkwardly. "I'm afraid that's not possible. Mr. Rivera only meets with guests or artists by appointment."

Artists? I could do that. Time for a bit of bluffing.

"Of course. My name is Savannah Caine. I'm sure he's heard of me. A number of my pieces have created a bit of a stir in the Chicago scene as of late. I'd really like to discuss my latest work with him before it goes on show next week, but there was just no way for me to arrange an appointment."

A little embarrassed at the ruse, I took a tip from the bitch in the garden and traced my finger over the guard's chest. "I'm sure you could make that possible."

A rosy blush spread over his tanned features like the magic paint on the artist's canvas. "Of course, Ms. Caine. Let me send word up to him, if you'll wait one minute."

He disappeared around the corner and spoke in hushed voices with another guard, who eyed me suspiciously. Two minutes later, he returned with an apologetic expression on his face.

"I'm sorry, Ms. Caine, but Mr. Rivera does not see anyone without a prior appointment. No exceptions."

I was tempted to press the matter, but I knew it would be fruitless. The other guard's expression was all iron and malice. Suddenly, he started toward me, suspicion burning in his eyes.

Making my exit as quickly as possible, I headed back to the garden as frustration tore me apart.

I was certain that if we could just speak to Alejandro, the brooding vampire would be sympathetic. Dragan had robbed him, after all. The only thing better than vengeance was vengeance twice over.

We just had to find a way to get his attention.

Temples throbbing, I glanced up at the vampire on his high balcony. I wasn't used to mingling with rich folk, but I could read people well. Alejandro Rivera was a king in his castle, and as far as he was concerned, we were peasants groveling for his entertainment.

At that moment, the king was leaning forward over the railing, intently watching the artist in the green smock paint. That hack with the magic brushes had the best position in the entire place, directly in Alejandro's line of sight.

My fingers flexed.

It was time to get noticed.

42

Savannah

I slowly circled the edge of the garden, subtly calling my magic, while watching the painter in the green smock. Though I'd concealed cars and people with clouds of shadow, and even made myself a shadow dress once, my plan would take fine control like I'd never used before.

I made a couple wisps of shadows slink across the painting and disappear.

The artist paused and looked around. As soon as he returned to painting, I did it again.

He stopped and rubbed his eyes.

After another few seconds, I did it a third time, letting the shadows crawl over him. I left a wisp clinging over his left eye like a veil, partially obscuring his vision.

With a yelp, he stood and began looking around wildly. The poor bastard probably thought he was going blind, but considering what an asshole he'd been, the trick didn't bother me.

He rubbed his eyes again, then headed to the bathroom in a panic.

As soon as he was gone, I rushed over, pulled his painting off the easel, and put up a new canvas.

Instantly, I could feel Alejandro's gaze boring into my back like an auger.

Showtime.

Before I could pick up my brush, a firm hand locked onto my arm, and the smoky scent of pine and earth and heat bombarded me, followed by a familiar growl that pebbled my skin. I stilled and met Jaxson's penetrating gaze.

"What the hell are you doing?" Anger rippled through his shoulders, and though his voice was calm and measured, it was laced with an underlying warning.

I pulled my arm free and tilted my chin up to him. "Getting a meeting with the vampire."

"What?" Jaxson grunted, his eyes challenging me. "This wasn't part of the plan."

"The bid on the brooch isn't working. Alejandro isn't biting. While you were busy making eyes at that woman in the garden, I decided to improvise."

Jaxson's nostrils flared, and his eyes momentarily dropped to my mouth. "*Making eyes?* What the fuck do you mean by that? I was working my connections."

"You were working *something*," I snapped.

As soon as the words left my mouth, I blushed, feeling like a jealous teenager throwing baseless accusations at the hot guy she had a crush on.

I could feel the outrage emanating off him—an intoxicating cocktail of jealousy and frustration and desire. What the hell was it that made me want to push his buttons, even at a time like this?

You want him.

Screw that.

I brushed my hair out of my eyes. "Look, Jaxson, that was off base, and I'm sorry. But I think this can get his attention."

"Hijacking an easel? That's going to get his attention for sure and get us kicked out."

I met his furious gaze with pleading eyes. "I have a feeling about this. Just trust me. Can you do that?"

He worked his jaw in frustration, then looked around. "All right. But if this goes south, we're out of here."

I nodded, dabbed my brush in the paint, and squeezed my eyes shut, trying to calm my mind. It didn't work. Jaxson was looming over me, his signature practically shouting at me with desire and frustration. A flurry of heat rose between my thighs, and I had to grit my teeth against the shiver that purred through me.

I opened my eyes and gestured with the brush. "You're distracting. Stand back and make sure no one tries to haul me out of here—particularly a guy in a green smock."

Jaxson glared and stepped away, and I turned back to the terrifyingly blank canvas.

What the hell was I going to do?

I had to create a painting that would *demand* Alejandro's attention, and fast. Unfortunately, I didn't have a clue what kind of art he liked, and if the pieces he was auctioning were any indication, then his tastes were wildly eclectic.

We only shared one thing in common.

Dragan.

I took a deep breath to steady my nerves and looked around. People were beginning to take notice.

Jaxson gave me a nod. Somehow, the simple movement spoke volumes: *Do it. I trust you.*

I gave him a thankful smile and turned back to the canvas.

All I had to do was earn that trust. Unfortunately, I had no idea how to paint—I'd really only worked with pencils and ink.

With no other options, I dipped the brush in black and began to sketch with it like a pen as best I could.

There was no time for grace or subtlety. I had to work fast, before the man in the green smock returned. Before the guards took notice and threw us out.

I let the memories flow through me and slashed at the canvas. Each stroke was like the strike of a knife, driven by fury and hatred.

I was here because of Dragan. He haunted my dreams and waking life and sent wolves and demons to hunt me. He'd drained my blood and even tried to cut out my soul.

Fuck him.

Paint flowed like blood across the canvas as my fury rose, and my breath became ragged. Everything, *everything* was Dragan's fault.

My trance broke when I fumbled the brush from my aching hand.

How much time had passed?

Suddenly self-conscious, I sat back and looked around. I was surrounded by richly dressed men and women with shocked expressions. There were guards, but Jaxson stood by my side like a bouncer, challenging anyone to lay a finger on me.

I turned to my painting and finally took in the image I'd created. Horror skated across my skin, and my shoulders jerked as a cold darkness settled into my bones. The canvas held a memory that had been seared into my brain.

The moment I'd ripped Dragan's soul from Kahanov's body.

It was etched on white with brutal strokes of pigment.

The snaking vines of the cave in Forks moved across the page, reaching out, threatening to drag me into the earth. Blood dripped from the wound in Kahanov's chest where I'd sunk the Soul Knife. A combination of agony and madness cut across his face as his mouth twisted in anguish.

But it was the image of Dragan that drew the breath from my lungs.

His specter seemed to rise from the page, his crazed eyes fastened on me with a hatred so deep, I trembled. It was like I could feel his fingers raking across my skin, hear his voice reaching through my memories.

I will have my vengeance.

"My God. Are you part of the auction?" A woman's voice with a heavy accent startled me back to the present.

"What?" I took a shaky breath, gazing up at the couple who were frowning at me.

"Are you for sale?" a man answered, his voice tinged with irritation. "I *must* have you for my collection."

For sale? Rage burned behind my eyes. *Who the fuck were these monsters?*

"No, I'm not," I snapped as I stood and looked up to the balcony.

Alejandro Rivera gazed back with piercing eyes. Even from across the garden, I could sense his emotions.

Curiosity. Want. Desire.

"Gotcha," I whispered.

Prickles spread across my exposed skin as a tingling coldness swept over my senses. The smell of pinot noir with earthy undertones of spice. It was the strangest thing...like the vampire was reaching out to me with his signature. How?

A wave of fury and possessiveness drowned everything out, and I turned to Jaxson. His honey-gold eyes were locked on Alejandro and filled with hate.

Great.

Before I could open my mouth, the looming vampire began to slowly applaud, each clap echoing off the towering walls. "Bring it to me."

I looked back to Jaxson, who gave me an approving nod. I

stood and hefted my horrific painting off the easel and headed for the stairs with my alpha in tow.

My entire body quaked with terror and relief. It had actually worked.

When we got to a narrow staircase, the guard stopped and looked between Jaxson and me. "I'm sorry, but Mr. Rivera is only interested in speaking to the artist."

"Where she goes, I go," Jaxson growled, letting his signature flare.

The guard shrank back, averting his eyes from the grouchy beast beside me.

I looped my arm around Jaxson's, trying to calm him. "What he means is, he's my muse. Didn't you see him inspiring me before I began my work? I'm sure Mr. Rivera won't mind."

Still terrified of Jaxson, the guard nodded meekly and melted away.

I passed my painting to Jaxson, then headed up the winding stairs with him just behind me.

My heart was pounding, and I was so tense, I feared my knees would seize up.

Jaxson put his hand on my back as we ascended. "So far, so good. You've got this, Savannah."

Heat crept along my bare back where his fingers traced my skin. I shivered with delight as Jaxson's presence exploded around me, pulling me into his orbit.

A little of the terror drained away. Finally, something was going to plan—well, at least going according to improvised plan C.

43

The stairs led to a dimly lit room decorated with floral tapestries and abstract artwork on the walls. Long-stemmed candles burned from the antique chandelier that hung from the ceiling, casting flickering shadows across the space. It was all very tasteful except for the weapons and chains interspersed among the paintings.

I sucked in a slow breath, hoping it would help calm my nerves.

The soft click of a door opening and closing whispered from an adjoining space.

A blur whipped into the room, and suddenly, Alejandro was there before me, pressing a kiss to the back of my hand. His signature of wine and earth tingled across my skin, and his kiss sent a shiver up my arm.

I blinked twice.

Holy *shit*, he was fast.

"Ms. Caine," the vampire whispered in a sultry voice, "so nice to meet you. I must confess, I was not aware of your work an hour ago, but it seems I have been terribly ignorant."

For a second, Alejandro sniffed, and his eyes dilated, but they quickly returned to normal.

"Rivera," Jaxson said, his expression blazing with barely restrained fury. "We've been looking forward to speaking with you."

The vampire released my hand and regarded Jaxson with disdain. He turned back to me. "Who is he? A model? I should be rather amused to see you paint him in the nude. Your work is filled with so much anger, I imagine you could capture his bestial nature quite well."

Jaxson started to move, but I braced him in place with my arm, and he clamped his jaws shut.

My mind raced faster than it ever had before.

By now, Alejandro had to know exactly who we were but not why we were here. He was baiting Jaxson deliberately. Clearly, this was a game, and I didn't know the rules, but I *did* know that if Jaxson wolfed out, we wouldn't get what we wanted.

I didn't have a presence like Jaxson, but I tried to push calming energy to him and lightly traced my fingers over his skin. "This is my muse, Jaxson Laurent, the Dockside alpha. He's inspired the most incredible transformation in my work."

Recognition dawned on the vampire's face as he poured three glasses of amber liquor. "*Laurent*," he purred. "From France?"

Jaxson freed his arm from mine. "Originally, yes."

"Fascinating." In a blur, he moved to a crystal decanter set on a mahogany cabinet along the back wall.

Alejandro returned and handed Jaxson and me each a glass, his fingers brushing mine. In another blur of movement, he disappeared and reappeared holding his raised glass. "Cheers to meeting new friends."

I sniffed my glass, noting the sweet, spicy aroma of the

tequila. Not wanting to offend our host, I glanced at Jaxson and took a sip.

Alejandro gestured to the painting tucked under Jaxson's other arm. "May I?"

Jaxson handed it over, and Alejandro raised the canvas to the light. "So much darkness. So much hatred. So much power. Two men, twisted in pain. One mortal and dying, the other dead and seeking new life."

Alejandro strolled over to the coffee table arranged between a set of antique couches and high-back chairs and placed the painting against the wall. "I love it. And it's strange, but I almost recognize this man. I feel like I know him."

"You do," I replied. "Victor Dragan."

The vampire's eyes dilated. "Indeed, I did. And what inspired this choice of subject?"

The terrible memories of that vile cave assaulted my mind. My hands began trembling, and I had to set my glass down. Fuck, I needed therapy.

Jaxson's hand slipped to my back, his touch sending warmth and calm through me.

Alejandro watched me intently as I swallowed. "Because I was there. I shoved the knife into the first man and cut Dragan's soul out of him."

The vampire gave me a ruthless smile. "I admire your dedication to your art. And tell me, what inspired you to paint this piece in the midst of *my* fucking auction?"

Instantly, the temperature of the room dropped.

Trepidation fluttered in my stomach, but I pushed on. "You have his finger, and we want to borrow it."

Alejandro tilted his head back and laughed deeply. He wiped a tear from the corner of his eye and smiled. "Even if I did have such a thing, what makes you think I would give it to you?"

"We'll make it worth your time," Jaxson snarled.

The vampire sipped his drink, looking bored. "Hmm. I doubt it. I only trade in things that are priceless."

"Dragan is on a warpath and wants vengeance on all who've wronged him," I blurted. "We need his finger to cast a spell that will stop him from possessing others and keep him in the underworld. You can think of it as insurance."

"Insurance?" The vampire's eyes rounded with surprise, and he snorted. "Against what?"

"You cut off his finger. Once he's extracted vengeance on those who killed him, I imagine you'll be next."

Alejandro tapped his ring against his glass. "Perhaps, perhaps not."

My gaze flicked to Jaxson. "There must be something we can offer?"

The vampire's eyes dilated again, and he flashed me a lewd grin. "I'd say a drink of your blood might settle it."

My heart stilled. *Of course.*

Instinctively, I glanced down at my chest. A dark stain had seeped into the halter of the dress.

Goddamn it.

Jaxson stepped forward protectively. "Not a chance."

"Well, then"—Alejandro shrugged and pressed a button on his desk—"no deal. Please see yourselves out."

A door opened, and three thugs in suits stepped in.

Great. Negotiations were over.

"Let's go." Jaxson took my hand and all but dragged me toward the door before I could process what was happening.

"Good luck on your quest to stop Dragan," Alejandro remarked. "I do hope you succeed. He truly was a foul creature."

I slammed my platform heels down and tore free of Jaxson's grip. "There must be something else."

Alejandro shook his head pityingly. "That finger is a warning to anyone who tries to fuck with me—which raises the question, why are you trying my patience? Get out!"

Jaxson pulled me, but I resisted with all my strength, and shouted, "A drop!"

Alejandro froze, eyes locked in like laser sights, and I broke out of Jaxson's arms before he could drag me away.

Jaxson reached for me, but the vampire raised his hand, and the thugs pulled out their sidearms. "Silver bullets, Mr. Laurent. I would let the woman speak, lest they make you both bleed. Then there will be no holding me back."

Jaxson snarled.

I looked at him and gestured for him to calm down.

On the day I'd met her, my aunt had said, "First lesson you need to learn: never give your blood to anyone. On any account. Ever."

But this wasn't for sorcery or potions. This was a drink.

I turned back to the vampire. "I'll give you a drop from my finger. I'll make the cut myself and drip it in your glass."

He laughed. "That's nothing."

"Please. Five drops. Ten drops. I'll fill your damn cocktail glass. Help us defeat this bastard."

Alejandro leaned over and pressed his hands against the desk. "Let me make this clear: this is not a negotiation. I drink from the source. It's all or nothing."

"It's nothing," Jaxson growled, his eyes narrowing on me. "Don't do this, Savannah."

I stepped out of his reach, trying to keep our options alive. "Why do you even want my blood?" I asked Alejandro. "You have plenty of people dying for you to drain them."

The vampire inhaled deeply and sighed. "Because your blood is so wonderfully different than that of the others of your kind. I can smell the power flowing in your veins, Ms. Caine, like two dragons fighting for control. To tell you the truth, even with my age and strength, it is all I can do to hold myself back. If I were a younger man with less restraint, I would have just taken what I wanted."

"Touch her, and I'll rip your heart out," Jaxson growled deep and low, causing my skin to prickle. The scent of his rage and hatred billowed through the room, practically choking me.

"Now don't do anything stupid, Laurent, or I will have my men put a silver bullet in your heart and hers."

"We're leaving." Jaxson strode forward and grabbed my wrist, pulling me toward the door.

Alejandro laughed as we headed into the stairwell. "Hilarious. After all that, you must not wish to stop Dragan at all."

But I did. We both did, desperately. If we didn't get those bones, if Dragan succeeded in summoning the Dark Wolf God, he would leave Magic Side in ruins and steal the souls of our pack.

In comparison to that, what did a drink of my blood matter in the end? Hell, Casey had been with a vampire, and it looked like she'd taken a sizable bite out of him.

I ripped out of Jaxson's grip and stepped back into the room. "I'll do it. A two-second sip in exchange for Dragan's bones. Final offer."

44

Before I could move a muscle, Alejandro was at Savannah's neck. "You don't want me to make a mistake, do you, Jaxson?"

I froze. The bastard was far faster than I'd imagined.

Savannah's teeth were clenched and eyes wide. The vampire's fangs were at her pulsing jugular. I could feel her heartbeat and taste her fear.

"Let her go, or I'll ram my claws into your heart."

Savannah shifted in Alejandro's grasp. "Both of you, back off. I've made my decision. Alejandro gets a drink, we get the bones, and we get the fuck out of here to stop Dragan from bringing Armageddon down on Magic Side. Simple deal."

The horror of the situation twisted my mind. She was *mine*, and yet, she was going to willingly let this fucker violate her in front of me. Rage filled my thoughts until I could barely see. "You are my mate. Don't do this. It means more than you think."

"Since I came to Magic Side, people have been hunting me for my blood. This is a chance to do something useful with it. I'm doing this for the pack."

"Don't worry, Jaxson, I promise to be gentle," the vampire

purred as he moved her hair aside, exposing the pale flesh of her neck and causing her to flinch.

Fuck the bullets.

I lunged forward, but my roar was cut short as Alejandro became a blur, and something wrapped around my neck. My body whipped backward and slammed into the wall as silver chains wrapped around me, searing my skin.

Alejandro was at my side in an instant. "Meet my favorite restraints. The more you struggle, the tighter they'll become."

"What are you doing?" Savannah screamed at him.

"Putting your dog on a leash!" the vampire snarled, fangs out.

In an instant, Savannah had her Soul Knife out. "Let him go!"

The guards swung their weapons at her, and fear seized me. I pulled against the chains, but they only tightened, forcing my wrists and head back against the wall. I could feel my power draining rapidly into them, sapping my strength.

Alejandro raised his hand. "Nobody shoot. We're almost all civilized here."

"This wasn't the deal," Savannah snapped, keeping the blade between her and the vampire.

He was behind her in a blur of movement. Before she could react, he shoved her against the wall and pinned her knife hand back. "Then tell me, Savannah, what *was* our deal?"

Her heartbeat pounded through every inch of my body, and the taste of her terror seared my throat. I tried to shout, but it only came out as a strangled growl as the chains around my neck tightened sharply.

Eyes burning with rage, she hissed, "The deal was that you get a two-second drink, we get the bones, and then we get out of here. There was nothing about fucking silver chains or men with guns."

"Or daggers," he whispered against her neck. "Tell you what, I'll get rid of mine if you get rid of yours."

He ordered his guards out, and she reluctantly dismissed her knife.

She bared her teeth in defiance. "Now let Jaxson go."

"One drink, and you both walk away with what you came for. I promise. On my oath."

For a second, she met my eyes, then turned her head, exposing the pale skin of her neck. "Do it."

My wolf tore at my heart, demanding to be released. But it would fare no better against the silver chains than I had.

Alejandro brushed the hair from her neck. "Try to relax, Savannah, this shouldn't be painful. Honestly, most people absolutely love it. That's why it's all the rage."

"Just get it over with." She raised her chin confidently, but she refused to meet my eyes.

She gasped as Alejandro sank his fangs into her neck. Fury rolled through me, and my restraints clanged as I pulled against them—but the harder I fought, the stronger my bonds became until I was practically immobile.

She moaned, her eyes dilating with fear while she pressed her back against the wall. Alejandro groaned, his heady desire filling the room while he gently lapped at the blood spilling from her neck.

A guttural roar squeezed from my tightly bound throat as the scene before me burned into my mind.

Savannah's lids grew heavy, and she sighed, her body relaxing as she leaned back, giving herself over to the magic that coursed between them.

The sweet scent of her unavoidable desire mixing with his shattered my mind. My heart collapsed inward as despair crushed me tighter than any chain ever could.

Fight for our mate, my wolf snarled. *Kill. Take what is ours.*

"Savannah—" I choked out.

For a second, her eyes fluttered, and she tried to push Alejandro away, but he pinned her hands back, his eyes a deep and unnatural red.

Blood madness. Something only new vampires were said to get.

Alejandro sunk his fangs back into the side of her neck and began to drink viciously. The heat of her desire turned to pain and terror, and her eyes opened wide.

My claws extended, and fur erupted from my arms as my wolf surged inside me.

Our mate is in danger.

Blood rushed in my ears as something inside me snapped. A primal howl of rage released in my soul as new strength coursed through my veins—strength that I'd never had before. I surged against the chains, my fury dulling the pain digging into my wrists and neck. The silver devoured my strength as it poured forth, but my rage was unending and couldn't be contained.

A metallic crack sounded as a chain link snapped, and suddenly, I was free.

Alejandro was on me in a second, a red-eyed monster tearing into me with his fangs and claws.

I rammed him into the wall with a crack. He gasped and struggled free, but before he could escape, I gripped one of the loose chains, tore it from the wall, and wrapped it around his neck.

Alejandro hissed in fury with Savannah's blood still dripping from one corner of his mouth and staining his teeth. He surged to his feet and hurled his body into mine, sending us careening through the air.

My back crashed into the wall with a crunch, but I wrapped another length of the chain around the fucker's neck and pulled, the tension straining my muscles. His trachea was crushed, and though it wouldn't kill him, it would hurt like hell.

This was just the beginning of what I was going to do.

He struggled to dig his fingers under the chain, his face contorted in pain and fury. In a flash, he arched his back and flung himself forward to drag me down.

We flew into his desk, sending it to splinters. I was on my feet in seconds, driving my fist into his jaw with a crack. I slashed his chest with my claws, feeling the tug of his flesh as I shredded his suit.

Savannah hurled herself into him, ramming him into the wall. "Chain the bastard up!"

But he was too fast. In seconds, he stood across from Savannah with a demented grin spread across his face as he looked at her. "I will drink you dry."

She held out her blade. "Try it, and I'll cut out your soul."

Fuck.

Alejandro whipped around her, but I lunged left and clotheslined him with my arm, my elbow cracking from the force of the impact. He groaned and dropped to his back like a brick, and then I was on him, pinning him with one arm. With my other hand, I reached for the shattered remains of a vintage chair and snapped one of its legs off.

Alejandro grabbed my throat, and I raised the makeshift stake above his heart—

"Stop!" Savannah's voice boomed through the space, and she seized my arm.

I could hear her fear and distress, but it didn't matter. I could stop, but I knew from the madness in his eyes that Alejandro never would.

I had to protect my mate.

I tore my hand free of her grip and rammed the stake down.

45

Jaxson

"What the hell, Jaxson?" Savannah screamed as I stood, the fight completely drained out of me but my anger still fresh.

"This is on you." I threw the bloody stake to the side. "He would never have stopped. Just like the drugged-crazed bikers."

I did what needed to be done. I'd done far worse to protect my sister, once.

"You don't know that," she snapped, dismissing her knife.

"I do," I snarled, closing the distance between us in a single step. "The moment he had a taste, it wasn't enough. Couldn't you see the madness in his eyes, or were you too drunk with pleasure?"

She hauled back and slapped me. It was then that I noticed the bastard's bloody fang marks marring her neck.

Fire burned in my veins as rage and frustration strangled me. "I told you not to give yourself over to him. Why didn't you listen?"

She turned away. "We had a deal. I did it for the pack. Now he's dead, and we still don't have the finger bone, thanks to you.

It was all for nothing." Her voice was venom, and her body quaked with fury, which only added to mine.

"You shouldn't have let him drink your blood!" I roared, stepping up to her. "I would have rather ripped my arms from their sockets than stand by while he fed on you."

She backed away slowly. I was already walking a fine line between man and beast, and the way her fear and anger mixed with the intoxicating scent of her arousal was enough to drive me over the edge.

A knock sounded on the door. "Master Rivera, Mr. Bronte is ready for you."

Fuck.

Savannah dashed toward the door, Alejandro's blood staining her dress and arms. "Alejandro and I need a few more minutes," she said breathlessly. "Come back in ten?"

The man outside grunted but turned and left.

Savannah locked the door and turned to me. "Now what?"

I reined in my emotions and focused on the shitfest before us. I'd deal with Savannah later. While she glared daggers at me, I pulled out my phone and called Damian. "We have a problem."

"How big of a problem?" the fallen angel asked, his tone implying that he could guess.

It was all I could do to not shatter the phone in my hand. "Alejandro is dead, and we made a lot of noise. I figure this whole place is going to be on lockdown in about two minutes. Worse, we don't have the bone."

"Fuck. Then we need to get out before all hell breaks loose."

"Not without the bone. Have you found a way in?"

"I've identified the location of his vault. We'll have to hope the impending chaos will distract from a break-in. Are you sure you want to try this?"

"Yes," I growled. Everything depended on that now.

"Meet me in the back of the garden." He hung up.

I glanced at Savannah, who'd surely heard the conversation, and tensed. She was rubbing the bite on her neck. Images of Alejandro licking her throat pummeled me. I strode up to her, boxing her in against the door. "This conversation between us isn't over."

"Agreed," she said defiantly, though her voice was shaking. "This is neither the time nor place. Now how the hell do we get out of here looking like this?"

She motioned to our bloodstained clothes. We'd have a dozen guards on us instantly if we took the stairs.

"The window," I said, as I lifted a dresser and dropped it in front of the door with a thud. "This should buy us some time."

"Shit." She stepped around Alejandro's body, looking away in revulsion. "At least we don't have to worry about him cutting off our fingers. Or selling people."

"Don't mention that fucker again. *Ever*," I growled.

Savannah narrowed her eyes at me and crossed to the window. I shoved it open and helped her out. She hitched up her dress, dug her claws into the stone, and scrambled down the wall.

With a final glare at the vampire's corpse, I climbed out and dropped to the garden below.

Guards were posted at the windows, so Savy wove shadows to help obscure us from view as we dashed through the well-manicured plants.

"Jaxson," Damian whispered from the darkness. "Over here."

He was waiting by a foliage-hidden hall at the back of the building.

"What the hell happened to you two?" he asked once he saw our bloody clothes.

"Savannah took things into her own hands," I growled, ignoring the way her body tensed with anger.

Damian held up his hand as a guard appeared around a

corner and stopped in front of a door. The guard punched some buttons into a keypad, waited, and then turned and left.

"Let's go." He slipped into the hall.

Savannah stepped around me and grabbed my arm. "We'll deal with your drama later, Jax, but right now, we focus on getting the damn fingerbone and staying alive. Got it?"

I glared at her and growled again. She was right, though. My mind and body wanted to rage, but we needed to focus on the task at hand if we were going to survive this party. "Stay close to me. And if I give you an order, you listen. Got it?"

"I'll try." Flashing me a look that could kill, she turned and headed toward Damian.

The door was made of solid steel, and the magic from its enchantments zinged the air around us.

"We have fourteen minutes before the guard checks the vault again." Damian moved his hands in an arc, and a series of glowing runes appeared in the air. Like moving pieces on a chess board, he rearranged the symbols by touching and dragging them into position. I'd seen him do this once, and I'd heard rumors that he could *sense* objects like a Seeker.

"Then we move quickly," I said.

The runes flickered and disappeared, and the door opened with a *snick*. I started my watch timer, and Savannah and I slipped through as Damian nodded and shut the door behind us.

Sweet citrus incense burned my nostrils. We descended a narrow set of stairs into a rock-hewn room lit by golden flames that licked out of dagger-like sconces arranged along the walls. Tendrils of steam rose from a central pool of dark water, wafting over the walkways on either side like fog.

Savannah paused and shuddered. "Are those bats?"

I followed her gaze to the ceiling, where I counted at least a dozen large creatures hanging motionless in the corner. A devilish cross between a bat and a monster, their feet were all claws, and two single talons adorned the edges of their wings.

"Something like that," Damian whispered. "Let's not find out."

She nodded and started around the pool, moving quietly, then hissed, "Shit!" and staggered as her left leg bowed. I caught her waist before she landed on her knees, but something rolled off the walkway into the pool.

Plunk.

"Damn." She felt around the steam that covered the floor and picked something up. She glanced over her shoulder at me, fear flashing in her eyes. "A bone. It looks like...part of a femur. Human?"

A few squeaks, and then the fluttering of wings reverberated above us.

I shoved her forward. "Go!"

Sharp pain sliced my shoulder blades as a heavy weight landed on my back. Reaching around, I ripped the hellish creature off me, but not before it sunk its talons into my arm. I snapped its neck and cast it aside as another swooped in.

Damian plucked it from the air and slammed it into the wall, knocking it out cold.

Ahead of us, two creatures dove for Savannah. She ducked under one and swung the bone like a baseball bat, hitting the other and sending it careening into the pool.

She glanced over her shoulder at us as I noticed darkness snaking in from the walls. "Run! I'll draw my shadows."

We slipped around her into the hall ahead, slashing the wings of two more bats, while she drew the darkness. I'd seen her weave shadows many times now. With each attempt, her skill seemed to be growing. In seconds, the room behind was pitch black, the light from the sconces blanketed by her magic.

She stepped out of the dark, her lips pursed in worry when

her eyes landed on the blood dripping from the puncture wound in my arm. It was already healing.

The bats quieted in the other room.

A dozen chambers opened onto the hall, all barred with grated iron doors that buzzed with magic that allowed us to see inside.

Caged objects, prisoners as much as the artists in the auction.

Savannah peered inside several of the rooms. "Holy shit, he has a lot of stuff."

Dismay darkened my thoughts as I glanced inside the closest chamber. Stacked to the ceiling along all walls of the twenty-by-twenty-foot room were Mesoamerican antiquities—ceramic masks, stone sculptures, and a giant circular astronomical relief.

"Damian?" I growled, frustration edging into my voice. "Where is it?"

The fallen angel's signature pulsed, and he strode down the hall. For a moment, he hesitated, then stopped in front a door. "It's here. But it's going to take me a while to get in. A word of advice: don't touch the iron doors. They have some sinister enchantments on them, and I don't know what they do."

He didn't have to warn me. The strange magic vibrating off them made me want to retch.

This was an accursed place.

Damian knelt by the enchanted door and began to work his magic. I was about to join him when the astringent stink of rotting meat with fruity undertones drifted into the room.

Something wasn't right.

My ears twitched at footsteps coming up behind. Ducking, I spun and blindly rammed into the attacker, my shoulder connecting with his gut. A shrill woman's voice pierced my ears as I landed on *her*.

I pinned her arms down as she tried to claw my face, and

that's when I noticed her ashen skin and fangs. Vampire. And not the civilized kind.

"Jaxson, behind you!" Savannah screamed.

A blur moved down the hall. *Fuck!*

Gripping the vampire beneath me, I rolled onto my back and shoved her into the air. She collided with whatever the blur barreling toward me was, and both crumpled to the floor. They had a similar theme going—pasty gray skin, long, tangled hair, sharpened nails, and black, soulless eyes.

These weren't typical vampires. What had Alejandro done?

Savannah gave a cry, and I shot to my feet.

Another vampire had her pressed up against the wall, her hands wrapped around Savannah's neck. Savannah rammed her hands into the creature's chest, and a crack of her magic ricocheted down the hall. The vampire flew backward and landed twenty feet ahead, arms and legs splayed out wide.

My mate has bite.

Damian was on his feet, a burning sword held out at his side, looking from one end of the hall to the other.

"Get the fucking door open!" I snarled. "We'll handle the bloo—"

Two hissing fiends lunged at me, cutting my words short. I caught one by the neck and slammed her into the wall, but the other moved with lightning speed and grabbed me from behind, sinking her fangs into my shoulder.

Pain rippled through me, and I jerked backward, feeling her bones crunch as we connected with the opposite wall.

The other dug her razor-sharp claws into my arm. I tossed her sideways and tore a sconce off the wall, spinning and shoving it through her chest as she lunged for me. Clutching the weapon, she sucked in a sharp gasp and collapsed as her body desiccated and crumbled into dust.

What the hell?

She must have been half demon.

As I regained my footing, the second shrieking vampire leapt at my back. I spun, driving my elbow into her face, and then hurled her head over heels down the hall.

Behind me, Savannah was holding another vampire off Damian. I sprinted down the hall toward them, but the creature dodged and leapt onto the ceiling.

"I'm in!" Damian shouted as he pushed through the open door.

I whipped my head toward Savannah. "Help him find the bone!"

She looked at me for a beat, then slipped around me, her intoxicating scent sending urgency through me as I took up a position in the hall.

Protect our mate, my wolf snarled.

The two remaining vampires had regrouped and stood side by side, hissing. Perfect.

My fangs erupted as I released my claws. "Come and get me, ladies."

46

The hollow shrieks of the crazy-looking vampires sent shivers down my spine as I scanned the contents of the room. Ceramic vases, lamps, and marble busts. Dozens of boxes, all collected and forgotten.

"Where the hell is it?" I whispered to Damian as I began to rummage.

He dumped out the contents of a vase. "There are so many signatures here, and I've never seen it, so it's hard for me to tell. Somewhere close. Keep looking."

I glanced over at Jaxson as he slammed one of the fanged harlots into the wall and rammed his claws into her chest.

Quick, quick, quick.

I scanned the room, searching for any kind of clue, as Damian ripped the lid off a wooden crate.

On the shelf, there was another large crate with a label that read, *Temporarily Off Display.*

My breathing stopped. The finger would have been a warning once, and Alejandro had probably displayed it prominently.

Could that be it?

As Jaxson's growl shook the hall behind us, I brought down the crate and dug my claws under the lid. I tugged, and the wooden panel lifted, pulling nails up with it. Inside were a dozen glass boxes padded with straw.

I lifted one out and peered inside. It held a single thorn. A fading label read, *From the Crown of Thorns.*

"Holy shit!" I gasped, looking through the crate. A big, square box had a mummified head with a label that read, *Possibly the Head of St. John the Baptist.*

These were relics, which meant...

Bullseye.

Damian joined me as I dug deeper and handed him boxes. "It's in there, you're close," he said.

Finally, I pulled out a small, black, leather box labelled, *Finger of Dragan the Thief.* Inside was a mummified index finger resting on a wad of gauze. "We got it!"

Damian and I darted outside just as Jaxson staked one of the vampires. By the looks of it, he'd made quick work of the other one. The woman's skin withered until she was nothing more than a pile of ash.

He was covered with blood and lacerations, but he didn't pause for a second. "Probably half of Mexico knows Alejandro is dead by now. We've got to go."

My muscles throbbed from the exertion as we charged down the hall. Thank God my Todorovas were like wearing my magic boots, just not as fast.

We raced back through the cave. Damian slashed one of the bat creatures from the air with his burning sword, while Jaxson repelled another.

I could see the stairs ahead, and my adrenaline spiked. We were almost there...

Fuck, why didn't I grab the head of John the Baptist?

Probably fake, my wolf chuckled.

We ground to a halt in front of the exit, my heart hammering.

The sound of alarms throbbed from outside as Damian pushed the door open.

I wiped my sweaty palms across my thighs. "Okay, now what?"

Damian grimaced as he looked between us. "How do you feel about stealing a car?"

47

___

The walls of Jaxson's apartment shook as he slammed the door shut.

Suffice it to say our escape from Mexico was not our finest hour, but with my shadows, Damian's wings, and Jaxson's ability to hotwire a vehicle, we didn't die.

Frankly, it was a freaking miracle. Maybe Alejandro's relics were real after all, and a bit of God's own luck had rubbed off on us. I'd need whatever I could get to deal with *the beast* in the room.

He stood at the counter, his eyes golden and body rigid. The tension in the air between us was so thick, I swore I could taste it zinging off my tongue, electric and violent.

We'd been deathly silent the entire way home from Damian's house, but there was no way we were going to outrun this fight.

"You're angry," I said flatly. Understatement of the *millennium.*

"Angry?" He slowly stalked around the room, circling me, his fists clenched. "That was a fucking disaster."

Indignation tore at me as I backed away. Mixed with the

aftereffects of Alejandro drinking my blood, I felt absolutely combustible.

"You say that like it's my fault. But tell me, Jaxson, what exactly was a disaster? The part where I got us an audience with Alejandro Rivera like we wanted? Or the part where *you* wolfed out and staked him through the heart *before* we got the finger?"

His jaw tensed, and his fists tightened. "Alejandro would have drained you dry. Had I known how he'd react, I would have murdered him the moment we arrived."

There was no doubt he meant every word.

I kept my distance as we circled each other. He watched me like a hunter, ready to strike, and though my instincts rang out, telling me to run, I was glued to him like the Earth orbiting the Sun—a tiny space rock inching closer to its fiery demise.

"In hindsight, it was a bad decision. But it was my decision, not yours," I said. "And you didn't have to kill him!"

He approached me slowly, his body shaking with frustration, as we continued our dance. "Do you think Alejandro would have stopped once he'd had a taste of you? I thought maybe it only affected werewolves, but your blood is a drug. Had I let him live, he would have hunted you to the ends of the earth."

But I knew it was more than that.

My blood heated, and my fingers tingled. "Were you worried about protecting me or about your own ego?"

Resentful fury burned in his eyes. "What do you mean by that? You're my mate. You were in danger and being tortured before my eyes. My very *soul* was insane with horror and rage."

I knew it was true, too. I'd felt his pain, felt his soul dying as he watched while Alejandro helped himself to my blood.

Jaxson had ripped through the magical chains and tore down the wall to protect me. But as much as that made my pulse race, it didn't excuse his actions.

"You were insane with jealousy and possessiveness," I hissed.

His jaw tensed. Before I could take a breath, he was in front of me, his hand gripping the back of my head. He tilted my face to his. "That is *also* true. Because you're mine."

His words released an inexplicable shiver of delight along my skin while the electricity of his touch arced through his fingers and sent a burst of heat to my core. My eyes dropped to his lips, inches from mine, begging to be tasted.

But in spite of that, righteous indignation burned under my skin.

"I am *nobody's* property." I twisted out of his grip.

"You know what I mean," he said gruffly as I evaded his grasp.

"No, actually, I don't, Jaxson." I was taunting the devil, but I couldn't help it. The flurry of emotions that he was throwing out was making *me* crazy and confused.

"You're my mate!" he roared in an almost bestial voice. "How could I stand by while you offered yourself freely to a vampire?"

I gestured violently to my neck as anger pumped through me. "To drink my blood, Jaxson. Not to keep, not to fuck."

He tilted his head in disbelief, bitterness tinging every word. "Do you think those two are any different for a vampire?"

"It's different for me," I snapped.

His expression darkened, and his voice dropped low. "I saw the way you swooned. How different was it?"

Indignation cut through me like a bullet.

I backhanded him across the face, smacking his head around. Pain rang through my knuckles, but it was nothing compared to my delight at seeing the disbelief in his eyes.

That's right, this bitch has bite.

Fury flashed across his face, but I could smell his arousal, which only ratcheted up mine.

"Do you think I wanted that freak sucking my neck?" I

snarled, shooting daggers at him with my eyes. "We had to get Dragan's finger, so what I did, I did for the pack."

"The pack didn't ask *that* of you, and neither did I. We could have found another way," he said, moving closer, inch by threatening inch. "All I asked was for you to stop, which you ignored."

His smoky pine scent wrapped around me and fogged my brain, and my back bumped against the wall. "So what's this about, Jaxson? That I let Alejandro bite me, or that I disobeyed you?"

He narrowed his eyes and closed the gap between us, his body taut with barely restrained fury. "Both. You should have listened. I'm your alpha."

Between the wall and him, I was trapped. A riot of emotions exploded in me. Rage. Frustration. Unabashed arousal and need.

Rebelling against how hot his dominance made me, I grabbed him by the lapels of his suit and flipped us around so that his back was suddenly up against the wall. I tilted my head and whispered in his ear. "You're my alpha, huh?"

A low growl of arousal rumbled from his throat, making my treacherous center burn with desire.

I shoved him so hard that the plaster on the wall cracked, and I stepped back to escape my emotions. "News flash, Wolf King: I don't have to listen to you."

Before I could get away, he grabbed my wrist and yanked me back to him, leaving our faces just inches apart. "I don't want to *make* you listen. I want you to *want* to listen. To *trust* me, godsdamn it."

My heart raced. I did trust him, didn't I? And if I did, why was defiance such a drug?

I needed space. His closeness and heat were both suffocating and alluring, and I couldn't sort out my thoughts. What the fuck was he doing to me?

Pushing free, I latched on to my anger to defend myself because that's what I knew best. "So what about listening to me? Trusting me?"

In a heartbeat, he surged forward and boxed me in against the wall again, his arms on either side of my head. My breath hitched as his emotions barraged my senses. Frustration. Betrayal. A need to control. "You asked me to trust you when you were painting. It was insane, but I did. I kept the guards and onlookers at bay so you could finish."

I raised my chin, refusing to be cowed. "And it worked. I got us an audience."

He brought his mouth near mine. "True. And when I told you not to let Alejandro drink, *that* was when you should have trusted *me*."

And as much as every inch of me wanted to ram my hands into his chest and blast him back with my magic, I didn't fight or try to get away. Instead, my treacherous lips brushed dangerously close to his, teasing and tempting. "And when I told you it was the right choice, that was when you should have trusted *me*."

Inches apart, we glared venomously at each other, neither of us willing to concede, apologize, or admit our need.

And then we were kissing madly, violently.

Our lips clashed as our mouths dueled for control. Sparks of ecstasy cascaded though my body, and his tongue stroked mine, causing the rivers of my body to meet.

No longer able to restrain the beast of lust within me, I shoved Jaxson to the couch. He grabbed my wrists and pulled me down onto his lap so that I was straddling him, but he kept my arms restrained behind me.

His hard body pressed into all my soft places, and a throbbing ache settled between my legs. I moaned loudly, driven by instinct. The need to fuck. To be one with my mate.

But he wasn't letting me.

In frustration, I leaned forward and sank my teeth into his lower lip, and the metallic tang of his blood set my senses aflame. He growled but released my hands.

Free at last.

"Savannah—"

"Shut up and fuck me now." Tearing his suit jacket off, I ripped the buttons of his shirt open, dragging my hands down his rock-hard abs. He gripped my thighs, shoving my silk dress up as his hardness pressed into my center. I ground my hips against his, desperate for friction.

I needed him inside me.

Unfastening his belt, I undid his pants and slipped my hand within. He groaned and tore his lips from mine, his eyes glazed with desire. "Are you sure?"

"Yes," I said, gripping his generous length. I needed him inside me now. His body tensed, and a deep rumble escaped his throat.

"And is this what you want?" I whispered.

"Yes," he growled from the painful edge of need.

Tilting my head down to his neck, I brushed my lips against his ear. "This doesn't mean I'm yours, and it doesn't mean you've claimed me or own me. This is no strings attached."

In a flash, he flipped me onto my back, his hand slipping between my legs as the rigid angles of his body pinned me. His gaze was locked on mine as he slid his fingers up my thigh, dragging them over my drenched panties. "We'll see how you feel afterward."

Cocky bastard.

And yet, I bucked against his touch, needing more resistance, but he held me down.

"You can't control me, Jaxson. I'm nobody's property," I

snarled in protest. "Will you be able to let me go, or will you be like Alejandro, and this won't be enough?"

A grin ghosted his lips as he pushed the lace aside and stroked my center. "I've warned you before, Savannah: my wolf is possessive."

His fingers found a rhythm, and I gasped at his touch, my back arching against the couch, desperate for a relief that didn't come. Anger mixed with the lust in my veins. He was toying with me. Teasing.

"Damn it, Jaxson," I hissed. He *always* had to be in the driver's seat. I tried to push him back, but he resisted. "Don't you *dare* hide behind your wolf," I said. "Who's in control, the man or the beast?"

Leaning down, he slipped two fingers around the edge of my panties and dipped them deep inside me, sending tremors of need through my body. He brushed his lips against mine as he worked my center and whispered words that sent a deep ache pulsing through my core: "Why don't *you* tell me, Savannah? Who do you want in control? The man...or the beast?"

His gravelly voice grazed my skin, further igniting my desire and anger.

"Me," I moaned, as I bucked my hips and rolled him onto his back so that I was straddling him. Then I slipped my hand between us, finally freeing his length.

He growled with unrestrained arousal and sat up, gripping my hair and kissing along my exposed neck. "One day soon, you *will* submit to me."

The pain of overwhelming desire throbbed within as I pushed up on my knees and pulled my soaked panties aside.

"I. Will. Never. Ever—" I said huskily, slowly sinking onto him before his size cut my breath short. I gasped as he stretched me in ways I'd never been before. "Oh. My. God."

"Fuuuck," he growled, every muscle in his body going rigid. "You feel so fucking good."

And then our bodies were moving. Still holding my hair, he licked my throat where Alejandro's puncture wound had healed while he thrust up into me over and over. Dominating, claiming, destroying me. I groaned, the combination of pain and pleasure sending fireworks through my nerves.

His grip released, both hands moving to my rocking hips, positioning me in a way that sent agonizing pleasure searing through my center. Sweat dripped down our bodies as the heat that was between us grew. Claiming his mouth with mine, I devoured him with everything I had.

Suddenly, he pushed me back and onto my knees so I was over the back of the couch. He pushed into me, deeper than before. I moaned with delight and pressed my ass rhythmically back against his hips, savoring the feeling of his control.

Pleasure and fire pooled in my center, building and mounting, until agony and delight exploded, moving through every nerve ending in my feverish body. My head tilted back, and a moan tore from my throat as wave after wave of ecstasy demolished me. Jaxson tensed and groaned, his desire pulsing as aftershocks rippled down my spine. I pressed back into him, chasing the last bits of my ecstasy.

Holy God.

Chest heaving, I collapsed onto the couch. He scooped me up and brought me to his chest as he lay back down. Our bodies were sweaty and bruised, our anger spent in a blaze of violence and delight.

"You're right," he said at last as my head rose and fell on his chest.

"Of course I am," I mumbled, still too exhausted and out of breath to think. "But in what way?"

"I'm like Alejandro. Now that I've tasted you, it'll never be enough. You're my mate, and I can't resist."

The truth of his words vibrated through me. Possessiveness. Desire. Need. Against my wishes, his words and signature sent a new tremor of pleasure through me, but I fought it down, trying to seize control. Determined not to betray myself.

I pushed up off him and met his eyes. "You can't play this game with me, Jaxson. You made it very clear in Forks that you didn't want me as your mate. And that's fine, but you can't have it both ways."

A dull ache had blossomed in my chest, growing and spreading. I hadn't realized how deep his rejection on the beach had cut me. Even though I'd been horrified at the idea of a mate bond, even though I hadn't wanted it myself...it was contradictory and irrational, but it still hurt.

The room suddenly felt constricting, too small for the both of us. I tried to get up, but he caught my wrist. "Things have changed."

He looked up at me with eyes that bored into my soul, that called me to him as surely as our bond pulled us together.

I lifted my chin in defiance, fighting the new surge of desire that threatened to bring me to my knees. "What's changed? I'm the same as I was then."

He sat up and traced the tattoo on my shoulder. "I thought you'd become a wolf against your will. But now that I know—"

Pulling free of his grasp, I adjusted my dress and walked to the other side of the room, turning my back to him. "What? Now you know I was born a wolf? And what difference does that make? I'm still the same *person*. So either you want me as your mate, or not."

Jaxson rose, and the heat of his presence warmed my back as he drew close. With deliberate control, he slowly coaxed me around and cupped my cheek.

Reluctantly, I met his gaze. The fire from earlier was gone, and in its place was something else. He pressed his lips to my neck and kissed me softly, sending a cascade of shivers across my flushed skin.

Delicately, he traced his mouth up my neck. "Either *you* want me as your mate, or not."

I tensed as the tables turned. I looked away, my heart pounding in terror. I wasn't ready to answer the question I'd asked.

I slipped away. "I'm sorting things out, Jaxson."

Buttoning his trousers, he nodded and walked over to the black counter. The man was covered with scars and blood, sweat and the scent of my body. A testament to what he would go through for me.

Silence stretched between us until finally, he spoke.

"It was Billy."

"What?" I asked, confused.

Jaxson shook his head absently and sighed. "He and my sister, Stephanie, were true mates. We failed to protect her, and she died. It broke him, Savannah. And in the end, he betrayed the pack. That haunts me. The threat of a bond so deep that you would throw away everything you stood for."

With sorrow emanating from him as strongly as his presence, he glanced my way. "I'm alpha. I don't know that I can risk that. Everything is so fragile as it is."

I could feel the pain twisting inside of him, and I could see it in his eyes—haunting visions of a past he was helpless to change.

My body was drawn to him, pulled forward by the need to heal and to help and comfort. I reached up with my fingers and brushed his cheek. "I know you, Jaxson. I know you would never betray the pack. It's who you are, and there's no changing that."

I kissed him softly on the lips and hung my head on his

shoulder, thankful we didn't have to answer any questions about what we were today.

After a moment's silence, Jaxson lifted me up with effortless grace and quietly carried me to his shower. Stripping me of my clothes, he washed my body, and the blood and water flowed down the drain—like our fates, spiraling together into inevitable darkness.

Once he'd laid me on his bed, he turned off the light and left me to snuggle in his sheets alone.

48

My body shook roughly.

"Wake up, Savannah."

I groaned and rolled over, and then, with a yelp of surprise, I pulled the sheets up around me. "Jaxson?"

He usually never came into the bedroom when I—

Oh. *Shit.*

With a wave of horror, the events of the night before came rushing back to me. As soon as we'd stepped through the door, we'd fought, and then, in a fit of adrenaline-powered rage, we'd fucked like animals.

I wanted to die of shame. We'd hadn't even taken the time to wash the vampire blood off our bodies.

It was so dirty, but lord, it had been *hot.*

An aching heat throbbed in my center, and embarrassment flashed through me as I looked out the window, trying desperately to hide the faint smile that spread across my lips. I covered my flushed face as the truth of it all sank in. "Oh. My. God."

"My thoughts exactly, *mate,*" Jaxson said, a slight smirk

tugging at the corner of his mouth as he opened the window blinds, letting in the bright sun.

I wanted to slap that smirk right off his face.

And then throw him down in bed again? Wolfie asked with fake innocence, already knowing the answer.

My cheeks burned as need fogged my mind.

Was my brain ever going to work right again? That, or other parts?

I started pulling the sheets up around me as if more layers could shield me from the consequences of what I'd done. "Okay, we need to talk about what happened, because—"

"No time. They found Tony."

"What?" My heart skipped a beat, and my skin turned ice cold.

That meant Dragan.

Trepidation froze me to my spot. "Is he…"

"According to Sam, he doesn't remember what happened. Not even driving up to Michigan. But he doesn't seem possessed, if that's what you're wondering."

No relief came.

"He could be faking it. That, or if Dragan jumped ship, he could have slipped into anyone Tony met—even whoever it was that found him."

"I know," Jaxson growled, not even hiding the concern in his voice.

This was a disaster. Not last night, or our *vampire murder spree* in Mexico.

This.

When Dragan had been inside Tony, we knew who to look for. Now, he could be anywhere.

"Do you think you could tell if he was possessed?" Jaxson asked, crossing to the bedroom window that looked out on the city.

Could I?

Dragan inhabited a new body each time. Kahanov. Grayling. Tony.

But I *knew* his signature. I'd felt it at Pere Cheney, and when I first saw Grayling.

Bile rose in my throat. "I'd know that fucker on sight, no matter who he was hiding in. He tried to force himself on me. I'll never forget that signature."

Jaxson turned. "Good. Our second problem is that we've got Dragan's finger, but the witch said we needed to find someone who could cast a curse to bind him to it."

I sat up and reached for my phone, still holding the sheets around me. "I asked Neve about that yesterday. She knows a woman at the Order, Devi Coltrane, who works with dark enchantments or something and might be able to help us. I got her number, but I wasn't sure about working with someone at the Order you didn't know—"

"Thanks, but in this case, there's no room for division. You can call her from the road. Get your clothes on, and let's go see if Tony is clean or still possessed."

My new Vera Wang red silk dress was draped over a chair. Once beautiful, it had been reduced to ribbons and stained with dark patches of blood.

A deep pang of loss reverberated through my soul.

I hardly knew you, but I loved you, little dress.

Lord knew where my pumps were. My eyes widened. I hadn't remembered taking them off... had I screwed Jaxson with shoes on? I didn't think so, but it didn't matter. Today called for jeans and my trusty ass-kicking boots.

"Ahem," I said, and looked emphatically from Jaxson to the door.

"But we—"

"Get out," I ordered.

With a grin that was a little too self-satisfied, he ambled to the door. "Be quick."

The drive to the Docks was awkward.

I called and made an appointment with Devi, but after that, silence set in. Neither of us wanted to talk about what had happened or deal with the consequences.

I was lost in my own thoughts, anyway.

Dragan was out there. How would we find him?

I wondered if Damian could locate people as well as objects. If so, that might be our only way of tracking Dragan down.

We were so *fucked*.

Why is that a bad word? Wolfie asked, her voice teasing. *Because last night—*

Shut it, Wolfie.

We passed through the dockyard checkpoint, and Jaxson slowly drove over to an area with three dozen stacked shipping containers.

"Where are we going?" I asked, looking over my shoulder at one of the massive freighters being loaded with cargo.

"Tony's under lock and key until we debrief him," Jaxson said. He turned the wheel and stopped outside of a rusty red container, where Sam was waiting for us.

"He's inside?" Jax asked as he slipped out of the truck.

"All wrapped with silver chains," Sam said.

Jaxson looked at me with an inquiring expression, then back at Sam.

Oh, shit. If she'd found Tony, Dragan could have jumped into her.

I reached out and touched her signature—a rich floral scent of lilac and almonds with an undercurrent of something else.

Nothing out of the ordinary. Relief flooded through me. "She's clean."

"What?" Sam asked, looking between us.

"Savy thinks she'll know if Dragan has possessed someone—their signature changes," Jaxson said, striding over to the container. "Ready to see if he's still in Tony?"

I nodded and summoned the Soul Knife. Jaxson's eyes flicked to me, his unease palpable.

"Don't worry. I'm not going to stab him," I said.

Jaxson undid the latch and swung the door of the container wide with a metallic creak.

The early morning light shone in, revealing Tony sitting on a stool with his hands bound behind his back, his head down, and completely wrapped in silver chains.

He looked up and smiled, a few teeth missing from his familiar off-center grin. "Hey, boss."

My stomach churned. Bruises darkened his cheeks, and his nose had been broken. He looked like hell.

I closed my eyes and concentrated on his signature, which I knew well. He'd driven me all over town and quietly put up with my antics for days.

No sign of Dragan, though I could feel the residual taint of his presence. Not hesitating, I rushed over and gave Tony a hug—perhaps the first time we'd ever touched. "He's clean, Jax. It's just Tony."

"Good," Jaxson said flatly. But beneath his tone, I could hear the deep relief and sorrow. One of his packmates had been returned to him, and I knew in that stoic moment that it meant more to him than anything.

"Just Tony?" the battered man asked, giving me a playfully sharp look. "That's rather demeaning."

I couldn't help but laugh at his feigned outrage. "I mean,

you're not possessed by a psycho ghost anymore. What happened to you?"

His cuts and bruises twisted my gut. I looked at Sam leaning in the doorway, hoping we hadn't done this to him.

"Car accident," Sam said, reading the apprehension in my voice. "They found him this morning, unconscious in his Jeep, which was wrapped around a concrete barrier."

"And you don't remember a thing?" Jaxson asked, looming over the man.

Tony shook his head. "Last thing I remember was loading guns at Eclipse before we headed to Michigan. After that, nothing until those cops found me."

Truth. I could feel it all the way in my bones. Jaxson could, too, because he turned to Sam and motioned to his wrists. "Keys."

She tossed them over, and he began undoing the locks on the chains. "Sorry about this, Tony, but we had to be careful. Who found you? Our people?"

"Nah. Some non-shifter cops. Folks from the Order," Tony said as I bent down to help unbind him. "They wanted me to go to the hospital, but Sam came and got me." He laughed. "As if werewolves don't heal on their own."

The Order. My fingers itched as trepidation rose in my throat. "And where did they find you?"

"Outside the Hall of Inquiry."

I froze, chains dangling in my hands. "Fuck."

"What?" Jaxson asked.

"That's not a coincidence," I said, my palms suddenly sweaty despite the cold metal. "Dragan could have gone anywhere, but he crashes Tony's Jeep outside the Hall of Inquiry? He was wanting to be found so he could jump hosts. He's trying to infiltrate the Order!"

"Maybe." Jaxson pulled the chains from around Tony and

hurled them aside. "But we don't know for sure. Tony could have been resisting possession, and the Jeep crashed. You fought against Dragan's dominance."

That was a good point. "The result is the same. Cops found him. We should at least warn the Order."

"Gretchen Mays. I'll call her now," Jaxson said. "Sam, can you work your contacts to get the names of the cops who found Tony?"

She nodded.

I pulled out my phone. "I'll call Devi."

Unfortunately, neither of us got through.

"What do we do now?" I asked as I hung up after dialing a second time.

Jaxson stepped out of the container and looked out across the dockyard. For a moment, he was silent, reflecting on something. Perhaps a memory.

At last, he sighed. "We head to the Hall of Inquiry and find Devi as planned. We can warn her about Dragan, and she can warn the proper personnel. Maybe she can even help us track down the cops involved. Most importantly, we need to get Dragan's bones enchanted before we run into him—otherwise, we won't be able to trap him."

"And if he's already infiltrated the Order?" I asked, joining his side.

"Then we might be screwed."

I swallowed hard. "What do you think he's after?"

Jaxson turned and studied me with hard eyes. "I have no idea, but whatever it is, you can bet it will be *very* bad for us."

49

Savannah

Fifteen minutes later, we'd parked along the Midway and were walking up the front steps of the Hall of Inquiry. The stone gargoyles on the roof looked particularly foreboding against the overcast sky.

We checked in with the two guards at the front, and a woman walked out of the elevator a couple minutes later, her heels clicking on the marble floor. Her silver hair was tied up in a bun, and she wore slacks and a tucked-in blouse. Her signature zinged around us with floral hints of lavender. "Jaxson and Savy?"

"That's us," I said. "We can't tell you how grateful we are for your help."

She gestured for us to follow and lowered her voice conspiratorially. "No problem. Just don't mention what it is we're doing."

Great. The last thing we needed was to get her in hot water with the Order.

Her office was on the third floor, and she shared it with at least three others who were presently absent. Grabbing a cloth bag from behind her desk, she ushered us into the break room and shut the door. "Let's see this thing."

Jaxson handed her the black leather box, and she opened it and whistled. "A finger. Wow. Creepy."

"*Creepy* doesn't even come close to what we had to do to get that," I said, taking in the dirty dishes in the sink and what smelled like day-old coffee in the pot. Jaxson tensed beside me, and the heat of his repressed fury practically blistered my skin.

Devi raised an eyebrow and gave me an appraising look. "Now I'm interested."

I glanced at Jaxson. "Uh, maybe over a drink sometime."

"Fair, especially since I've only got a few minutes." She revealed the contents of her bag: a tall red candle with dried wax on the sides, some twiggy herbs and feathers, a jar of white powder, string, and a piece of polished onyx.

"Is everything all right? This place seems a little on edge this morning," Jaxson said.

"You noticed?" Devi's eyes flicked up as she poured the white powder into a circle on the table in the center of the room, then lined it with twigs and feathers. "Something's going on at Bentham. A prison riot, by the sound of it. That's why I was called in this morning."

"A riot?" I asked, glancing at Jaxson nervously.

Bentham was jam-packed with some of the world's most dangerous Magica criminals, and as of two nights ago, a couple dozen more shifters. I shivered just thinking about my first time visiting the prison with Neve and Amal. "Anything to be worried about?"

"Don't think so, but after everything that's happened at Bentham this past year, we can never be too careful." She lit the candle and placed it in the center of the circle, then gingerly took out Dragan's finger and set it next to the candle. "This will only take a minute, but you two should step back."

I glanced at Jaxson and backed up after recalling what had happened with the lycanthropy test at Alia's apartment. At least this didn't require blood or any other bodily fluids.

We stood in the corner next to the coffeemaker while Devi closed her eyes and began moving her hands like she was rolling a ball in them. She whispered in a language I didn't recognize. The shadows of the room lengthened, drawing inward toward the flame. For a second, it felt like I was being pulled in, but Jaxson caught my arm.

The candle's flame flickered, and Devi picked up the black gemstone, cupping it above her lips before tossing it into the circle. It landed beside Dragan's finger with a thud, not bouncing, but rather almost sticking to the table. The candle's flame curled upward in a blinding explosion of light.

I shielded my eyes with my arm and froze when I peeked at the table. Dragan's withered finger began inching toward the onyx like it was tied to a string and being pulled by an invisible hand. As soon as it touched the gemstone, the candle extinguished in a plume of smoke, and the ring of white powder ignited in a bright burst of fire.

A wave of magic blasted outward, pushing us back against the wall.

Perspiring, Devi held her hands over the object as if feeling an invisible force, and then she clapped her palms together and smiled. "It's done."

"That's it?" I frowned. The white powder had completely burned away, leaving only the candle and the gemstone on the table. The finger was...gone.

She retrieved a tiny black linen pouch from her bag and used it to carefully pick up the gemstone, which she handed to me in its new wrapping. "Hey, it might have looked like nothing, but that was a pretty hefty spell."

I looked at the strangely warm object in my hand. "Sorry, that's not what I meant. I just imagined it would be different."

She flashed me a friendly smile. "People always do. Now, give it a minute to cool off. The magic is still fresh, and the stone will scald you."

"How will it work?"

"You'll want to keep this talisman on your person at all times, holding it in your palm, if possible. It's instilled with Dragan's essence, so it will lead you to his soul if you concentrate on him."

Holy shit. It was like a Dragan divining rod.

"Now, trapping him will be trickier," she continued. "Once you've found his soul or ghost, you'll need to overpower his will to draw him into the stone. Once you do that, he's trapped."

"Overpower his will? How exactly do I do that?" I asked, dread sinking into my chest.

"Your magic?" She looked at me like I was an idiot and then turned her attention to Jaxson. "I'm sure the two of you could work together and pool your magic. That should be enough to beat the bastard into submission."

Fear wrapped around my pounding heart. This was the weapon we'd been searching for, but now that we had it, I wasn't sure I was up to the task. Dragan had possessed me and nearly taken over. Would I be strong enough to defeat him?

Jaxson pressed his palm to my back, and a cool wave of calm radiated from his touch. "We'll get him. You and me."

Together. I wasn't in this alone anymore. Jaxson had my back, and so did the pack. "Let's get this asshole."

"All right, I've got to go. Sorry I can't show you out." Devi packed up her supplies and handed me the box that had held Dragan's bones.

"And what about the finger?" I asked.

Devi paused at the doorway. "It's in the onyx. I guess I should have mentioned that before. Hope you didn't need it." Her phone began vibrating. "Crud. That's my boss. Gotta run. Good luck!" She shuffled out of the break room and disappeared.

I gazed down at the black talisman in my hand. It was still warm to the touch and so smoothly polished that I could see my tiny reflection in it. Closing my eyes, I concentrated on Dragan, recalling the face I'd seen in the cave in Forks, the chilling feel of his soul when he'd possessed me, the sound of his voice...

My mind drifted for a minute, and then, like a missile radar locking on to its target, it fixated on something. And though my body was firmly rooted in the break room, my mind was towed somewhere else.

An image began to unfold, and the all-too-familiar sensation of Dragan chilled my skin. Gray concrete walls rose around me, and the smell of bleach and sweat tugged at my memory. This place was familiar, I'd been here before...

A large tower appeared in the center of the vast, circular space as the vision in my mind expanded. But its base didn't reach the ground—it was suspended. The faint sound of voices filtered in, chaotic and hysterical, and in between it all, a rhythmic chanting. Skin prickling with fear, I moved through the vision as it unfolded. *Where are you, Dragan?*

A gasp seized my lungs as all around me, figures materialized. Faces I'd seen before, others I hadn't, and among them, a bald, monstrously muscled man who towered over the other prisoners. He was shirtless, and his blue veins shone through his pale skin.

Though I had no recollection of this man, I knew who he was, or at least who was in the driver's seat. Victor Dragan.

As I stepped closer, he paused and seemed to look right at me with glassy, pale gray eyes. The others followed, and it was then that I realized that their eyes were distant white orbs like those of the bikers at the rally.

Where was this place?

Heart racing, I looked around. Lining the walls of the circular chamber were hundreds of prison cells, their barred doors all facing the central tower. The tower I was standing below.

Shit.

My eyes flew open, and I found myself in the break room once more. Jaxson towered over me, his hands on my shoulders and worry on his face. His shoulders relaxed when he realized I was back. "You screamed. What happened?"

I had?

"Dragan," I panted, somehow out of breath. "He's got a new host, and he's in Bentham."

50

Savannah

Jaxson grabbed my arm. "We need to catch Devi."

We bolted out of the office and followed Devi's scent. People rushed by in all directions, too busy to ask who we were.

Finally, we reached a pair of large doors, behind which we could hear a din. Without pausing, Jaxson pushed through.

Dozens of people filled the large book-lined chamber. They all went quiet the moment we stepped in. My eyes were drawn to a giant screen with a CCTV feed.

I recognized the place immediately from my vision. Bentham.

Inmates were running about the prison, though many more had barricaded themselves in their cells. The picture flipped to the inside of a control room. There were several dead guards on the floor and inmates shuffling through papers.

A low voice with an Australian accent boomed from across the room. "What the hell are those people doing in our gods-damned operations room in the middle of a riot?"

I turned to see a golden-haired man striding toward us.

Lightning practically crackled around him, and all the people in the room stepped back.

The signature of his magic hit me like a blast of wind roaring over the plains. It had the sound of thundering hooves, and the rich scents of hickory and earth. I sensed that he was something powerful, but I didn't know what.

The painfully handsome man stopped short when Jaxson turned around. "Laurent? What the hell are you doing here, of all places?"

"Ethan. Seems you have a problem in Bentham," Jaxson said as he stepped up, leaving them just inches apart. The air practically shook between them as their signatures clashed.

They were a study in opposites. While Jaxson was rugged, with rippling muscles and a black beard, Ethan was clean shaven with perfect hair and blazing topaz eyes.

Jaxson was a wolf. The mage felt more like a lion amid his pride.

"I *know* I have a problem in Bentham, which is why I need you to get your ass out of here," Ethan growled. His voice was pitched so low, I almost felt it in my bones.

"We can help," I said, albeit with less confidence than intended.

Ethan looked around the room. "Damn it all! Who let these people in?"

Devi pushed through the crowd. "I'm sorry, Archmage. Laurent told me he had some information, and I asked him to come in."

She gave me a look that said, *Just go with it.*

"We know who's behind this," Jaxson said. "And we need to go in to stop it."

Ethan shook his head and pointed at the screen. "I know who's behind it. The riot is being led by the Crusher, one of the most notorious serial killers in Bentham. He bashed in the heads of three people with his bare hands. His only defense was that he liked the way it felt when their skulls popped, and now he's done the same thing to two of my guards. So unless you want more people to end up like that, let us do our work."

"Whoever that is, it's not the Crusher anymore," I snapped at the archmage. "He's been possessed by Victor Dragan."

He looked at me with a cold expression that made my bones hurt. "Dragan was killed years ago, missy."

Archmages were not people to whom one spoke harshly. According to my aunt, they were masters of their art and included many of the most powerful people in the city in their ranks.

Pushing down my trepidation, I stepped forward. "Getting killed didn't stop him—it just made him angrier. He's a ghost and can jump bodies. I've seen him do it twice."

The archmage studied me for a moment, letting his topaz eyes bore deep into me. "How certain are you of this?"

"One hundred percent." I pointed to the inmates on the CCTV screen, who had their hands raised and were chanting, though we couldn't hear the words. "They're performing a ritual to summon a dark god from werewolf lore. I've seen that before, too."

"What? When?"

"A day and a half ago. We interrupted the ritual with the help of Agent Harlow Blake. Dragan recruited cultists from the local MCs. They were arrested and locked up in Bentham." I pointed to a biker in a jumpsuit on the screen. "Apparently, Dragan found a way to let them out."

Ethan followed my gesture and stared furiously at the TV. I could smell his rage and irritation.

"Ethan, this is real. Trust us. We know what to do," Jaxson said.

He turned. "Devi, since you let them in, take them and debrief them. Get any information we can use."

Jaxson grabbed Ethan's arm, and the archmage's eyes flared. "You need to get us in there," Jaxson insisted.

He shook his head. "Bentham is an Order issue. We'll resolve it."

I stepped up and gave him *the look*. "Not without our help. No matter what you do, Dragan will just find another host. We have the only means of containing him."

"And we know Dragan. We know what's at stake," Jaxson growled.

Ethan pulled his arm free. "That's dandy. But the rioters took over and initiated a lockdown. They have control over the entire place, and they're making sure that no one gets in or out. So as you can see, the situation is, at the moment, a bit fucked."

"You must have an entry," I pleaded. "Get us in. We know how to stop him. We've done it before."

Ethan laughed. "Yeah, I'm not letting the irreputable alpha of Dockside through the back door of Bentham. I wouldn't have a single werewolf locked up there within a week."

Without a second's hesitation, Jaxson growled, "I'll take a blood oath to never reveal its location or use it without your permission. Savannah and I both will. But we need to be part of the team that goes inside."

Ethan looked incredulous. "You're kidding. You're that eager to join a prison riot?"

Jaxson's rage boiled over, and his savage energy pulsed through the room. Although his claws and fangs erupted, he kept his voice low and hard. "I will do whatever it takes to protect my pack. If Dragan succeeds, their souls will be at stake. This *city* will be at stake. I would fucking make a deal with a necromancer, if that's what it took. If that's not your mindset right now, then you'd better get there, because the fucking apoc-alypse is coming."

Everyone in the room grew deathly still, and I could feel their fear rising.

Neither Jaxson nor Ethan moved.

Finally, the archmage smiled warmly. "Well, then, I guess it's good that I only have to make a deal with a werewolf and not a demon. Tell me, how much do you hate getting wet?"

51

Savannah

The cold spray soaked me to my bones as the Order's Zodiac Sea Rib screamed across lake Michigan, jackhammering through the waves. I'd quickly grown numb to the chill, jarring impacts, and earsplitting roar of the engines.

The only thing on my mind was Dragan, and I couldn't tear my eyes away from Bentham Island.

A dark storm had formed above the prison, building in whorls like a slow cyclone—just as the clouds had appeared above the graveyard. That meant Dragan's ritual was already underway.

"Not good," Jaxson said, as if reading my mind.

I let my gaze sweep over our team, wondering if they shared my ominous feeling. In addition to Jaxson, our boat held Devi, Ethan, and two agents I didn't know, plus a captain and deckhand.

Not much for facing down an entire prison of psycho murderers.

Our team was small on purpose. According to Ethan, the entrance to the prison was underwater and could accommodate only a few people at a time. We would have to dive down, infil-trate the prison, and get to the control room to bring an end to the lockdown so that the rest of the mages could get in.

Jaxson leaned over and whispered, "If you get any tenser, your claws are going to come out and tear through the side of the Zodiac."

Heat flushed my cheeks, and I jerked my hands away from the inflatable hull. There were a few nuances about being a werewolf that could sneak up on you.

Hoping the others couldn't hear my whisper over the roar of the engines, I bent my head close to his. "Last time we faced Dragan, we had over a dozen people on our side, and he still got away. This time, he's got a whole prison at his disposal."

Jaxson smiled. "True. But all we have to do this time is take the control room back. The prison was built to handle riots, just not sabotage from within."

I looked up at the storm forming over Bentham as trepida-tion sank further into my heart. "Well, those clouds tell me that we might run out of time."

Jaxson gently traced my jaw and brought my eyes back to his. "The only one who's run out of time is Dragan. We have the talisman. This is it."

I touched the tiny drybag in my pocket that contained the talisman Devi had made. I felt the conviction of Jaxson's words and wished I could believe them.

As we approached the towering walls of the prison, the Zodiac slowed. The captain consulted his GPS and began to maneuver the craft into position.

Ethan unzipped a black duffle and began passing out full face masks. "The entrance is at the base of the island. Each of these masks is enchanted to provide thirty minutes of fresh air, but we shouldn't need more than ten. They also have intercoms, but they're shit."

"So we just swim down to the bottom and what, find a door?" I asked as I tried to figure out how my mask worked.

"Essentially correct. I'll head down with a line and secure it. When I tug three times, you'll all follow me down, one by one. Give the person ahead of you about a ten-second lead. When you get to the bottom, do your best not to kick up sediment. Whatever you do, don't panic. If you can't manage the swim, return to the surface, and the captain will take you back."

"That won't be a problem," I said, more confidently than I felt. "Will we need fins?"

"No. I'll take some because I have to hunt for the door. But you all can just descend the line. After I've disabled the warding spells on the entrance, Jaxson will help me open the hatch. Follow me down the tunnel, and then we'll swim up to an exit pool. After that, we'll review the plan from there. Any questions?"

We all shook our heads.

Ethan turned to the captain. "Are we in position?"

He gave the thumbs-up.

"Okay, everybody, masks on." He fitted his over his face and tightened the straps. Turning a switch on the top of the mask, he flicked on an integrated head lamp.

I did my best to imitate him and turned on my light. Once Jaxson had his own mask on, he checked that my straps were tight.

"—ound che—" Ethan's voice crackled over the intercom.

We all checked in one by one. He sighed and shook his head as he pulled on a pair of fins. "All the magi—in the—orld, and you think the Ord—could find masks to enchant that weren't a piece of sh—*fzzzzzt.*"

His voice crackled out.

Great.

Ethan picked up the end of a silver spool of line and positioned himself on the side of the boat. He gave a thumbs-up to the captain, who shifted into neutral and flashed the sign in return.

"—lip backward, like this." And with that, Ethan tumbled over the side into the lake with a solid splash. The silver line zipped as it fed into the dark below. One of the agents kept their hand on it, letting it run through his gloved fingers.

Then we waited.

Every so often, the line went loose for a while, and the agent pulled slack in. But it always fed back out.

Minutes ticked by as we rocked in the waves. My stomach lurched with every bob, and I very soon realized that I hadn't calculated seasickness into the equation.

I hope I don't barf in my mask.

I was totally unprepared for this shit. There'd been no time to change, and I was still dressed in jeans, a T-shirt, and boots.

Man, this is going to suck. Wet jeans and sloshy speed boots. Chafe city.

This is why I think clothes are silly. Fur just makes so much more sense, Wolfie observed.

Obviously, we were far beyond the limits of safe operation protocols, but it seemed that protocols were things that went away when shit hit the fan. I guess when someone was threatening to bring a wrathful wolf god down on the city, the paperwork could go to hell.

Finally, the line jerked in the agent's hand once, twice, three times.

Ethan was on target. The agent passed the line to one of the deckhands and gave us the thumbs-up. "Everyone ready?"

I added my thumbs-up to those of the group.

"Follow my lead, one at a time," the agent said. Then he grabbed a bag off the bottom of the Zodiac and backflipped over the side with his hand firmly on his mask to keep it in place. As soon as he surfaced, he gave an okay sign by touching the top of his head.

The remaining agent pointed at me. "I'll go last. You're next. You look like you're gonna hurl if you don't get off soon."

I gave Jaxson an apprehensive look, then shimmed myself so I was balanced precariously on the side of the rocking Zodiac. Devi gave me a broad grin and two thumbs-ups. "See you on the bottom!"

After making sure the talisman was safely secured in my zip pocket, I put my hand on my mask and took a deep breath. "Bombs away!"

I launched myself backward and hit the water with an icy splash. When I surfaced, Jaxson was leaning over the side. "You all right?"

I gave the okay sign. "Yeah, but I'm beginning see why you hate the water. Here I go."

With my hand on the silver line, I did a half dive and descended into the cool, dark lake.

Kicking with my boots should have been almost impossible, but they jetted me downward like a pair of fins. Apparently, the appellation *Swiftley* applied underwater as well.

Within seconds, I'd caught up to the agent ahead of me and slowed my kicking. The hazy light faded as we descended, though the headlamp and my werewolf vision compensated for the darkness and allowed me to make out faint shapes.

Slowly, the bottom resolved into view as we reached the rocky side of Bentham Island.

Ethan's light flashed below. He'd tied the line off to an old bit of rebar, but he was twenty feet over, waving his hands. The agent ahead of me cleared off the line and, careful to not stir up the sediment, swam over to Ethan to help illuminate his work.

Jaxson and I followed to make room.

Ethan was weaving his hands in the water, tracing runes over the rocks, much as Damian had done in Mexico. I assumed he was reciting a spell, but he'd turned his coms off.

Slowly, the stone began to glow, and then the runes dissolved in a sparkle of gold light, revealing a round white hatch with a crank wheel in the middle of it. Ethan touched his mask to switch on his coms. "I have to unl—k the spells prote— ing the door. This will take a couple m—tes. Hold tight, and—n't swim off."

He nodded to Devi and the last agent as they swam over, then returned to tracing golden lines on the hatch. I shivered from the cold. Hopefully, this would go quickly.

With nothing to do but wait, I looked out into the dim waters surrounding the base of the island. Trash was nestled every- where among the rocks. An old tire. Bits of wood covered with zebra mussels. A plastic six-pack holder. Corroded cans.

My mouth went sour with disgust. People were horrible.

Something flickered in the distance, and my pulse skipped a beat. I peered through the gloom. My werewolf eyes allowed me to pick out the details of a jumble of old wood resting on the rocks.

Then it happened again—a faint flash of pale green.

My heartbeat accelerated, and I grabbed Jaxson's hand.

His voice crackled over the intercom. "What is it?"

I shook my head. "Just thought I saw something."

Devi and the others tensed and looked around.

It happened again, but this time, instead of a flash, it was a rolling image that appeared for a second and faded away. A translucent wooden boat positioned where the timber lay.

My breath caught. It was an old shipwreck. I'd seen a ghost ship.

I shivered again, this time not from the cold.

Suddenly, the wound on my shoulder began to itch and throb. I turned around as an apparition moved toward me across the rocks—the ghost of a sailor. His face was drawn, and his ethereal skin was rotting.

My stomach turned.

For one second, he looked at me, and I heard him speak in my mind. *Beware, young lass: it took our ship, and now it's coming for you!*

Just as quickly as he'd come, the ghost disappeared.

Fear iced my skin, and I squeezed Jaxson's hand. "Something's coming, and I don't think it's good."

Ethan paused and toggled his mic. "I'm al—st done. Don't get jumpy."

I twisted back to glare at him. "I'm not jumpy. A ghost just told me the thing that killed him is coming our way."

"A ghost?" Devi asked.

"Everybo—get ready," Jaxson said. "This is real."

His body hardened next to mine, and he moved slightly in front of me, even though we had no idea which way the thing was coming from.

I felt it first, like a current rising and pushing against us. Something big enough to disturb the water column. I looked back at the flickering image of the shipwreck. *Shit.*

I began summoning my magic. "Whatever is coming, it's big enough to sink a ship."

"Get that h—tch open, Ethan," Jaxson growled over the crackling coms.

52

Savannah

My pulse pounded in my temples, fogging my mind. A sea monster was headed our way. What had attracted it? Our sound? Our lights?

My lips were dry, and I tried to think. "Okay, nobody talk. I'm going to make a dome of darkness around us, and maybe it won't be able to see us."

Praying that the creature used vision and not scent or sound, I called my magic and shaped the midnight blue shadows around us. My muscles strained as I pushed the darkness outward. Instead of just creating a cloud, I created a dome—hollow like a bowl, so our headlamps would still work within.

Devi gave a start as the sunlight overhead faded, leaving us in blackness except for the anemic beams of our lights.

Everyone looked around frantically, but only I could see beyond the veil of darkness. And what I could see was beyond my imagination.

At first, a massive shadow formed in the deep blue-green of the water. Then it resolved into the long, sinuous form of an eel winding its way toward us. My heart clenched while my muscles ached from the strain of keeping the shadows around us. Its body was silver-blue and at least three feet in diameter. Two twisted horns sprouted from its head, and strange peaked plates ran along its back.

Most significantly, its jaws were open wide enough to swallow a person whole.

I stood frozen, concealed in the magical darkness. *Please don't notice us.*

The serpent came within twenty feet, but it looked past us with its pale eyes and just kept swimming.

I pulled Jaxson close, trying to calm my beating heart. If only he could see it. Then I wouldn't be the only one who had to stare death in the face.

Every part of me wanted to scream, but I stifled the sound as the enormous creature slowed and cautiously skirted the dome of darkness I'd created.

Waves of pressure pushed against us as its undulating body churned the water. Momentarily knocked over, Ethan looked up and uselessly scanned the darkness. I gestured frantically at the door with both hands, willing him to *get it open now, damn it!*

At last, the thing's impossibly long tail passed us as it swam to inspect the remains of the wreck.

"Jaxson. I need a hand," Ethan whispered over the coms.

Kicking powerfully, Jaxson jetted toward the hatch. He grabbed hold of the wheel, and together, they heaved against it. I could hear them straining over the coms.

Then there was a heart-stopping squeal of metal grinding as the wheel began to turn.

My blood turned to ice water, and I glanced toward the shipwreck. The creature was gone.

The crack of a breaking seal reverberated across the rocks, and the hatch groaned as Jaxson slowly forced it open.

A shadow appeared in the distance, and then the monster

surged into view—no longer lazily winding its way through the water but barreling directly toward the source of the sound. Us.

"Everyone in now! Sea serpent coming right at us!" I yelled over the coms. In my panic, I inadvertently released my magic and the shadows around us dropped. "Go, go, go!"

In a frantic cluster, we swam to the hatch and slipped though one by one as the thing hurtled for us with jaws opened wide. Jaxson grabbed me roughly and shoved me through headfirst, then slipped in behind.

Our headlamps flashed around the chamber. Six swimmers. With all of us in, Jaxson and Ethan pulled the hatch shut. For one second, as it closed, I saw a brief flash of silver-blue scales pass through in the light of Jaxson's headlamp. Then he and Ethan began to spin the wheel to seal the door.

Suddenly, the whole chamber shook as something huge slammed against the hatch from outside, buckling the metal.

Ethan and Jaxson strained to turn the wheel, but it barely budged. Ethan shook his head. "Okay, the door just became a problem for later. Let's go."

I grabbed his arm. "We need to get out of here fast. That hatch is almost the exact diameter of that thing's body."

He nodded and pushed between us in the crowded tunnel. "Point taken. Follow me."

In single file, we swam down the tunnel. Every so often, Ethan stopped to do something, tracing runes along the side of the walls, and every so often, a dull shudder reverberated from behind us.

The corridor branched several times, and I was certain that I didn't want to know what devious traps lay down the wrong passages.

At last, we reached a silo-like chamber that ascended into the gloom above. Ethan waved us forward, and we spiraled up as a group.

Finally, after what must have been a hundred feet, I broke the surface, Jaxson at my side. Our headlamps traced the walls with beams of light as we looked around. It was a small, rectangular concrete chamber.

Jaxson heaved himself out of the water onto the crumbling platform. Smiling through his foggy mask, he reached out his hand. "Well, we lived."

I clasped his hand, and he hauled me out of the water. I stood, yanked off my mask, and pulled my hair into a dripping ponytail behind me. "Great. We'll defeat Dragan, but we'll die of hypothermia."

Ethan was the last out of the water. He took off his mask, and then, using it as a flashlight, followed a pair of conduits to a metal box. He popped it open and flicked a breaker. "Welcome to Bentham Prison."

Light illuminated the room.

It was wholly unimpressive—just a concrete tunnel with a pool at the end. After surviving a near devouring, I'd frankly hoped for a little more.

Ethan unzipped an agent's bag as the rest of the group pulled off their masks. "Sorry, that was a little more harrowing than intended. But it makes a nice warmup for a prison riot."

"What the hell was it?" Devi asked. "I couldn't see anything."

Still shivering from the cold, I shook my head. "I don't know. It was like a giant eel or snake the diameter of a barrel. It had spiked ridges down its back and horns."

Ethan let out a long breath. "Misiginebig."

"Michigan what?" I asked.

"A horned serpent, one of the legendary beasts of the lake. Good thing we got out of the water when we did." He pulled a map from the bag and looked straight at me. "Do you really talk to ghosts?"

I shrugged. "Yes, apparently. It's new."

"Well, it saved our life, so I'd keep at it." He unrolled the map on a dry patch of ground, though it was immediately dampened by water dripping from his clothes. "This is a plan of Bentham. This corridor isn't on the map, but we'll pop out in a closed-off room, here." He pointed to one of the many rings on the map.

With no time for pride, I said, "I have no idea what I'm looking at."

He nodded. "Okay. They call Bentham the donut because it's shaped like a ring. The prison cells are on the outside. There is the mirrored glass observation tower in the center. The guards in the tower can see into all the cells, but the prisoners don't know whether they're being watched."

Right. I recalled seeing this in my vision when I used the onyx talisman.

Ethan looked up. "The design is called a panopticon. It dates from before CCTV and video camera were invented. It was manned by unsleeping demons who were always watching."

Jaxson crossed his arms. "Considering recent events, it might be best to go back to demons."

Ignoring Jax, Ethan traced his fingers over the map. "We have to get to the operations center in the control tower here. From there, we can end the lockdown and let the rest of the archmages and agents in. We'll also be able to initiate riot suppression protocols."

"Let me guess—Dragan has people guarding it," I said.

Ethan nodded. "Someone would have had to overrun the guards in the tower to release the prisoners in the first place. You can bet the rioters have it secured."

"So how do we get there?" Devi asked.

Ethan pointed to the control room. "Well, the problem is that the tower doesn't actually reach the ground. It hangs on struts over the exercise courtyard so that watchers can monitor from above. We'll have to cross a bridge on the eighth floor to get to it, but that means we need to go through one of the cell blocks to get there."

"So fight our way there, and then fight our way in," Jaxson grunted.

Ethan shrugged and rolled up the map, then passed us each a potion bomb. "With Savannah's ability to shape darkness, we might be able to sneak in. I have a feeling that the place is going to be a madhouse."

53

Jaxson

Ethan led us through the endless concrete corridors. We were on our way to face a madman in a madhouse.

Savannah was shivering in her wet jeans and T-shirt, and I could sense her exhaustion from using her magic. I pressed a little of my energy into her. I needed her strong for the battle ahead.

Finally, we reached the entrance, a hidden door Ethan revealed through more of his tedious, mind-numbing spellcasting. The prison above us was a ticking timebomb, and we were playing hocus-pocus.

Ethan shoved the secret door. "Shit. It's jammed."

I pushed the pretty boy out of the way and rammed my shoulder into it. A cacophony of crashing and falling objects sounded from inside, and the door opened.

The light from Ethan's glowstone lit the interior of a storage closet. Buckets, brooms, and canisters of cleaning fluid had spilled everywhere, and I picked my way over the debris.

"You could have made a bit more noise," he said.

"We're in," I grunted, and moved to the supply closet's door. "You said this was supposed to be an empty room."

"It was. In the fifties."

There was no sound coming from outside, so I cracked the door open. No sign of movement.

I carefully slipped out and looked around, but the hall was deserted. As was the one on the next level, and the next, as we ascended the back stairwells to the eighth floor.

"This place should be crawling with inmates," I muttered as we reached the access to level eight.

"Apparently, everybody's busy," Savannah whispered.

Not a good sign.

We moved out of the stairwell into the eighth-floor cellblock. The access to the central observation tower was through there. A short corridor led inward and terminated at a large red door marked *H-Block*. Ethan cast a quick spell, and it unlatched.

As soon as it cracked open, the sound of chanting greeted our ears. It was a thunderous and maddening cascade of arcane syllables, but it sounded far away.

"I think we know what everyone is up to." Slowly, I pushed the door inward, revealing the prison within.

Even though I'd been to the maximum-security wing before, the full panopticon was terrible to behold. Ring after ring of prison cells were stacked one on top of the other, all facing inward. The hanging central observation tower was sheathed in black glass so there was no way to tell who was watching from within. This time, however, some of the iron bars at the front of the cells had been opened.

I gave Ethan a dark look. "What an inhumane way to treat people."

He frowned. "It's not that simple. Supernatural powers make everything complicated. With claws and horns and innate magic, it's very easy for inmates to find ways to put guards and prisoners at risk."

I grunted, emphasizing my contempt for the place. "Honestly, if I had to live here, I'd start a brawl just to be thrown in isolation."

Our position at the door allowed us to peer down into the prison. The rings of cell blocks descended seven levels below us. At the bottom, there was an open courtyard filled with tiny figures moving about. I couldn't tell what they were doing, but we could hear them. In the barbaric language of magic, they were summoning the Dark Wolf God.

Our access to the hanging tower was across a narrow bridge connected to the catwalk that ringed our level, like all the others above and below. The sides had high railings, which I supposed were to prevent inmates from shoving one another over the edge.

Or jumping to their death.

"There's no way to obscure our approach. They'll either see us or a big floating cloud of shadow," I growled.

"So we better move fast and catch them before they have time to react," Ethan said. "Ready, everybody?"

I darted out and ran quietly along the catwalk. The clanging of our footsteps reverberated around us, but they were drowned out by the amplified sound of chanting. The whole prison was like an echo chamber, magnifying every noise.

Madhouse is right. I would go insane living there.

Many inmates were still in their cells. Most were curled up with their hands over their ears to block out the sound of the twisted voices from below. It seemed that Dragan had released those who were compliant and left everyone else to rot. At least that explained why the place was deserted.

One of the inmates came to the bars of his cell. "Who are

you? Can you help me? I don't want to be a part of this! Just let me out!"

Ignoring the poor soul, I slipped across the narrow bridge and positioned myself beside the blast door that led into the observation tower, the only part of the structure not covered in glass.

If there was anyone in there, they knew we were here.

Ethan crept up behind me with the two agents at his back. "Ready?"

I nodded.

"I'll knock them down. You clean them up." Ethan keyed an entry code on the access panel. Nothing. With a low curse of frustration, he quietly traced a sigil on the door.

A single ringing knock reverberated through the prison, pulsed through the catwalk, and vibrated me to my core.

The door slid open.

Ethan swung out of the way as a bolt of fire lanced past his head, then dropped low and release a concussive blast of magic that warped the air around us.

"Go!" he shouted.

I charged into the room and leapt over an overturned desk. A white-eyed wolf charged me, his jaws wide and teeth dripping with spit. I ducked out of the way, caught him in midair, and hurled him, howling, into a man in an orange jumpsuit.

Werewolves with their claws out attacked from both sides. I snapped one's arm as she reached for me and slammed the other's head into the deck.

The bastard in the orange jumpsuit leapt to his feet and crossed his hands to cast a spell. I dove as a firebolt ripped through the air.

Devi charged through the room and hurled a potion bomb at the man's chest. It exploded in a flash of light—a stunner.

Ethan blasted one of the werewolves as it charged, but the

wolf I'd tossed whipped in from the right, sank his teeth into Devi's arm, and dragged her to her knees. Her scream cut through the air.

I vaulted back over the desk and grabbed him by the jaws. Arms straining, I pried his mouth open, then snapped his neck and hurled him over the railing.

A roar erupted behind me, and I was flattened to the ground as the desk splintered over my back. With a growl, I rolled out of the wreckage and kicked my assailant in the knee. This did absolutely nothing because my assailant was an enormous bear.

Werebear. *Fuck.*

His claws sank into my leg, and he hurled me into the railing, which bent to match my form.

Ethan blasted the thing back, and Devi and the agents simultaneously hit him with three stunner bombs.

Slowly, the creature staggered forward, opened his mouth, and slammed down onto the ground.

A few burning sheets of paper fluttered through the air.

It was over.

I gingerly rose and took stock of my injuries: a few broken ribs, a shattered collarbone, and something horrible had happened to my shin.

"God, Jax, are you okay?" Savy asked as she slipped through the door.

"Fine." I'd heal eventually.

Ethan chuckled. "When I said, 'clean up,' I didn't plan for you to try to solo the whole room."

"Devi helped," I grunted. "What now?"

Ethan and the agents surveyed the wreckage. "Well, we pray we didn't destroy the computers that control the mechanical security protocols, and we see if we can break the lockdown."

54

Savannah

My breath caught as I looked around inside the tower. The walls were all glass, and I could see out into the prison cells perfectly. I'd known what to expect, but seeing it in person was unnerving.

The practical reality of zero privacy.

Every time I looked at the glass, it rippled with magic and magnified the world outside. Everywhere I looked, it was like having binoculars.

I could see some of the orange- and gray-clad inmates curled up in their cells, hiding from the echoes of the ritual below.

A helical ironwork stairway spiraled down around the inside of the observation tower. It was easy to imagine unsleeping demons walking up and down the stairs with their relentless eyes trained on the inmates.

I peered down over the railing, and my stomach lurched with vertigo. The bottom of the control tower was glass as well, allowing observers to continuously watch activity in the court-yard below.

Looking back at Ethan, I asked, "What do you need me to do?"

He and the agents were busy going over a pile of notes and fiddling with the computer systems. "We just need to override the system. Give us a minute. I'm an archmage, not tech support."

I immediately descended the stairs.

Jaxson followed. "Where are you going?"

"This tower overhangs the courtyard with all the chanting freaks, and I'm betting that Dragan's still down there. I want to see what he's doing for myself, and in here, I can do it without him knowing I'm watching."

I moved down the spiraling stairwell quickly, then paused and looked up at Jaxson behind me. "I'm practically stomping, but my boots aren't making a sound. Why is that?"

"The stairwell is probably enchanted, so creatures with acute hearing—like werewolves—can't tell when people are moving inside."

"This place is so creepy," I said as I continued down the stairs.

"It has a reputation," Jaxson grumbled.

I wondered how many members of the pack had spent time in there. Or how many members of my family, for that matter.

If Casey had been here, he would have asked if the guards had to watch everybody do their business, or something equally inappropriate. Sorrow and loss twisted through my heart as I stepped out onto the all-glass floor.

I reached for Jaxson's arm. "Whoa, this is freaky."

You could see everything below. It was like flying. What I saw, however, disturbed me far more than the vertigo.

The base of the tower was on level with the third ring. Below us, the perimeter of the second ring and the courtyard were lined with prisoners, far more than I'd seen in my hazy vision.

They were chanting, and their collective voices buffeted the building as magic sparked in the air.

The highly polished courtyard floor was covered with strange symbols and radiating lines that reminded me of my aunt's workshop, but these had been crudely written in red with broad, sloppy strokes.

Blood.

The source was obvious. The dismembered corpses of two guards were crumpled off to the side. Dragan had apparently used their arms to write with.

Without hesitation, my stomach unloaded itself onto the glass floor.

Jaxson touched my shoulder lightly, but I shook him off and wiped my mouth with the back of my hand. "I'm going to destroy that fucker."

He wasn't hard to find.

A massive man stood in the center of it all, his arms raised and chanting. The Crusher, possessed by Dragan.

He must have been eight feet tall, and his shoulders were twice as broad as Jaxson's. He wore no shirt, revealing muscles that were inhumanly swollen and distended with bright blue veins. The video cameras and my vision hadn't done him justice. Seeing him in person, I had no doubt that he could crush my skull with a single hand.

As I looked on in horror at the monstrous man, his head wrenched back and shifted into that of a wolf. His left arm sprouted hair, and claws erupted from his hands. He howled, then reverted to human form.

Dragan couldn't control his host.

The grotesque image made me think of something I'd heard about Dragan—that he'd had a split soul, each half vying for control.

My skin went cold. Wolfie and I had fought for control at the start. Could that have been our fate?

The sickening transformations didn't stop Dragan from continuing his spell, however, and I shook my head to focus. How close were they?

Wild energy crackled through the room, and dark shadows spiraled along the walls. Even as we watched, I felt the intensity building.

The chant of Dragan's possessed cultists reverberated through the walls of the prison—dark, grating words that felt like they were gnawing on my skin.

"Ethan? How close are you?" I shouted up at him.

"Working."

I clenched my fists with worry.

Then the tower shuddered as a shockwave erupted from the courtyard below.

When I regained my footing, I could see that some of the chanting prisoners had collapsed, and the dark shadows swirling around the room had multiplied. My skin prickled. Were those faces in the shadows?

I ran to the bottom of the stairs and started ascending. "Ethan, we need to do something *now*! Shit is getting wild down there."

Devi leaned over the railing above. "We've got it. We're going to initiate riot suppression procedures to interrupt the ritual. Then Ethan will let the archmages in to deal with Dragan and the more powerful prisoners."

The tower shook again. "We might not have that long!"

An alarm horn blared, and the sound of a woman's soothing prerecorded voice echoed though the prison. "All inmates must return to their cells. Inmates who do not return to their cells will be incapacitated and subject to isolation procedures."

"You think they're going to comply?" Jaxson roared incredulously as he vaulted up the stairs behind me.

"Of course not!" Ethan shouted from above. "That's just an automated recording. But this might get them to listen up."

The tower reverberated with a drone that made my stomach churn and head spin. I reached for a railing to keep from falling, and I was glad I'd already emptied my stomach.

I could tell the effect was far worse down below. The prisoners looked around in wild confusion, and those still in their cells on our level threw up.

"What the hell was that?" I screamed.

"Vibrations to disorient. It won't hurt their ears, but at least we've stopped them from chanting. Now we put them to sleep," Devi shouted to us as we returned to the platform.

Plumes of pink-gray gas began pouring from vents along the edges of the tiers. Some of the haze lingered in the walkways, but most cascaded down like a waterfall to pool in low clouds in the open space below.

The Order team had the cameras working again, and the chaos played out on the array of monitors.

A few prisoners ran for the doors. A couple made it through the exits, but more began to stagger and drop to their knees in the clouds of gas, quickly passing out. But the werewolf cultists regained their balance and continued their chant.

Dread twisted along my spine. "It's not strong enough! They're not stopping!"

"It'll take longer for werewolves. The gas needs time to build up," Ethan muttered as he flipped through a notebook of instructions.

I looked down in horror at the scene below us. A dark storm was brewing, whipping the clouds of gas into a spiral around the walls. Ethereal ghosts swirled along with the wind, their mouths open in silent cries.

This was bad.

"Can you see the ghosts?" I asked Jaxson.

He nodded.

Okay, *really* bad.

I returned my attention to the cultists on the monitors. One werewolf's head lolled to the side, but his mouth kept moving, and his arms remained raised in the air.

"Shit!" I shouted. "They're like zombies or automatons or marionettes. They're not going to stop, even as they fall asleep!"

Jaxson grabbed two gas masks from a locker with riot gear and turned Ethan. "Can you vent the gas? We've got to go down there to stop this ourselves."

"Yes, but we need the other archmages," Ethan shouted as he held up a pile of notes and some prison schematics. "This place isn't meant to be reopened once it's locked down. I need to take the defenses down one by one to get them in without letting the prisoners escape."

"Well, we're out of time." I took one of the gas masks from Jaxson and tugged it down over my face. "It's up to us to disrupt the ritual."

As we darted for the door of the control room, Devi and one of the agents joined us. "We're coming with."

I nodded. "Thanks. And good luck."

Jaxson pressed the button on the blast door. It flew open, revealing two white-eyed werewolf inmates with their claws out, waiting for us.

Well, no one said it was going to be smooth.

55

Jaxson

The two possessed fuckers lunged as soon as the door opened.

I charged forward and rammed my shoulder into the chest of the first and sent him flying to the other end of the bridge. The second werewolf rammed his claws into my chest and pressed me backward so I was leaning half over the guardrail.

I hooked one leg between the bars of the railing so that I didn't slip, and then, with a single swift motion, I seized the bastard and heaved him up and over my head. His claws tore into my flesh, but they ripped free as he fell. I turned to watch his body disappear into the whirling maelstrom of magic and sleeping gas below.

Savy was on the other werewolf before he could get all the way up. She slapped her hand on his back and released a jolt of magic that drove him straight down into the ground.

I ran over and prodded him with my boot, but he was unconscious.

Whether Savy was aware of it, her power was growing. *Fast.*

Chests heaving, we peered over the side of the bridge. The

lower levels of the prison were in chaos, and of course, Dragan in the body of the Crusher stood in the eye of the storm. He looked up at us and pointed with a massive grin.

Suddenly, werewolf cultists from the second level swung themselves out onto the railings and began climbing toward us, moving from level to level.

This was going to get messy.

I turned to Savannah, Devi, and the agent. "I'll go this way to keep them distracted. You three take the stairs, and I'll join you at the bottom. We need to take out Dragan before his ritual is complete!"

I turned, grabbed the guardrail, and hurled myself to the seventh-floor railing below.

I wrapped my claws around the bars of the guardrail that fenced in the landing and looked down. Having already reached the third floor below me, the werewolves were using the same route to climb up.

The metal posts reverberated next to me, and I whipped my head around.

It was Savy, clinging to the guardrails for dear life.

"What are you doing here?" I growled. "I said take the stairs! Are you trying to break your neck?"

"I'm trying to break Dragan's neck," she snapped, then dropped a level to the railing of the sixth floor below.

A madwoman. My mate was a madwoman.

I jumped down to her position, catching the railing with my claws and swinging to her side. "Are you crazy? Two weeks ago, you were afraid to climb down a cliff."

"The thought of the Dark God loose in Magic Side really puts things in perspective. Anyway, you jumped first." Then she leapt down to the fifth level, and with a grunt of frustration, I followed.

We were only two levels above the ascending werewolf

cultists. One howled in mad delight, and they scrambled upward toward the fourth floor.

At that moment, Savannah cloaked the lower railing in shadow. There were shouts of surprise as the werewolves flew into the darkness, and then a metallic clang and sounds of scrabbling. One howled and dropped from the shadows.

"Hoped I'd get more of them," Savy grumbled, and then she jumped down into the darkness.

"Fuck!" I shouted. Did she forget I couldn't see in there, just like the werewolves? Or was she so hot under the collar that she was going to take them on solo?

Well, that's what you were planning to do, my wolf observed.

That's because I'm a godsdamned alpha. I flipped down onto the fourth-floor walkway as a bloodcurdling shriek echoed out from the patch of darkness. A werewolf flew back, sparking with Savy's magic.

I flipped myself over onto the catwalk, then rushed forward on foot into the darkness. "I need to see, godsdamn it!"

The black cloud of shadows vanished, revealing an inmate with white eyes clinging to the other side of the rail. I recognized him as one of the bikers from Pere Cheney. Reaching through the high bars, I grabbed him by the head, which I rammed against the metal rails again and again until his grip loosened. He dropped unconscious to the ground below.

"Nice wo—" Savannah's shout turned into a scream as the entire railing suddenly shuddered and bent inward. Her grip slipped.

I lunged forward and caught her hand before she plummeted, then pulled her up and over the twisted rail onto the catwalk.

Dragan had landed on the railing only twenty feet away. His new host was more like a giant than a man, a behemoth of flesh and swollen muscle. He couldn't have weighed less than four hundred pounds, and his landing had bent the railing inward.

The monster heaved himself over the crushed rail onto the catwalk and eagerly flexed the fingers of his hands that were the size of my head.

The Crusher.

Before we could move, he hurled himself down the catwalk toward us with deceptive speed.

I pushed Savannah out of the way and took the brunt of his blow.

My body hurtled backward through the air, and I slammed into the bars of a jail cell. Pain shot through my newly fractured ribs, and I wheezed for air.

But there was no time to breathe.

The monster swung at Savannah. She moved like the wind, and his fist rammed into the wall. It cracked, and concrete crumbled away. One blow could kill a man.

He pulled back, but Savannah shot low beneath his grasp, gouging his leg with her Soul Knife.

He roared, and his head shifted into that of a wolf. She dodged his snapping jaws, but his backhand caught her and sent her skidding across the ground.

"You could have been like me, Savannah. But now, you will become nothing!" He flicked his hand and sent a wave of fire in her direction.

With his back turned to me, I sprang forward and sunk my claws into his neck. But his muscles were so thick, it was like cutting into steel. He rammed himself into the wall, trying to crush me, but I twisted away just in time.

"You think you can stop this? That time has passed!" he roared as the chanting of the possessed inmates surged from below, resounding to a fever pitch. With a single swift motion, the beast seized a cell door and ripped it off its hinges. He swung, bashing me backward down the walk.

I rolled to my feet as the sound of the door smashing into the railing reverberated through the silent prison.

Silent?

No more chanting. Just a void

Not a good sign.

Dragan grinned and hurled the door at Savannah, and then the monster turned and ducked through the level two exit. He spun and slapped something on the opposite side of the wall.

I charged forward as a warning horn blared and a blast door shot down.

No!

I leapt and held the bottom of the door as it dropped, my arms straining to slow its fall. My joints and tendons screamed. The door shuddered and whined as it fought to continue.

My claws tore into the metal as I struggled to keep it up, but it was slipping.

Savannah appeared at my side. "I'll find something to wedge it!"

The gears whined, and I dropped to one knee as the door lurched down. Only a foot remained. "No time! Go! Open it from the other side!"

My claws scraped as they tore into the metal.

Savy read my face, then dropped and rolled through the gap.

I heard her slapping a button. "Jax! It's not working! It says, 'Lockdown procedures in place. This door will be unlocked in five minutes!'"

With a growl of frustration, I heaved the door upward with all my strength. It rose an inch.

Then metal tore, and the blast door slipped through my grasp. It sealed with a thunderous clang, trapping Savannah alone with Dragan on the other side.

Savannah

"Shit!" I snarled as the blast door crashed into the ground. I checked over my shoulder, then pounded on the steel hatch. "Jaxson!"

The only response was a dull beat from the other side.

I mashed the buttons on the control panel once again. No response. The red timer just kept counting down the seconds: 4:36 remaining.

Great.

I spun and searched the hallway. Should I wait for backup or pursue?

Dragan was long gone, but if I could catch him and stall him, Jaxson might be able to find another way through.

Go time.

The hallway curved off in either direction. I wasn't familiar with the scent of Dragan's new host, but I could tell that a werewolf who reeked of malice and sweat and toxic amounts of testosterone had gone to the right.

The Crusher, for sure.

Although I wanted to charge after him, I moved cautiously

down the hall and pulled the shadows around me. *What do you think the chances are that this is a trap, Wolfie?*

Oh, a hundred percent, my wolf responded. *Let's go get him.*

Dragan knew I was isolated. There wasn't any reason for him to run from me except to lure me into an ambush.

I cautiously peered through a side door into an enormous weight room. I didn't see any sign of Dragan, and his scent continued down the hall.

Hmm, my wolf said.

What? I asked as I pressed myself against the wall and started moving again.

On second thought, Dragan is inhabiting the body of a four-hundred-pound monster. Why would he need to ambush us? He could crush us with his left hand.

I paused as I reached the entrance to a stairwell. I cautiously cracked the door and peeked in. Empty, but I could smell that he'd gone that way.

It was like the stairwell we'd used to get to level eight. Flights of concrete steps zigzagged back and forth, leaving a small gap in the center rising to the top.

Fading footsteps echoed from above. He was moving up, *fast.*

If it's not an ambush, why is he running? I asked.

Well, maybe he just doesn't want to stick around for whatever is going to happen next, Wolfie said.

"Aw, shit."

For one beautiful moment, I'd hoped that just maybe he'd been running from me. It had been a nice, empowering thought. But the asshole was running away before his damn ritual or the Wolf God or something else blew us all to kingdom come.

That probably meant we didn't have much time to catch him and stop whatever was going to happen.

Throwing caution to the wind, I ran.

My boots propelled me upward with blinding speed. I took

the stairs three at a time and used the railing to slingshot myself around corners.

Each level had a door, but I flew past them. The echo of footsteps and the scent of big bad wolf told me my quarry was still ahead.

But I was faster.

The levels raced by. For one brief second, I saw his shadow on the stairs ahead, and then a thunderous explosion shook the building. I tumbled and skidded to my knees.

My heart froze as a cascade of rubble poured down from above. I rolled out of the way, taking shelter against the wall as chunks of concrete rebounded off the stairs and a rain of debris filled the air.

There was a wild, metallic groan, and then an iron railing tumbled down into the dark.

When the noise abated, I pulled myself unsteadily to my feet in the cloud of dust. *That was one hell of a blast.*

I paused and listened to my thundering heart and the reverberating groans of the building. Once I was sure that the rain of destruction had ceased, I cautiously continued up the winding stairs until the consequences of the explosion came into view.

The blast had completely destroyed the top of the stairwell. All that was left of the last few flights of stairs were bent iron girders and broken concrete steps.

The sky shone through the gaping hole in the roof. Dark clouds spiraled overhead, but I could also discern a faintly shimmering dome—the magical forcefield above the prison. If it was still intact, Dragan wouldn't be able to escape, but I had a sinking feeling he wasn't actually running away.

Cautiously, I made my way up to the point where the stairs had crumbled into nothing. I craned my head to look up at the tangled mess of beams and rebar, and then down to the distant pile of rubble ten flights below at the bottom of the stairwell.

This is going to be just like climbing a tree. Except if I fall, I'm going to be a shish kebab on rusted rebar.

I leapt, grabbing hold of a protruding bit of metal, and then began hauling myself upward. Hand over hand, I climbed up the shattered stairwell until I came to the edge, where the roof had collapsed at an angle, but not all the way.

Huh. Monkey hands are actually more useful than paws from time to time, my wolf teased as I caught my breath.

Slowly, I poked my head over the ledge, relief trickling through me. *Gotcha.*

Dragan was wreathed in a spindle of neon flame. The twisted signature of his sorcery tainted the air around us as glowing green runes appeared one by one across the surface of the roof.

I had no idea what he was doing, but I got the feeling that I didn't have time to figure it out.

Preoccupied by his spell, Dragan didn't see me. His back was turned.

Give me speed, Wolfie.

I'd only have one chance, and I had to make it count.

Crouching for a sprint, I launched myself forward and summoned my Soul Knife. Our feet pounded the rooftop, moving faster than I ever had before. Dragan began to turn, and I—

Unbelievable pain cascaded through my body as I slammed into a solid, invisible wall.

I felt my left wrist snap on impact, and I ricocheted off the unyielding barrier.

Agony jumped from limb to limb as I rolled onto my side. Darkness pressed at the corners of my vision, and I couldn't breathe.

From his pillar of fire, Dragan laughed. "Savannah, you are always so entertaining. Sorry I had to lock you out of the party."

It hurt too much to even think about rising, but I managed a jagged breath. "The party isn't over, Dragan."

"Oh, but it is. You're too late. The ritual is complete."

I laughed. "Then why are you hiding up here? Where's your Dark God?"

"Watching. Waiting for the final sacrifice to be made." He turned and flashed a malicious grin. "You."

57

Savannah

Fear and rage poured through me. Dragan's evil delight, his arrogant confidence, the way he'd toyed and tormented *me* for weeks on end—I'd had *enough*.

"Fuck you," I growled as I tried to push myself up. My left arm exploded with pain, and I crumpled while the bastard laughed.

Let me take part of that load, Wolfie said. Suddenly, some of the agony drained away, and my thoughts cleared.

Thank you.

Just make this count, she whined, and I could hear the suffering in her voice. She'd taken on my pain.

Shakily, I rose and pressed my right hand against the wall. I felt the toxic strength of Dragan's magic, and it made my skin crawl.

The flames around him lowered as the runes across the roof took on a brighter glow. "The Dark God commanded that I perform a ritual for him, and he promised he would deliver the sacrifice. Well, here you are. I will offer him you and your pet alpha, and all the archmages and prisoners in this place!"

He raised his arms and voice to the sky. "I have prepared your altar, great one! A sacrifice unlike any before."

Altar? I looked around at the rune-inscribed top of the prison. Oh, shit, the whole damn thing was going to be his altar.

Horror chilled my veins. The Order's top people were entering the prison now, and I was pretty sure the place was about to go up like a nuclear bomb.

Do something, Savy!

I summoned my Soul Knife and pressed the point against the invisible wall, hoping that somehow, we could break through. I felt my wolf's power pour into me like heat and ice, but my blade didn't budge.

I could feel Dragan pushing back with his mind, repelling my own power. He laughed, a low, thunderous sound coming from the body of the Crusher. "You think you have the strength to stop me? My cultists have charged me with the power of their souls. You are nothing."

He raised his arms, and the runes that had formed over the top of the building leapt into pillars of green fire. A green glow formed in the sky above, and a radiant, twisting funnel cloud began to rapidly form.

My blood grew ice cold. A sorcery-infused tornado was about to drill down into the prison and rip it and its occupants apart. Hundreds of inmates, as well as the agents and arch-mages, all sacrificed on the altar of the Dark God.

Jaxson.

My will surged, and I screamed and threw myself into the wall. Dragan's vile magic lanced through me, and it felt like pushing through the barrier would rip apart my soul.

And then it did.

Pain beyond imagination cascaded through me, and I staggered back as the shadow of a wolf leapt from my chest and through the barrier. *My wolf.*

How was that even possible?

She hurtled forward, dodged the blazing runes like land mines, and tore into Dragan.

My shadow wolf was as fast as the wind. She struck and was gone, leaving red trails across his pale white skin.

He bellowed in rage as she tore into his calf. He swung his massive fist, but like a stream of smoke, she vanished and reappeared, then brutally attacked again.

The invisible barrier in front of me flickered, and I felt its magic weaken as his concentration broke.

I charged forward and rammed my blade into the wall, pushing all my magic into it.

Black shadows streamed off me, and frost formed on my skin, but a green crack split the air in front of me. With a concussion I felt more than heard, Dragan's magic shattered.

I was through the barrier in an instant and charging across the minefield of runes.

The twister above us had formed to a point, like a glowing green dagger plunging toward the roof.

Dragan had lost control of his form as well as the barrier, and his arms and head and chest shifted at random, from man to wolf to man again. The giant brute stumbled and twisted as he tried to incinerate my wolf with bursts of green flame.

I lunged forward, but he spun at the last second. His backhand slammed into me like a steam shovel and flipped me into the air.

I crashed down onto the roof, and my knife ricocheted from my hand and vanished into smoke. Unable to hold in the pain, I gasped and arched my spine.

And then Dragan was on top of me.

My shadow wolf tore at him, but he shook her free and lunged forward with blinding speed. I resummoned my blade, but he slapped it from my grip and slammed his giant hands on either side of my temples. Pain exploded through my skull, and stars swam through my vision.

The Crusher.

My wolf ripped and tore at his arm, but he didn't budge.

I screamed in blinding agony, and he smiled. "This is the proper way to sacrifice before a god."

Suddenly, his right hand ripped free, and he staggered back.

My head ricocheted off the pavement, and the world spun.

Get up! my wolf roared in my mind.

I shoved myself to my knees and saw Dragan the Crusher with his wrist clamped in the mouth of a massive gray wolf.

Jaxson.

Before I could move, the beast of a man swung his arm, sending Jaxson flying free. He tumbled and skidded across to the edge of the roof.

Dragan roared as the Crusher's upper body turned into a half man, half wolf.

Jaxson climbed to his feet, and dread filled my heart. Crimson blood seeped from a deep, gaping wound in his side where a piece of rebar had impaled him. Charging forward, he leapt onto the Crusher's chest, his jaws sinking into the monster's throat.

The Crusher bellowed and gripped Jaxson's head. With one quick movement, he ripped Jaxson free and bashed him down on the roof. Nightmare screams filled my mind as horror ripped through me.

Then the monster bent down, gripped Jaxson with his massive arms, and heaved him up over his head, as if offering him to the tornado above.

"Wolfie! Strength!" I shouted as I charged.

The shadow wolf slammed into my back. We merged as one and shot forward like a bullet.

The world was nothing but a blur. I had half a breath to

summon the blade before I collided with the Crusher's back. I drove the Soul Knife deep into his spine and poured my magic into the dagger. Black shadows boiled off my arm like smoke, and my skin burned as it turned to ice.

The Crusher opened his jaws and roared.

Gritting my teeth, I dug in with the blade, feeling the taut resistance from Dragan's soul. He clung to his host like iron, and the knife wouldn't cut.

Help me!

My wolf's power flowed into me like sweet nectar, and the blade grew white hot. Then, with a gut-wrenching tear, it swung free. There was an explosion of magic as it sliced through Dragan's soul, and I stumbled back.

The monstrous beast dropped to his knees, then fell face-first onto the roof, bringing Jaxson down with him.

The Crusher's head twisted toward me, his mouth open in a lifeless scream of horror. Thunder ripped through the sky above as the white light in his eyes went out and dissipated in smoke.

I pulled the talisman from my pocket, waiting for the moment that I knew would come—just as it had after I'd cut Dragan's soul from Kahanov.

My wound began to burn as a pale, spectral apparition rose from the corpse.

But it wasn't Dragan. It was the Crusher. He loomed just as large as he'd been in life.

My arm dropped, and I stepped back.

The ghost of the Crusher spread his hands wide, and his voice roared in my mind. *You little bitch! I should've caved your head in! How I would've loved to feel the slick pieces of your skull slip between my fingers.*

He lunged forward, hands outstretched. *I'll haunt you unt—*

The phantom dissipated into wisps of smoke as a translucent green spirit ripped through it.

Dragan.

I will possess you! the spirit screamed, a silent vibration that shook the rooftop. *I will force you to rip out the throat of your mate with that little knife of yours.*

He shot forward and dove into me as I raised the talisman.

Fight him! Wolfie cried from within my soul.

My arms began to shift between human and wolf as Dragan fought within me, trying to take hold. I felt all the poison and hatred in his soul as he thrust himself into me.

No!

With a scream of rage, my soul pushed against his. Wolfie joined her strength to mine as Dragan struggled for dominance.

I raised the black talisman high overhead. *That* was where the fucking evil bastard belonged.

Black shadows billowed from my skin as I concentrated my will, and with a final burst of power, I thrust the green specter out of me and into the onyx.

His unearthly scream was cut off as the last tendrils of green light drained from my body. The black stone glowed with a radioactive light, and the charm seared its shape in my hand.

I dropped it to the ground, and a trail of smoke curled up off it.

The tornado above me exploded into clouds and began to drift apart, but I had only one care in the world.

Jaxson.

58

Savannah

Heart pounding and pain searing through me, I stumbled to the side of the enormous gray and brown wolf. His body was savaged by deep cuts and wounds, and the side of his head was battered and matted with blood.

Oh, God.

Forcing my stomach to still, I dug my hands into his fur and felt his heartbeat. Strong and powerful.

Joy leapt through me.

I didn't know what Jaxson was to me. A lover? My alpha? A mystery? All I knew was that I couldn't let him slip away. That I needed him, and the pack needed him.

How do we heal him? I asked my wolf, panic straining at the edges of my mind.

I'll guide you, she said weakly. *But I don't know how much we can give.* I closed my eyes and let her take control. My hand pressed against him, and we pushed with our magic, searching for that connection that bound him to me.

I could feel it, that unbreakable thread.

My magic began to flow. Not cold and shadows, but

warmth and light. It poured out of me, like a torrent of life. The world sharpened, and euphoria filled my veins. I didn't know how much time had passed, but every part of me became alive, even as the last of my strength drained from my body.

I slipped sideways, barely catching myself with my weakened arms as the euphoria faded and my head spun.

The great wolf lying before me suddenly thrust upward. He shook his head, then looked at me with radiant golden eyes that pierced into my soul. Eyes that I could lose myself in forever. Ignoring the pain that racked my damaged body, I wrapped my arms around his furry neck. "You're alive!"

Without warning, the savage beast shifted beneath my arms and lifted me upward. I yelped as I suddenly found myself wrapped around a naked man.

"Savy," he practically purred. Dragging his fingers through my hair, he brought my mouth to his and kissed me deeply. Passion, desire, and need flashed through me, dulling my pain, but the kiss was more than that. It was deeper. It was an unspoken promise between us, that we would always protect one another. Whatever Jaxson was to me, I knew he would always have my back.

Shouts echoed across the roof.

I dropped from Jaxson's arms with a moan and summoned my knife while he shifted into a wolf.

It was Devi and Ethan. My shoulders relaxed, but the aches and pains in my body screamed as the adrenaline wore off. I was drained.

They surveyed the white rooftop with wonder. It was covered in burned sigils and streaks of blood.

"What the hell happened up here?" Ethan asked.

I tilted my head toward the corpse lying face-down on the roof. "Well, I almost learned why they call him the Crusher."

Ethan grunted. "Looks like that bastard's reckoning finally came due."

Turning to survey the wreckage, I shrugged. "As for what else happened here. I'm not exactly sure. He was casting a spell. I don't know what it was, but it was powerful enough to turn this whole place into a sacrificial altar for his god."

Ethan crouched down and inspected the charred remains of the runes. "It's crude but powerful sorcery. Fates, was that lunatic going to nuke the entire prison? Himself included?"

I nodded. "That checks out. He'd really drunk the Kool-Aid."

The Dark Wolf God had promised him a new form.

Ethan rose. "I don't know how close it got, but if you hadn't killed him when you did, chances are we would've all been dead, and this place would've been a charred pile of rubble."

Setting the Dark God free and leaving Magic Side without its archmages. Man, we'd been really close to disaster.

Devi dropped down beside the massive corpse of the Crusher and inspected the talisman she'd made. The onyx pulsed with its sick light.

"Did it work?" she asked.

My heart skipped a beat at her question, and I looked at her, wide-eyed. "Are you telling me there was a chance it *wouldn't* work?"

She rose and dusted off her hands.

"No. Of course it would work. I didn't have a doubt," she said, clearly lying.

Oh, God.

But it *had* worked. That's what mattered.

I took her hands. "Thank you. Without your spell, he'd still be out there."

Devi smiled. "Just glad it did its job. Now we have to figure out what to do with it."

Ethan knelt and reached for the talisman, but Devi stopped

him and shook her head. He stroked his chin, studying the vile, pulsing thing. "We could lock it in our vault. It's a labyrinth with a few billion combinations. No one would be able to get to him, and he'd never be able to get out if he broke free of the enchantment."

If he broke free? More like *when*.

Jaxson grunted. "We need to destroy him. For good."

"How?" Devi asked.

Silence hung in the air.

"I think I know how," I murmured. "My aunt has a way."

The Sphere of Devouring.

But that meant I'd have to face her. And Casey. I wasn't sure if I was ready for that.

Taking a moment to myself, I walked to the edge of the roof and looked out across the channel toward Magic Side. *Home.*

But was it? I couldn't go back to the LaSalles, knowing what my aunt had done to me. And staying at Jaxson's was out of the question. I knew we shared a mate bond—we had since birth—but I needed space to sort out what that meant.

And certainly, I couldn't spend my life sleeping on Sam's lumpy couch, for the sake of both our friendship and my back.

But even though I was homeless, Magic Side was still home. And today, it was safe.

I'd never seen the city from this vantage. It was beautiful. In the north, the towering skyscrapers were lit with fierce sunlight. The south was a sea of red brick apartments. The center of the island was cut by the green expanse of trees and parks where I'd run with the pack for the first time. The sky hanging over the city was bright blue.

But not over Bentham.

I craned my head back. Dark clouds still spun above us, and a cold wind tore at my wet and blood-soaked clothes. We had our own micro-climate on the island.

A deep dread settled in my gut, and I swallowed hard.

When we'd disrupted the ritual at Pere Cheney, the storm clouds had dissipated. But not now. While the glowing funnel cloud was gone, the vortex remained, spinning slowly and ominously.

We weren't finished here.

I scooped up the glowing talisman and turned to Jaxson. "Take me to the Indies."

59

Jaxson parked out front of the big red house that had become like my second home—or at least, it *had* been before I'd almost killed Laurel in front of Casey.

Jaxson turned off the truck and looked over at me. "Are you sure this is a good idea?"

I wiped my sweaty palms on my bloodstained jeans and sucked in a breath. "It's the only way we can be sure that Dragan stays dead."

The front door opened, and Laurel stepped out onto the porch, concern cutting her face.

"Do you want me to come in with you?" he asked.

Jaxson's signature pressed into me, and my nerves settled. Dried blood streaked his skin and beard, and I couldn't help the pangs of desire that rang through my body. He was savage and lethal, and maybe it was the aftershocks of near death, but at that moment, I wanted all of him. First, however, I needed to settle the score with Dragan.

"I've got this one." Scooping up the black pouch with the talisman, I squeezed Jax's hand and carefully slid out of the cab.

We'd picked up a couple of Alia's healing potions from Sam on the drive over, but my body still felt bruised and broken.

Laurel went rigid as she took in my form, which I'm sure was a sight. My clothes were torn and caked with blood—my own and others'—and my hair was a wild mess.

"Are you injured? Do you need one of Pete's healing potions?" she asked calmly, though I could sense her fear and concern. She glared at Jaxson, who'd stayed in the truck, as she opened the front door and ushered me inside.

I recalled how Casey had protested about Uncle Pete's potions after he'd busted his ankle at the Magic Moon Motel, and a sharp pain lanced my heart. "No, I'm good, but thanks. Is Casey here?"

She slid the locks on the door into place and turned to me. "He's not."

The pained expression on her face told me everything she couldn't, and a lump of sorrow rose in my throat.

"What can I do for you?" she asked.

Pushing aside my grief for my cousin, I opened my palm, revealing the black linen pouch. "We got him."

The weight of those three words finally settled over me.

Laurel sucked in a sharp breath and pressed her hand to the base of her throat. "My gods, you did it. *How*?"

"Thanks to you, we tracked down the art dealer and retrieved Dragan's finger. A contact at the Order used it to make a talisman, and...well, long story short, we got the asshole." I fought back the horrors that bombarded my mind: Alejandro, the vampires, Bentham, the Crusher squeezing my skull... I swallowed hard. "Now I need to destroy this thing. For good. I was hoping we could let the Sphere of Devouring put an end to this madness."

Laurel reached out to touch me, but I flinched, and she dropped her hand to her side. "You've been through so much,

Savannah. Too much for one soul to bear, and I'm so sorry for that. Let's get rid of Victor Dragan for good. Come on."

I followed her into the drawing room and took a seat on the antique red couch, where all of this had started. I no longer was the same naïve girl. I had blood on my hands and darkness inside of me now. Would I ever be whole again?

Laurel retrieved the wooden platter that held the Sphere of Devouring and set it down on the coffee table in front of me. I recognized the nine-pointed star and ring of runes. Once, they'd seemed alien, but now they were familiar.

She pulled away the velvet cloth that was draped over the sphere, revealing the floating black orb. Worried that somehow, after all of this, Dragan might find a way to escape, I clutched the cursed talisman tightly as Laurel traced her fingers across the runes. They glowed blue, and then the magic of the sphere exploded around us.

Vertigo turned my stomach, and I braced my free hand on the couch. But this time, I didn't feel like I was falling into an abyss.

"Ready?" Laurel asked, seemingly unfazed by the energy whipping off the orb like a million magic lightning bugs pulsing at once.

"What do I do?" The last time the sphere and I had interacted hadn't ended well, and I didn't want it devouring my magic along with Dragan's.

Laurel watched me closely, her expression serious. "Offer the talisman to it but be clear with your intentions. The Sphere will try to take whatever magic it can, including your own. Let it know what it may and may not take."

My heart thrummed against my chest as my stomach knotted.

Don't get us killed, Wolfie said.

I opened the pouch and slid the talisman into my palm. It

was warm to the touch and gave off a pulsing green glow that felt wrong. I looked to the Sphere of Devouring, unsure of exactly what to say but certain that it had to be precise.

"I offer you this talisman that is holding the soul and magic of Victor Dragan. You may only take it, and nothing more." I glanced at Laurel, and she nodded.

"Goodbye, Dragan," I whispered. The instant I moved my hand that was holding the talisman, a force pulled it toward the sphere.

"Do not touch the sphere!" Laurel said. "Use your magic to counter its force."

I gasped and pulled back, my fist inches from the black orb of devouring. My muscles ached, and my arm felt like it was being torn from its socket, but I couldn't open my fist to release the talisman.

Help me, Wolfie.

My strength isn't what you need. Call your magic, she answered anxiously.

My arm was shaking from the strain, but I closed my eyes and focused on drawing my magic. It came forth easily, like the sphere was drawing it out. Cool waves of energy flowed through me, and I opened my eyes. Shadows coalesced around me, and a dark tendril snaked around my arm, enveloping my clenched fist.

Release it, said the oddly familiar voice I couldn't quite place.

The force that was tugging me lessened, and all the tension in my body released.

This was it.

I opened my fingers, and the talisman flew into the black orb. Gone. An explosion of energy cascaded from the orb, knocking Laurel and me back, and shaking the house. In seconds, it was over, and everything was still.

Tension twisted in my stomach, and I looked to my aunt. "Did it work?"

Laurel leaned forward and swept her hand over the runes, and the magic in the air extinguished as each of the glowing blue symbols faded. She covered the Sphere of Devouring with the velvet cloth and gazed up at me with a broad smile. "You did it, Savy. You succeeded where we all failed. You destroyed Dragan. For good."

The wound on my shoulder burned. I glanced around the room but saw nothing. An uneasy heaviness hung in the air, and I couldn't shake the feeling that something wasn't right. "Are you sure?"

"You saw it for yourself. The sphere devoured the talisman. Whatever goes into the orb is destroyed. Dragan is gone, my dear. You can rest easy."

"Right." I stood and rubbed my hands on my jeans, feeling unsure of what to do next. "Thanks. We couldn't have done it without you."

Laurel stepped around the coffee table and pulled me into an embrace. I recoiled, but there was nowhere to go—she had me pinned.

"I'm so proud of you, honey. I know you're still upset, but know that we love you and that you always have a place here." She released me and left the room.

My aunt was offering me an olive branch. Could I forgive her?

Maybe if you forgive her, Casey would forgive you, my wolf said.

Maybe Casey and I both needed some time to come around. I sighed and headed to the front door.

"Savannah, wait." Laurel strode down the hall toward me and pressed something into my palm.

A small key.

I glanced up at her. "What's this for?"

She shrugged. "Your mother sent it many years back. She never said what it was for, just asked that I keep it safe for her. I never looked into it, but I suppose with everything that's happened...maybe you should."

Another mystery, but maybe one that would yield some answers. "Thanks. For everything."

I could feel my voice tightening, so I spun and unlocked the front door, and stepped outside. Laurel waited for a second, but then the door closed, and I heard the locks slide into place. I sighed in relief. I couldn't believe it was all over.

Jaxson was still in the truck. I rubbed the wound on my shoulder, which was beginning to really ache, and headed down the front steps. I'd need to figure out what was going on with it and how to get that missing piece of my soul back befo—

A thunderclap reverberated through the heavens, and I stumbled on the lawn before looking up.

Chills skated over my skin, and my breath stilled as a deep dread settled in my gut.

The sky had darkened, and enormous thunderheads roiled above. As I watched, the clouds gradually resolved into the shape of a wolf. Its face had no eyes, but I could feel it watching me, and I shivered as memories flooded back.

Several weeks ago, when I'd sleepwalked down the stairs into the clutches of the Noctith demon, I'd seen that same form in the dark clouds rising in the starlit sky. In that moment, a voice had spoken in my mind, a voice that shook my thoughts and being to my very core: *I will free you, if you free me.*

It hadn't been the voice of my wolf, but of someone else. The same voice I'd heard but couldn't place just moments ago in Laurel's drawing room, urging me to destroy the talisman. The same voice I'd heard when I'd attacked Laurel days ago.

Oh, my God.

Your sacrifice is accepted, little wolf, the voice boomed. *Together, we will bring darkness upon the world.*

"No!" I choked out as understanding dawned like a thousand puzzle pieces falling into place.

That voice...it had been the Dark Wolf God speaking to me all along. Urging me to do his bidding. He'd released my wolf. Laurel didn't understand how it had been possible, but now it all made sense.

No, no, no.

Jaxson must have seen me freaking out, because he was out of his truck and striding toward me. I doubled over, panting heavily as his arms wrapped around me, pulling me to his chest. "What happened?"

The clouds overhead dissipated, revealing a bright blue sky. I shook my head and twisted from his grip. "What was the prophecy?"

Jaxson paused and frowned. "What's going on, Savy?"

"Tell me what the prophecy said, Jaxson."

Confusion tugged at his features, and his muscles tensed. "That Dragan would bring back the Dark Wolf God."

I dug my claws into his arm and burned my words into him with my eyes. "No. *Exactly* what the prophecy said."

He studied me with concern. But it was the dread and fear enveloping him that sank my heart. How had I missed it before?

"Please."

A darkness settled over him, and his voice turned cold and detached. "A twin-soul will come to power. They will be the harbinger of destruction. When the moon has turned her back, they will make a sacrifice before the Dark God, and in seven days, he will walk the earth once more, spreading madness among the living. The twin-soul will steal the wolves from every werewolf who resists them and will leave your people weak before the Dark God."

The world spun as the weight of his words sank into my soul. By trapping Dragan and delivering the talisman to the Sphere of Devouring, had I completed the ritual and released the Dark Wolf God? Had he been playing me like a puppet the whole time?

Nausea overwhelmed me, and I stumbled as my knees grew weak.

Jaxson grabbed me and held me upright. "Savy, what happened?"

I began to tremble. Dragan's words played on repeat in my mind: *If they knew what you truly were, they'd kill you where you stand, Savannah Caine. They'd kill you without a second's hesitation.*

We've got to flee. We've got to get out of here, I thought to my wolf.

My heart was beating so fast I thought it would explode. I pulled out of Jaxson's arms and backed away, but he grabbed my shoulders. "Where are you going? Tell me what's wrong."

I shook my head. "I can't."

He tightened his grip. "It's me, Savy. You can tell me anything."

Could I tell him that his mate was the one responsible for releasing the Dark God? That she was the one who would destroy his pack? The pack meant more to Jaxson than anything, even me.

I went limp in his grasp, despair taking my will to fight.

Jaxson's eyes were dark with concern. "Tell me what the hell's going on."

With no courage left in my soul, I whispered, "He's free."

I had to warn him, after all.

Jaxson's brow furrowed, but the way his body tensed indicated he knew who I was referring to.

Tears flooded my eyes, and my trembles became quakes. "The Dark Wolf God is free. And I released him."

Jaxson froze, and I struggled out of his arms, taking several steps back. "Dragan completed the ritual, but *I* gave the final sacrifice by destroying the talisman. The Dark Wolf God just told me that my sacrifice has been accepted."

"I don't—"

"*Dragan* was the sacrifice! The prophecy was never about him. It was about *me*. I'm the twin-soul, Jaxson. I'm the harbinger of destruction. Because of me, he'll return."

Jaxson didn't move, but his emotions bombarded me, one after the other. Fear. Anger. Disappointment. And rage.

I felt my heart cracking. I had to protect him. Protect the pack.

"No." He looked up at me with a piercing gaze that made my knees quake. "We'll stop it."

"Jaxson. The prophecy says that I will steal your pack's wolves and leave them weak when he returns. I have the fucking *Soul Knife*, for God's sake. It's me."

"Not my pack, *our* pack," he growled. "And you would never—"

"Of course I wouldn't. But he's a god—what if he takes control of me? Dragan nearly possessed me. It won't be a problem for a god. What happens if he makes me cut everybody's souls out? If it comes down to me or the pack, who will you choose?"

He didn't speak, and I saw the agony in his eyes.

"That's right. You'll choose the pack, and you should. I'm a LaSalle, Jaxson, not one of you anymore. You have to let me go before I destroy us all." Tears pooled in the corners of my eyes, but I fought them back as I inched away from him.

He was on me so fast, my heart didn't have a chance to beat. While he'd held me firmly before, he was ruthless now, and he sank his claws into my wrists. When he spoke, however, it wasn't with a savage growl, but with quiet, calm strength. "No. You're mine. You are *not* leaving."

My magic coursed through me, frigid like melting snow. Shadows coalesced at my feet, waiting for my command. How had it all come to this?

Run! Wolfie said, sorrow and anguish in her voice.

Tears spilling down my cheeks, I raised my palms toward Jaxson and released a clap of magic. He flew backward, landing hard on the sidewalk.

He was on his feet in a heartbeat and striding toward me, anger and worry on his face. I drew the shadows around him, blocking his vision.

"Savannah, what are you doing?" Fear tinged his voice as he searched for me.

I swallowed hard, trying to keep from sobbing. "Leaving. I'll find a way to stop this, but I won't risk the lives of you and the pack. I'm sorry. Goodbye, Jaxson."

A cry tore from my throat as I turned and ran.

Yet it was Jaxson's roar that demolished the remaining pieces of my heart. My feet pounded against the pavement, and though every fiber of my being screamed to turn back, I couldn't.

I had to leave, to buy Wolfie and me some time, while I figured out a way to stop the Dark Wolf God from returning.

We appreciate you joining us on this wild adventure! If you've got an extra minute, please leave us a review on Amazon (mybook.to/Dark-Lies) and Goodreads. Reviews make a *huge* impact. They help us become better writers and keep us going through the difficult pages!

Ready to find out what happens next? *Shadow Kissed*, the final book in Savy and Jax's story, is available now: mybook.to/Shadow-Kissed

And if you didn't get a chance to read the prologue of the series and you would you like to know more about the first run in with the rogue bikers that kicked off *Wolf Marked*, sign up for our newsletter here to get access to an exclusive, insider only copy:

https://dl.bookfunnel.com/wgkpoqcjqa (you can unsubscribe at any time).

Finally, if you're interested in learning more about the archaeology and history that inspired this book, keep reading!

AUTHOR'S NOTE

Thank you for reading *Dark Lies*!

This installment of Savy and Jaxson's story was inspired by a few places we have yet to visit—the cemetery at Pere Cheney being one of them. The historic town was founded in 1873 in northern Michigan as a stop along the Michigan Central Railroad. Unfortunately, an outbreak of diptheria wiped out most of the population, and by the early twentieth century the place had become a 'ghost town.' Local legends about the abandoned town abound, but perhaps the most popular is the legend of the witch who cursed the village after she was banished to the woods. Many people believed that she was to blame for the outbreak of disease and the death of most of the town's population. She was later hanged from a tree and buried in the cemetery.

Pere Cheney cemetery itself is located to the south of the historic town and contains the burials of at least ninety people, one of whom is rumored to be the witch. Unfortunately, many of the headstones have been vandalized over the years and only a few remain—hence why the witch in our story asks Savy for an unbreakable tombstone! If you venture out to Pere Cheney cemetery today, tread lightly over the strange mossy grass that grows in the area, and keep your eyes peeled—you may catch a sighting of a ghost!

We recently travelled to Mexico and decided what better place to stage a meeting with a notorious vampire art dealer. The colonial-era town of San Miguel de Allende is located in the central highlands north of Mexico City. The town is well known for its baroque Spanish architecture and thriving art scene, attracting artists and aesthetes from all over—including our vampire, Alejandro Rivera. You'll recall that Savy, Jax, and Damian arrived through a portal at Cañada de la Virgen (The Virgin's Glen) on the House of the Thirteen Heavens. This is an archaeological site that was recently excavated and is located within striking distance of San Miguel de Allende. The ancient complex consists of seven pyramid structures that were constructed by the indigenous Otomíes and in use until around 1050 AD. The whole complex functioned as an astronomical observation site, and the House of the Thirteen Heavens, where our characters arrived, was built in perfect alignment with the movements of the Sun, Jupiter, and Venus. This is definitely on our list of places to visit!

And finally, our book wouldn't be complete without a bit of Chicago history and lore. You might recall the two-horned serpent in the final battle—the Misiginebig or Mishi-Ginebig. Chicago was built on the ancestral lands of indigenous tribes, which had extensive trading networks in the Great Lakes region prior to European contact. The Misiginebig was an underwater serpent common in the legends of the Algonquian people who populated the Atlantic Coast, much of Canada, and the Great Lakes. This mythical creature was said to lurk in lakes and eat humans. While disease and relocation had a tragic impact on the tribes in the Chicago area, the city has maintained a diverse and thriving indigenous population to this day.

That's all that we have space for right now, but we'll be

posting more detailed notes about more of the inspiration for this book in our newsletter. You can sign up at: https://www.veronicadouglas.com/newsletter

Shadow Kissed, the epic conclusion to Savy and Jax's story is available now! Read it on Amazon here: mybook.to/Shadow-Kissed

Come check us out in our Facebook Reader group (Veronica Douglas' Magic Side Insiders) if you'd like to chat more about the books, interact with fellow readers, and get the scoop on what's up next. You can join here:

https://www.facebook.com/groups/veronicadouglas

Thanks again for reading and stay in touch!

-Veronica Douglas

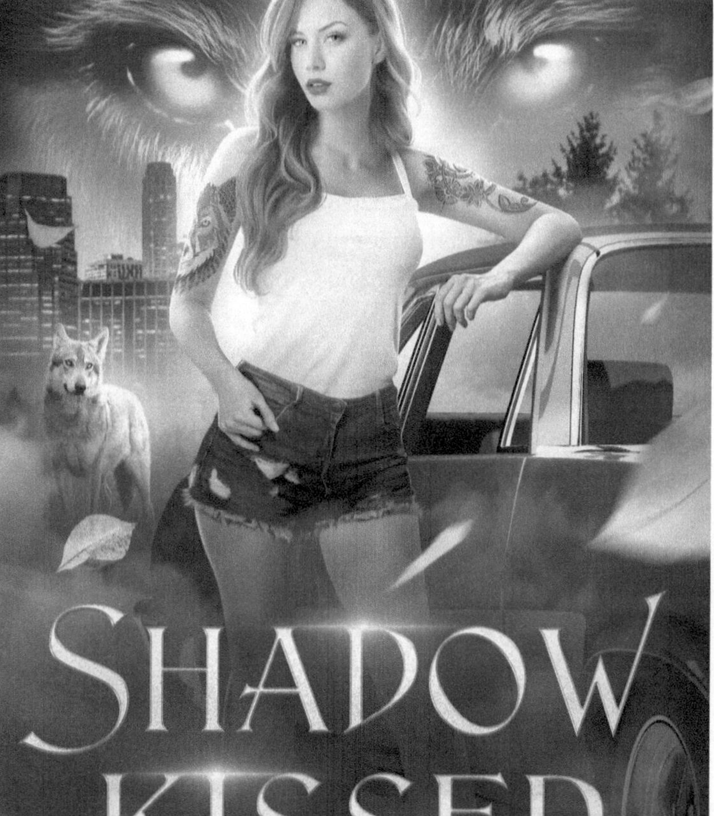

SHADOW KISSED
MAGIC SIDE: WOLF BOUND BOOK 4
VERONICA DOUGLAS

SHADOW KISSED

MAGIC SIDE: WOLF BOUND, BOOK 4 OF 4
PREVIEW

I released the Dark Wolf God. Now he's using me.

Last week, I defeated a monster hellbent on killing us all. I thought I was stopping a prophecy, but it turns out, the dark omens were about me all along.

Now I'm destined to steal the souls of the pack—*my pack*—and help the Dark God bring destruction down on the world. Jaxson Laurent, my fated mate, is determined to help me fight back, but what if he has to choose between me and his wolves?

The Dark God is beginning to take control of me, and unless I can heal the wound in my soul, I won't be able to resist his call. Worse, if I can't heal the centuries-long blood feud between my family and the pack, our city won't be able to stand against his wrath.

Unfortunately, my only choice may be to betray them all and do the one thing Jaxson may never forgive me for. It seems my destiny is to destroy everything I love.

The fates have a wicked sense of humor.

Good thing I've never been one who follows the rules.

Book 4 of 4

The epic conclusion of the Wolf Bound series.

Read Shadow Kissed now on Amazon here: mybook.to/Shadow-Kissed

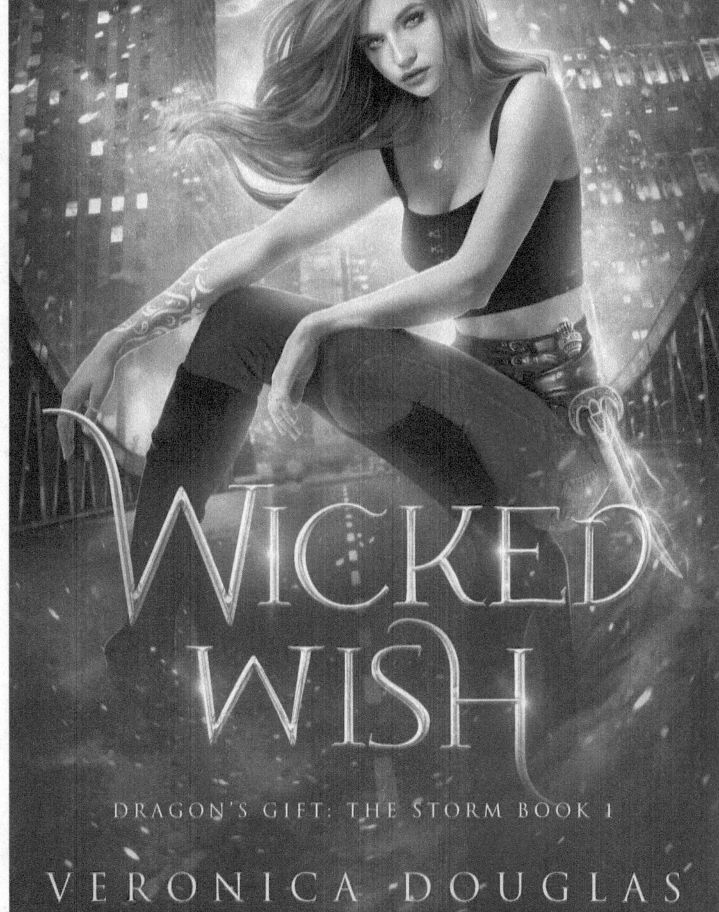

WICKED
WISH
DRAGON'S GIFT: THE STORM BOOK 1
VERONICA DOUGLAS
LINSEY HALL

WICKED WISH

DRAGON'S GIFT: THE STORM, BOOK 1 PREVIEW

If you're ready for more Magic Side adventures and want to read a complete series right now, try: Wicked Wish (co-authored with Linsey Hall).

I'm at the mercy of a fallen angel.

I work for the Order of Magica, the supernatural version of the FBI. Sounds fun, right? Except I spend my days chained to my desk, writing reports, and wishing that I was out solving crimes. *Well, be careful what you wish for.*

When my best friend is abducted, my life in Chicago turns upside down.

I'll do anything to get her back—even work with Damian Malek, a wanted criminal, notorious crime lord, and dangerous fallen angel. He's hot, lethal, and he's the only one who can help me master my dangerous powers. I don't want anyone to know about my magic, but I have no choice if I want to save my friend.

Here's the catch: if the Order finds out that I'm working with Damian, I'll get canned. Maybe even be hunted for what I am. But if I don't give him what he wants, he'll reveal my secret to the world.

Wicked Wish features a rebel heroine, a dark angel hero, and slow burn romance. Prepare yourself for edge-of-your-seat adventure amongst ancient ruins and fantastical worlds.

If you enjoyed the archaeology, history, and daring in Linsey Hall's original Dragon's Gift books, this adventure is for you!

Begin the adventure now: mybook.to/Wicked-Wish

ACKNOWLEDGMENTS

VERONICA DOUGLAS

Thank you to all of our readers and friends who have been so supportive. This book took much longer than we'd planned, and your encouragement and support helped get us through the tough times.

Thank you to Jena O'Connor and Ash Fitzsimmons for your patience and amazing editing skills! You two are incredible.

Thank you to the amazing readers on our advanced review team! And extra special thanks to our beta readers Penny, Susie, Aisha, Loren, and Amanda—your eyes are so sharp!

Many thanks to Lauren Gardner for all of your hard work. You are absolutely a lifesaver! And thanks to Caethes, for all your efforts to keep us rolling. We'd be lost without you both.

And finally, a huge shoutout to Orina Kafe for designing yet another mind-blowing cover! You truly are the best!

ABOUT VERONICA DOUGLAS

Veronica Douglas is a duo of professional archaeologists that love writing and digging together. After spending an inordinate amount of time doing painstaking research for academia, they suddenly discovered a passion for letting their imaginations go wild! A cocktail of magic, romance, and ancient mystery (shaken, not stirred), their books are inspired, in part, by their life in Chicago and their archaeological adventures from around the globe.

This is a work of fiction. All reference to events, persons, and locale are used fictitiously, except where documented in the historical record. Names, characters, and places are products of the author's imagination, and any resemblance to actual events, locales, or persons, living or dead, is coincidental.

Copyright 2022 by Veronica Douglas, Magic Side Press, LLC

Published by Magic Side Press, LLC

All rights reserved, including the right of reproduction in whole or in part in any form, except in instances of quotation used in critical articles or book review. Where such permission is sufficient, the author grants the right to strip any DRM which may be applied to this work.

www.veronicadouglas.com

 Created with Vellum

www.ingramcontent.com/pod-product-compliance
Lightning Source LLC
Chambersburg PA
CBHW030700190726
48286CB00001B/108